STOLEN *dreams*

STONE BAY SERIES

BOOK FOUR

USA TODAY BESTSELLING AUTHOR

PERSEPHONE AUTUMN

BETWEEN WORDS PUBLISHING LLC

STOLEN *dreams*

STONE BAY SERIES
BOOK FOUR

USA TODAY BESTSELLING AUTHOR

PERSEPHONE AUTUMN

BETWEEN WORDS PUBLISHING LLC

BOOKS BY PERSEPHONE AUTUMN

Lake Lavender Series

Depths Awakened

One Night Forsaken

Every Thought Taken

Devotion Series

Distorted Devotion

Undying Devotion

Beloved Devotion

Darkest Devotion

Sweetest Devotion

Bay Area Duet Series

<u>Click Duet</u>

Through the Lens

Time Exposure

<u>Inked Duet</u>

Fine Line

Love Buzz

<u>Insomniac Duet</u>

Restless Night

A Love So Bright

<u>Artist Duet</u>

Blank Canvas

Abstract Passion

<u>Novellas</u>

Reese

Penny

Stone Bay Series

Broken Sky—Prequel

Shattered Sun

Fractured Night

Fallen Stars

Stolen Dreams

Raptured Souls

Standalone Romance Novels

Sweet Tooth

Transcendental

In Knots For You

Poetry Collections

Ink Veins

Broken Metronome

Slipping From Existence

Poisonous Heart

Beneath Wildflowers

PUBLISHED UNDER P. AUTUMN

Standalone Non-Romance Novels

By Dawn

CONTENT WARNING AND AUTHOR'S NOTE

Stolen Dreams is a contemporary romantic suspense story. Graphic content, domestic violence, physical assault (not between the main characters), sexual assault (not between the main characters), kidnapping / abduction, child neglect (off page), addiction / substance abuse, and person for ransom in certain scenes may trigger emotional distress in some readers. If you are sensitive to the listed triggers, this story may not be for you.

Please use your own personal judgement before proceeding.

Dear reader,

After writing Stolen Dreams, I searched high and low for content sensitivity readers. With a Native American Indigenous heroine, I wanted to make sure I wrote her with the utmost respect.

That said, I was unable to secure North American Indigenous sensitivity readers.

So, I combed through Stolen Dreams with a fine-tooth comb and read every detail in reference to the heroine, her family, and their ancestry over and over. I believe I have written her, her family, and their culture with the respect they deserve.

Prior to writing this book, I did online courses and read books about Inuit history and culture, but I acknowledge this does not make me completely knowledgeable, nor does it allow me to understand the full personal experience of the North American Indigenous peoples.

If you read Stolen Dreams and discover a piece of those elements needs adjustment, please reach out to me on social media or via email so I can research and update the content.

xo

Persephone

This one's for the #foodporn lovers!
Bon appetit!

INUIT WORDS IN STOLEN DREAMS

Anaanatsiaq – **a-NAA-nat-si-aq** – maternal grandmother
Anaanatsialirqiuti – **pronunciation unknown** – great-grandmother
Angakkuq – **a-NGAK-kuq** – shaman
Ulaakut – **oo-la-coot** – good morning
Anaana – **a-NAA-na** – mother
Panik – **PA-nik** – daughter
Nalligivagit – **na-GLEE-ghee-va-geet** – I love you
Unukut – **oo-new-coot** – good evening
Irngutaq – **IR-ngu-taq** – grandchild (singular)
Qallunaat – **qal-lu-NAAT** – white people (plural)
Unusakut – **oo-nah-sa-coot** – good afternoon
Aakuluk – **AA-ku-look** – dear
Ataatasiaq – **a-TAA-ta-si-aq** – grandfather
Inuuhiqatsiaq – **pronunciation unknown** – cheers; good health
Kuluk – **KU-luk** – dear one; cute one; wee one (term of endearment)

Sources:

- Words of the Inuit: A Semantic Stroll through a Northern Culture by Louis-Jacques Dorais

- https://inhabiteducation.com/2021/12/09/inuit-nipingit-inuit-sounds/
- https://www.frobisherinn.com/speaking-the-inuktitut-language.htm
- https://www.omniglot.com/language/phrases/inuktitut.php
- Saqiyuq by Nancy Wachowich
- Indigenous Canada online course via Coursera

PROLOGUE

RAY

"I never wanted this!" Brianna flails her hands dramatically around the room. "To be a mother. To be... *attached* to the same person for the rest of my life."

Crossing my arms over my chest, I snort then laugh without humor. "Bit late for that, Bri." I glance down the hall toward our bedroom, praying our fight—one of several over the past two and a half years since learning we'd be parents—doesn't wake Tucker. "You *are* a mother. I *am* a father." I gesture between us. "We *are* parents. And we will always be *attached*—to each other and our child."

Her entire frame stiffens as she curls her hands into tight fists at her sides. "Don't talk to me like a fucking idiot, Ray," she grits out between clenched teeth. "Just because I gave birth doesn't mean I *want* to be a mother. Doesn't mean I have to be. Maybe someone else should take him."

Spinning on her heel, she heads for the door and dons her coat.

"What the hell does that mean?"

Brianna keeps her back to me as she picks up her purse and riffles through it. An exasperated huff floats through the room as she tosses the purse down and darts around me for the hallway. "Did you take my keys?"

I bolt after her, hoping to stop her from turning the bedroom upside down with Tucker in his toddler bed. When Brianna gets like this, she doesn't care about anyone except herself.

Well, that's not entirely true. There is one other thing she cares about.

Several months ago, I walked in on Brianna in the bathroom as she popped a couple pills into her mouth. Concern wrinkled my forehead as I met her gaze in the mirror. Worried she had a cold and needed isolation so Tucker didn't catch whatever she had, I opened my mouth to ask what was wrong and how I could help.

But I snapped my mouth shut the moment I glanced down at the vanity. An unlabeled prescription bottle sat uncapped on the counter. None of the pills inside the small container the same shape or color.

In a flash, a million questions ran through my head.

What is she taking?

How long has she been taking them?

Does she take them when alone with Tucker?

As I held her gaze in the mirror, I asked the first question. She'd given me a plausible answer.

"I've been getting migraines. A guy at work said he used to get them and tried a few medications before he found one that worked. He gave me a few to try."

At the time, like a naive fool, I believed her. The stress of parenthood, plus working insane hours on opposite schedules so we were with Tucker as often as possible, took its toll on us both. Brianna hadn't given me a reason not to trust her, and the last thing I needed to do was divide us with my irrational thoughts.

But I should have pushed the subject. I should have asked more questions or taken a closer look at the pills.

Not long after that day, Brianna morphed into someone else. Someone unrecognizable.

As her sparkle dulled, my guilt and concern multiplied.

I should've said more that day in the bathroom. Should've offered to adjust my schedule and give her more downtime. Should've paid closer attention after the night she popped those pills.

There's so much I should've done but didn't do. In my own way, I care for her. Trust her. And she played me like the gull I am.

"No, Bri, I didn't take your keys," I whisper-hiss in the dimly lit bedroom.

She shuffles everything on top of the dresser, not giving a damn about the noise.

Tucker squirms and rolls over in his toddler bed, less than five feet from my side of our queen mattress. But he doesn't wake, thank goodness.

Brianna continues the hunt for her car keys, tossing things on the floor as she moves from one spot to the next. When she starts toward the nightstand between our bed and Tucker, I step in front of her and extend my arms.

"No," I whisper with firm authority. "Your keys aren't over here. And you will *not* wake and scare Tucker by throwing shit near him."

Brianna tries to push past me, but I hold my ground.

"Asshole." The insult echoes loudly off the walls before she pivots and storms out of the room.

Dropping my arms, I inhale a slow, deep, steadying breath.

I can't do this anymore.

I glance over my shoulder at my sweet, jovial, innocent son.

He shouldn't have to live like this either.

Exiting the bedroom, I ease the door shut but leave it open a few inches. As I enter the living room, my gaze drifts to Brianna as she upends the sofa cushions and digs between the cracks. Frenetic energy floats throughout the apartment as she knocks over pictures and keepsakes without care.

"We should move to Stone Bay."

My words make her freeze. Straightening her spine, she peers over her shoulder, a scowl carved into her features. "So that's how it is?"

Narrowing my eyes slightly, I tilt my head, confused. "How what is, Bri?"

"Life gets shitty, so you run back to Mommy and Daddy."

I fight the urge to act as childish as she is, knowing it won't better the situation. "Who said anything about running?" Inching closer to her, I reach for her arm. Extend a proverbial olive branch. "We need help, Bri. And my family would love to be there for us and Tucker."

She scoffs and shakes her head. "Of course." Disdain coats her tone.

And just like that, I'm over being the nice guy. Done bending over backward for this woman who seems to give no fucks about me or our son. "Of course, what?" I ask, my tone and volume matching hers.

The corner of her mouth twitches. A twinkle dances in her eyes. As if me going toe to toe with her brings her some perverse sense of joy. Before I have time to explore why, a deadpan expression replaces her scorn.

"What about *my* family, Ray?" She stabs the center of her chest with a finger. "Do they not count?"

"That's not what I said. Don't put words in my mouth."

Turning her back on me, she goes back to searching for her keys.

"You don't talk about your family much, Bri. And the little you have shared..." I drag a hand through my hair. "You haven't painted a pretty picture."

Eyes downcast, she shoulder-checks me as she passes and enters the open kitchen. "They weren't the best parents, but they're still my family."

Now she is throwing bullshit to see what will stick. Fine. If that is how she wants to play, I can throw it right back.

"Really?"

She pauses and peeks over her shoulder, eyes narrowed, but doesn't say a word.

"We've been together how long?" Before I give her a chance to answer, I continue. "Not once have we or you spent time with them. Not once have you texted or spoken with them on the phone." As each word leaves my lips, the irritation flowing through my veins builds, expands, becomes borderline explosive. "Do they even know about Tucker?"

Whipping around, she stomps across the room and shoves at my chest. "Fuck you."

Am I the asshole for that last jab? Yeah, I am. My parents would reprimand me for saying such a callous thing to the mother of my child. Regardless, the question needs to be asked.

Brianna and I need help raising Tucker. Period.

It isn't about money. If finances were an issue, I'd ask my parents for a loan. They'd happily lend me whatever we needed and wave me off every time I tried to pay it back.

What we need is someone willing to help with day care. Sure, Tucker could go to a place nearby and develop social skills early. He could play with other kids around his age and start preschool learning before most children. The list of perks is extensive.

But the bill for childcare would eat up most of one of our salaries. One or both of us would have to shift our schedules to accommodate the day care's business hours. We'd have to work extra hours to foot the bill and still have enough to live after.

Which is why our schedules are the way they are now.

"It's a shitty question." And not one I regret asking. "Doesn't make it any less valid."

Fists trembling at her sides, she works her jaw back and forth. Any moment, I expect Brianna to swing. To punch or slap me in the face. To scream and tell me to go to hell.

Instead, she spins around and storms to the fridge. She whips the door open, shuffles the contents from one side to the other, grabs a bottle of beer, then lets out a squeal of delight.

I hear the jingle of her keys as she takes a step back. A smile I haven't seen in far too long lights her face as she closes the fridge door and faces me. It's the same smile that lured me closer to her. The smile that gives me an ounce of hope.

"Bri…" Her shortened name is soft on my tongue.

"Just let me have tonight," she pleas, her anger and frustration from a moment ago gone. "We can talk about it tomorrow."

Tomorrow is one of those rare occasions we both have the day off. It's the perfect time to sit down, talk about the future, and map out what steps to take next.

"Sure. Yeah." I glance toward the bedroom door. "Maybe lunch at the park with Tucker."

Her smile grows impossibly brighter. "Sounds like a wonderful idea." Stepping into me, she wraps her arms around my middle. "Sorry for yelling. It's not fair to dump on you like that."

The swift change in her demeanor is pleasant yet unsettling.

I hug her tighter to my chest. "Your stress is mine too. We need to be able to talk about what's bothering us. It's the only way we'll get through this together."

She releases me and takes a step back. "Still, I said some pretty shitty things."

Yes, she did. But I wasn't nice either.

Lifting a hand to her cheek, I brush the hair out of her face. "Tomorrow, everything will be better." As the words leave my lips, I will them into existence.

Brianna nods, pushes up on her toes, and kisses my cheek. Then she turns for the door, swipes up her purse, drops the beer inside, and reaches for the dead bolt. "Shouldn't be long. Don't wait up."

Something about those last three words and her tone twists my insides. But I shove it down, remind myself she is the mother of my child and I need to trust her, then promise myself to address it in the morning.

"Be safe, Bri."

Her dark hair swishes as she peeks over her shoulder, that radiant smile on her lips. "I will." Then she's out the door.

Over the next hour, I tidy up the mess she made throughout the apartment. I turn off the light in the living room and kitchen but leave the hood light over the stove on.

When my head hits the pillow, the weight of the evening crashes down on me hard. But I don't mull over it. Instead, I tell myself we will clear things up tomorrow. One more sleep, then Brianna and I will sort out the future.

With that final thought, I let go of my worries and pass out.

Sunlight peeks through the blinds as I wake the next morning.

I tilt my head left then right, cracking my neck. Twist in place, waking my muscles. Stretch an arm and find the spot next to me in bed empty and cold.

After last night, it honestly wouldn't surprise me if Brianna slept on the couch. When things get heated or she stays out past midnight, her crashing on the couch isn't abnormal.

Tonight will be different. Once we air our concerns and come up with a resolution, we will start anew.

Pulling back the covers, I swing my legs off the bed and sit up. As it does every morning, my gaze automatically goes to Tucker's bed.

Empty.

I glance at the alarm clock—a little after eight. Usually I'm up with him around seven, but I must've been so exhausted that I slept through his morning routine of waking me up. He's probably on the couch with Brianna, watching his favorite show on the tablet.

After I use the bathroom and brush my teeth, I slip on a pair of sweatpants and head for the living room.

"Who wants panca—" The word dies on my tongue as I enter an empty, still tidy living room. "Bri? Tucker?"

No response. No sound. Nothing.

"Fuck!"

I race back into the bedroom, grab my phone off the charger, and open my text history with Brianna. Tapping on her picture, I glance down to see her location, but there's no map. My pulse whooshes in my ears as I scroll down, thinking maybe my phone updated and the map moved.

But there is nothing.

Closing the contact info, I type out a message and hit send.

> Did you take T out for breakfast without me? lol

Red flag one: I can't see Brianna's location.

Red flag two: the text bubble is green instead of blue.

Red flag three: there's no indication the message has been delivered like usual.

This is not happening.

I tap on her profile picture again, tap the phone icon, and bounce in place as it rings in my ear. The call connects.

"We're sorry, the person you are trying to reach is no longer reachable at this number. Please try again later."

No, no, no.

"Where the fuck are you, Bri?" I all but yell as I storm to the bedroom and open the blinds.

I dash to the closet, my eyes immediately dropping to the floor. Tucker's three pairs of shoes are missing. The small supply of diapers we keep while potty training him is gone. My gaze drifts up to the hangers, several of Brianna's empty.

How the hell did I not hear her emptying the closet?

My limbs start to shake. My vision blurs. White noise fills my ears as I gasp for air that won't seem to come.

I bolt for the dresser and open the drawers reserved for Tucker. Empty.

Pressing the heal of my palm to the center of my chest, a sob rips from my throat. Sharp pain ricochets through my legs as my knees smack the floor.

"What d-did you do, Bri?"

Hands trembling, I tap the phone icon, dial the number no one ever wants to call and lift the phone to my ear.

"9-1-1, this is a recorded line. Please state your emergency."

I inhale a shaky breath as tears roll down my cheeks. "My son has been taken."

ONE

KAYA

Present

The end of the school year is always the hardest yet most rewarding time. Farewell hugs go on for days. So do the teary eyes and choked-up words. But when the kids share their gratitude at having me in their lives, incomparable joy fills my soul.

Those small sparks of appreciation remind me of why I chose this career path. To help guide children when they feel lost or out of place. To listen to their happiness and heartache, especially when they feel no one else cares. To give them a voice when they often feel silenced.

Constantly bombarded with expectations while trying to figure out who you are, it's hard to be a kid. Add in the ever-changing influences online, peer pressure, trends, and feeling the need to grow up years ahead of your time, it's a wonder why more kids haven't totally lost it yet.

Thankfully, I get to be one of their sounding boards. A safe space. An adult they can share their feelings and opinions with and not feel judged, forgotten, or degraded when they leave my office. If anything, I teach them it's okay to feel the way they do.

It's okay to be upset or angry or frustrated. What matters most is how they channel and release their emotions.

I may not be the best behavioral specialist in Washington, but I am the best in Stone Bay. A hallmark I wear with pride.

A couple half-packed boxes sit on the credenza behind my desk. Colorful pictures in crayon, marker, pen, and colored pencil stowed carefully. Thank-you letters in tidy and messy scrawl folded neatly and stashed in an envelope. A thick stack of photos with countless smiles and bright eyes.

Although my office will be the same next school year, I like to pack up special mementos from the current year and take them home. Add them to the scrapbook I started last summer after my first year in this role. Small tokens that make me smile and drive my love for helping children be their best selves.

A muffled buzz distracts me from my task. I open my desk drawer, pull out my phone, and tap on the text notification.

CLARISSA

drinks later?

I smile down at the screen as I type out a response.

Count me in. What's the occasion?

is that a serious question?

Light laughter spills from my lips, a gray bubble dancing on the screen as she continues to type.

I survived another year of teenage angst, being told I have no idea what I'm talking about because I'm old, and being told I'd be hot if I knew how to take care of myself. I'm still in my 20s. I am NOT old.

I laugh harder, grateful I'm not on the high school campus with Clarissa right now. Being the only person in my field in the

Stone Bay school system, my time is split between the elementary campus and the middle and high school campuses, which are side by side with the shared administration offices between them.

> You are not old. And I told you, don't let the kids get to you.

> I know... *insert dramatic eye roll with a huff*

Ringing through the room pulls me out of my conversation with Clarissa.

I press the speaker button on my desk phone. "This is Kaya."

"Hi, Kaya. It's Mia."

"Hey, Mia. What can I help you with?"

A heavy sigh echoes through the line. "I'm sending a student your way. Tucker Calhoun. He's been acting out most of the year, but I've managed to redirect the behavior. Today, no such luck. He riled up the class in no time and won't calm down."

A pang blooms in my chest. Most children act out for a reason, and it typically stems from a painful source outside the classroom.

"Thanks for the heads-up, Mia. I'll talk with him and hopefully figure out what's going on."

"He's a good kid. Just has some pent-up frustrations."

"I'll keep you apprised of what we talk about."

"Thanks, Kaya."

The line disconnects.

I type out a quick text to Clarissa before I stow my phone back in my desk.

> Duty calls. When and where for drinks?

A knock sounds on my open door, and I look up to see an office assistant with who I assume is Tucker.

Genuine smile on my face, I step around my desk and toward the door. "Are you Tucker?"

Arms crossed over his chest, he screws his lips tightly and

stares at the floor. He doesn't acknowledge my presence or my question, but I don't take it personally. Anger radiates off his aura like thick fog.

I glance at the office assistant. "I'll take it from here, Enola. Thank you."

They smile and nod, then head back to the front desk.

"Come in, Tucker." I gesture to the guest chairs near my desk. "Have a seat."

Tucker stomps across my office and plops down in one of the chairs, an exaggerated huff leaving his lips.

Closing the door, I cross the room and take a seat in the guest chair next to Tucker, twisting so I'm angled in his direction. Silence stretches out between us, a quiet I don't disrupt.

Both my position in the room and my reticence serve a purpose. Sitting next to Tucker as opposed to the other side of my desk, I appear less an authority figure and more a friend. Remaining quiet for a couple minutes gives him a moment to collect himself and his thoughts.

He undoubtedly thinks he was sent here to be punished for his behavior in class. But I'm not here to discipline. My job is to find the root cause of his troubles, talk him through it, share the possible ramifications, and guide him on what to do when he feels this way in the future.

I extend a hand toward Tucker. "Don't think we've met, Tucker. I'm Ms. Imala, the school behavioral specialist. But my students call me Kaya."

His eyes flit to my proffered hand, then go back to staring at the desk.

I lace my fingers and rest my hands in my lap. "Ms. Cambridge tells me you've been upset. Do you want to share what's bothering you? Whatever we talk about in here stays between you and me."

As I say the last part, Tucker's shoulders relax a little and his expression softens. Progress.

"When I was your age, kids in my class picked on me."

With a slight tilt of his head, he peeks up at me, curiosity in his eyes.

I nod. "It's true. Because I didn't look like most of the girls in my class, they called me names and teased me about my heritage. They spoke to and about me with no regard to how it'd make me feel." I pause and let my words sink in a moment. "Words hurt people. Sometimes worse than cuts."

Throughout most of my childhood, many of my peers made me feel less than, unattractive, incapable, and as if I didn't belong. Being the center of their censure, abhorrence, or discrimination came too easy for some of my classmates. What's worse is they felt no shame, guilt, or remorse over the horrid names they called me or pranks they pulled at my expense.

I am not the only Native American my age or in my generation in Stone Bay, but there are fewer of us in town than when the Imalas journeyed here more than a hundred years ago and connected with the local Indigenous, the Stonewater tribe. As our numbers have dwindled over the generations, more of our history and culture have gotten lost, dismissed, or ignored.

My family strives to keep our ancestors' memories alive. We share our stories, pass them down to each generation, and learn the suppressed and forgotten ways of our people. We take pride in who we are and where we come from.

When a student enters my office, their struggles may be unique and slight compared to others, but they are still valid. Each person deserves the opportunity to be heard, seen, and supported. I do everything within my power to provide this to my students.

Tucker's brows scrunch together then relax.

"When those kids said mean things about me, it made me so angry. I wanted to yell and hit something." I lean a little closer to Tucker and lower my voice. "I wanted to hit *them*."

This garners his attention. Wide hazel eyes stare up at me with dozens of questions. "Did you?"

An empathetic smile tugs at the corner of my mouth as I sit

back and slowly shake my head. "No, I didn't hit them. When I got home from school, my *anaanatsiaq* felt my sadness and anger."

"What's an anaa—"

I cut off his fumbled pronunciation with a smile. "*Anaanatsiaq*," I repeat. "It means grandmother."

Tucker's brows and lips twitch. He's likely repeating the word in his head. Trying to master the speech pattern.

It isn't often I use Inuktitut with people who don't speak the language. But like most dialects, if you don't speak them regularly, you start to forget. Considering the Inuit side of my family migrated to Stone Bay, some of the language and traditions have slipped away over the generations. Ahnah—my *anaanatsiaq*—works tirelessly to keep who we are and what we do know alive.

"How did she feel your anger?"

I shrug a shoulder. "Some people are born empaths. They just know how other people feel."

Eyes lifting to mine, Tucker tilts his head and narrows his gaze. "Are you an empath?"

The corners of my lips turn up as I shake my head. "No. I have my own gift."

His fingers wring the bottom hem of his shirt. "You do?"

"Yes. I've always been good at helping other people find peace when they're upset."

"Oh." He tucks his chin to his chest and studies his fumbling fingers in his lap.

"Would you like to tell me what made you upset earlier?"

He clutches one hand with the other, squeezing until his knuckles blanch. "I don't snitch."

Interesting. Maybe he was a part of something and has since been rejected, hence his outbursts.

"Remember, Tucker, whatever you share with me stays between us. I promise."

Lifting his chin, he studies my expression with narrowed eyes. Silence hovers around us as he reads the lines of my face, searching for any indication of deceit. He isn't convinced I'll keep my word, and it hurts my heart someone so young feels such a high level of distrust.

"Tucker, my job is to help you navigate your feelings in a healthy way. Unless someone is hurting you or the other way around, I won't share our conversation with your teacher or family."

"Really?" So much hope surrounds the single word.

My chest aches as I nod and draw an X over my heart. "Swear."

Once more, he tucks his chin to his chest. Inhales a deep, shaky breath as his hands twist in his lap. "Kids in my class are saying mean things to me."

The pang in my chest intensifies as I soften my tone. "I'm sorry that's happening. I bet it hurts."

Back slumped and shoulders caved, he nods and stays quiet.

"Do you want to share the mean things they're saying?"

His chin trembles a moment before he sniffles then drags the back of his hand across his nose. Tucker shrugs then mumbles, "Stuff about my mom and dad, and me."

I don't make a point to learn everything about all the students enrolled at the elementary, middle, and high school. It'd take weeks, if not months. Typically, I dive into their file and homelife after they visit my office or a teacher or administrator brings up their name.

This is the first time I've seen or heard anything about Tucker, so I have no context on his history.

"Do you want to tell me the mean things they're saying about you and your parents?"

An audible huff fills the room. "Kenny called my mom a bad word. Said she doesn't love me anymore."

Kenny is a little jerk.

"It must've hurt a lot when he said those things." I reach over and touch Tucker's shoulder a moment. "But Kenny doesn't know what your mom feels."

"Maybe he's right," Tucker mutters.

My brows bend in confusion. "Why would you say that?"

His lips turn down at the corners as he tucks his chin closer to his chest. "Before I was here, I lived with my mom. We lived in a bunch of places, but the last had lots of noise and scary people." He wrings his shirt until his knuckles blanch. "I didn't know my dad until two Christmases ago. He says him, me, and my mom all lived together until I was almost two, but I don't remember that."

A twist of pain settles beneath my diaphragm as emotion swells in my throat. I take a slow, steadying breath as I shove aside the gut instinct to wrap him in comfort. Swallowing, I say, "A lot of parents don't live together. Doesn't mean they don't love their child."

"What if they're never home? What does that mean?"

Another crack lines my heart. "Was your mom away a lot?"

Tucker nibbles on his lips and shrugs. "She was always with one of her boyfriends."

"At home or not?"

"Sometimes at home. Sometimes I didn't see her for two days."

My stomach cramps as my skin heats with anger. Quietly as possible, I inhale for a count of three and exhale just as long, trying to remain calm. It takes quite a bit to light a fire in my veins. In most cases, it's when a child is mistreated by an adult.

"Is it better with your dad?" *Please say yes.*

"I guess." He sniffles as a forlorn look consumes his expression. "He works a bunch."

"When you're not at school and your dad has to work, what do you do?" *Please tell me you're not home alone for several hours.* The last thing Tucker needs is to go from one irresponsible parent to another.

A hint of his sadness is replaced with reverence. "I stay with Grandma Angel, Papa RJ, GG Grace, or Auntie Abi."

"GG?"

"She's my great-grandma."

As part of the Seven—the Stone Bay registered founding families—I am familiar with some of the more prominent families in town. Although the Calhouns aren't part of the Seven, they have made a name for themselves over the years. They've also become good at keeping tidbits about their family—Tucker and his mother —out of the limelight.

I know *of* the Calhouns, but I don't know them.

"Well, I'm glad you have people who love you here," I say with heartfelt honesty.

"Yeah, I guess so."

"I don't know your dad, but I bet he works hard so you can have everything you need." I reach out and touch his shoulder again. "It's okay to tell him what you want." My hand falls back into my lap. "Some parents don't realize they're not giving you what you need. Lots of kids want toys and other fun stuff. But some kids want a day with their mom or dad. Both are okay to ask for."

His chin wobbles. "What if he says no?"

My heart squeezes at his question. "What if he says yes?" I counter.

Tucker turns in his seat and looks up at me, his hazel eyes glassy but brighter. "I like you, Miss Kaya."

"I like you, too, Tucker."

His entire face scrunches to the middle. "What about Kenny and the other mean kids?"

After hearing of this group of cruel fourth graders, I plan to have a conversation with the staff. Obviously, we can't be in all places at all times, but it is our job to make sure situations such as this don't fester and become worse. Left unchecked, kids like Kenny eventually switch from using words to hurt others to inflicting physical harm with their fists.

I refuse to let that happen on my watch.

"Although it's hard, you have to ignore his mean words. Especially the bad ones." I rise from my seat and move around my desk. "Most bullies have their own sadness. To keep their hurt hidden, they pick on other people. They pass it on so no one sees their pain." I open one of my desk drawers and sift through the small open box inside. "Do you have a favorite thing to do? Or a favorite color?"

"I like it when I get to help my dad cook. He got me a bright-red apron with my name on the front."

"Red like this?" I hold up a small piece of tumbled garnet.

Tucker shakes his head.

I riffle through the box again and stop on a Matchbox fire truck with a moving ladder on top. Scooping it up, I show it to Tucker. "How about fire-truck red?"

"Whoa!" He wiggles out of his chair and pins himself to the front of my desk, his eyes the brightest I've seen them since he entered my office. "I love fire trucks."

Closing the drawer, I move back to the other side of the desk. "Fire trucks are pretty cool. But this one"—I hold it between us in my open palm—"is special."

"It is?"

"Yes. It was made just for you."

His brows tug together in confusion. "But it's like all the other ones in the store."

"True," I agree. "Want to know why it's different?"

Tucker nods rapidly.

"I have a box of special items I save in my desk. When I'm in a store, sometimes small items call out to me."

"They talk to you?" he asks in wonderment, his eyes widening.

"Not like how people talk. It's more of a feeling." I lay a hand over my belly. "The items let me know that one day soon, someone I see will need them." I hold the fire truck closer to Tucker. "When I was shopping two days ago, this fire truck called out. It knew I'd need to give it to you."

Tucker stares at the fire truck, speechless.

"I want you to have it, Tucker. Every morning, I want you to hold it in your hand and say, 'Today will be a good day.' Can you do that for me?"

Gingerly, he reaches for and takes the fire truck from my palm. "Yes."

"Good. In the afternoon or evening, I want you to do something different. It sounds funny, but I want you to tell your fire truck about your day. The good things that happened and the stuff that upset you. This fire truck will keep all your secrets safe."

"Can I play with it?"

"Only after you do those two things, but not in school. You can carry it in your backpack, but it's best to only have it out at home." I tap the fire truck in his palm. "Special secret keeper."

He stares at the toy that is now a way to release his frustrations. "The most special secret keeper," he whispers before he shoves it in his pocket. "Thank you, Miss Kaya."

"You're welcome, Tucker. We should get you back to class." I cross the office and open the door. "Don't tell anyone else, but I think the fourth graders are getting a pizza party for lunch."

"Yes," he hisses then fist-pumps the air.

When we reach the front, I ask Enola to escort Tucker back to class. Once they are out the door, I audibly inhale.

Such a wonderful little boy. If only he got the attention and affection he so desperately craves.

Clarissa clinks her wineglass with mine. "Cheers to three more days of endless teenage hormones."

I laugh, and the sound blends with the pub music. "So you know, I'm not drinking every night this week."

Clarissa sticks out her tongue. "You're no fun."

"Maybe. But at least I won't be on death's door when one of those teenagers comes into my office tomorrow."

"Yeah, yeah, yeah." Clarissa brings her glass to her lips and drinks a healthy sip. Then her body language shifts. She leans forward and shows a touch more cleavage.

Great.

I follow her line of sight across Dalton's Pub to see who she is making eyes at. A man with salt-and-pepper hair sits on a stool at the end of the bar. Broad shoulders and a tall frame, he is dressed in a sharp, dark-colored suit. No tie around his neck, the top two buttons of his dress shirt undone. He appears to be alone, nursing a pint.

Clarissa has him in her sights, but he has yet to notice her.

I wave a hand in front of her face. "Want me to leave so you can flirt with Mr. Anonymous?"

"Not yet."

"Gee, thanks."

"Joking, Kaya." Clarissa rests a hand over mine on the table. "Can't help but admire a beautiful man." She arches a brow. "What about you?"

Knowing exactly where this is headed, I play stupid. "What about me?"

"Anyone catch your attention recently?"

"You already know the answer."

Clarissa downs the rest of her wine, then holds the glass up until the bartender nods. "You need to date more. I worry about you."

I roll my eyes. "No, you don't."

She spins the stem of the glass between her fingers. "All the heavy stuff we deal with, it's important to take care of ourselves. And not just our mental health, but also our sexual health."

As the last words leave her lips, a full glass of wine is deposited on the table.

My face flames with embarrassment. My skin undoubtedly sunburn red. Once we're alone, I give her a pointed stare. "Can we please *not* talk about my sex life in public. Ever." My plea is more a statement than a question.

"Fine," she says with faux exaggeration. "But you're too young to become a recluse with hundreds of porcelain statues you talk to and call your friends."

"I have plenty of actual people to talk to, so no need to worry."

I take a small sip of my wine. "Plus, I've told you, right now, work and family are my priorities. When I have a few more years of work under my belt, I may consider a romantic relationship."

"But sex..." The word comes out a mile long. "How can you live without sex?"

Chuckling, I drop my gaze to the table and shake my head. "Believe it or not, it's possible." I squeeze her hand. "It's called focus."

"You're so weird sometimes."

I lift my chin. "I'll take that as a compliment."

Clarissa drinks half of her second glass before I get through half of my first. Her gaze flits between me and the guy at the bar. And if I'm honest, all this talk of relationships has killed my barely-there buzz.

When she finishes her second glass, I slide mine in her direction. "Here. Drink mine and go meet Mr. Anonymous."

"But I want to spend more time with you," she whines playfully.

"I love you, Rissa. But I need to call it a night." I nudge my head toward the guy at the bar. "And if he knows what's good for him, he'll make your night much better."

"Are you sure?"

I shoulder my purse and slide off my stool. "Absolutely."

Clarissa hops off her seat and wraps her arms around my neck. "Love you."

I laugh at her tipsy sentiment. "Love you, too. Get home safe, okay?"

She swipes up the wineglass. "I will."

I kiss her on the cheek and head for the door. Before I exit, I peek over to the man at the bar and see a brilliant smile on his face. When my gaze shifts to Clarissa, her expression mirrors his.

One day, I'll smile at someone like that. One day, I will find love. But not yet. Not until I'm ready.

TWO

RAY

"Where's my salmon, Cam?"

"Coming, Chef," Cameron hollers as she pivots away from the range, sizzling pan in hand, and rounds the pasta and salad stations for the plating area.

Bent over the marble top, I spoon pomegranate forbidden rice into a crescent-shaped mold on the center of the plate, packing it tightly before removing the mold. As I strategically lay green beans on an angle beside the rice, Cameron sidles up to me with the quinoa-crusted salmon filet.

Taking the thin spatula from her, I set the salmon atop the green beans. "Great work, Cam."

She draws in a sharp breath. "Th-thank you, Chef." And then she scurries back to her place at the range.

Head down, a hint of a smile curves one corner of my mouth as I create art with the seasonal salmon dish. By no means am I oblivious to Cameron's crush on me, but I will never exploit her with it.

After Chef Beaulieu hired me last year, he asked me to interview candidates for two more positions. People who were versatile in the kitchen and loved food as we did. Cameron was my first interviewee. Her knowledge base and competence blew my mind. Her kitchen skills were impeccable as she cooked a dish for me and Chef Beaulieu. But it was the way she blushed when I complimented her expertise that caught my attention most.

Although I'd never cross the line with an employee—no one needs that kind of drama in their life—the faint rouge on her cheeks at my praise was the main reason I hired her. Yes, her culinary expertise was top-notch. Her time management was flawless. But her humble nature won me over.

Many in our field are arrogant and determined. We all dream of the executive chef title, of running our own restaurant. We work tirelessly to perfect our craft. And oftentimes, those qualities give us a superiority complex.

Cameron is an exception. She doesn't have a pretentious bone in her body and is by far the most selfless person I've met in this industry. But her brilliance and innovative thinking outweigh her timidity. Her wild passion and outspoken nature shine when she conjures a new dish.

An expert in our field, I admire Cameron. But that's where my feelings for her end.

I add a small spoonful of orange-ginger marmalade between the salmon and rice, followed by a slow-roasted garlic clove. I garnish the plate with dots of spicy orange-miso sauce, large to small, from the edge of the plate to the fish. For the final touch, a teaspoon of salmon roe and an edible flower atop the fish.

Straightening my spine, I turn the plate and look at it from every angle.

Perfection.

Plate in hand, I pivot and slide it across the marble counter of the pass-through window. The server opposite me takes the plate along with another and crosses the dining room to a couple in my line of sight. I stare on as the dishes are presented, my breath caught in my throat as I wait for their reaction.

The woman's eyes light up, a hand coming to her chest. When

the salmon is set in front of the man, his mouth forms an *O* as his brows lift with excitement.

Their reaction is one reason why I love what I do. Seeing someone light up at the sight of my food, hearing their praise before they leave the restaurant… it's a high like no other.

"Another hit of magic," I say loud enough for everyone in the kitchen to hear. "Proud of you, team."

Shortly after I started at Calhoun's Bistro, I came up with the term *hit of magic*. It's the phrase I use with my kitchen staff to tell them we are on our *A* game. And since the kitchen is open to the dining room, it's also a way to keep our vocabulary in check while on the clock.

If you think sailors and truckers have a colorful dictionary, you should step inside a closed kitchen. Other than dish names and culinary terms, fuck is the most used word away from customer earshot.

"Thank you, Chef," they sound off as they work.

The rest of the night passes faster than anticipated. By quarter to eleven, half of the stations are being cleaned and prepped for tomorrow. Once the final dishes for the night leave the kitchen, the rest of the kitchen is scrubbed spotless.

"Fin, you still good to stay?"

His attention shifts from the steel counter he washes to me, and he nods. "Yeah, man. It'd take an act of God to keep me away."

I laugh. "Noted."

Once the last table clears and the staff head home for the night, I prep for another *job* I've come to love. Filming online food porn videos.

Before Chef Beaulieu brought me on board, I worked with my dad at RJ's Diner. I had a lot of freedom in that kitchen. Dad let me come up with fun, unconventional creations to attract regulars more often as well as entice newcomers.

I recorded myself as I worked and figured out how to edit the clips down to a reasonable amount of time. Most of the videos were simple—me in the kitchen doing what I love. The first few months, a couple hundred people viewed my videos. Occasionally, someone left a comment and applauded my culinary skills.

One of those comments tipped the first domino to me going viral online. A follower asked if I would share a fancy meal anyone could make at home for a special occasion. I gladly acquiesced.

With Stone Bay being a coastal town, I decided on a seafood dish. As a bonus, I also made a romantic dessert.

Jerk shrimp with rice in pineapple bowls and chocolate lava cake is the video that garnered more than a million followers on social media within a week. A unique yet simple dinner for two is what skyrocketed me from an ordinary line cook in a small-town diner to sought-after sous-chef in a gourmet restaurant.

The food in the video isn't what boosted my culinary career. *How* I made the food is what made me an overnight sensation.

For decades, I've watched cooking videos and shows. Studied culinary masters and absorbed as much knowledge and expertise as possible. Followed countless foodies and drooled over their content.

When it was time to share my own abilities, I mirrored other foodies and used the same hashtag—#foodporn.

The night I filmed the fancy romantic meal video, I elected to make it literal food porn. From how I ran my finger through the splayed spine of the shrimp to the way I rapidly flicked my fingers through the melted chocolate for the cake.

Food. Porn.

The viewers wanted more. So, I gave it to them. It's been a whirlwind since.

Arms loaded with ingredients, I amble out of the walk-in and set everything on the prep station counter. Heading for the back room by the office, I unbutton my chef coat, toss it in the dirty hamper, and swap my work shirt for a fresh, white T-shirt that fits like a second skin.

Fin is waiting when I return to the kitchen, his hip against the counter as he scrolls through his phone.

"Thanks for another great night, man," I say as I sort the ingredients in order of when I need them.

He locks his phone and stows it in his back pocket. "Tonight was fire. How many plates went out?"

Calhoun's Bistro is more of an experience than the average restaurant. With fifty-four seats in the dining room and our doors open for six hours in the evening, it's rare for us to fill tables twice Monday through Wednesday. Thursdays are hit or miss. And the private rooms seldomly book during the week.

Weekends are a different story. Friday, Saturday, and Sunday reservations are fully booked three months in advance and further out for holidays. Private rooms are reserved as far out as six months to a year, but we keep one off the reservation list and available in case a large party calls in. The only exception we make on the weekend is for the Seven or close friends with my grandfather, Ray Calhoun Sr., or his business partner, Roger Kemp. If a founding family calls and asks for a table last minute, we do our best to squeeze them in.

"Sixty-three," I answer with pride. "A damn good night."

"At one point, I checked my phone to see what day it was." Fin laughs. "Tonight felt more like Thursday than Tuesday."

"Agreed."

Fin surveys the ingredients on the counter. "What's on the menu tonight?"

Tuna, salmon, chicken, shrimp, precooked sushi rice, vegetables, sake, and wonton wrappers are spread across the counter. I still need to grab ingredients for the sauce and tempura batter.

"Bento box, Tré style." I use the nickname many call me when my dad or grandfather are present. Mom tried to make my middle name *cute* when I was young, but I vetoed Georgie as my sobriquet before age ten.

Fin hums as his eyes roam the ingredients again. "Love it."

After I collect the remaining ingredients, I hand Fin my phone.

Not long after he started here, Fin asked to join me when I film. Sounded fun, so I agreed. After a couple videos, he learned being in front of the camera wasn't for him. Still wanting to be involved, he offered to help record. Not only did it make the process more entertaining, it also cut recording time in half.

The next hour and a half flies by as I slice sashimi, roll sushi, fry tempura, steam dumplings, and grill chicken. Every move I make is planned. Intentional. The way I trail my fingers over the meat and between the slices. How I dip my first and middle fingers in the batter and flick them rapidly back and forth. How I dunk my middle finger in the teriyaki sauce then glide it over my tongue.

The raunchier I make the videos, the better.

Lucky for me, Chef Beaulieu encourages my social media presence. *"We've seen a boom in business since you joined us,"* he told me during my ninety-day evaluation. A month later, he created his own account and started sharing his own passion for food—chocolate and pastry. A literal chocolatier and master in the kitchen, his following surpassed mine in a matter of days.

Oftentimes, he attests the restaurant's success to my provocative videos. But I wave off the notion and tell him it's *us* and our team who are responsible for the growth at Calhoun's Bistro.

Once we get a shot of the completed food, Fin and I devour every morsel. When we finish, I clean the kitchen and Fin records.

Everything back to rights, we shut off lights and grab our stuff to leave. As we near our cars, I pause and spin to face him.

"My place in the morning? Film a couple easier dishes."

"Ten?" Fin unlocks his SUV.

"Perfect. Gives me time with Tucker before school."

Fin opens his door and slips behind the wheel. "See ya in the morning."

I get in my own car and wave before I shut the door. Cranking the engine, I wait for Fin to drive off and then follow. Not a soul on the road, we drive the same path until we reach Granite Parkway. As Fin turns left at the light, he sticks his hand out the window and waves. I do the same as I turn right.

Stars glitter in the sky as my tires eat up the miles. Trees blend in with the darkness and pass in a blur. The scent of pine and earth mingle in the crisp night air as it dances over my skin.

I turn onto Fossil Mountain Highway then take the narrow two-lane road for the Calhoun estate. The property is sizable but minuscule compared to the properties of the Seven. Three grand houses sit nestled between a thicket of trees—mine, Mom and Dad's house, and one for my grandparents. On the north side of the property, past acres of trees, is Stone Bay Country Club with its beloved golf course.

Our property may be on the outskirts of town, but I love the incomparable peace and quiet.

I steer my car down the drive to my parents' house. A single light on in the living room tells me one of them is awake, waiting.

"Shit," I mutter as I put the car in park and cut the engine.

Most nights, I slip into their house undetected, grab Tucker from bed, and leave with him without waking anyone. Every now and then, one of my parents waits up to talk.

Tiptoeing into the house, I ease the door shut and head for the living room. Wrapped in a blanket, Mom is curled up on the couch with her eyes closed. On light feet, I pad across the room to turn off the light. As my hand reaches for the lamp switch, Mom's eyes flutter open.

"Hey, sweetheart. How was work?"

In the food and hospitality industry most of their lives, my parents know what it's like to work crazy early or late hours.

"Busier than usual."

She scoots back and sits up straighter. "That's wonderful." Lifting a hand to her mouth, she stifles a yawn. "And you got another video in?"

I nod. "One. Fin and I plan to meet up after Tucker's at school tomorrow."

Reaching up to rub the back of her neck, her expression turns pensive as she hums. "Speaking of Tucker…"

This is why she's on the couch.

"What?" I ask, keeping my tone neutral.

"You need to spend more time with him." A hint of sharp determination in her sleepy voice.

At least she got straight to the point. "I'm trying, Mom. You know my schedule is hectic."

Lips in a flat line, she subtly nods. "I also know you're working more hours than necessary. That you've gone in to help on a day off several times over the past month."

In a blink, I feel like a teenager again. Every move scrutinized. Every imperfection thrown in my face.

Downfall of working in a place your family owns, they have easy access to everything, including schedules and clocked hours. Last I checked, my time card registered no less than sixty hours a week for the past six weeks… which doesn't include the time I spend filming for social media.

Irritated as I am with Mom for pointing out my flaws, my indignation fizzles out. Guilt wiggles its way in and sits like a brick in my gut.

"Was worried the kitchen would get bogged down with the number of reservations," I say.

She tugs the blanket tighter around herself. "I get it, sweetheart. Your father and I both do. Being in the kitchen is part of who you are. It's in your genes." A sympathetic smile tugs at the corners of her mouth. "But Tucker needs to be higher on your list of priorities."

Deep in my bones, I know she is right. I need to spend more time with Tucker. I need to show him one of his parents cares about him, loves him. After years of searching for him, after all the anxiety-filled days and sleepless nights, after all the bullshit Brianna put him through, I need to be more present.

What kind of parent am I if I fight to get my kid back only to not spend time with him?

More than anything, I want time with Tucker. To make up for our years apart. But damn is it hard to find work-life balance with conflicting schedules. Not to mention, working extra hours pads my paycheck and helps me give Tucker the life he should've had all along.

But if we're never together, am I really providing him with a great life?

"I'll talk with Chef Beaulieu. See if Tucker can be at the restaurant a few hours after school and during the summer."

Her shoulders relax as her smile gentles. "I'm sure André will go along with the idea. One of us can pick Tucker up before dinner and watch him until your shift ends." She swings her legs off the couch and stands. Resting a hand on my arm, her eyes bore into mine. "Tell André you need more time with Tucker. He'll understand and find a way to make it happen."

A pang flares in my belly.

Tucker is of the utmost importance. But I don't want André to think I'm incapable of working my appointed shifts and managing my personal life. The last thing I want is a culinary genius I admire to see me as incompetent.

Had I not missed close to six years of Tucker's life, everything would be different. Tucker would be a normal nine-year-old kid. He'd get upset over trivial things like not getting his way. He'd have a sense of belonging with peers and family. The hurt and confusion he wears daily would be nonexistent.

Had we spent those monumental years together, we would've grown into daily routines and schedules with ease instead of fighting the current at every turn. Love would highlight his life instead of abandonment. Jokes and laughter would color his world.

In the past week, since he met Oliver Moss—his current musician idol—at the Memorial Day Festival, Tucker has been better. Happier. But he's still a scared little boy. He still fears the future. Questions if he will ever fit in.

And it breaks my damn heart.

I want a simple, easy life for Tucker. Daily smiles and shrill laughter as I tickle the spot on his ribs beneath his armpit. Grand adventures he brags to his friends about and fun cooking lessons he can't get enough of. Stability that offers him the chance to grow into who he is meant to be without concern over what *could* happen. Above all, I want him surrounded by love.

It isn't a monumental wish, but achieving it is harrowing.

"Promise I'll talk with André in the morning."

Mom pats my shoulder. "Good. Now take our boy home and tuck him into his own bed." Mom leans in and kisses my cheek. "Night, sweetheart."

"Night, Mom."

I collect Tucker's belongings and then scoop him up from the bed in his room at my parents' house. He stirs a moment, curls into me, and falls right back asleep. I buckle him in the car, deposit his backpack near his feet, hop in the car, and drive to our house on the property.

As I tuck him into his bed, I study his face, which looks so much like my own at his age. Visually trace his little brows and wild, curly hair he inherited from his mother. But it's the softness in his expression while he sleeps that shreds my heart to pieces. The softness he hides behind a steel mask of hurt while awake.

It kills me I missed so many years of his life.

Brianna moved around often enough I had trouble tracking them down. Just as the investigator received a tip on their whereabouts, Brianna packed their bags and left the area. Not sure if she knew I was on to her or her restless, vagabond soul needed to move.

Brianna never wanted to be a mother but stole our son and used him as a financial pawn. She robbed me of time and memories—precious commodities I'll never get back. She ripped Tucker away from a loving parent for years, all for selfish, nefarious reasons.

What she did is repulsive and unforgivable.

I only hope Tucker finds peace and moves forward.

Tiptoeing out of his room, I close the door except for a few inches. Move down the hall to my room and go about my bedtime routine.

When my head hits the pillow, my mind zips into overdrive. Mom's words play on repeat as my mind tries to solve the issue before sleep. After what feels like hours, exhaustion wins out. As I drift off, I think of how everything I do is for the little boy in the room across the hall. It also dawns on me to ask him what *he* needs rather than assume.

THREE

RAY

groan into my pillow. Eyes heavy with sleep, I blindly reach in the general direction of my current archnemesis and slap anything and everything on the nightstand until the alarm quiets.

Five more minutes.

When the alarm blares again, I curl the pillow around my head and pin it to my ears for one, two, three jolted heartbeats. On a heavy sigh, I release the pillow, shut off the alarm, throw back the covers, and force myself upright.

Last night's conversation with Mom weaseled its way into my dreams. Woke me up a time or two. Stole a decent chunk of the fleeting sleep I get on film nights. Still has my mind whirling with questions, possible solutions, and how this will impact my role at the restaurant.

Swinging my legs off the bed, I drop my elbows to my knees, head in my hands. "There has to be a way," I grumble into my palms before combing my fingers through my hair.

Tons of single parents work forty to fifty hours a week and still have time with their child. Granted, most of them probably work while school is in session and only miss an hour or two together after school ends.

Unfortunately, I don't have the luxury of working anything other than nights. Aside from private parties and events, Calhoun's Bistro only serves dinner. Early afternoon to midnight is a typical workday, and I don't see any way around it.

As Mom suggested, I'll talk with Chef Beaulieu later. I may not see a feasible resolution, but André's mind is always firing off new ideas.

Rising from the bed, I cross the room for the dresser, grab a pair of sweats, and tug them on. After my morning bathroom routine, I pad across the hall to Tucker's room.

"T-Man," I call out softly from the door. He squirms but doesn't wake fully. I step into the room and go to the foot of his bed. "Tucker. Time to get up, bud."

A displeased grumble filters through the room, and I clamp my lips between my teeth to keep from laughing. Early mornings —one thing Tucker and I would happily forfeit if given the chance.

I rest a hand on his foot still under the covers and give it a little jostle. "Going to make breakfast, bud. Any requests?"

At this, Tucker's eyes ease open. He blinks a few times then nods. "The pancake cootie tray."

We usually rotate through a list of breakfast options on weekdays. Most mornings, Tucker wants cereal. Occasionally, he asks me to cook. Weekends are reserved for entertaining breakfasts, visits to the diner, or creating something new with Tucker. Sunday, we make a list, load a cart at the grocery, and restock the fridge and pantry.

A couple weeks ago, Tucker asked for pancakes. Rather than make him the usual stack with a side of fruit, I assembled a pancake charcuterie board. I piled it high with toppings—butter, syrup, a handful of seasonal fruits, chocolate chips, hazelnut-cocoa spread, peanut butter, whipped cream, and caramelized cut apples.

When he slid onto his seat at the table, I'd never seen his eyes so wide or bright. He loved every minute of that breakfast. He tried to pronounce charcuterie twice before giving up and calling it cootie instead. I didn't have it in me to correct him. Instead, I melted at the sight of my little man happy at something so simple yet memorable.

I tap the footboard of his bed twice. "One pancake cootie tray coming up."

While I head for the kitchen, Tucker goes through his own morning routine. One he didn't need me to set, but I made a few adjustments to.

It broke my heart that my little man had to grow up faster than most kids his age. His mom loaded him with burdens far too early.

Over the past year and a half, I learned Brianna never made him breakfast—or any meal. If he wanted to eat, he had to figure out how to make a meal with what was in her apartment. When he went to school, he found out what hygiene was because other kids said he smelled, and the teacher pulled him aside. Tucker learned basic life skills before third grade and was responsible for his own well-being.

My stomach sours every time I think of the mayhem Brianna put him through.

I wish I could turn back time and change the past. Suggest moving to Stone Bay sooner. Be insistent yet reasonable. I wish I had heard Brianna packing that night, woken from the slightest noise, and stopped her from taking Tucker. But more than anything, I wish I was able to save him from years of traumatic experiences and me from trust issues.

Regrettably, the past is irreversible. All I can do is focus on the present and how it molds the future.

As a single parent, my work schedule needs a massive overhaul. No sense in denying it. But I do everything within my power to let Tucker be a kid now. When he helps in the kitchen, I reiterate it is *my* job to get groceries and prepare meals. Although he knows laundry basics, I make sure he's aware it isn't his responsibility to put his clothes in the washer, start the load, then move them to the dryer after.

Of course, he has chores. But they're standard chores kids his age have—clean up after yourself, tidy your room, dirty clothes in the hamper, help clear the table after a meal. As he gets older, I'll tack more on. For now, I just want him to enjoy his childhood. You only get so many years to be a kid, to live a more carefree life. Kids shouldn't bear the same pressures as adults. They'll have decades to shoulder all that stress.

As Tucker steps into the kitchen, I slide the last batch of pancakes onto the cutting board. Fruits and the other toppings decorate the rest of the space. A cup of juice sits in front of his plate and coffee in front of mine. The timer on the range beeps as Tucker takes his seat at the kitchen island.

Bacon sizzles as I pull the pan from the oven. Hickory wafts through the air as I add the strips to a plate, take the seat beside Tucker, and set the plate between us. "In case you want something salty."

"Ooh. I'm gonna make a pancake sandwich."

A hum as my shoulders cave, the first sip of coffee works its magic. From the corner of my eye, I watch Tucker as he assembles his own breakfast creation.

Tongue peeking out, he hesitates on what to add next. When he slaps a pancake on top and makes a *ta-tum* sound, I twist his plate and study his masterpiece. Pancakes in place of bread, a thick layer of peanut butter on both cakes, banana slices, mini chocolate chips, and several strips of bacon—it reminds me of Elvis.

I manage to bite back my laughter as he eats the messy breakfast sandwich too big for his mouth. Crumbling in his hands and falling onto the plate, Tucker carries on, undeterred. Before long, he swallows the last bite and finishes his juice. Without me asking, he takes his plate to the sink, rinses it, and puts it in the dishwasher. He comes back for his cup, but I shake my head.

"Finish getting ready. I've got the rest."

His forehead wrinkles for a second, then he nods. "'Kay."

I finish my breakfast, drink the last of my coffee, and start clearing the counter. Once the leftovers are stowed and the dishes are in the dishwasher, I head upstairs for a shirt and shoes.

As I near the bedrooms, Tucker says something in a hushed tone. Curious what he's up to, I tiptoe toward his cracked door and peek inside. Sitting on his bed with his back to the door, he has something small and red in his hand. A toy car, maybe? He holds it but doesn't play with it.

I angle my head to hear him better.

"Today will be a good day," he says softly. "If someone is mean, it's because they're having a bad day. Their madness isn't my fault."

As quietly as I approached, I retreat. Entering my room, I close the door and slump against the wall. My rib cage contracts, compresses, feels too small for my lungs. I press the heel of my hand to the center of my chest, a doleful ache blooming beneath it as my heart weeps.

Someone is bullying my little man?

The room blurs as the backs of my eyes sting. The ache beneath my sternum morphs into a million little pinpricks, jabbing over and over.

Is this why he acts out at random? A classmate picks on him. Says cruel, detrimental things.

A different sensation surfaces and takes hold. My nostrils flare as my nails dig into my palms. Sweat licks my skin, a turbulent heatwave pulsing, expanding, staining my neck and face. Red clouds my vision, my rage a molten hydrothermal vent ready to burst.

A growl rattles my chest as I close my eyes and take a slow, measured breath. Then another. And another until the fiery storm wanes.

Regardless of my anger, I can't approach this with a hot head. With Tucker's past, I need to tread lightly. Find a way to broach the subject in regular conversation. I want answers but can't demand them.

Talking with the toy must be an outlet. A way to release the hurt. Say what he feels in a safe space. The last thing I want Tucker to think is I eavesdrop on his privacy. He deserves refuge. A space free from harm or intrusion.

Instead, I'll talk with Mom and Dad. Ask if he mentioned anything after school yesterday. Then I'll reach out to Tucker's teacher. Question if there's a bully in the classroom. Bring this shift in Tucker's behavior to their attention.

Shirt and shoes on, I exit my room and act as I do every other school day. "Train leaves the station in five, T-Man."

"I'll be down in a minute," he hollers.

As I pocket my wallet, he flies down the stairs. We exit the house through the garage and hit the road a minute later.

Every cell in my body begs me to pry. To ask him if a classmate is harassing him. Somehow, I bite my tongue and resist the urge. When we reach the only stoplight in town, I turn on music and let the upbeat track steal my attention.

Two songs later, I steer the car into the school drop-off line. Tucker kicks his feet to the music and mumbles the lyrics. Bops his head, the corners of his mouth turned incrementally upward.

This is the most at ease I've seen Tucker since I got him back. I soak up every single second.

Is this because of his talk with the red toy?

As we inch forward, the need to say *something* surfaces. "You excited for summer, bud?"

He stares out the backseat passenger window and shrugs. "I guess."

I wait, but he doesn't elaborate.

"When I was in school, I counted down the hours during the last week. I was so excited to play outside all day and sleep in."

"Yeah," he says wistfully, his feet stilling. "Will you be home?"

That constriction in my chest from earlier makes a rapid comeback. I swallow past the sudden dryness in my throat. "We'll have so much more time together, bud."

The hint of a smile brightens his expression as we reach the drop-off spot. "I'll start thinking of all the things I want to do." He grabs his backpack, unfastens his seat belt, and opens the door. "Bye, Dad."

"Bye, T-Man. I love you. Have a good day."

His eyes meet mine for a second. "Love you, too." He closes the door and bolts through the crowd, disappearing inside the building a moment later.

On my drive home, I set a reminder to reach out to my parents and the teacher in a couple hours. Hopefully it's nothing to worry about, but I'd rather err on the side of caution.

As I park in the driveway, my phone rings, Fin's name flashing on the screen. I hit accept. "Morning, sunshine. You're up early," I say with exaggerated cheer in my voice.

"Are you always this loud in the morning?"

I cut the engine and exit the car. "Only for you, Finny."

If eye rolls made a noise, I'd hear it through the line right now.

"You're ridiculous." He huffs out a breath. "Just like my neighbor who thought no one would care if he used an electric saw in his open garage at seven in the morning. Ugh."

Unlocking the front door, I step in the house and toe off my shoes. "Dick move."

"Yeah. And now, I can't sleep. Was wondering if you wanted to knock out filming early."

Not really. The plan is to nap an hour before Fin comes over. But I guess there's always time after.

"Sure. Head over when you're ready. I may power nap on the couch until then."

"I'll be sure to bang loudly on the door, *sunshine*."

I laugh. "Appreciate it."

When the call disconnects, rather than sit on the couch and close my eyes, I head for the kitchen. Pull ingredients from the fridge and pantry for three more videos. Thankfully, some of the ingredients overlap for the recipes and I can use some footage more than once.

While I wait for Fin, I check my stats for the last few videos. Millions of views display on each post. As I work my way through the comments, liking and responding to as many as possible, Fin bangs on the front door.

"Wakey, wakey, porn star," he shouts loud enough for it to carry through the trees to my parents' house.

As I open the door, I roll my eyes. "Really, Fin? My parents will scold you every day for the rest of your life if they hear you."

Goofy smirk on his face, he strolls past me and into the house. "Lucky for me, they aren't home." He kicks off his shoes and heads for the kitchen. "What meat are you molesting for your groupies today?"

Following in his wake, I peel my shirt off and toss it on the dining room table. "Something moist and juicy."

"Should've known." He chuckles as he surveys the ingredients on the counter. "I'm ready when you are."

For the next three hours, I do what I love most. Cook and entertain.

FOUR

KAYA

From an early age, the desire to help others lived in my bones. It was different from that of my parents. My path was more abstract, profound, visceral. Scalpels, sutures, bandages, and medications will never be in my healing arsenal.

I mend the spirit. Restore the soul. Alleviate a different type of pain.

Sadness and heartache, hurt and frustration, anger and anxiety—my spirit cries out to heal the darkness in others. Show them ways to move past life's hiccups and hurdles. Point out the good when they can't see beyond the devastation. Guide them back toward the light and be a pillar when they need it most.

When I was a small girl, my *anaanatsialirqiuti*—great-grand-mother—told me she saw a great energy around my spirit. Great-grandmother said it had been many years since she encountered such a powerful spirit in a person. Both my *anaanatsiaq* and *anaana*—grandmother and mother—had gifts too, but theirs was differ-ent. As unique as we were. She said this gift I had been given was my calling. That I am *angakkuq*—a shaman.

I remember asking her if that meant I would work with my mother or father at a doctor's office or the hospital. She told me no. That my gift was distinct from theirs. I would heal people in a greater way, not with pills or thread, but with my heart and words.

It wasn't until years later that I truly understood what it meant to heal someone's spirit. When I neared the end of high school and started looking at college courses, it hadn't been difficult to narrow down my major. Finding a way to blend my culture with modern healing and the need to relieve others' anguish, I elected to study psychology. A year into my studies, after several conversations, a professor took me aside and said I'd be a phenomenal behavioral specialist. That I had a rare gift and saw more than a person's superficial layer.

Working with children in Stone Bay has been… interesting, but I wouldn't change a single moment. Once we overcome the hurdles and struggles and get to the root cause of their hurt, it opens a door for joy and gratitude. Nothing is more rewarding than seeing someone find their peace again. Gaining priceless connections with the town's youth is an additional perk.

When the final bell rings this school year, many will silently rejoice. Naturally, I'm the oddball. The one who wilts in their absence. The one who wants to check in with her students over summer break.

And as I pack up office number two, a gray cloud looms overhead and has me melancholy.

"Why are you frowning?" Clarissa asks from her spot in one of the guest chairs.

Snapping me out of my gloomy introspection, I blink a couple times and school my expression. "I'm not."

She peers up from her phone and arches a brow. "You were." Her gaze drops back to the screen as she chuckles.

"What's funny?"

"You're the only person at school sad about not seeing students for three months."

My eyes lose focus as I recall recent conversations with other school staff. Teachers, administrators, janitors. Several expressed their excitement for vacation and rest, but no one explicitly said they were thrilled to have student-free days.

I mentally wave off Clarissa's comment and return to packing. "I'll see some of them at the rec center throughout the summer." Fetching an empty manilla folder from the filing cabinet, I fill it with drawings and paintings middle and high school students gifted me this year. "Though it'll mostly be the elementary students."

"What else are you up to this summer?"

Unless my answer includes the word *vacation* or *relaxation* or some other variation of *I'm not working*, she won't like my response. Focusing on my task, I mentally prepare to be read the riot act. It's inevitable. A huge advocate of self-care, Clarissa is always on me about taking time to rest and restore.

Unfortunately, she's unable to grasp how spending time with and helping kids is one of my forms of self-care. Seeing their smiles, hearing their laughter, knowing I've made their day better… it's a balm for my soul.

"Not sure yet. Maybe some gardening. My grandfather has been begging me to go fishing with him again. It's been a while."

Clarissa lifts her gaze from her phone and pins me with an inquisitive stare. "Don't you garden all the time?"

I keep my expression light, neutral. "Yes, but gardening is different from one season to the next."

She stays quiet for a beat. The only sound in the room is of me boxing up memorabilia. As I put the lid on one box, she breaks the silence. "You should come to the beach with me next month."

My stomach pitches then plummets. "As fun as that sounds, you know I already promised to help out at the rec center."

A subtle shake of her head, she shrugs. "Give them plenty of notice and take a long weekend. I'm sure they won't mind."

"Rissa…"

"Picture it, Kaya. Endless sunshine, golden sand, hot guys everywhere you look." A devilish smile curves the corners of her mouth. "Maybe you'll find someone to help relieve your stress." She waggles her brows.

With a roll of my eyes, I laugh under my breath. "I'm not spending a long weekend in Southern California to"—I peer at the office door to make sure we're alone, then drop my voice—"have sex with random strangers."

"Boo." She pushes out her bottom lip in an exaggerated pout. "You're no fun."

"Yet you still love me," I tease.

She lifts a hand and rests it against her chin as a huge smile brightens her expression. "I do. Not sure what I'd do without you."

"Going soft on me, Rissa?"

Dropping her gaze back to her phone, she taps the screen. Music floats through the room as her smile turns devious. "Only for a sec." She laughs. "Maybe you don't need to go out of town for hot guys."

My brows furrow. "Do I want to know what that means?"

Clarissa rises from her seat and sidles up to me at the desk. Turning her phone so I can see the screen, she taps it and a video plays. "Stone Bay's very own celebrity."

On the screen, a man in a shirt tight enough to be a second skin makes a crust out of crushed cookies. Seconds later, there's whipped cream or frosting in a bowl. And then...

I gasp as my skin heats everywhere.

"Mm-hmm," Clarissa acknowledges.

His fingers are in a bowl filled with batter, flicking back and forth in a quick, suggestive way. Then his fingers are in a piece of fruit, juice squirting out.

I swallow, inhale a ragged breath, and hold it. The good girl in me says I should look away. Go back to what I was doing. But my racing heart, searing skin, and the subtle ache between my thighs keep my eyes glued to the screen.

The video turns tame for a few seconds as the dessert gets plated. In the next shot, all I see are abs. Tan rippled panty-soaking abs. He drags his tongue up a slice of cake before his eyes meet the camera and he blows a kiss at the audience. Then, it starts over.

For the first time in years, I'm speechless, at a true loss for words.

Clarissa, on the other hand, has plenty to say. She fans her face. "Mm-mm-mmm. That man can cook for me any day of the damn week." She stares at the screen as the video loops back to the beginning again. "Preferably naked."

"Rissa," I admonish.

"What?" She swipes the screen and different music echoes around us. "If he fucks as good as he cooks—"

"Rissa!" I whisper-shout and hook a thumb toward the open door when she looks up.

She rolls her eyes. "The office assistants are probably glued to their phones. None of them are listening to us."

"Either way…"

"Kaya, you cannot tell me this man doesn't do *something* to your… nether region."

A flush of heat crawls up my neck and spreads across my cheeks as I widen my eyes and mouth, *"Really?"*

"Could've said worse," she mutters and shrugs.

If we weren't at work, I would've let the comments go without a word. Still would've gotten hot watching the video. Still would've been self-conscious over the… sensations it elicited. But I would have otherwise left it alone.

I am far from a prude. Just prefer to keep certain thoughts to myself. Like the countless obscene thoughts that surfaced as the man-made dessert magic. The way my mouth watered… and not just for the food.

Am I ashamed? No, just private when it comes to partners, love, sex, and the emotions they come with.

Needing a subject change, I search for a safe topic. Her California trip comes to mind, but I quickly shut it down. It'd steer us back into Kaya-needs-a-man territory. Hmm.

"I mean, how can you look away?" Clarissa shoves her phone closer to my face as the guy practically molests a chicken with oil and herbs.

"Have you gone swimsuit shopping for your trip?" I blurt out, hoping the conversation will shift.

She bites her lower lip. "He can slather me in oil and herbs then lick me clean."

I pinch the bridge of my nose. "Rissa…" I drag her name out like a pouty child.

She lifts her gaze and pins me with mischievous, sparkling eyes.

Oh, no.

"I know the perfect way to celebrate the end of the school year," she declares, voice a little too chipper.

I swallow past the unfettered energy climbing up in my throat. "Oh yeah?"

"Mm-hmm." Her devilish smile from earlier makes a reappearance. "Dinner and drinks at Calhoun's Bistro."

Relief washes over me as my shoulders relax and I exhale the breath I was holding. "Nice as that sounds, they're booked months in advance."

Her wicked smile grows impossibly wider. "There are exceptions for *some* people."

She's talking about the fact that I'm Seven—a status I don't care to use—and can get a table whenever I want. All I have to do is make a call and flaunt said title.

I shake my head. "Let's go to Bay Chowder House or Gigi's. It'll be less crowded."

She props a hand on her hip. "Good as those are, I can go anytime. Can't say the same about Calhoun's Bistro."

No matter how much I push back, Clarissa will hold her ground. When she wants something, she is a force of nature.

I love and hate this side of her.

Minutes of silence pass before she sets her phone down, claps her hands together in prayer beneath her chin, and pushes out her bottom lip. "Please, Kaya. I'll even make the reservations."

I close my eyes, subtly shake my head, and take a deep breath. "Have I told you lately how pushy you are?"

"No." Her tone is lighter, buoyant. As if she *knows* I'll say yes.

Opening my eyes, I narrow my gaze on her. "Well, you are."

"But you still love me," she singsongs.

"Maybe," I tease.

She hooks an arm around my shoulders. "Say yes, Kaya. What've you got to lose?"

A heavy sigh leaves my lips. She's right, not that I plan on telling her. "Fine," I huff out. "Yes."

"Eeeee!" she squeals loudly, and I shrink away. After a quick kiss to my cheek, she picks her phone up and taps the screen several times. Lifts it to her ear and sets reservations for us.

Saturday at seven thirty.

At least I'll have most of the day to mentally prepare for our night out. And by prepare, I mean meditate for hours.

Clarissa ends the call then dances in place. Infectious as her excitement is, it doesn't quash the slow-building pang in my belly. Saturday feels different than our typical night out. More than a bite to eat or drinks as we celebrate another successful year. Saturday feels life altering, and I don't know why.

Change is good. It wakes you up. Gives you fresh perspective. Makes you question life.

Were my grandmother at my side, she'd tell me to be brave and do what makes my stomach flip upside down.

So, rather than let my jitters consume me, I embrace the unknown. With a smile on my face, I knock Clarissa's hip with mine and do a little jig. I open myself to something new.

FIVE

RAY

"Sick move, bud," I call out to Tucker as he rolls past me on his skateboard. By no means is Tucker able to do actual tricks on his board. But he's come a long way already.

For Tucker's ninth birthday, I got him a skateboard. I'd noticed him eyeing a few kids at school when I dropped him off at the car circle last fall, a hint of envy in his gaze. I asked him if skateboarding was something he wanted to try. With a shrug and emotionless half smile, he'd muttered, "I guess."

I may have missed years of Tucker's life, but I connect with my little man in a way no one else does. DNA isn't the only thing we share. In so many ways, Tucker is a mini version of me. His smile and laughter. His sense of adventure and willingness to try new things. And his tendency to bottle up his feelings and guard his heart once someone has broken it.

Sad to say, both our hearts were broken by the same person. Unfortunately, Tucker won't recover as quickly as I did. It's one thing for me to move on from a girlfriend who slowly slipped away, then carried out unforgivable, atrocious exploitation. Tucker was ignored by his mom for years. Feeling unloved and unwanted by her the entire time, and then being handed off to me, who he didn't remember because Brianna ran off with him at such a young age and warped his memories... it scars you in a way nothing else will.

Now that I have Tucker, now that he has a loving parent at his side, I'll fight nonstop to offset the hurt Brianna caused. I will do whatever it takes to give Tucker a happy life. My little man deserves the stars, and I'll hand him every single one.

Until recently, he rarely smiled. Most were forced. But the days his smiles come easily and shine brightest are at the indoor skate park. I'd bring him daily just to see more of those smiles.

The slap of wheels hitting concrete echoes through the space as I sit on a bench on the sidelines. Tucker glides from one side of the room to the other, arms slightly extended at his sides, eyes darting from the ground to what's ahead.

On our first day here, a teenager took him under their wing. Taught Tucker the basics and talked him through his fears of falling. Before we left that day, I asked the teen what days they were at the park and if they minded showing Tucker the ropes more.

With a little financial incentive, Jordan happily agreed to spend one or two days at the skate park with Tucker.

It eases my anxiety and warms my heart that Tucker has someone to look up to who's closer to his age. Someone he can make a lifelong friendship with.

A few weeks back, Jordan declared Tucker was ready to move on to something other than flat surfaces. The idea of Tucker flying through the air on his skateboard made my stomach flip—with thrill and unease. But I put my trust in Jordan's capable hands, and it was the right choice.

I stare on as Tucker sails past me and heads back to the line for the smallest ramp in the park, one specifically in place for learning.

Waiting his turn with a glowing smile on his face, Tucker inches forward and prepares to take off. As soon as the person in front of him clears out of the way, he kicks off and charges forward. The ramp's subtle incline teaches him how to build momentum safely. He flies up the ramp, crests the ridge of the low pyramid with a quick hop, coasts across the flat surface, then glides down the opposite side with a blinding smile on his face.

"Yeah, T-Man!" I cheer. "That's what I'm talking about."

I have yet to be told by Tucker I'm an embarrassment. So, I cheer him on as often as possible and pray it boosts his confidence.

An hour passes way too soon. We say our goodbyes to Jordan and leave the skate park. Tucker tells me how awesome it felt to do *bigger kid stuff* today. In response, I tell him he *is* a bigger kid.

A few blocks up the street, I park at the pizza place, and we head inside. Order drinks and a small pizza—Tucker's half with cheese and mine with everything. As the server walks off, I nudge Tucker's foot with mine under the table.

"You were awesome at the park today, bud. So proud of you."

He bops in his seat to the song playing in the restaurant. A hint of a smile on his lips. "Yeah." He sits a little straighter. Taller. "My moves were pretty dope."

Dope. Yet another word to add to the list of slang Jordan is teaching Tucker. At least none of the words in his new vocabulary are curses, derogatory, or hurtful.

"Jordan's a good teacher. Glad we met them."

Tucker plucks a crayon from a cup on the table and starts doodling on his place mat. "Me too. Jordan said I'm like the best little brother." The admission enlivens Tucker's expression.

My heart squeezes at the sight.

I love that Tucker has a role model, someone considerate and supportive he can talk with who isn't his therapist.

"That's amazing, bud."

The server deposits Tucker's root beer float and my Pepsi on the table, says the pizza will be out soon, then disappears again.

Eyes on his glass as he pokes the scoop of ice cream, worry creases Tucker's forehead. He takes a tentative sip of his float then sags in his seat. The sudden shift in his mood has my dad senses tingling. In an instant, a gray cloud swoops in and wipes away his happiness, and I don't like it.

I nudge his foot under the table again. "What's up, bud?"

He shifts his tight lips from side to side, unsure.

Ducking closer to the table, I peek up into his eyes and give him an encouraging smile. "Whatever it is, you can tell me." I gesture between us with a finger. "Remember, this is a safe space."

His brows bunch together in what I assume is hesitancy. Slowly, they relax, but not fully. Eyes still downcast, he asks, "Have you told Mom about Jordan?" His voice is so soft, timid, I barely hear his question.

My heart squeezes again but for a completely different reason. An achy tightness because my little man may never see or hear from his mom again. Tucker may be too young and unintentionally oblivious to grasp the finer details of why she is no longer in the picture, but he isn't too young to experience the everlasting side effects.

The one and only time Brianna reached out since abandoning Tucker at Dad's diner was two days after Tucker's birthday. She called the diner, asked Dad for my number, then called me from a blocked number and asked for money. She didn't ask about Tucker. She didn't ask me to tell him happy birthday from her.

Brianna spoke to me as if Tucker didn't exist at all.

Thoroughly repulsed by her attitude and behavior, I told her to lose my number and hung up.

Any time Tucker brings up Brianna, I tread lightly. His invisible wounds are still too fresh. He struggles to convince himself his mom doesn't want him—something he will work on for years.

It's natural for Tucker to ask about her, to want her to love him. Hurtful as the truth is, I refuse to lie. I refuse to give him false hope. But I will soften the truth.

"Not sure, bud," I answer with as much tenderness as possible. "I told you about the last time she called." Twisting my glass on the table, I watch the condensation roll down. "Don't remember all the things we discussed."

The corners of his mouth turn down as he nods.

"Promise I'll tell her about Jordan if she calls again."

"'Kay," he mutters.

Every protective bone in my body rages at the sight of Tucker's forlorn expression and wilted frame.

Fuck Brianna. Fuck her for doing this to Tucker.

Hate is not a strong enough word for how I feel about her.

You want to take off and traipse around who knows where doing who knows what? Fine. It's your life. You want to dick people over and ruin every relationship you've ever had? I don't give a damn. Go. Be an irresponsible idiot. Live like rules don't apply to you. You're the one who lives with the consequences.

But do *not* use *my son* as a pawn. *Ever.*

Tucker deserves the world. He deserves to be a kid, to not stress over food or bills or housing. He deserves to smile and laugh, to be carefree and happy.

If I have to make a wish on every falling star, birthday candle, dandelion, and wishbone, I will. All I want is for him to know life will move forward without her. That her actions and opinions don't shape his future, he does.

Needing to brighten the mood, I switch topics. "Did I tell you about the cooking school?"

Tucker peeks up from his drink and shakes his head.

"Chef Beaulieu came up with the coolest idea," I say, smile on my face and in my voice. "Summer cooking school for kids."

A soft glow twinkles in his hazels, and I love the sight.

"And guess what?"

"What?" Tucker asks, curiosity edging his tone.

"You're the first kid signed up."

Tucker goes quiet. Eyes glued to the ice cream in his cup, he swirls the straw and blends it with the root beer. I don't interrupt his thinking. Don't push him to respond. Don't force him to feel one way or the other about the news.

For most of his life, Tucker has had most of his choices taken from him. At an early age, he was forced into adulthood. Callously, Brianna stole the light in his eyes and used his innocence for her own personal gain.

I may have already signed Tucker up for the kids' culinary classes, but if he says he doesn't want to go, I won't make him.

The server returns with the pizza and sets a plate in front of each of us. I put a slice of cheese on Tucker's plate and add two supreme slices to mine. As I'm about to take a bite, Tucker finds his voice.

"Will…" His brows scrunch together as lines mar his forehead. "Will you be there?"

Shit. I didn't mean to leave that part out.

"Yeah, bud." I nod. "I'll be there. I'm teaching the class with Chef Beaulieu."

Tentatively, he picks up his slice of pizza, takes a bite, and sets it back down. Mulls the news over as he chews. And it's like watching a butterfly emerge from a chrysalis, the way the light filters back into his features. Zeal dances in his eyes. Excitement tips up the corners of his mouth. And this undeniable effervescence makes him fidget.

"Are we gonna make weird food?" he asks, voice garbled as he talks around the bite in his mouth.

I chuckle. "Don't talk with your mouth full, bud."

He swallows, then takes a sip of his drink. "Sorry."

"It's okay, bud." I reach across the table and ruffle his curls. "And yes, we'll probably make some weird, fun recipes."

"Yes!" he says then does a fist pump. "When does it start?" He picks up his pizza. "How many kids will be there?" Bringing the pizza to his mouth, he goes to take a bite then pauses with the slice an inch from his mouth. "Do I get to wear a chef hat like you?" He shoves the pizza in his mouth, takes a monstrous bite, and stares at me wide-eyed, waiting.

God, I love his enthusiasm. Love the light in his eyes. And I'll do whatever it takes to make sure it stays.

While we devour pizza, I share all the important details of the kids cooking school. When it starts. How many kids will be there. How many weeks it will be. And that we will get to spend almost all day together.

What I leave out is after the kids cooking school ends in August, I'll have a new schedule. One more flexible and in line with Tucker's schedule.

When I approached André to discuss my hours, he told me about the cooking school concept. I immediately loved the idea. Although most kids were likely signed up for summer programs months ago, neither of us worried about filling spots. Thirteen kids—a baker's dozen. Parents will fight to get their children in.

The classes will bring new life to Calhoun's Bistro.

Once the summer classes end, André wants to start adult classes. Monday through Friday, I'll be teaching cooking basics and how to make decadent dishes without breaking the bank or your kitchen. After we have several classes under our belt, we'll offer beginner, intermediate, and advanced classes.

The best part? On the days I teach, my evenings in the kitchen will be shorter. Several hours shorter.

If everything goes according to plan, between now and the end of the year, I'll spend half the day teaching and the other half leading and prepping the kitchen. I should be home an hour or two before Tucker's bedtime. If everything goes according to plan, next year, I should be home well before dinner.

The initial stab felt as though I lost my sous-chef position. But the more André and I talked, the more he explained this change as an advancement in my culinary career, not a step back.

"All chefs dream of running their own kitchen and restaurant, but the ultimate reward is passing on your knowledge. Watching someone create their first dish with the skills you taught them is the greatest gift."

His words took time to sink in, but once they did, it was a shot of dopamine to my bloodstream.

As Tucker and I leave the pizza restaurant, I peek at him in my periphery. Take in his sunny disposition and bounce in his step. Soak up his happiness and let it seep into my bones. Let it remind me everything I do, every decision I make, is for him.

If Tucker is happy, so am I.

Sweat beads my brow and I take a deep breath to cool down. Twisting, I press my forehead to the sleeve of my chef's coat then return my focus to the plate.

I spoon red wine demi-glace over the roasted quarter chicken on buttery, mashed cauliflower. Top it with a caramelized clove of roasted garlic and chiffonade of basil ribbons. After a quick wipe of the plate rim, I move the dish aside and follow the same process on the next plate.

The kitchen works like a well-oiled machine as tickets come in. André weaves through the kitchen, observing everyone at their stations, delivering praise and sharing tips. A moment later, he sidles up to me and does the same.

"Exquisite plates this evening, Chef Calhoun. Guests have sent compliments to the kitchen all night."

My cheeks warm at his praise. "Thank you, Chef Beaulieu."

As we do every night in the kitchen together, André and I fall into a harmonious dance. Tickets come in, we call out orders, and magic happens as each dish is plated under his hand or mine.

I love every minute—the rush, the stress, the pure chaos, and the art we create. I live for the thrill, the surge in my pulse. It's why André and I work so well together.

After another dozen plates are sent to the dining room, the tickets slow. André and I move about the kitchen, checking in with the cooks.

"Chef Beaulieu," a server calls from the pickup area.

He crosses the kitchen. "Yes, Ginny?"

Hands clasped at her waist, Ginny smiles. "A guest is requesting to speak with the chef."

In some restaurants, a cook or chef may be concerned if a guest asks to speak with them. At Calhoun's Bistro, we live for the requests.

André peers over his shoulder at me, pride highlighting his

expression. "Chef Calhoun"—he gestures toward the dining room —"would you mind?"

I nod. "Yes, Chef." I wipe my hands on a towel and toss it in the dirties bin off to the side.

Exiting the kitchen, I follow Ginny to the outskirts of the dining room. She pauses and nonchalantly points to a table across the room. "Table eight."

From here, it's difficult to make out the guests at the table. All I see is long, dark hair.

"Thank you, Ginny."

"You're welcome, Chef."

Straightening my chef's coat and smoothing my hands down my floor-length apron, I walk through the dining room toward table eight. Several guests stop me momentarily to sing their praise over tonight's meal. I thank them and casually move on.

As I near table eight, muted conversation and faint laughter hit my ears. The light, whimsical sound warms my skin and quickens my pulse. I suck in a sharp breath and hold it as I step closer.

Clasping my hands at my back, I slowly exhale. "Good evening, ladies. You asked to speak with the chef?"

The woman to my right meets my gaze, a sparkle in her eyes and suggestive smile on her lips. She's vibrant, beautiful. Just not the kind of beautiful I prefer.

"Yes." The woman bats her lashes as she taps her fork on her plate. "Best steak I've ever had." She spears a piece, pops it in her mouth, then slowly, seductively, slides the fork from between her lips. "So juicy..." Her eyes trail over my chef's coat. "Chef Calhoun."

A few years ago, when I had fewer responsibilities and would take anyone to bed, I would've flirted with this woman. Asked for her number. Had a wild night with her without a second thought.

But I'm not that man anymore. I can't be, not with Tucker. The moment he was in my arms again, I made a promise to myself—and him, in essence.

No more frivolous relationships. No random hookups with strangers.

If I introduce a woman to Tucker, I want her to be someone who will stick around. Someone I've spent time with and gotten to know. Someone who won't break my kid's heart if things don't work out with us.

I've had my fun. Hell, fun got me where I am now—fatherhood, dream career.

But now it's time to be more selfless.

"Thank you. I'll pass along the compliment to my kitchen." I shift my gaze to the other plate on the table—a half-eaten piece of grilled halibut with citrus segments, diced onion, and minced jalapeños. "How's the fi—" My voice catches when I lift my gaze to the woman on my left, and I clear my throat. "The fish. How is it?"

Shimmering copper-brown eyes stare up at me from beneath dark lashes. A faint dusting of pink colors her cheeks. The hint of a smile lifts the corners of her lips a beat before she swallows.

Unabashedly, I stare at her. Marvel at her rare beauty. Get lost in her sparkling, red-brown irises. Revel in the flush coloring her golden, light-brown cheeks as she holds my gaze. Take too much pleasure in her reticence as her hands fidget in her lap.

Damn, she makes me breathless, thoughtless, jittery in a way so foreign yet alluring. In a way that makes me want to know more about her. In a way that frightens me more than anything.

SIX

KAYA

MY CHEEKS AND NECK FLAME AS HIS UMBER EYES LOCK ONTO AND hold my gaze. The *whoosh, whoosh, whoosh* of my pulse thrums in my ears as I inhale a shaky breath. I twist the napkin in my lap then release it.

In his videos, the man is undeniably sexy and charming. In person... he's infinitely more captivating. So striking looking away feels impossible.

I blink out of my trance, wipe my palms over the cloth napkin in my lap, and give a subtle nod. "The fish is wonderful. Delicious." The compliment comes out soft, a touch raspy.

Clarissa snorts and garners both his and my attention.

"Wonderful?" she repeats in a teasing tone. "Delicious?" Muffled laughter drifts across the table as she covers her mouth with her hand. Her gaze turns playful. "Your moans suggested it was a bit more... *titillating*." Clarissa arches a brow, lifts her wineglass to her lips, and smirks. "Wouldn't you agree?" She tips the glass and takes a hefty sip of wine.

I am not a violent person. But god, do I want to kick Clarissa's shin right now. Hard.

Instead, I plaster on an over-the-top smile and mutter, "Seriously, Rissa?"

The wicked minx Clarissa is, she presses her arms closer together to make her already ample cleavage more pronounced. A mischievous smile curves up one corner of her mouth as she twists in her seat to face him more fully. "What, Kaya?" Eyes on him, she licks her lips. "Not like he's never heard his food is provocative."

My skin heats for a completely different reason, and I tuck my chin closer to my chest to hide my embarrassment. Timid is not a word I'd use to describe myself, nor would anyone who knows me well. But leave it to Clarissa to awaken my practically nonexistent bashful nature.

I love Clarissa. Truly. I love how easily we became friends. Love her out-going, resolute, brazen personality. How she goes after what she wants without shame. I love the way her strengths complement my own. How we lift each other up and support each other without reservation.

What I do *not* love is her putting me on the spot, especially with a guy, and she knows it. But she is hell-bent on pushing my boundaries and *getting me out there* more.

Smirk on his face, he chuckles. "Ah, so you know who I am then?" His gaze shifts back to me, his smug grin morphing into a vibrant, breath-stealing smile. The type that makes you forget your name.

The tip of his tongue peeks out and licks his lips a beat before he traps the bottom one between his teeth. The corners of his mouth twitch, and it's then that I realize I am full-on staring at his lips. For far too long.

I blink away, pick up my fork, and poke at the food on my plate. My face is on fire and undoubtedly a vivid red.

"Doesn't everyone in the restaurant know who you are?" Clarissa carries on, flirting without shame. "That's why we're here." She rolls her eyes. "Well, one of the reasons. We're also celebrating." Clarissa takes another hefty gulp of wine.

His gaze darts from me to Clarissa, then back to me. "What's the occasion?" Inching closer to the table, he leans forward. "I'll send dessert when I return to the kitchen," he says, a breath above a whisper.

Immediately, flashes of him sucking batter off his fingers and licking sliced cake pops in my head.

I clench my thighs.

"The end of school," Clarissa answers, appearing completely unaffected. Resting her forearms on the table and pushing up her breasts more, she bites her lip. "You make damn good dessert."

"Thank you." He chuckles and straightens to his full height. "You're teachers?"

"God, no," Clarissa says, tone derisive.

"Rissa," I admonish before meeting his gaze. "Excuse her candor. Sometimes she's *too* forward. We work in the main office." I point to Clarissa. "High school guidance counselor." Then I rest my hand on my chest. "Behavioral specialist for all three schools."

At this, he lights up. His joviality feels familiar. As if I've seen it before. I sift through my memories, and it isn't long before realization hits.

The boy in my office earlier this week—Tucker Calhoun—this is his dad. Ray Calhoun. Not sure why I didn't piece it together sooner. I blame my libidinous daydreams since he approached the table. Fair excuse.

But now I've connected the dots. Now, I see him a bit differently.

He's not just a chef or social media superstar. He's also a man working hard to make a better life for his son. And that makes him more attractive than any of his other attributes.

Ray squats and rests his forearms on the edge of the table. "Chef Beaulieu and I are offering our first kids culinary school this summer. Last-minute idea, but we're not worried about filling spaces."

"Sounds fun," I admit. "They'll love it."

Clarissa sits back and sips her wine. "Sounds like torture," she teases.

Ray ignores Clarissa and gives me his full attention. "Could use some help wrangling the kids." He doesn't outright ask me to help, but I hear the suggestion in his voice.

Beneath the table, Clarissa knocks my foot with hers. "Kaya is great with kids, and they love her."

I glance across the table at my friend, kick her shin like I wanted to minutes ago, and smile. "Thank you"—I turn back to Ray—"but I'm working at the rec center this summer." I give him a sad smile. "Sorry."

Clarissa's eyes widen as she tilts her head at Ray. "Shift some stuff," she says. "The rec center has plenty of workers and volunteers during the summer. I'm sure they'll be fine if you miss a few hours a day."

I glare at her. "I promised my time, Rissa. They're counting on me being there."

Clarissa opens her mouth to say something but stops as Ray stands up.

Reaching into his pocket, he pulls out a business card. Unclipping the pen hooked on his chef's coat, he writes on the card. He caps the pen, hooks it back on his coat, and then hands me the card.

"If you're able to swing it, let me know. The kids would love to see you, I'm sure." He takes a step back from the table. "My personal cell is on the card. Call me. We'll sort out the details." Dazzling smile on his face, he takes another step away from the table. "Thanks for coming in, ladies. Was nice to meet you, Kaya."

My cheeks warm as my name rolls off his tongue. I swallow and nod. Open my mouth to say it was nice meeting him as well but don't get the chance. Before I return the sentiment, he spins on his heel and retreats to the kitchen.

Every molecule in my body begs for me to turn and watch him walk away. To soak up a few more seconds of him. To ogle his broad shoulders and swagger. But I don't. I train my eyes forward and stare at Clarissa's shocked expression.

"Oh. My. God." Her hand smacks the table. "Oh my god," she repeats. "He likes you."

My brows shoot to my hairline as I shake my head. "What? No, Rissa." I glance down at the suddenly hot card in my hands, his number scrawled on the back. "He's being nice because he needs help."

"You can't be serious." Clarissa scoffs. "Has no one flirted with you before?" With a slight tilt of her head, she arches a brow. *"Was nice to meet you, Kaya,"* she says mockingly.

I roll my eyes.

"I openly flirted with him the entire time. Practically shoved my tits in his face."

"Rissa," I whisper-hiss as my gaze roams nearby tables.

She waves me off. "Point is, it doesn't matter. He wasn't looking at me." Sly smile on her face, she glances toward the kitchen then meets my gaze. "That man only saw you."

Lips rolling between my teeth, I drop my gaze to my plate. Load a bite of fish onto my fork, but don't bring it to my mouth. Turn immobile as my eyes lose focus. Clarissa's words repeat in my mind over and over.

"That man only saw you."

Each reiteration heats my blood more. Has my pulse thrumming harder, louder in my ears. Makes my hands tremble in my lap as nervous energy flutters in my belly.

I flashback to the way he held my gaze, piqued interest in his rich-brown irises. I examine the way he smiled at me versus Clarissa and note the clear differences. How he leaned more in my direction than hers when he moved closer to the table.

Body language doesn't lie. I hate to admit it, but Clarissa is right, to some degree.

A soft hum dances beneath my skin, and I take a deep, methodical breath to settle my nerves. I revel in the feeling and question what it means—for me and the future. But I don't ruminate long.

As quickly as the buzz sparks to life, I shut it down. It doesn't matter what it means.

First and foremost, his son is a student under my care. Relationships between staff and parents of students are a conflict of interest and presumed to be—but not stated—forbidden.

Second, a romantic relationship is off the table for at least another five years. When I graduated college, I promised myself I'd focus on my career until I had a strong foothold. I don't want my students to suffer because my attention is elsewhere.

If, by some miracle, those reasons are of no consequence, it still doesn't matter. In the end, my parents will undoubtedly disapprove. My future isn't dictated or set in stone by my family, but I do value their opinions. I cherish their love and guidance. I respect them and want to make them proud.

And no matter which way I spin it, I don't see my future including a man such as Ray Calhoun.

SEVEN

RAY

"Why do you get to go out for breakfast, but I don't?" Tucker grumbles as I tug a shirt over my head.

"It's a work meeting, bud." I ruffle his hair as I pass him for the bathroom. Squeezing product in my hand, I add it to my hair then run a brush through it. I glance at him in the mirror and shrug. "Lots of talking about boring stuff."

Tucker crosses his arms over his chest and huffs. "Yeah, with yummy food." His gaze hardens as his lips purse in obvious annoyance.

Washing my hands, I fetch the deodorant from the counter and swipe some on. Then I add a hint of cologne. "Grandma makes some of the best breakfast in town." I breeze past him as I exit the bathroom and head for the closet. Sneakers in hand, I sit on the foot of the bed and slip them on. "No one's stuffed French toast is as good as Grandma's."

Tucker steps up to the bed on my right and kicks at the end of the comforter. "But she doesn't make it with chocolate chips or whipped cream," he grouses.

"T-Man." I wait for him to look up. When he finally does, I bite my cheek to resist laughing at his forced pouty expression. Unfolding his arms, I hold his hands in mine. "Grandma makes gourmet candies and chocolates every morning she works, bud. I bet if you asked her, she'd make something with chocolate chips and whipped cream."

A hint of hope glimmers in his eyes. "Really?"

I nod. "Really," I assure. "Now, go." Slipping my hands from his, I dig my fingers into his side and wiggle them. "Finish getting ready."

Squeals of pure joy fill the room as I tickle Tucker. The biggest smile plastered on his face, he swats at me and pushes me away. "S-s-stop." He snort-laughs and shoves harder. "No m-more." A hefty dose of hysterical laughter. "I... I... I'm gonna p-pee my p-pants."

After one last wiggle of my fingers, I release him, and he runs for the bathroom.

Rising from the bed, I glance around the room, checking if I need anything else before heading downstairs. I pocket my phone, wallet, and keys, then head for the hall.

"Finish getting ready, bud. I'll be downstairs. Go time in five minutes."

"'Kay," he shouts as the sink turns on.

Downstairs, I wait for Tucker on the couch. Sifting through a folder about the summer cooking school, I double-check André and I didn't miss anything. As I skim the last page, Tucker plods down the stairs with his backpack over his shoulders.

"Did you pack your swim shorts?" I ask as I close the folder and rise from the couch.

He reaches around and pats his bulging backpack. "Yep. And my water blaster, fin, and flippers."

When I asked Mom and Dad if they minded watching Tucker for an hour this morning while I went to a meeting, they offered to keep Tucker a little longer. After our talk, I told Mom I didn't want to burden her with watching Tucker longer than necessary. She dismissed me with a wave of her hand and said spending time with her grandson is never a bother. She only wants to make sure I'm getting enough time with him.

"You've missed so much already, sweetheart. Don't want you to miss anything else. Tucker needs his dad, and you need your son."

It's really that simple.

I may have seen Tucker take his first step, may have heard him say his first few words, but I missed countless milestones after. Like seeing him kick his first ball or jumping and dancing on his own for the first time. Watching him draw his first picture. Answering all his questions about animals and sea creatures and people. Being annoyed with his pouty nos and inquisitive whys. Learning what foods he loves and which ones he can't stand.

I still have years to experience a different version of those with Tucker, a future full of other firsts, but I'll never get a chance at the ones I missed. I'll never get those stolen moments back, and neither will he.

Rushing to his side, I scoop him up off the floor and pin him to my chest. I poke the side of his neck and he tucks his chin to fight me off. "Where are those gills?" I tease as I carry him toward the door.

His giggles fill the air and warm my heart. "S-stop it." He laughs harder. "I don't have g-gills."

I wiggle my fingers across his neck. "I know they're hiding somewhere around here." Giving him a moment of respite, I enter the garage and unlock the car. As I set him on his feet, I give him one last tickle around the neck. "All that time you spend at the pool with Grandma and Papa, I swear you're turning into a shark."

He opens his door, tosses his backpack across the bench seat in the back, and climbs in. "'Cause sharks are dope."

There we go with the *dope* again.

"Yeah, bud, they are."

The engine barely has time to warm up before we reach my parents' house. We exchange morning greetings and hugs. Mom tells me to take my time; she and Dad will be at the country club pool with Tucker until lunch.

I kiss the top of Tucker's head, ruffle his hair, and tell him to have fun at the pool. Then I bend closer to his ear and remind him to ask Grandma for chocolate chips and whipped cream.

He gives a sly thumbs-up then runs off to the kitchen.

"Go to your meeting, sweetheart." Mom hugs me again. "We'll entertain our little man."

I pull her into another hug. "Thanks, Mom."

Gravel crunches as I back out of their driveway and drive off the family estate. My knuckles blanch as I wring the steering wheel and turn onto Fossil Mountain Highway. My stomach does a small flip when I reach Granite Parkway and steer the car toward the heart of town. As the miles disappear, my left knee bounces faster. Sweat slicks my palms, my grip slipping on the leather.

"It's just a meeting," I mutter to myself.

Cranking the air conditioning, I aim the vents at my face and armpits, praying I don't look like a swampy heathen when I arrive. My thumb taps the volume button on the steering wheel, and I let the rock music steal my attention. I drum my fingers to the beat, belt out the lyrics, and get lost in the song.

By the time I reach Poke the Yolk—a breakfast and brunch restaurant owned by my family and the Kemps—every ounce of calm I gained during the drive goes out the window. I weave through the packed lot and park in a spot near the back. Cutting the engine, I drop my head against the rest, close my eyes, and take a couple deep breaths.

A meeting. Not a date.

Snagging the folder off the passenger seat, I take one last deep breath, then exit the car. Crossing the lot, I enter the packed restaurant and scan the tables and diner counter. I deflate a little when I don't see her. Glancing at the clock on the wall over the kitchen pass-through window, I note I'm early.

"Looking for someone, sweetheart?"

I startle and turn my attention to the older woman in a Poke the Yolk shirt and apron. The corners of my mouth curve up as I meet her gaze. "Meeting a friend." More like a stranger, but she doesn't need to know.

"Give me a minute to clear a table." She winks.

I scan her name tag quickly. "Thanks, Trudie. Appreciate it."

From my spot near the door, I survey the crowded restaurant, a hint of pride coursing through my veins. The Calhouns and Kemps may not be founding families, but we sure as hell have made a name for ourselves in Stone Bay.

As far back as records show, the Calhoun family has been a staple in the community. Bakers and stew makers. Produce and meat suppliers. As the way people ate evolved, so did the food we offered. Stored in old wine boxes in my grandparents' house are stacks of photos of past generations cooking for and serving the residents of Stone Bay. Our love for food has been with us for several generations. It may be more complex and intricate now, but our passion is the same.

While the Kemp family also served food to the community, they are best known for their coffee beans and loose-leaf teas. Their process from plant to cup was unmatched and still is. When the two families decided to join business forces, it was a match made in Stone Bay heaven.

"Follow me, sweetheart." Trudie grabs two menus and leads me to a table near the window. "Here you are." She sets the menus on the table. "Can I get you started with something to drink?"

"Coffee, please."

"Sure thing. Be right back."

I peruse the menu to distract myself while I wait for my coffee and Kaya. As I decide on the caprese omelet, the chair across from me is pulled away from the table at the same time Trudie returns with a coffeepot and creamer.

Flipping over the mug in front of me, Trudie fills it almost to the rim. "Morning, sweetheart." She sets the creamer down and turns toward Kaya. "Coffee?"

A soft smile lifts the corners of Kaya's eyes. "No, thank you. Hot tea would be wonderful."

"I'll give you a moment to look at the menu and be back with your tea." In a heartbeat, Trudie disappears toward the server alley.

I wipe my palms down my thighs beneath the table, swallow past the nervous ball of energy in my throat, and plaster on what I hope is my best smile. "Good morning. Thanks for agreeing to do this."

Kaya unwraps her silverware, sets it on the table, and places the napkin in her lap. "*Ulaakut.*" A faint blush colors her cheeks. "Good morning. Sorry if you've been waiting long."

Sparkling copper-brown irises meet mine and I forget how to breathe, how to speak, how to do anything other than look like a bumbling fool.

A small teapot being set on the table snaps me out of my daze.

"Brought you a variety," Trudie says, placing a wooden caddy with several tea options on the table.

"Thank you." Kaya gives her a bright, genuine smile.

Pen poised on a guest check, Trudie glances at me. "Ready to order?"

I peer over at Kaya, and she nods then sifts through the tea selection. Picking up the menu, I hand it to Trudie. "Caprese omelet, home fries, and bacon, extra crispy."

Trudie scribbles furiously. "And for you, sweetheart?"

Kaya hands over her menu. "Smoked fish bowl, poached egg, heavy on the toasted sesame oil."

Is it too soon to fall in love with what she eats? Probably. But there is nothing like a woman with a unique food palate.

Awkward silence dances between us the moment Trudie walks away. It's not uncomfortable, just odd. Different than what I'm used to.

I've never been this enchanted by a woman yet so gobsmacked in her presence. When I want something, self-control is my biggest weakness. Anyone who knows me will agree. Without argument, they'll call me uninhibited, flirtatious, typically the life of the party. A ladies' man. That I'm more likely to make spontaneous, unwise decisions. Act the fool to make others laugh.

Quiet, subtle, or discreet are not adjectives my friends use to depict my personality.

But something about Kaya urges me to pause and pay attention. To absorb the subtle yet formidable way she takes up space in the room. To bask in the addictive, enthralling energy she exudes so effortlessly. To revel in *her*.

In a single glance, her coppery-brown gaze warms me more than the summer sun. And I eagerly indulge in her light.

Kaya dunks a tea bag in the pot, my eyes glued to the delicate way she moves. Almost as if it were a dance.

"So…" The single word on her tongue brings me back to reality, though I'd rather stay in her haze. "Tell me more about what I signed up for."

Ah, yes. The actual reason she agreed to meet for breakfast.

Setting down my mug, I hand her the folder. Her eyes roam the cover before she opens it and thumbs through the small packet and brochure. I give her a moment to peruse the details before I interrupt with my spiel.

"The program is six weeks of classes, and we skip the first week in July." I lean back in my seat and lay my hands in my lap. "Half a day, Monday through Friday."

My gaze roams her face as she stares down at the packet, and I get momentarily distracted when an endearing smile tugs at her perfect lips. So full, so pink. A hint of gloss.

Quit staring at her lips.

Shaking my head, I pick up where I left off. "Week one is more verbal instruction than hands on as we teach the kids basic skills and kitchen safety. But we have an incredible lineup each week and plan to show them something new every day."

Kaya opens the brochure André had Skylar at CKI—the queen of marketing for Calhoun-Kemp Industries—put together. I study Kaya as she skims over the gourmet food, kitchen, and chefs' images. Do my best to only read her body language and not ogle like a creep. Her gaze stays in one spot longer than anywhere else, but she isn't reading.

When I sit straighter to see what's caught her attention, she closes the brochure.

Her gaze meets mine, and I'm trapped in a swirl of cinnamon and honey. Her lips move, but I don't hear a word.

"Sorry." I blink, lean forward, rest my forearms on the table, and curse my distracted mind. "What was that?"

Biting her bottom lip to repress a smile, Kaya pours tea into her mug and clasps it with both hands. "I asked what I'll be doing with the kids."

Get it together and quit embarrassing yourself.

"André"—I start then correct—"Sorry, Chef Beaulieu and Finley Boland, a cook in our kitchen, will join the class during the first week. Primarily to make sure everyone is following safety protocols and to help guide them if they're not." I take a sip of coffee and lean forward more. "A couple parents have volunteered to help here and there. Staff from the various Calhoun-Kemp restaurants also offered their time. But other than me and you, no one is available throughout the entire course." I drop my gaze to my mug as I lift a finger to trace the rim. "You'll be working alongside the kids, chopping and cooking"—a corner of my mouth crooks up as I meet her addictive gaze once more—"and helping me translate chef speak into kid talk. Maybe assist me with keeping them in line."

Light, whimsical laughter bursts from her lips as she lifts a hand to cover her mouth. "Sorry." She continues to laugh as her neck and cheeks turn a delicious shade of pink.

I unabashedly stare at every inch of her flushed skin.

Soft. I bet her skin is so soft, so warm.

After a moment, she collects herself, her radiant smile still firmly in place. "Kid talk and keeping them in line," she says in a teasing tone. With a subtle shake of her head, her hand falls away from her mouth. "I'll do my best but won't make any promises."

My lips twitch and I bite the inside of my cheek. "Thanks." The way this woman always makes me smile—or want to smile— she must've cast some hocus-pocus on me.

I lift my mug to my lips, and her eyes follow the action. Heat ripples over my skin like a skipped pebble. When I lower the mug and her gaze stays on my mouth a breath longer, I mentally groan. But it's when those coppery-brown irises lift to mine that I lose it. Understated fire burns just beneath the surface, and I'll be damned if I miss a single singe of that flame.

"Should've known it was you."

I startle at the new, unexpected voice and look up to see Oliver Moss—a Stone Bay rock star and Tucker's current idol—standing at our table with a loaded tray.

My brow furrows. "Sorry, what?"

Oliver grabs a bowl from the tray. "The smoked fish bowl. Only a few people order it. Should've known you'd be one of them."

"Appreciate the flattery, man." I shake my head and gesture to Kaya with my hand. "But I'm about to disappoint you."

Bowl midway to my place mat, Oliver's extended hand pauses as he shifts his attention to the other side of the table. "Really?" he asks, the single-word question loaded with disbelief and awe.

Kaya shrugs. "Guilty."

Oliver sets a rice bowl piled high with smoked salmon, colorful vegetables, and a poached egg in front of her. "Huh." His gaze darts between us a beat before he places the other dish in front of me.

I tilt my head at his blatant intrigue. "What?"

"Nothing." He waves me off then nods to my mug. "More coffee?"

"Please." I resist pushing him further. *Another time.*

"Kirsten's making rounds. I'll let her know." And then he spins around and winds his way through the tables, checking in with guests on his way back to the server alley.

"He's fascinated that *I* ordered the unconventional breakfast dish and not you."

I bring my attention back to Kaya. "Yeah, I guess." Unrolling my silverware, I set my napkin in my lap. "His tone," I mutter as I spear a piece of potato. "Felt like he wanted to say something else."

"He did."

As I open my mouth to ask Kaya how she knows, a woman I'd seen several times when I worked at RJ's with Dad sidles up to the table with a pot of coffee.

"Ollie said you need a refill."

I nod and slide my mug toward her. "Thank you."

Cup filled to the brim, her eyes dart between us. "Anything else you need?"

Kaya shakes her head as I say, "Good at the moment."

A smile brightens her face. "Holler if you do." As she turns away, the faintest *hmm* hits my ears.

It's on the tip of my tongue to shout, "What's so damn interesting?" But when I glance across the table, the humor in Kaya's expression steals my attention.

Over breakfast, I share a little about myself, and Kaya does the same in return. I mention Tucker, and a softness takes over her features as she tells me she's met him. As we get to know one another, I take small bites and chew slower than usual. Pause more often than necessary. Do whatever possible to drag out our time together.

Minutes feel like seconds as I squeeze in more personal questions. The restaurant fades away. The chatter around us morphs into a dull murmur. Without effort, I ignore everyone and everything except her. Absorb her every word. Bask in her charismatic aura. Get lost in her addictive copper-brown irises.

Kaya. Damn, is she ravishing. Spectacular. An undeniable force.

For an hour, all I see, all I think about, all I *want* is her.

When Trudie delivers the check, Kaya argues—poorly—when

I refuse to let her pay. Breakfast was my idea. This... meeting could have been anywhere and without food involved. It's only right I pay. At least, that's what I tell myself when a voice in the back of my head screams *date*.

With the tab settled, I walk her to her car. My fingers twitch at my side, eager to touch her, feel her warmth, make contact with her soft skin. It takes every ounce of strength to curl my hands into tight fists and refrain.

"Thanks for breakfast," she says when we reach her car. "And a heads-up on what to expect with the kids."

"My pleasure." I shove my hands in my pockets. "Glad we got to know each other a little."

Unlocking the car, she opens the door and sets her purse inside. For a moment, we linger, neither of us sure what to say or do next.

Not wanting to make her uncomfortable, I take a reluctant step back, remove a hand from my pocket, and wave. "Enjoy the rest of your weekend."

The early June sun shimmers in her eyes, but her radiant smile shines brighter. "You, too. See you in about a week."

One step, then another, I slowly make my way to my car. As I slip behind the wheel, she pulls out of the parking space and drives toward the exit. And when her car vanishes from view, the bubble of euphoria I've been in the last hour pops.

In an instant, reality hits me full force. Slaps me in the face. Reminds me what happened last time I was so smitten with a woman.

Fingers curled around the steering wheel, the leather complains as my knuckles burn. I close my eyes, let my head fall back, and take a deep breath.

Kaya isn't Brianna.

No matter how many times I repeat it, the truth doesn't stick. No matter how much I want it to, my mind refuses to believe someone else won't ruin my life the way Brianna did.

For three years, she told me she loved me. And for three years, I was a goddamn fool.

Irrefutably, Kaya is nothing like Brianna. In every way, they are complete opposites.

But it's of no consequence.

The last time I handed over my heart, the last time I trusted someone fully, she all but laughed in my face, stole the most important person in my world, and ran off as if it were no big deal. Brianna kept Tucker from me for almost six years—not because she loved him, but because he was *useful*, and she was wretched and self-absorbed.

I despise Brianna for what she did. Refuse to forgive her for the hurt she so carelessly inflicted. With one selfish act, she wrecked our lives. Scarred our futures. Robbed us of countless memories.

An ache blooms in my chest as my pulse throbs in my ears. Sweat dampens my skin as outrage simmers in my veins. The car feels unsteady beneath me as my breath gets caught in my throat.

Breathe, I command myself. *Deep breath in for five. Hold it for three. Exhale for five.*

I hate how Brianna still has her claws in me. I hate that because of her, I have trust issues. But most of all, I hate how I refuse to let anyone in fully. How I reject happiness, fearing Tucker and I will be hurt again.

Kaya isn't Brianna.

If I repeat it enough times, maybe I'll start to believe it. If I repeat it enough times, maybe I'll learn how to trust again.

EIGHT
ERASER

"WHERE THE FUCK'S MY MONEY, COOK?" I REAR MY FOOT BACK, then drive it forward until it meets her rib cage with a sickening crunch.

Face down on the living room rug, her violent coughs echo through the room. She clutches at the spot where my boot made contact but doesn't otherwise complain.

"I had t-trouble with the last batch," she says, tone meek as she pushes up from the floor, arms trembling.

"Trouble?" I growl out the single word as I fist her greasy hair and yank her up. A whimper falls from her lips, but I ignore it as I hold her at eye level. "As in you and your buddies smoked all my shit and fucked until you passed out?"

Her eyes widen with fear, and she attempts to shake her head. "No."

Liar.

"Don't fucking play games with me, Cook." I wrench her higher and hear some of the hair rip from her scalp. "You will lose." I send my knee into her gut and release her hair. "Every. Fucking. Time."

Pathetic cries filter through the air as she clutches her stomach.

How did I get myself into this? How did I cave so easily to her advances? Not as though I haven't fucked half the city. Not as though I haven't tasted and fucked better cunts than hers.

So why did I let her get close? How did I get *here*?

I stare down at her pitiful, withering body and gaunt face and curl my fingers into fists at my sides. A promise, that's what got me into this insufferable mess.

Fully dressed, legs on either side of my lap, pussy grinding against my unimpressed dick, her dainty fingers trail down my chest. "I know what you want. What you need," she purrs.

Playing along, I reach up and tug a lock of her hair. Wrap the curls around my finger. "Do you now?"

"Mm-hmm." With a gentle rock of her hips, she does her damnedest to wake my still disappointed dick. She leans in closer and runs the tip of her tongue along the shell of my ear. "To own this town. To put fear into those who don't respect you."

She isn't wrong.

Fisting her shoulders, I force her back and away from my face. "And how would a pretty thing like you give me what I want?"

Her fingers tease my abdomen as she drifts lower. "I'll cook for you. Cut you a deal if you let me keep a little chalk." She pops the button on my jeans. "We both win."

I grab her wrist as her fingers go for my zipper. "What makes you think you get to set the terms?" With a shake of my head, I peel her hand away from my pants. "You're in my house, Cook.*"*

Bony hips rock against mine as she licks her lips. "Then tell me what you want." She thrusts her tits in my face. "I'll give you anything."

Damn, this bitch is desperate for a fix.

"Trial run. You cook for a week, produce quality ice, make my friends happy, and then I'll let you know what you get out of it."

"I'll have to sample as I go." Her eyes lose focus as she daydreams about testing *it. "Make sure it's perfect."*

Junkies… they're all alike. Tunnel vision for their next high.

"Only when I'm in the room, Cook." I fist her chin and crush her jaw. "You steal from me, you'll regret breathing."

Tilting her head, she bats her lashes with false innocence. Lifts a hand to her chest and draws an X over her heart. "Promise I'll be good."

Since that day, this bitch has been nothing but a nightmare. One *honest* mistake after another.

No more, though. I am fucking done.

"End of the month, Cook. I want every penny you owe in my hands by the end of June."

With shaky limbs, she pushes herself up until she's on her knees. Lifeless eyes stare up at me as she figures out what to say or do next. "I'll cook more. Twice as much for free."

I study her hollow cheeks and emaciated body for a beat. Let her think I'm considering the idea. The moment a glint of hope sparkles in her full eyes, I howl with laughter. Openly. Unabashedly.

"Cooking for me got you into this predicament. You really think it'll get you out?" I shake my head. "Don't have time to babysit you, Cook."

She crawls closer to me and plasters on her best seductive expression, which looks disturbing as hell in her physical condition. "Promise I won't do anything but cook. No samples. Nothing off the top."

I scoff. "Not a chance in hell you'll be alone in my kitchen anytime soon." Taking a step back, I growl out my irritation. "Now I have to pay someone to watch you when I can't."

Shuffling on her knees, she closes the distance I added between us. "I, uh, know of another way to pay." She bites down on her chapped, burned bottom lip.

Sad and fucking pathetic.

"Do you now?"

Her head bobs in a wobbly nod. "Use me. However you want. Whenever you want."

I rake my gaze over her body, and it does nothing for me. Not a flicker of desire or twitch of my dick. It's tragic.

Years ago, before the drugs gnawed away at her body, she was attractive. Not my type, but pretty in her own way. All buxom curves, fiery eyes, and fierce determination. Now, all she has is hunger for her next fix.

She does nothing for me, but at this point, why the hell not? Let her pay off a microfraction of her debt with her body. So long as I wrap up when I fuck her cunt, I have nothing to lose.

"Alright, Cook. Let's make a deal."

"Anything." The single word is loaded with too much hope as she blinks up at me.

"I fuck you whenever I want. If it's good enough, I'll shave off some of your debt."

Her cracked lips stretch into a creepy smile.

"Make no mistake, Cook. You still owe me thousands. I will collect."

She stumbles forward on her knees, lifts her hands to the waistband of my pants, and fumbles with the zipper. "You'll get everything I owe." She tugs down my jeans, then my underwear, and licks her lips. "I'll make everything right again."

And as she strokes my dick, my mind drifts to the curvaceous woman I had in my bed two nights ago. Her thick thighs clamped to my ears as I ate her pussy. Her full, soft breasts bouncing as she rode my cock. Her moans as I pinched her nipples just before she came.

And as Cook takes me to the back of her throat, I close my eyes and get lost in the memories of another woman.

This won't pay off her debt, but it will assuage my anger, for now.

NINE

RAY

Rolling onto my stomach, I wake before my alarm. The soft light of dawn filters through the edge of the curtains, and for a moment, I enjoy the peace that comes this early in the morning. The calm before the daily hustle. Those first breaths when everything is still and undisturbed.

The soft patter of rain hits the deck and trees outside as I shift the pillow and hug it to my chest. For a moment, I zone out to the rhythmic thrum. Let it lull me as the fogginess of my dreams fades and reality trickles in.

As it does most mornings, my mind skims through a mental to-do list. Monotonous daily activities. Tucker's short but tedious routine. And eventually, things specific to today. When the reality of what day it is sinks in, everything in me stills then swiftly jolts to life.

Cooking school starts today.

A surge of energy swirls in my chest a beat before my pulse echoes in my ears. I roll onto my back, stare at the ceiling, let the rush flow through me unrestrained, then slowly sit up. Closing my eyes, I cross my legs and take a few meditative breaths. When my eyes open, I feel energized yet centered. Ready to take on the day.

I welcome the unstable throb beneath my rib cage. The irrefutable hum dancing beneath my skin. The thrill and impatience pulsing through my veins. More than anything, I delight in the buoyancy in my limbs—something I haven't felt in a long time.

Kicking off the sheet, I swing my legs off the mattress, plant my feet on the floor, and stand, stretching my limbs. I amble over to the wall of windows and fling open the curtains. Gaze out at the tall evergreens lining my property, the Bay Cliff Mountains in the distance. Take a moment to appreciate all the good things in my life.

When André and I spoke about adjusting my hours, I feared my culinary career would die an early death. But the more time I've had to digest what this change means, the more I've let his optimism take root, the more excited I am to take the next step.

Since our conversation a couple weeks ago, I've worked hard to focus on the positives. In doing so, I've seen how much they outweigh what I thought I'd be losing.

I may not be in the kitchen when all the chaos happens. I may spend less time with the friends and family I've gained since I put on my Calhoun's Bistro chef's coat. But I don't regret a single step forward. When I finally accepted this was the path I was meant to take, I felt dizzy. Exhilarated. Ready to go.

Just the thought of teaching Tucker what I know, sharing one of my passions with him, showing him how fun it is to create in the kitchen... a fiery storm blazes in my chest. I love how eager he is to learn. How excited he is to *play with food.*

It makes the reward of this next step that much sweeter.

I cross the bedroom for the bathroom, stripping my briefs as I go. Tossing them in the hamper, I crank the water in the walk-in shower and give it a moment to heat up. The glass fogs as I step in and set a towel on the far end of the bench.

The hot spray wakes up my muscles as I go through my shower routine. Hair washed, I squirt bodywash in my palm, coat the other, and lather my chest and tattooed abs. As my hands drift lower, my mind wanders to more libidinous places.

I close my eyes as my slick palm strokes the length of my cock. Slow. Measured. Squeezing a little harder as I near the head. Root to tip, over and over, I pump my cock. An inferno blazes beneath my skin. Expanding. Pulsing. Begging for relief.

An image of Kaya flashes in my mind. Her coppery-brown eyes peeking up at me from beneath her lashes. A faint blush on her cheeks and neck.

"Fuck," I growl out as my free hand slaps the glass and takes some of my weight. *I'm going to hell.*

I strengthen my grip, pulse my cock harder. Cling to the image of her and let it fuel my uninhibited thoughts. Of what it would feel like to trail my fingers over her golden-brown skin. How she would look beneath me, jaw slack and gaze wanton. What her breath would feel like on my skin as her moans fill the room. The way her body would quiver as we edge closer to climax.

My balls draw up as fire licks my veins. "Jesus. Fuck." As my thumb strokes the head of my cock, I come undone, painting the glass. Legs shaking, I glance down at my swollen cock. "Definitely going to hell," I mutter.

But oh, how glorious the trip would be.

After I finish in the shower, I towel off and pull on a pair of sweatpants. Poke my head inside Tucker's room to see him still asleep. Once I rouse him, I jog down the stairs and get started on breakfast.

Tucker plods into the kitchen, hands rubbing his eyes, and takes a seat at the island.

Thinly sliced ham warms in the oven while I scramble eggs on the stove. When the eggs are only a little runny, I cut the heat and put a lid on the pan. I grab a couple croissants that I picked up from the bakery yesterday and slice them in half. Turning off the oven, I swap the ham for the croissants. While they warm, I slice some brie.

Across the bar, Tucker watches with complete fascination. "Will we make breakfasts like this?"

I pull the croissants from the oven and start assembling the breakfast sandwiches.

"Yep. We made an amazing list of fun foods." I set his sandwich in front of him. "Can't wait to make them all with you."

Tucker presses down on his croissant and squishes his sandwich. "Me either."

He devours his food in no time, hops off his stool and takes his plate to the sink. Before he runs off to get ready, I call after him.

"Hold on a minute, bud." I rise from my stool and wipe my hands. "Follow me." I lead him to the living room and fetch the bag on the couch. "Got something for you."

"Really?" His excitement palpable as he bounces beside me.

I pull out the junior-sized chef's coat, unfold it, and hold it up. "What do you think?" I point to the left breast where his name is stitched.

"Whoa!" He shuffles forward and gingerly takes the coat. "This is for me?"

"You know it." I ruffle his hair.

Hazel, glassy eyes stare up at me with so much love, appreciation, and a hint of disbelief. "This is so dope." He tries and fails to hide his sniffle. "Thanks, Dad."

I bend and press a kiss to his head. "You're welcome, T-Man. Now, go"—I pat his butt—"get ready."

Tucker talks my ear off as we drive to the restaurant. He tells me all the food he plans to make and how he will be a chef one day. And while he chatters on, I tap the steering wheel over and over. Watch the odometer tick off tenths of a mile, one after another.

To say I'm nervous would be an understatement. Hell, I haven't been this jittery in years. And it has nothing to do with teaching thirteen kids how to cook or use sharp knives.

No, this endless effervescence in the center of my chest is because I get to see her again.

Kaya.

Sure, I can lie to myself. Do my best to shove down this foreign, fizzy feeling beneath my diaphragm. Deny how I come alive whenever she is within reach. Argue that it's only attraction and nothing more.

But deep down, I know it's more than lust. Avoiding the truth is pointless.

For now, though, I need to focus on what is important and keep my thoughts to myself.

I steer the car into the lot and park on the side of the restaurant. Open the back door, grab my work backpack, and shoulder it. When Tucker joins me at the trunk of the car, he takes my hand and gives it a small squeeze.

"Don't be nervous, Dad. You're the best cook ever." He tugs me toward the door. "Everyone will love you."

With such a simple statement, a weight lifts from my shoulders. Tucker makes me feel like I can take on the world. He and the other kids are why I am here. They are my priority. If they're happy, so am I.

The restaurant is too quiet as we weave through the employee area in the back. We pass linen storage, followed by the back-of-the-house server stations. I guide Tucker down a short hall that leads to the kitchen and point out the walk-in cooler and freezer. He stares wide-eyed at the large door when I tell him we have to wear winter coats if we are in there more than a couple minutes.

"Hey, little man," Fin says as we enter the kitchen. "So cool you get to hang out with us all summer." Fin holds out a fist and Tucker bumps it with his own.

Tucker points to his name embroidered on his chef's coat. "It's just like yours and Dad's," he says with so much pride it makes my chest ache. "I'm never taking it off."

Fin squats until he's eye level with Tucker. He brushes off Tucker's shoulders, smooths down the sleeves, and double-checks the buttons. "Just remember"—Fin holds Tucker's gaze—"appearances are important when you're a chef. Messes are expected, but we always want to look our best." He tugs on the bottom of Tucker's coat. "And that means you need to wear an apron to protect your clothes or wash your coat every day."

Tucker's expression turns serious. "Promise I'll look my best, Mr. Fin."

"Good man." And then Fin sweeps Tucker off his feet, clutches him to his chest, and digs his fingers in his rib cage. "Now, let's have some fun."

"Sss… sss…" Tucker snort-laughs as he swats at Fin's hands. "Stop it."

God, his laughter is infectious. My little man may have been through a lot already, but he still has an air of innocence. And damn, do I want him to have it as long as possible.

After a minute, Fin plants Tucker on his feet. "Come on, bud. Let's go set up before everyone gets here."

Without another word, Tucker follows Fin to the classroom to help organize the tables.

While he's distracted, I go to the office, review schedules and checklists, and talk with André about how we can balance prepping for the cooking classes, kitchen, and events. Although the kids will be doing most of the work, we still need to prepare some of the ingredients in the main kitchen outside of class hours, store the ingredients, and mark them so staff don't accidentally use them.

Quarter after eight, André and I head for the front. He unlocks the door and a handful of students come in, their parents waving and promising to return in a few hours. Fin and Tucker appear long enough to lead the new arrivals to the classroom.

As I linger near the door, I can't help but scan the parking lot for Kaya. André does one last review of what we will do with the kids today. But the moment I spot her powder-blue SUV, I don't hear a word he says.

Kaya exits her car, and I swallow past the sudden dryness in my throat.

Damn.

A pair of soft-apricot palazzo pants sit high on her hips and draw attention to her legs. The pristine-white scoop neck top shows a hint of her collarbones, and I lick my lips. But it's the white sneakers that tie it all together and give her an effortlessly casual energy. In the sun, her loosely braided dark hair has subtle red undertones.

"Chef Calhoun."

I blink a couple times and turn my attention to André. "Sorry, Chef."

He chuckles. "Maybe I need to work more of these classes with you." He nudges me with his elbow. "Make sure you're actually teaching the kids instead of eyeing the assistant."

Heat crawls up my neck. "You know I'd love to have you at my side every time I'm in the kitchen."

"That I do." He clears his throat. "I said we should video a little of each class, snap some photos, and post them online. Create more buzz for future classes and the restaurant other than an article in the Gazette. Show us instructing but edit out faces of the students."

Distracted, I only hear half of what he says as my gaze flits back to Kaya as she enters the valet loop. "Brilliant idea," I say, my eyes still on her. "If we get any shots of the kids, maybe we can make a video for the parents. A nice keepsake."

André pats my shoulder as he takes a step away. "Fin promised to film a little each week when he helps. Maybe you can ask your... assistant if she'd mind taking pictures and recording a few videos."

The way he says *assistant* makes me want to slap him—in a playful way, of course.

"I'll be sure to ask," I say, not giving him any more fuel.

As she nears the door, André crosses the restaurant. "Can't wait for you to introduce her."

I roll my eyes, take a deep breath, and plaster on my best smile as I open the door for Kaya. "Good morning. Please, come in."

"*Ulaakut*. Good morning." Kaya steps past me and surveys the restaurant. "I'm not late, am I?"

With a shake of my head, I say, "You're perfect." And then, I mentally slap myself and try again. "Still have another ten to fifteen minutes before we get started." Not trusting myself, I clasp my hands behind my back. "Let me show you where we're hosting the classes."

I lead Kaya to one of the event spaces in the back.

Most of the sizable rooms are set up for large gatherings and celebrations. Several tables, chairs, and couches with softly lit sconces and chandeliers. A personal bar stocked with all the essentials, a grand fireplace with tall wine racks lining either side and a large window overlooking the bay.

Thankfully, my grandfather and his business partners, Ray Sr. and Roger Kemp, opted to furnish one of the restaurant's event spaces with a colossal kitchen and enough seating for thirty. The space has only been reserved a few times since I've worked at Calhoun's Bistro. Different occasions when the party wanted a personal chef and set menu or to cook for their significant other with our guidance.

"Here we are." I open the door and am hit with excited chatter.

Tucker glances our way and lights up. Scrambling out of his seat, he rushes across the room. "Miss Kaya." Before I can stop him, he slams into her and wraps his arms around her middle.

My cheeks heat as I wince. "Tucker..."

Kaya chuckles. "Hi, Tucker." She gently wraps him in her arms, then releases him. "I wondered if I'd see you today."

I tap Tucker's shoulder. "How about we let Miss Kaya come in."

He drops his arms and shuffles back. "Sorry."

"No need to apologize." A soft smile plumps her cheeks. "I'm happy you're here, too."

For a moment, I'm struck speechless. Bewildered. A little thrown off at how easily Tucker and Kaya interact with one another. How comfortable they are in each other's company.

What did she say her title was at the school? Behavioral specialist.

The way they smile and chat tells me Tucker is at ease with her. Delighted. Glad he has someone familiar here.

She told me over breakfast she'd met Tucker. But why? At the time, I was too enamored with her to ask.

I would know if something happened at school, wouldn't I? If Tucker caused trouble and was sent to the office, someone would call or email. I flashback to him talking to the toy a couple weeks ago. If someone bullied him and he spoke with Kaya, she would reach out. Right? It's on the tip of my tongue to ask, but I stop myself. Resist the urge to question why the school's behavioral specialist is acquainted with my son. This isn't the place.

Another time.

Tucker bounds off to hover near Fin and the other kids.

"Once everyone's here, I'll give a more eloquent speech about your role," I say as I inch closer to Kaya. "But all we're asking is that you help keep the kids focused. We expect them to be boisterous and a little loud, but we don't want to detract from why we're all here."

Smile still on her face, Kaya stares at the kids and nods. "If you need me to do more or less at any time, just let me know."

I shuffle back to see her in more than my periphery. And for a moment, I simply breathe her in. The delicate slope of her nose and plump bottom lip. The subtle curve of her brows and the way her thick, long lashes fan out. A light blush highlights her soft cheekbones, a hue darker dusted on her eyelids.

From the corner of my eye, Fin glances at us, a wicked smile tugging at one corner of his mouth. It's enough to snap me out of my Kaya-induced haze.

"Chef Beaulieu wanted me to ask if you'd mind taking pictures or videos occasionally. Otherwise, we're good for now."

André comes in with the rest of the students. Everyone finds their designated seat and we go around the room and introduce ourselves. The class is a good mix of ages ranging from eight to sixteen. We let the kids know that Kaya, as well as some parents, are here to help make the class fun.

While Fin and I go over the basic outlined schedule, André retrieves the chef's coats we got for everyone. We pass out the coats and help the kids put them on. Rather than hand Kaya hers to put it on herself, I offer to help.

"I'm quite capable," she teases as I hold the coat open for her.

"Don't doubt it. Just thought I'd help."

Before she spins around, I spot the heat coloring her neck and cheeks. "Thank you."

Guiding her arms into the sleeves, I step closer as I set the coat on her shoulders. An earthy, rose scent wafts up my nose, and my gaze drops to the nape of her neck.

Does she dab perfume there? The spot just beneath her hair.

I want to lean in closer, skim my nose down the curve of her shoulder, inhale every inch of her skin, and learn exactly where that smell is. Take a long pull and store the scent of her skin in my memory.

With a slight turn of her head, she peeks over her shoulder. "Is everything okay?"

No.

"Yes. Sorry." God, this woman must think I'm a nitwit. "Been a bit foggy today. Not used to working so early."

Lies.

I shift my hands to fix the collar on the coat as she starts to speak. But the moment my fingertips graze the nape of her neck, we both freeze, her words dying on her tongue.

An insatiable hum dances up my arms and settles in my chest. When she takes her next breath, it's shaky. Ragged. Telling.

She feels it, too.

There is no chance in hell I'll only ever be acquaintances or friends with this woman. Not after today. Not after the charge that just passed between us.

But what if I don't have what it takes to be... *more*? What if Kaya walks away and shatters me like *she* did?

I yank my hands away and clutch them behind my back. "Sorry," I mutter.

She spins around and faces me, so close the warmth of her breath ghosts the front of my throat. "Don't apologize," she whispers as she meets my gaze. "To live is to feel, to experience, to hope. I'd rather feel all those things than nothing at all."

Yep. It's official. I'm done for.

TEN

KAYA

Death Valley–level heat roars beneath my skin as embarrassment paints me in red splotches.

Why did I say that? Because for whatever reason, any time I am near this man, my brain short-circuits.

"I'd rather feel all those things than nothing at all."

Dig the hole and bury me now.

Tingles dance over my skin where his calloused, capable fingers grazed my neck. An infinitesimal, simple touch that was more than a surface-level connection. My hands flutter, eager to reach up and let my fingers sweep over the point of contact, to imprint it permanently on my skin.

But I don't. Instead, I curl my fingers into loose fists at my sides and ignore my impulses.

Heavy silence looms over us as I study his striking umber irises. Eyes that tell a story yet give nothing away.

"I'm—" I start at the same time he says, "Me—"

I tuck my lips between my teeth, fighting my smile, as he chuckles and says, "Go ahead."

For three heartbeats, I capture the sound of his understated laughter. Commit the deep, throaty tones to memory. Let it take up residence in my soul like the feel of his fingers on my skin has.

I like his laugh. Quite a bit. More than I should.

Releasing my lips, I set my smile free. "Was just going to apologize." I drop my gaze and fumble with the buttons on the coat. "Seems I made things awkward."

His hands appear at his sides, fingers twitchy as I fasten the cloth-covered buttons. My stomach flips at his restlessness, at his inclination to touch me again.

"Not awkward," he mumbles.

When I reach the last button, I lift my gaze and am taken aback by the warmth in his eyes. We barely know each other, but his visceral reaction every time he sees me is undeniable. Significant. As if it's impossible for him to conceal his feelings. It's refreshing.

I like an unreserved man. A man willing to open himself up to vulnerabilities. A man unafraid to flaunt every facet of himself, including the side most are taught to suppress because it makes them appear *weak* or *less than.*

"As you said, there's nothing to apologize for." The corner of his mouth tips up in a crooked smile. "I agree with you."

My eyes dart between his as my brows pinch together. "Agree?"

With indiscernible ease, he leans closer, invades my space, breathes my air. "I'd rather feel all those things than nothing at all, too."

I suck in a sharp breath as he straightens and inches back. Several heart-pounding seconds pass as I stand slack-jawed and speechless. Dumbfounded. Unable to articulate a coherent thought or find my voice.

No man has stunned me silent before, not like this.

A click sounds behind me, and I turn to see a shock of red hair. Eyes scanning the room, Phoebe Graves enters with a bag slung over her shoulder and a semi-cheerful smile on her face. Although Phoebe and I are descendants of the founding families, we aren't familiar with each other beyond names and basic public information.

Most of her life, Phoebe has been dubbed the *most frigid* person in Stone Bay. Until a little more than a year ago, most people—including myself—steered away from her. With a single glare from her harsh gaze, she would've turned anyone to ice.

It took a serial killer threatening to rob her of someone she'd fallen in love with—Delilah Fox, another of the Seven—to thaw her arctic heart.

I'm still a bit hesitant on how much I share or interact with her. A tiger may not change its stripes, but I'd like to think perhaps she was a chameleon blending in with her environment until ready to show her true self.

Phoebe scans the room full of kids, then breathes easier when she spots me and Ray. She crosses the room for us, smiles... and it appears genuine. Happy. A touch skittish.

"Kaya." She tips her head in my direction then turns toward Ray. "Tré," she greets. "Great turnout."

Brows pinched in confusion, Ray tilts his head. "What brings you in, Phoebe?"

Phoebe glances to the front of the room, where the kitchen is, and juts her chin. "Chef Beaulieu asked me to come in, take pictures, and write up a feel-good story for the Gazette on the restaurant's first cooking classes."

Ray peers over his shoulder at the front of the room as his fingers rub his palms at his sides. When he turns back to us, he rolls his shoulders and nods, his expression vacant and all business.

"He mentioned the paper, but I missed the details." He folds his arms over his chest. "Seats are assigned. Look for an empty spot without a tent card," he says, voice colder than usual.

Phoebe rolls her eyes. "I'm glad to be here, too," she says in a mocking tone, then gives us her back. Hiking the bag higher on her shoulder, she wanders off to a table in the corner.

The desire to console Ray once she's out of earshot blooms in my chest. Words dance on the tip of my tongue, eager to comfort him. Tell him not to worry about the nosy reporter and focus on why he's here—to do what he loves and share it with the next generation.

On instinct, I reach out and rest a hand on his forearm. The heat, the hum, the undeniable connection we shared moments ago flares back to life. An inferno blazes anew. Tingles ripple up my arm to my chest. Need pools low in my belly.

I yank my hand away and swallow. Watch as his hand flexes then extends at his side. Inhale a slow, deliberate breath as I meet his mystified gaze.

"Focus on why you're here and ignore the rest." My voice is sandpaper as I clutch my left wrist and stroke the beads on my bracelet. "You'll do great."

The lines around his eyes deepen as a soft smile tugs at the corners of his mouth. "Thanks."

"Chef Calhoun," Chef Beaulieu calls. "Shall we begin?"

With a wink, Ray walks off and I take my seat. Tucker gives a gleeful "Yes!" when he learns we are at the same table. Everyone quiets down, and I turn my attention to the front of the room as Ray greets the group.

After introductions, Ray, Fin, and André outline some of the *boring* but important safety measures the kids will learn this week before the fun starts. They share the kitchen tools we will use, how sharp the knives and graters are, and how important it is to focus on your tasks and hands.

Fin abandons the counter to hand out thickly sliced cheese as Ray instructs everyone to pick up the butter knife at their setting.

"Before we introduce sharp knives, we'll practice basic techniques with gentler tools," Ray says as he picks up his own butter knife. He shows the kids how to hold it properly, where to place their other hand, and how to cut without hurting themselves.

The entire time, I salivate in my seat at how capable he is. Peek at him every once in a while from under my lashes. Do my best to focus on why I am in this room.

I'm here to assist, to work, not ogle.

Although the kids didn't cook anything today, lunch is served before class ends.

Rice-shaped and decorated to look like different animals. Vegetables sliced into stars, hearts, and other various designs or left whole. Thin cuts of chicken with teriyaki sauce on the side. A small bowl of fresh fruit. The younger kids are thrilled by the adorable display. And thankfully, the chefs made "adult" versions of the same lunch for the teens.

As plates are delivered, I can't help but notice I'm the only person with fish instead of chicken.

Ray has seen me eat twice, and both times, I've had fish on my plate. That he's paid attention and remembered such a detail makes me bite my cheek throughout lunch.

As we clear and wipe down the tables, I spot Ray in my periphery. Huddled with the teens, he promises things will be more exciting soon. Lips pursed, one of the teens shrugs and mutters something inaudible. The others appear a little more accepting and appreciative.

Taking the last of the trash from our table to the bin, I approach Chef Beaulieu at the front of the room.

"Thank you for a wonderful first class, Chef. It's great that you're offering this for the kids."

An amiable, genuine smile brightens his features as he extends his hand for me to shake. His skin is more calloused than I expect, but his grip is gentle, firm yet supple. "I should be the one thanking you, Ms. Imala. Your time is valuable, and we appreciate you spending it with us. Your assistance eases our stress and helps the kids focus better. And please, call me André."

I lean closer and whisper, "Only when the kids aren't around." I straighten and see Ray heading our way. "While class is in session, they should address you as Chef."

His affectionate smile morphs into this pulse-pounding beam.

It's impossible not to be pulled in and enthralled by the sight. "Of course, you're right." Brilliant smile still in place, he winks.

Is that a requirement to work at Calhoun's Bistro? An addictive smile the patrons will melt over.

Ray sidles up to me at the counter, the heat of his gaze on my profile. "Good first class?"

My body hums as I turn to meet his waiting stare. He's close. Much closer than expected. I swallow and nod. "Great." Perspiration dampens my skin and I pop the buttons on my chef's coat. "Kids really enjoyed it."

I don't miss the way his intense focus falls and latches on to my fingers as I undo each button. How the muscles in his jaw flex as I reach the last one. The way his Adam's apple bobs as I peel off the coat.

The way he can't take his eyes off me… this man likes me in a chef's coat. Would undoubtedly prefer it to be his and nothing else. But the fire in those dark irises as each button pops free… he aches for the slow, torturous way I take it off more.

"Did you?" Ray asks, voice low, gravelly.

I fold the coat and drape it over my arm. "Did I what?"

His dark gaze drifts up and locks onto mine once more. "Enjoy the class."

Right. "Yes." Peeking around the room, I inch closer to him and lower my voice. "But I do prefer gouda over cheddar." I straighten and bite the inside of my cheek.

His eyes dart between mine for three erratic heartbeats. "Noted."

A student says goodbye as they exit and it snaps my attention back to reality. I glance at my watch and see it's just after one.

"I should head out." I amble back to the table and collect my things. Ray follows in my wake like a proprietorial shadow. "They need me at the rec center," I say as I shoulder my bag.

"Let me walk you out."

I open my mouth to tell him it isn't necessary but can't form the words. He would ignore my dismissal anyway.

We weave through the dining room in comfortable silence. A low hum in the air between us. When we reach the door, he holds it open and gestures for me to exit. I expect him to linger on the threshold and say his farewell from the door. But as I step into the sunshine, his shoes clap the stone pavers behind me.

The last time a man pursued me, *really* gave chase, was in college. I didn't make it easy for him, but that was part of the thrill. Although I was career-focused and not looking for a relationship, one man snuck in and cross-wired my lifelong plan. For the first time in years, my career wasn't my only priority. Eager but scared to leap, I needed him to prove I'd be more than one night between the sheets. He didn't disappoint.

At the start of my third semester in college, Ren Tajima sat several seats from me in cultural anthropology. The course wasn't crowded, but the occupied seats outweighed the empty ones.

I remember the first day our eyes met. The twinkle in his dark hazels made my stomach flutter.

During the second week of class, we arrived within seconds of each other. As we scurried for our seats, we bumped into one another, and my notebook fell out of my hands. Ever the proper gentleman, he bent down, picked it up, and handed it back with a soft, apologetic smile on his lips. He introduced himself, asked my name, and what year I was in. The conversation was cordial, if not a little generic, lasted maybe a minute, and then we took our seats.

Every day after the incident, Ren smiled at me before class started. And every time, his smile reached his eyes and emphasized that alluring twinkle. When the opportunity struck, he sat closer. It wasn't long before friendship sparked. By the middle of the semester, he asked me on a date, and I said yes.

I liked Ren. I enjoyed spending time with him. But as time ticked by, I knew we'd never be *more*.

In my sophomore year of high school, my primary focus had been my studies. By mid-junior year, most of my attention centered around my eventual career. If something or someone disrupted my plan, I tended to shove it or them aside. The more my career goals solidified, the more concrete those tendencies became.

After a handful of dates with Ren, we took the next step. Unfortunately for him, it was also our last step.

I liked Ren. A lot. For months, he garnered much of my attention. Spending time with him felt right, perfect. So taking the next step seemed evolutionary, natural. But as we lay in his bed in coital bliss, it dawned on me how off course I'd drifted.

I didn't want to hurt him, but I refused to let myself be distracted anymore. Once we crossed the line, there was no in-between. So, I broke his heart and lost a great friend in the process.

At this stage of my life and in my career, the occasional date isn't off the table. But I refuse to let a romantic relationship smother my light, my work, my ambition, or my future. It's challenging enough to fight the strong, invisible current in my path. The last thing I need is an additional obstacle in the way.

With the right person, it's possible to have more than my career. Love and intimacy take work, but they shouldn't feel like barriers.

If Ray Calhoun truly wants a shot, I need to be more than one of the millions of people fawning over him online. I need to know I'm more than a distraction or good time. That he won't diminish my aspirations to boost his own.

I unlock my car and stow my belongings in the back seat. Opening the driver's door, I turn to face him. "Thank you, again. It was nice to see the students in an environment other than school."

He nods. "I don't get enough time with Tucker because of our schedules. But that's changing."

"I'm sure it'll be a positive transition for you both. Oh"—I hold up a finger—"I meant to ask earlier but didn't have the chance. Why did Phoebe call you Tré?"

Conflicting emotions dance in his eyes. "It's a default nickname. The simplest to use when Dad, Pops, and I are in the same room. Curse of sharing the same name." He chuckles. "I put my foot down and refuse to let there be a fourth Ray."

"I love Tucker's name."

"Thanks. Was my choice. His mother didn't care about his name." Melancholy laces his tone. "Was nice to see Tucker so happy today. Don't think I've seen him smile that much in a while."

The details of Tucker's past are vague, but after talking with him and spending time with Ray, it's easy to see they've experienced major bumps.

"Glad he has a parent who gives him that." I slip behind the wheel and reach for the door handle. "See you in the morning."

He reaches for the door, steps closer, and flashes me his dazzling smile. "Look forward to it." With a wink, he shuts my door and steps back.

I expect him to turn around and head for the restaurant. Go inside and say goodbye to others. But he doesn't move. Rooted in place, gaze on my profile, he watches me drive out of the lot. Fire licks my skin the entire seventeen seconds I see him in my rearview.

My pulse resumes its normal rhythm by the time I reach the rec center. I head inside, spend a few hours entertaining and corralling the grade school children, pass out snacks and sit through an animated movie I saw a dozen times last summer, and am thoroughly exhausted when the last child is picked up.

On the way to my car, I call Bay Chowder House for takeout. Order one of my favorites as I slip into the driver's seat and crank the engine. Melt into my seat and take a moment for myself when the call disconnects.

It's been a long day, but I wouldn't change a single minute.

As I turn into the restaurant lot, ringing sounds through the car speakers. I glance at the console and smile when *Anaana*—mother—flashes on the screen. Mom.

Pressing the answer button on the steering wheel, I greet, "Hi, Mom."

"Hi, my sweet *panik*. Hope I'm not interrupting."

In my preteens, there was this small window of time where I wished my mom called me something besides *my sweet daughter*. Most girls my age were called darling, cutie, peanut, or a similar term of endearment by their parents. I wanted so badly to have a *normal* byname from my parents. To be like the other girls.

When I grew out of my broody stage, I was glad my parents hadn't given me one of those nicknames. They didn't fit who I am or where I come from.

My smile widens at her warm, affectionate tone. "Not at all. Picking up dinner."

"Long day?"

As doctors, my parents are accustomed to long shifts and the exhaustion that comes with it. But we all agree the reward is worth the price.

"Yes. Working a couple programs this summer."

"I won't keep you. Only called to check in about Friday dinner."

No matter how busy life gets, my family gets together once a week. Although we see or speak with each other during the week, our family dinners are the one guaranteed time we have to catch up and strengthen our kinship. Most happen on Friday, but we switch them if too many conflicts pop up.

"I'll be there, *Anaana*. What can I bring?"

"Just that beautiful smile."

I pull into a parking space marked for takeout. "I'll be there. *Nalligivagit, Anaana*." I love you, Mom.

"*Nalligivagit, panik*." I love you, daughter.

When the call disconnects, I cut the engine and head inside to pick up my order. Bag in hand, I'm behind the wheel a moment later and driving to the Imala estate.

Music plays in the background as my tires eat up the miles. As the second song ends, I turn onto a road bearing our family's surname. Each of the Stone Bay founding families has a vast estate with a private road marked with their name. The only difference between the Imala estate and those of the other founders... the homes on our property.

Most of the founding families have grandiose mansions and a small home or two for guests. On the Imala estate, we have a larger house—four bedrooms and bathrooms—for the two eldest generations of the Imala and Stonewater. On the rest of the estate, we have smaller, quaint homes for the younger generations and guests. Our homes are modern, simple, and minimalistic. They provide shelter, warmth, and safety. As children, anytime my brothers or I would complain about not having *things*, an elder would tell us that beautiful trinkets will come and go, it's the things we need most that remain.

We live by those wise words.

I park in the garage, grab my dinner and bag from the back, and head inside. Setting my food on the kitchen counter, I go to my bedroom and change into sweatpants and a loose-fitting T-shirt.

From the fridge, I grab the wine and pour myself a small glass. Take a sip, carry my dinner to the living room, and plop down on the couch. With a heavy sigh, I sink into the cushions. Let my muscles relax for the first time since early this morning. Close my eyes, take a few deep breaths, and center myself.

I love my job. I love how rewarding it is to work with children and give them a safe space in a harsh world. But I also love coming home to an empty house and not having to attend to anyone other than myself.

Pulling the take-out box from the bag, I open the lid and stare down at the grilled shrimp and avocado salad. And without fail, I smile.

Because it makes me think of him—Ray—and how he's book-marked my favorite foods.

And after a long day, there's no better way for it to end.

ELEVEN

RAY

"Fantastic work, everyone." I applaud at the front of the room. Fin and André on either side of me join my praise of the kids, clapping. "Thanks for hanging in there as we mastered the *boring* stuff this week."

Smiles light up several faces as laughter floats throughout the room. Their exhilaration palpable as I scan the tables.

"Next week, the real fun begins… with breakfast foods."

A few of the younger kids wiggle in their seats while others do fist pumps and whisper-hiss, "Yes!" When their excitement tapers, I continue.

"Before we go today, I have homework for you." I hold up a hand to cut off grumbles and comments. "You'll like this assignment. Promise."

André and Fin pass out homework sheets. Briefly, my gaze pauses on Kaya, a shy smile on her lips. The corner of my mouth twitches a beat before I move past her.

"Between now and the start of dessert week"—murmurs filter through the room at the mention of dessert—"I want you to think about your favorite dishes or a family meal you really love. Write them on the paper as they come to you. Put as many as you want on the page." I hold up a copy and tap it. "The hard part of this homework is at the start of week six." Somber smile on my face, I add, "You'll have to choose the one you love most. Then we'll put them to a vote. The most popular dish will be made by me for everyone to enjoy."

Oohs followed by mumbled, animated words echo around us.

"Everyone's dish will get made and shared for the group to enjoy. They may not taste as good as the version you love, but we'll do our best. Any questions before lunch?"

Several hands go up and we answer each question, be it silly or serious, as lunch is brought in from the main restaurant. Once we've responded to everyone, André, Fin, and I take a seat at different tables with the kids and enjoy lunch.

I squeeze in a chair beside Tucker's and give him a tight side hug. "What'd you think of week one, bud?"

Tucker slurps a fettuccine noodle between his lips, alfredo sauce coating his mouth and splattering his face. Not that he cares. "Was good. Kind of boring, but okay."

Twirling pasta around my fork, I pierce a blistered tomato, grilled mushroom, and chunk of lobster. "Glad it was only kind of boring," I tease and then pop the bite in my mouth.

As light chatter fills the room, I listen and soak in everything the kids have to say about the class so far. From what I hear, they all seem pleased with the class but are happy the first week is done. That little tidbit of insight warms my chest in an incomparable way.

I can do this. I can take this next step and still feel a sense of achievement. Fulfillment. Exultation.

This new role is a step in the right direction, and I look forward to the opportunities it brings. Although the rush is different from what I get working in the main kitchen, it still thrums in my veins. I still feel as though I have purpose, am important. When I'm at the head of the room and glance around to see their attention zeroed in on me, it feels as though I've made it. As if I've unlocked an elusive dream I didn't know I was chasing.

I load my fork with another bite of pasta and lift it to my mouth. As it has countless times this week, my gaze flits to Kaya. At this point, it feels like second nature. Habitual. When my eyes lock onto her coppery-brown gaze, a sense of weightlessness settles in my chest.

How long has she been staring?

Had I met Kaya a few years ago, I would've rattled off some cocky comment when I spotted her checking me out. A one-liner to make her laugh or blush. Anything to get a reaction and make her lean a little closer or playfully roll her eyes and wave me off. Anything to hold her attention and lure her in.

In that regard, I'm glad I didn't meet her back then. Happy I didn't have the opportunity to ruin what may possibly be something great.

From the moment I laid eyes on Kaya, she's been at the forefront of my thoughts. The slight, natural upward curve of her full lips at the corners. How her lustered irises seem to reach for and capture the light in any setting. Shimmering. Captivating. The soft slope of her nose that leads to a septum piercing I don't remember seeing before today. Her soft, golden-brown skin with a hint of blush on her cheekbones. The overall radiance she exudes effortlessly.

Kaya is more than beauty and appeal. When she enters the room, an inexplicable magnetism sparks to life inside me. An undeniable awareness rooted in my marrow. It's more than temptation. Bigger than some carnal urge.

She calls out to and awakens the dormant side of my soul. Rouses new, irresistible desires.

Needing more than a silent conversation with her, I load my fork and bring it to my lips but don't take the bite yet. "How was class for you this week, Kaya?"

A faint blush pinks her cheeks. The sight heats more than my blood, and I discreetly adjust myself beneath the table.

Kaya glances at Tucker for a split second before meeting my gaze again. "Fun. Informative." A smile plumps her cheeks as she spears a blistered tomato and chunk of lobster. "Learned some great tips and tricks. You're an excellent teacher. Your skill set, expertise, and patience are noteworthy, especially with this crew." She visually sweeps the room, pausing on each child a moment.

Her praise turns my insides to hot honey.

"Thank you," I murmur then take a deep breath and sit taller. "Are you excited to slice, dice, sauté, and bake?"

Swallowing her bite, she takes a sip of water and nods. "Yes. I'm no stranger to the kitchen, but my competence is mediocre next to yours." Soft laughter leaves her lips. "Basic, simple meals are my specialty. The fewer ingredients, the better." She shifts in her seat, a soft glow about her as her entire body comes to life. "And I'm learning how to make traditional foods with my family. Ancestral recipes and delicacies we lost generations ago but have rediscovered."

The conversations around us fade into the background as I focus all my attention on her. "I'd love to hear more if you're comfortable sharing. Before culinary school, I trekked through parts of Europe and Asia. Experienced a plethora of cultural foods unlike what we see in the States."

Those months exploring the world changed how I looked at and thought of food. Of course, my family influenced my love for being in the kitchen. But the days and nights in Italy, France, Spain, Thailand, Japan, Vietnam, and the Philippines had the biggest impact on my culinary creativity.

It's one thing to be handed a recipe and make a dish from a list of ingredients. It's something wholly different to stand in a kitchen smaller than the average bedroom, sweating your ass off because there's no air conditioning and cooking the food you just caught or foraged. The experience humbled and motivated me in a way nothing else ever has.

When I returned home, I immediately signed up for culinary school. I knew it'd be years before I'd create anything as extravagant or awe-inspiring as the foods I tasted in my travels, but I had the patience to wait. And until that moment arrived, I created unique dishes on my own time.

Kaya tucks an errant hair behind her ear as the blush on her cheeks blooms a darker, more addictive shade of red. And damn, how I love my effect on her.

Bold, twinkling eyes meet mine as she sits back, rests her hands in her lap, and nods. "Sometime."

Her confident, relaxed energy is my new favorite obsession.

Setting my fork on my plate, I wipe my mouth then set my napkin down. Subdued grin on my face, I shift my attention to Tucker and his now empty plate. "Hey, bud, will you help clear the tables?"

Grumbling his acquiescence, he scoots his chair away from the table and takes his plate to the tub.

Without overthinking it, I move to Tucker's seat next to Kaya and inch closer to her. "Thanks again for being here." I do my damnedest to come off as casual. "I appreciate you taking the time."

What I really want to say is *you're the reason I've smiled all week,* but that seems over the top.

"I should be thanking you." She hands Tucker her plate when he returns to the table. "Had you not mentioned the class, I would've missed out."

We fall silent a moment, but it's far from uncomfortable. As the seconds tick on, as the end of class looms in the not-too-distant future, the warmth in my chest at her proximity morphs into buzzing anxiety.

Before I can stop myself, I blurt, "Can I take you to dinner sometime?"

Her eyes widen in surprise as the question registers. "Erm…"

I plaster on my best smile, the one most melt over, and inch impossibly closer to her. I don't miss the rapid rise of her chest at my nearness.

"Nothing extravagant. Dinner, maybe a little wine." I shrug

and try to remain outwardly composed. Inside, every cell in my body screams *please say yes* over and over.

Bucking up the courage to put myself out there is hard enough. It isn't only my heart on the line, but I'm willing to take the initial hit. For Kaya, I will risk my heart. Expose myself and be vulnerable. Endanger my peace and emotions for the possibility of what may be.

She shifts in her seat as her eyes scan the room. "I, uh…" Wrinkles line her forehead as her gaze meets mine. "I don't know."

Not a firm no. Which means there is room for a yes. Time to add more fuel to the kindling.

Twisting in my seat, my hand rests inches from hers. "I like you, Kaya," I say, voice soft, words laced with conviction. "And I'd like to know you better."

"Is that a good idea?" She tilts her head toward the kids and my coworkers.

"There's no rule saying we can't have dinner together." I almost said *go on a date* but quickly countered.

Skepticism dances over her expression. "The school frowns upon staff spending personal time with parents."

"School's out for the summer," I rush out. "We can cross that bridge later."

Her gaze drops to her lap a beat before it drifts across the room. "What about Tucker?"

With such a rough start in life, the last thing I want to do is disrupt the inkling of serenity Tucker has gained since I got him back. But Tucker isn't the same little boy I laid eyes on almost two years ago. Now, he has a safe haven, a sense of security, feels loved. He smiles, is genuinely happy.

After countless hours of overthinking this week, of going back and forth on whether I should attempt dating as a single dad, I decide yes. It's time to find what—who—sets my soul on fire. Yes, I am a parent. But it's not all I am.

"I'll talk with him. Figure it out."

I see the cogs turning as she mulls over whether to accept or decline. She doesn't make me wait long.

With a lick of her lips, she swallows then nods infinitesimally. "Dinner sounds nice."

I stop breathing for one, two, three erratic heartbeats. As I exhale, the noise around us filters back in. My cheeks burn as a smile stretches across my face. "I'll talk with Tucker and text you later."

She fights a smile and fails, and damn do I love how much it makes her glow. "Talk to you later."

TWELVE

KAYA

Friday family dinner is always a grand affair in the main house.

My grandmother, Ahnah, and her mother, Liuna, spend most of the day in the kitchen. Whether it's chopping fresh vegetables from our family garden, preparing fish or meat, or kneading dough for fresh bannock, their hands are busy post-breakfast until it's time to serve dinner.

Most Fridays, thirteen to fifteen of us gather. On rare occasions, twice as many join. Either way, I soak up every moment with each of them. Listen to their stories. Let them teach me nearly forgotten skills no longer necessary in everyday life. Discover more invaluable parts of our ancestry.

Our history and traditions were lost over generations, but we're slowly navigating our way back. Learning who we were, our ancestors' way of life, and finding ways to incorporate those pieces into our modern-day lives.

At twenty-five, my life isn't vastly different than other young women my age. I work forty-plus hours a week, go out with friends, have an unhealthy obsession with fashion, eat too much ice cream while watching sappy movies, and live for rainy days on the couch with a good book.

But there will always be a piece of me, unlike women my age, and I accept this. Although it's been a rough road, I have learned to love this part of myself more with time.

Years ago, my grandmother decided to do an online DNA ancestry test. When I asked what provoked the idea, she said, *"I love Stone Bay. It will always be my home. My heart. But sometimes it feels like a piece of our family is missing."*

She wasn't wrong.

A significant amount of saliva in a tube shipped off to a lab for evaluation changed everything. Within days of the results, she tracked down family we didn't know existed in northern Canada. After a few jittery weeks of mulling over what to do with the information, she sent a message to someone listed as kin. It's been a whirlwind since.

Same as my grandmother, Stone Bay is my heart and home. Stone Bay is all I've ever known.

But it soothes a piece of the soul to know where the Imala family originates. That more of us live outside our small town's borders. Grandmother has worked diligently to organize a reunion party. The largest gathering of multiple generations in more than a century.

The scent of smoked meat wafts up my nose as I enter the kitchen. A smell so comforting and familiar. Home. I inhale deeply and sigh. My stomach grumbles, and I rub my midsection with the silent promise to eat soon.

"Unukut, Anaanatsiaq. Anaanatsialirqiuti." Good evening, Grandmother. Great-grandmother.

Both their heads pop up, their tasks forgotten. Deep wrinkles line their eyes and lips as smiles brighten both of their expressions.

"Unukut, my darling *irngutaq."* Grandchild. "How was your first week of cooking classes?"

I walk around the large kitchen island and hug my great-grandmother, then grandmother. "Good. More tedious than anything."

Curious eyes so similar to mine but a hint darker stare back. "Tedious?"

Without being asked, I slice the red onion on the counter. "This week focused on teaching basic techniques and kitchen safety." My eyes sting and I blink a few times as I continue to cut. "Was dull because I already know most of those things thanks to you." I set the knife down and lean into her side. "You and Great-Grandmother have been my favorite teachers."

She kisses my hair. "As sweet as your *anaana*. Although, I wish we would've been able to pass on more."

Another side effect of my grandmother taking the DNA ancestry test... guilt. It isn't her fault, nor her mother's fault we lost so much of our culture. Yet, as the eldest living Imala generations, they still shoulder the burden.

It was Great-Grandmother Liuna's great-grandparents who decided to trek south for months in search of a better life. When the Europeans invaded what is now Canada, they stole so much from the Indigenous. From stories Great-Grandmother has shared, my Imala ancestors tried to cohabitate with the *qallunaat*. White people. But as time progressed and the *qallunaat* took over more Native lands, it became harder and harder to coexist.

Tekkeitsertok, my four times great-grandfather, said there had to be a place for his family to live without worrying about what the white man would do next. So, he packed up his family and they crossed the country south until they happened upon the Stonewater tribe in what is now Stone Bay. This was not long after Washington became a state.

The Stonewaters accepted the Imala family, which had dwindled from seven to five on the journey. For a time, the Stonewaters and Imalas lived harmoniously off the land. Washington was a new state in the Union, but much of the land still belonged to the Indigenous.

As more *qallunaat* arrived, it proved more difficult to defend their home. It was Lusa Imala, my three times great-grandmother, who bridged the gap between the Stonewater, Imala, and *qallu-*

naat. Over time, Lusa learned simple English and interpreted for her family and the white men.

Lusa Imala is the reason an Indigenous name is listed as a founder on the town charter. She fought to include the Stonewater name but was repeatedly denied. To assuage her exasperation, the town was named for the Stonewater people. Stone Bay.

It was not enough, but there was little more she could do.

Rather than fight, when land was *gifted* to each founder, the Imalas shared with the Stonewaters. The money the Imala family *earned* as a founding family was split with the Stonewaters. To this day, sharing everything we have with the Stonewaters is still in place. It is not a burden. The Stonewaters are as much our family as the Imalas still in Canada. Sharing the *gifts* given to us by the town is a moral code we abide by and will continue to honor with each generation.

I lift my head from her shoulder and kiss her cheek. "We will continue to learn." A soft smile tugs at my lips as I pick up the knife and resume my task. "The past cannot be changed. But the future is what we make it."

Her loving gaze warms my profile. "My smart girl with the biggest heart." She brushes fallen hair off my cheek. "The moment you came into the world, I knew you'd be a force of good."

We finish our individual tasks, load everything on platters, and carry them to the large dining table at the heart of the house. As is routine every Friday evening, the family filters into the room within seconds. Seats are taken, plates are passed and filled, and conversation carries on with ease.

As we dive into caribou burgers on homemade bannock buns, air-fried goose, roasted vegetables, pickled beets and cucumbers, my mom announces she has news. The table quiets and all attention turns to her.

She reaches for and takes Dad's hand. "Tikaani and I have been in touch with a medical facility in Colorado for some time. We've paid close attention to case studies that may be beneficial for some of our clients."

Animated murmurs sound around the table.

"Dr. Adriel Hatathli, a Navajo neurologist, has been dubbed the best of his generation," she continues, a glint of admiration in her eyes. "Tikaani and I asked if he would come to Stone Bay and give a seminar." Mom glances at Dad and he stares at her as though nothing exists but her. "Dr. Hitathli agreed to the conference. As a thank-you, we want to extend a dinner invite." Mom's gaze shifts to mine. "Kaya, I'd like you to join us."

Neurology may not be my area of expertise, but it would be wonderful to ask a specialist how to spot signs of neural issues that may appear as behavioral obstacles. My mind wanders as new ways to help children filter in, but I quickly shove them aside.

Something about Mom's tone as she suggested I join them doesn't sit right. Can't quite place it, but a voice in the back of my head says she has an ulterior motive.

"For the seminar?" I sit straighter in my seat and square my shoulders.

"Of course, the seminar."

As I exhale, a hint of tension leaves my muscles.

"And for dinner," she adds.

With three words, every joint in my body stiffens. Because this isn't just a courtesy dinner with a brilliant doctor visiting Stone Bay. This is my mother's way of trying to set me up with someone. Not an ounce of malice in her tone, I know her heart is in the right place. She sees this dinner as an opportunity for an extraordinary future.

But I've told her time and again why I'm not interested or serious about romantic relationships right now. I've worked hard to get where I am with my career. Serious romantic commitments are a distraction. A risk I'm not willing to take.

Then, an image of Ray next to me at the table in class earlier filters in. His proximity. His spicy, sweet scent with a hint of lavender. My agreeing to dinner with him.

Suddenly, the room is too hot, too small. Wildfire dances over my chest, up my neck, and sears my cheeks. My clothes cling to me as perspiration dampens my skin. Wringing the napkin in my lap, I draw in a deep breath. And as I relax my fingers, I remind myself Mom only has my best interest at heart.

"I'd love to attend the seminar. It'll undoubtedly help with how I move forward with my students." My eyes lose focus for a beat, then sharpen as I meet Mom's hopeful stare with a sympathetic smile. "But I'm not interested in a dinner date."

Dad's expression darkens as he looks from me to Mom, an invisible strain heavy in the air. The muscles in his jaw tic once, twice, three times before he takes a deep breath. Giving Mom's hand a noticeable squeeze, the shadows in his eyes fade. Another steadying inhale, he meets my gaze.

"Your mother and I fought against being set up, too. She was home between her sophomore and junior years of college. I was preparing to attend the same college in the fall. And our parents thought it'd be a good idea for us to have a *friend* from home."

He chuckles as he arches a brow and smirks at his parents a few seats down from him.

"We made excuses most of the summer to avoid an arranged date. Then our parents got sneaky. A few weeks before school resumed session, your grandparents said they wanted to take me out for a special dinner before college. I agreed. Little did I know the meal would be hosted in this exact room."

A slow sweep of his thumb over Mom's hand, my parents share a silent conversation for a breath.

"We refused a date for months, but the moment we were in the room together, I never wanted anyone else."

This isn't the first time I've heard how my parents got together. It's far from romantic, but I love how they clicked so easily. Once they set aside their irritation and spoke with each other, everything fell into place.

My grandmother speaks up next, sharing a similar story of how she and my grandfather came to be. Their love story has rougher edges. Grandmother says Grandfather was quite self-centered. A ladies' man with a pompous demeanor.

We all laugh at this.

Grandmother refused to take him as a husband for years. Made excuses and pushed back at every opportunity. Until Grandfather set aside his haughty behavior, she did not give him the time of day. And then, one day, he came to her home with a gift for her parents and an attractive, mature temperament.

That is when she fell in love with him.

But those were different times. The mid-1970s and 1990s may not be long ago, but so much has changed between each generation. Women no longer *need* a man to thrive or have access to things former generations were not allowed to have.

Women's independence is applauded more each day, given a place in the world. Of course, there will always be people who try to stamp out our light—those people will never go away. It's what we do when they come at us that defines what happens next.

I want to live life on my terms. Yes, I will continue to learn about my culture and where I come from. Yes, I will share those pieces of myself, so my story lives on. But I will not be defined by the past. My future is mine, and I want to write it.

"An arranged relationship can become one of love," Mom says, interrupting my reverie.

Part of me wants to tell my parents I agreed to a date with Ray Calhoun. That I'm thrilled to spend time with him. Learn more about the man behind the videos and his alter ego as a father. We may not have sorted out the details, but it's in place. And accepting a date with anyone else feels… wrong.

Another part of me wants to ask why they don't put as much energy into finding love matches for my brothers. Ask why they aren't hounding them more to marry by a certain age. Yes, they're younger, but not by much. And let's not forget, my parents have sought a suitor for me since my teens but left my brothers to their own devices.

I'd love to tell Mom and Dad how much I like Ray—more than

I have anyone in some time—but the sudden, dull pang in my side has me biting my tongue. The faint voice in my head says my family wouldn't approve of him. Not because he isn't a good man. And not because he wouldn't be able to provide for me.

Sakari and Tikaani Imala have a vision for my future. A mental picture of me with a man that looks nothing like Ray. A man with a specific career and ambitious life goals.

Their fantasy isn't bad. It's just not what I want.

Maybe I should fight back as Grandmother did. Stand strong, put my foot down, and tell them what *I* want. Whether it's independence or a relationship with someone of my choosing, it's time I use my voice.

Squaring my shoulders, I lift my chin and hold Mom's gaze. "I know, *Anaana*. But I want more than a relationship that eventually turns into love."

I want a love I can't breathe without.

A love I'd die without.

A love I'd kill for.

But I also don't want that love now. One day.

"Miss Kaya is going to love my room." Tucker does a little jig across the kitchen before he grabs his apron from the hook near the pantry.

"Did you clean your room like I asked?"

He nods with too much enthusiasm. "Yep. Spick and span." He lifts a hand and ticks off items on his fingers as he says them. "Clothes are in the basket. I made my bed. Kind of. Games and toys put away. Comics stacked on my shelf. Desk is clean."

Sometimes, your kid needs a little extra motivation. As in someone he thinks highly of coming over to your house and potentially seeing how neat and tidy—or not—you are.

"Good job, bud. Thank you."

Asking Kaya to have dinner with me took more courage than I anticipated. Sorting out the details before I messaged her had proven to be a minor challenge.

The last time I had a legitimate date was when Tucker was still with Brianna. There was no need to ask my family to look after him. There was zero potential of my parents prying into my personal life. Had I asked them to watch Tucker tonight, it would have been different. Sure, they would've said yes. They love him and would do anything for him. But their yes would've been followed by a barrage of questions as to why.

At thirty-six, I should be able to tell my parents I'm dating. Tell them a woman caught my eye. But I can't. I won't.

For over a decade, my parents paraded my sister around like a prize poodle. Tried to marry her off to a son of the Seven. All for notoriety and status. And last year, it backfired in their faces. Cataclysmically.

With the exception of Brianna, I've kept my relationships quiet. Had I not become a father, I'd have remained tight-lipped about her, too.

I love my parents. I love our small family. But their meddling is an unwelcome intrusion I'd rather live without.

So, I came up with a better date night idea.

Yesterday afternoon, I sat down with Tucker and asked if it was okay if Kaya came over for a special dinner. The way his face instantly lit up made my eyes sting. I anticipated him asking questions. Mentally prepared to give him honest answers. And to my surprise, only a couple of his questions made my stomach cramp and twist.

"Is Miss Kaya going to be your wife?"

"Will she be my new mom?"

So much hope sparkled in his hazel eyes as he waited for my answers. It gutted me to be candid and tell him no, that Kaya and I are only friends. His smile vanished, and he deflated faster than his pool floaties. His dejection was a dull blade to the heart. A sadness I was tempted to erase with empty promises.

Wanting to be more than Kaya's friend isn't a lie. Saying I'm ready to be more would be, though.

I could give Tucker false hope. But I won't.

If Kaya and I are never more than this—two people madly attracted to each other—and I lie to him, he may never forgive me. He'd never believe a word I say. I'd be labeled untrustworthy. A betrayer. He'd grow to resent me.

And I refuse to be another parent he loses confidence in.

I'd rather him feel the sting of truth now than the debilitating pain and heartache of careless lies later.

After our talk, I messaged Kaya and said Tucker would join us. Then I tossed out the idea of her coming to the house if she was comfortable with it. Texts suck at inflection, but her response came across as excited.

Since this morning, Tucker and I have been busy. Between tidying the house, running to the store for last-minute ingredients, and food prep, there hasn't been much downtime.

Tucker steps onto the short stool beside me and watches as I dice red onion for the salad. "Can I help?"

"Of course, bud."

I fetch another cutting board from the cabinet and lay it in front of him. Grab the paring knife from the magnetic block on the wall and set it on his board, but keep it covered with my hand.

"This knife is very sharp. You have to pay attention to what you're doing when it's in your hand. If you don't, someone could get hurt, including you."

Lips in a flat line and expression serious, he meets my gaze. "I promise to be extra careful."

"Always keep your eyes on the knife and your hands."

"I will." He nods.

Erring on the side of caution, at least until he gets used to the knife, I give him a cut-resistant glove to wear. "Put this on the hand not holding the knife." The last thing we need right now is to visit the emergency room.

Once he's gloved up, I demonstrate how to cut the broccoli florets. Rapt, he focuses on every move. I tell him not to rush— that's how accidents happen. After I've chopped a few florets into bite-size pieces, Tucker takes over. While he cuts broccoli, I dice cucumber, avocado, apple, and grape tomatoes. I rough-chop walnuts and set them aside to be sprinkled on at the end.

Tucker adds all the ingredients into a large wooden bowl as the doorbell chimes through the house.

Wood scrapes tile as he hops off his stool. "She's here! She's here! She's here!" Ripping the glove from his hand, he bolts for the front door.

"Hold up, bud." I jog after him. "Let's not scare her before she's in the house." I chuckle.

Too excited to contain himself, Tucker whips open the front door with a bright, toothy smile on his face. Before either of them says hello, Tucker rushes Kaya and wraps his arms around her waist.

I grumble under my breath, "Tucker..." My eyes dart up and find Kaya's surprised but happy expression, and I mouth, "Sorry."

Kaya shakes her head, mouthing, "It's fine." Her hand skates up and down his back, gentle and comforting. "Hi, Tucker."

Inching back, he unravels himself from her waist. "Hi, Miss Kaya." He beams up at her. "We're making dinner for you." Her hand in his, he yanks her inside. "Come on. I'll show you."

"T-Man," I say a bit louder to catch his attention. He pauses and looks over his shoulder. "Let's give Kaya a moment to set her stuff down."

His brow crinkles in momentary confusion. Then he nods, and his expression smooths out. "Yeah. Okay. Sorry."

Kaya sets her bag down on the chair in the foyer. "You don't need to apologize, Tucker. It's okay to be excited." She toes off her shoes and scoots them under the chair. Then she leans a little closer to him and lowers her voice. "Can I tell you a secret?"

His eyes widen as he slowly closes the distance.

"I'm excited too."

Warmth cocoons me as I witness their exchange. An unfamiliar flutter erupts in my chest. Breathless, speechless, I watch them in complete awe. Utterly enthralled.

It's one thing for me to be physically and intellectually attracted to Kaya. But seeing her easy relationship with Tucker and his thrill at having her here opens a hidden door deep inside me, a place with countless possibilities.

Falling in love is the easy part. Falling for someone who accepts you after you've been emotionally wrecked is tricky.

Not that I'm ready for love. Too much emotional baggage still left unpacked.

But seeing these little moments with Kaya and Tucker… damn, it'd be easy to fall for this woman. Hard.

Shifting his weight from one leg to the other, a faint huff under his breath, Tucker glances up. "Can I take her to the kitchen now?"

Ruffling his hair, I chuckle. "Sure, bud."

I follow in their wake, eyes locked on their joined hands. Bewildered. Rapt.

Adulation blooms in my chest and molds itself around my heart. Makes me dizzy, unsteady. I reach for the wall as the ground wobbles beneath my feet. Inhale a steadying breath then continue forward.

They disappear around the corner, and something twists inside me. I brace against the wall again. Close my eyes as anxiety swirls beneath my diaphragm and inches up my throat. Pinch my eyes tighter and take another deep breath. Press the heel of my hand to the center of my chest and ease my eyes open.

Fuck, am I screwed.

Sucking in a sharp breath, I push off the wall, straighten my spine, and put one foot in front of the other.

When I reach the kitchen, Tucker is on his stool again, adding salad ingredients to the bowl and narrating his work to Kaya. She gives him her undivided attention, asks what he cut, praises his work, and offers to help.

Completely and utterly screwed.

I set out everything for the salad dressing and tell Tucker how to make it. While he and Kaya whip it together, I distract myself with the main entrée—braised Korean short ribs, paprika and lime crushed potatoes, and brown-sugar-glazed, slow-roasted root vegetables. Short ribs have been in the slow cooker since midmorning. Root vegetables went into the oven before I started on the salad. The only thing left is the potatoes.

Carrying the pot of boiled potatoes to the sink, I strain them in the colander. Give them time to cool while I fetch a sheet pan. Then I load them on the pan, grab the potato masher, and crush each one until it's flat.

In my periphery, I spot the occasional glance from Kaya. The corner of my mouth twitches the longer her gaze lingers. Her unabashed staring while I do what I love is a heady rush. An incomparable high.

I want her twinkling, addictive eyes always on me, *only on me.*

Pivoting, I grab the sauce pot from the stove and drizzle garlic and herb-clarified butter over the potatoes. Sprinkle them with sea salt and freshly ground black pepper. Then pop them in the oven with the root vegetables.

"Did I do it right?" Tucker tilts the bowl in my direction.

I make a show of inspecting the simple vinaigrette. "It's perfect, bud."

"Yes!" He does a small fist pump.

I ruffle his hair, then kiss the top of his head. "Why don't you show Kaya your room while I clean up."

"Let me help," Kaya insists.

Lopsided smile on my face, I shake my head. "Not a chance. You're our guest. Go." I tip my head toward Tucker. "Let him show you around. His room has never been this clean." I chuckle.

"Are you sure?" Kaya glances at the stack of dishes. "I don't mind helping. It's the least I can do."

"Positive. I'm used to my kitchen messes. I'll have it cleared in no time."

Tucker hops off his stool, yanks his apron strings loose and tugs it off over his head. Hanging it back on the hook, he sidles up to Kaya, takes her hand, and starts for the staircase.

"You're going to love my room, Miss Kaya. Dad let me decorate it with my favorite things. I'll show you. Come on."

Just before she rounds the corner, Kaya gives me a what-did-I-get-myself-into smile.

I simply shrug. *Good luck.*

When their footfalls quiet, I inhale deeply, hold my breath and count to five, then slowly release it. Can't remember the last time I felt this... discombobulated. Thrown off. Indecisive on whether I should listen to my logic-spewing brain or my wild, exuberant, impulsive heart.

As I clean the kitchen, I mentally scribble a pros and cons list. Mull over worst-case scenarios if things went nowhere or ended with Kaya. Daydream what a real romance would be like—to have a loving, caring partner, someone you feel incomplete without, someone who adores and loves your child as if they were their own.

Pro: Tucker looks up to Kaya. He cares about her opinions. A lot.

Con: If Kaya and I go separate ways for whatever reason, Tucker will be devastated.

Pro: No awkward conversations about being a single dad. No need to explain Tucker will always come first.

Con: With Kaya's education, she may be more suitable to guide children than parent one. Maybe.

Pro: She's so damn beautiful. Otherworldly gorgeous.

Con: I have trouble thinking clearly when she is in the room. Which could lead to countless, unwise decisions.

Pro: She is as attracted to me as I am her, and it isn't swift lust that fades after a short time.

What I feel for Kaya is this perfect blend of magnetism, temptation, and something primal. An undeniable compulsion deep in my bones. An inarguable instinct I can't shake. An irrefutable urge to make her mine in every way that matters.

Even if it scares me to no end.

I load the last pot into the dishwasher and wipe down the counters. As I go to set the table, I pause and recenter myself. Take a meditative breath and clear my mind of its frenzied thoughts.

One step at a time. Focus on dinner and tonight.

I repeat this as I add plates to each place setting, as I set silverware on cloth napkins, as I put empty glasses on the upper right corner of each place mat.

Don't get ahead of yourself. Hasty decisions equal disaster.

Sweet and savory waft up my nose as I take the pans out of the oven. Rich umami floats through the air, my stomach growling when I take the lid off the slow cooker. As I transfer everything to serving dishes, Tucker bounds down the stairs with Kaya in tow.

"Smells absolutely divine in here." Kaya steps into the kitchen, her radiant smile aimed in my direction.

My inner zen becomes a distant memory. One compliment, all logic goes out the window. One dazzling smile, my uninhibited heart takes over.

Instead of fighting what I feel, instead of overthinking, I let go. Give myself over to instinct and float on.

Dinner passes in easy conversation about cooking school, Kaya's time at the rec center, and Tucker sharing his favorite summer activities. At one point, he asks if I'll sign him up for the rec center summer program. After I explain how he'd miss cooking school and time with my parents, he says to sign him up next year.

I sit across from Kaya and ogle her more than a *friend* would. But I don't miss how often her eyes meet and hold mine. Don't miss how often she hides her smile. Or how often that delicious blush stains her cheeks.

Tucker helps clear the table after dinner and brings out dessert —which he selected and assisted in making. It's one of Mom's old recipes from the early days of RJ's Diner before Calhoun's Confections opened. A beloved favorite at the diner Dad keeps on the menu.

"What's this?" Kaya holds up her plate and studies the layered treat.

"Heaven in a pan," Tucker announces. "It's Grandma's special recipe." He presses a finger to his lips. "Shh. You can't share it with anyone."

I chuckle.

"Promise I won't tell a soul." Kaya draws an X over her heart.

When Tucker rushes back to the kitchen for forks, I let Kaya in on a secret. "Actually, Mom calls it *sex* in a pan," I whisper. "For obvious reasons, we don't tell Tucker that."

A stunning shade of red paints her cheeks, neck, and exposed chest. She tucks her chin and swallows.

My dick twitches behind my zipper.

I doubt Kaya is *innocent*, but damn do I love her reactions.

"I..." She clears her throat, then takes a sip of water. "I understand why."

As she eats dessert, I openly stare at her. Fisting the napkin in my lap, I relish the way her eyes roll closed for a second after each bite. Revel in the way her lips wrap around the fork before she slowly slides it from her mouth.

I want to tell her what those small reactions do to me. The way she heats my blood. Makes me bite back moans. Has me eager to reach across the table and touch her.

But I don't say a word. Somehow, I maintain my composure and keep my hands to myself. I ignore my aching dick and focus on the current conversation.

"Can we watch my new superhero movie?" Tucker asks, mouth full, voice garbled.

"Don't talk with food in your mouth, bud."

He takes a sip of water then flashes me his *whoops* wince. "Sorry."

I glance at Kaya for a beat before meeting Tucker's waiting gaze. "Not sure if Kaya likes superheroes. Or if she'll stay to watch."

Guilt claws at my chest for the last part, but I deserve it.

This date is so different from any other. I have no idea if Kaya plans to leave after dessert. If she wants to watch a movie. But I hope she'll stay.

Kaya scoops up the last of her dessert. "Depends." She brings the fork to her lips. "Which superhero is it?" She pops the bite in her mouth.

Damn, I love her lips.

"The newest Spider-Man movie." Tucker bounces in his seat.

"Ooh." Kaya wipes her mouth with her napkin. "Hard to say no to Spider-Man."

"So, you'll stay?"

She reaches for Tucker's hand and gives it a squeeze. "Yes, I'll stay."

Chair legs grate against the tile as Tucker bolts out of his seat and wiggles his butt.

"Think I gave him too much dessert," I tease, and Kaya laughs. "Tucker, take your plate to the kitchen and wash up, please."

Without a word, he scurries to the kitchen.

"You don't have to stay," I whisper. I *want* her to stay. Damn, do I want her to. But I practically guilted her into it. And I don't want her to think she *has* to if that's not what she wants.

"I know." A gentle smile tugs at the corners of her perfect mouth. "But I want to." A faint *swish* filters through the air as Kaya gently glides her seat away from the table. She gathers her plate, fork, and napkin and starts for the kitchen.

Up and out of my chair, I step in front of her and cup her elbow. "I've got it." The buzz from earlier makes a reappearance. Humming. Pulsing. Dancing over my skin. I stop breathing as the air crackles between us.

Fuck, I want to kiss her.

Her lips part. A soft gasp hits my ears.

She feels it too.

She wants to kiss me too.

I inch closer, my fingers drifting up her arm. One breath, then another. She's close. So damn close. All I have to do is lean forward a few inches. Erase the last little bit of space between us. Press my lips to hers.

In three erratic heartbeats, her breath paints my skin. Every cell in my body vibrates as I close my eyes, lean forward, and duck my chin to meet her lips.

"Dad, can I have popcorn?" Tucker shouts from the kitchen.

My eyes fly open and lock onto Kaya's hypnotic gaze. Ignoring the impulse to steal a kiss, I inch back, lick my lips, and swallow. Neither of us moves, breathes, looks away.

"Dad!"

I chuckle, and Kaya grins. "Yes, Tucker, you can have popcorn."

"Yay!"

I take Kaya's dishes then collect my own. "Go relax in the living room. I'll be there in a moment. Need to make sure he doesn't burn the popcorn."

She laughs, but it's different—soft, nervous. "Smart plan. Do you need me to cue the movie?"

"Nah." I shake my head. "Want anything to drink? Wine, tea, water?"

She holds up a hand and pinches her thumb and forefinger together. "A little wine would be nice."

I get to the kitchen in time and stop Tucker from using the microwave's popcorn button, which is unreliable. I send him out to the living room with the important task of readying the movie while I make his snack.

When I meet them in the living room, Tucker has the lights off and the movie up. My heart catapults as I cross the room and take the only available spot on the couch… next to Kaya.

If I make it through the next two hours without touching her, it'll be a miracle.

Tucker presses play and then sticks out his hands for the popcorn. I pass it over then hand Kaya a glass of wine. She takes a considerable gulp before setting it down, and I resist the urge to laugh.

The first half hour is filled with endless commentary from Tucker. I don't think anything of it, but wonder if it bothers Kaya. When I peek at her, she appears unfazed.

I do my best to focus on the movie, to keep my eyes forward, but fail miserably. Less than a foot separates us, her hands in her lap while I drape an arm over the back of the couch. I drink the last of my wine then set my glass next to hers on the table.

As I sit back, my arm on the back of the couch caresses her shoulders. My skin prickles as that delicious buzz returns. Like an incoming tide, it rolls up my arm again and again. I roll my eyes shut and revel in the current. Let it take over.

But it's her sharp inhale that knocks me sideways.

That she feels this every time too… it seals my fate. Terrified as I am to pursue whatever this is with Kaya, I'd be an idiot to ignore it.

Tucker talks less over the movie. When a solid twenty minutes pass without commentary, I chance a look at him. Curled up with a pillow, jaw slack, his soft snores masked by the movie, Tucker is passed out.

I ease off the couch, take the bowl from his lap and set it on the table, then hoist Tucker into my arms. "Be right back."

Kaya nods.

Up the stairs, I pad down the short hallway for Tucker's room. Peel back the covers and lay him down. And as I tuck him in, he mutters something incoherent about missing the movie.

"We'll watch it again, bud," I whisper. "Go back to sleep. I'll see you in the morning." I kiss his forehead.

"Love you, Daddy."

My heart melts. When he's alert, Tucker calls me Dad. But it's these sweet, sleepy moments I love most. The ones where he's a touch more innocent. More the younger boy he didn't get to be while with his mother. The times when he calls me Daddy.

"Love you, T-Man."

As I back out of his room, he rolls onto his side and starts snoring again. I envy how easily he falls asleep now. After Brianna left him with me, he struggled to sleep for weeks. He never told me why, but I have a feeling it's the colorful company Brianna keeps. Plus, I was a stranger to him.

Knowing he feels safe enough to be vulnerable now is the best gift.

When I reach the first floor, Kaya is carrying our glasses to the kitchen. I pivot and follow her. "You didn't need to do that."

She sets them in the sink then turns to face me. "I know, but I wanted to."

The world stills as I shuffle closer to her. As I close the distance. Gazes locked, we soak up the sight of each other. Time passes in shaky, swift breaths and trembling hands. The longer we stay like this—inches apart and practically vibrating—the more I want to kiss her.

"Should head home," she whispers without an ounce of conviction. "Early day for us both tomorrow."

Against every greedy cell in my body, I take a step back. "Let me walk you out."

A thick, pulsing cloud of repressed desire blankets us as we walk to the foyer, as she slips on her shoes and collects her bag, as we cross the driveway to her car. In step with her the entire way, my fingers twitch at my side, eager to touch her. To get another hit of that delicious buzz.

A beep bounces off the trees as she unlocks the car, followed by a soft click as she opens the door and sets her bag inside. Unable to bear another second without touching her, I step into her orbit. A gasp echoes in the night as she spins around, her breasts grazing my chest. Barely a breath exists between us as her eyes glitter in the moonlight.

"I want to kiss you," I confess.

Lips parted, her chest rises and falls faster, her nipples hard beneath her top. Iridescent eyes on mine, her tongue peeks out and wets her lips.

"Can I kiss you, Kaya?"

Time stops until she gives the slightest nod.

"Need to hear you say it, Fire Eyes." The nickname rolls off my tongue as if I've said it a thousand times and not just the once.

"Yes," she answers a breath above a whisper, and it's all I need to hear.

Pressing into her, I cup her cheeks and lower my mouth to hers. Soft, warm lips meet mine. So delicate. So perfect. My eyes roll shut as an inferno sweeps through me and annihilates the buzz from earlier. Somehow, I don't lose control. Somehow, I suppress the moan begging for release.

I press a chaste kiss to her lips. Then another. And another.

She clutches my hips, her fingers gently fisting my shirt. With a faint tug, she pulls me impossibly closer. Presses her body flush to the length of mine.

She's everywhere. Invading all my senses.

Hands drifting to the nape of her neck, I thread my fingers through her hair. My tongue darts out and licks the seam of her lips, silently asking for more. To taste her.

She fists my shirt harder. Gives another tug. Then parts her lips and invites me in.

I moan without shame as I deepen the kiss. As I stroke her tongue with mine and taste her for the first time. As I memorize the feel of my body molded with hers. The kiss feels infinite and everlasting, yet fleeting and meager.

Fingers curling in her hair, I turn her head and plunge deeper. Lick and stroke and suck and taste until I don't know which way is up.

I want more. Need more. *Crave* more.

But I stop myself from taking the next step.

Not tonight.

Against every carnal cell in my body, I break the kiss but don't stop touching her. I'm not ready to.

I rest my forehead on hers. Toy with her hair as my other hand caresses the length of her spine. Catch my breath and give her a moment to do the same. Her fingers skim my lower back a beat before her arms circle my waist and hold me to her.

"Could kiss you forever, Fire Eyes." I drop my lips to hers, needing one last taste tonight.

"I won't stop you." Her admission takes me by surprise.

Groaning, I inch back. "I'll do my best to remember that." I press my lips to her forehead and keep them there a moment. "Don't want to, but I should let you go," I pout.

A tremor ripples from her chest as she laughs. Her grip on me loosens, her arms slinking back to her sides.

Unable to resist, I drop my mouth to hers. Kiss her again, then force myself to take a step back. "Go. Before I don't let you leave," I tease.

She slips into the driver's seat, an indefinite smile on her lips. "Good night, *Chef*." She closes the door and starts the car.

The way *Chef* rolls off her tongue makes my dick weep.

I'll deal with you soon enough.

Rooted in place as she backs out of the driveway, I wave, and she mimics the gesture. Until her brake lights disappear through the trees, my feet don't unstick themselves.

When I walk through the front door, the subtle scent of her perfume hits me immediately. A sweet, earthy rose fragrance that makes my blood sing. I cross the room, sit on the couch, pick up the throw pillow she was closest to, bring it to my nose and inhale. Any sane person would call me a creep for doing it. But I give zero fucks.

Falling for anyone, falling for Kaya, scares the hell out of me.

But disregarding what I feel for her, not giving whatever this is between us a chance, downright petrifies me.

FOURTEEN

ERASER

A low moan ripples through the room.

"You fuck like a nasty whore, Cook. Are you a nasty whore?"

In reality, she doesn't fuck at all. She either lies on her back and spaces out or gets on all fours and barely stays upright. She is a literal hole to fuck and nothing more.

She moans again, louder this time.

"It's okay if you are." I caress the angle of her bony hip, pretend she is someone else, someone with actual curves, then crack her ass with my palm. "I love all my whores."

Her body teeters forward with each thrust. Her arms tremble and buckle as she tries to hold herself up from face-planting into the mattress. Lucky for her, I keep her hips up and in line with mine.

Weeks have passed since I told her I wanted every penny she owed. Weeks since I started using her body as a poor excuse to get off. Fucking her those first few days felt okay. I came. Got what I wanted, to some extent. But with each passing day, with each *sample* she slips past one of us, the less interested I become in this part of our arrangement.

I love fucking… warm bodies that actually feel good. Borderline corpses who toss out exaggerated moans for effect do nothing for me or my dick. Not that she ever did anything for me.

"Got my money, Cook?"

She peeks over her shoulder, cheeks gaunt and eyes sunken, desolate. Something akin to a smile tugs at her cracked, burned lips. The look is haunting, disturbing. On the precipice of death.

"I am paying you." Her gaze drops to where I plow into her. "Didn't you say I could pay this way?"

Fuck no.

Pulling out of her, I shove at her hips until she topples over on the bed. I tuck my depressed dick into my pants and zip up. "No, Cook. I said that if the sex was good, I might shave off a little of what you owe." Lip curled, I flick my gaze up and down her pathetic body. "When I said you fucked like a whore, I was being nice. It's a good day if I get off with my dick in you."

She scrambles up to her knees, her hands spasming at her sides as her eyes shift uncontrollably. "I'll have it. I s-swear." She clambers off the mattress and stumbles over her shorts around her ankles. "I just need more time."

I move across the room to the door. "You've had enough time. Six more days. I want every fucking cent, Cook." I turn the knob and crack the door open. "No more games. And don't even think about stepping into my kitchen again."

On quick feet, she meets me at the door, her eyes bright with more fire than I've seen in them for months. "Let me cook for you. Promise I won't sample anything."

Raucous laughter bubbles in my chest before echoing throughout the room. "Your desperation is sad as fuck, Cook." I rake my eyes down her skin-and-bones frame and shake my head. "The only time you have life in those eyes is when I threaten to take you out of the kitchen. When I endanger your habit."

"Please. It's all I'm good at. Don't take it from me," she begs.

Pathetic.

"Does it look like I give a fuck?" I open the door wider and smack her with it. "Six days. You better have my money. All of it."

I take a step out the door. "I'd hate to take payment out another way. One you wouldn't benefit from."

"W-what?" A deep, raspy cough fills the room. "I don't understand."

"You are expendable, Cook. As are the people closest to you." I take another step and start to close the door. "Six days, or I'll *show* you what I mean."

FIFTEEN

KAYA

When Ray asked me to be a part of this, I wasn't sure what to expect. Rowdy kids, basic recipes, and a lot of leftovers, perhaps. But that's not the case. Quite the opposite.

The kids are a bit wild in the morning but overall well behaved and friendly. They quiet down when Ray or another chef speaks. The older students assist the younger ones if they run into trouble with cutting, mixing, or measuring. They smile and joke for hours while they work.

Great people, fun environment, delicious food. What's not to love?

Monday's breakfast was a twist on a classic—cheesy scrambled eggs, brown sugar bacon twists, garlic and herb biscuits, and crispy home fries with caramelized onions and bell peppers. A simple way to test everyone's skills and comfort in the kitchen and a gentle introduction of what is to come.

Tuesday, yesterday, and today were more fun and unique. Nutella-stuffed pancakes topped with fresh berries and bananas paired with a creamy pineapple and strawberry smoothie. Bacon, egg, and cheese breakfast sandwich with hash browns in place of the bread alongside a unicorn hot chocolate. Scrambled eggs, sausage, and country gravy breakfast pizza on a biscuit crust with fresh-squeezed orange juice and fruit medley on the side—my favorite so far.

Tomorrow, we end the week with a sun-dried tomato, fresh mozzarella, and pesto quiche with a decaf iced mocha.

If they offered yearlong classes, I'd be first in line.

Speaking of classes…

Sunday night flashes in my mind. An unforgettable date night with Ray and Tucker. Ray made the entire meal—well, Tucker and I contributed to the salad—without breaking a sweat. He moved effortlessly and delivered mouthwatering dishes. Created magic in his home.

And if I'm lucky enough for a repeat, maybe I won't need cooking classes. Ray can teach me personally.

I initially brushed off our fancy date night dinner as Ray trying to impress me, but I know that's not entirely true. Every time he steps inside a kitchen, his love for food comes to life.

Was he pulling out all the stops Sunday night? Of course. It was a date.

Did he cook outside his wheelhouse? I doubt such a thing exists for Ray.

Wonder what he'd think of my family's dishes. Intrigued and curious, I imagine. Eager to learn more.

"Hey, Fire Eyes," Ray whispers as he squeezes a chair in on my right and sits. His warm, brown eyes meet mine for a breath, then shift to Tucker on my left. "Hey, T-Man. How's the pizza?"

"Soooo good." He stares at the pizza and moans. "We *have* to make this at home."

"Yeah?" Ray asks, and Tucker nods vigorously as she takes a massive bite. "What about the pancakes a couple days ago?" Ray takes a bite of his own pizza.

"Mm-hmm." Tucker swallows his bite then washes it down with juice. "Those were like dessert for breakfast." His expression turns dreamy as he licks his lips.

A heart of pure gold, Tucker is one of the cutest kids I've met.

Ray leans into me and I still, fever blanketing my skin. Beneath the table, his leg presses the length of mine with no promise of retreat. Such a simple move, but it makes me dizzy.

Dropping my chin, I try to hide my dopey smile. Mask the inferno flaming my face. I inhale—*one, two, three*—and exhale—*three, two, one*—to steady my erratic pulse while every nerve ending in my body lights and sparks like a chain of firecrackers. Clutching my napkin, I fight the urge to drop my hand beneath the table and touch him.

His leg is magnetized to mine the entire time we eat. Tucker asks what the class is making tomorrow, and Ray rattles off the menu. When a groove forms between Tucker's brows, Ray translates it to Tucker terms.

"Remember the pizza I made with the creamy green sauce?"

Tucker nods.

"It's kind of like that, but a breakfast pie version."

Tucker's eyes narrow as if he's trying to picture it. Then he shrugs and resumes eating. When Tucker's plate empties, Ray asks him and the other two kids at the table to help clear plates and wipe down tables. With a playful roll of his eyes, followed by a half-hearted groan, Tucker slides out of his chair and takes his plate, mine, and Ray's to the dirty dish bin. The others at our table get to work without complaint.

Ray opens his mouth to say something, but I cut him off. "I need to get to the rec center before the other counselors rip out their hair."

Checking his watch, he chuckles. "Thought my days were busy."

Scooting my chair back, I rise and start unbuttoning my coat. Ray unabashedly stares at my fingers as each button pops free. And when I reach the last one, his gaze meets mine. I don't miss the fire in his dark eyes. The hint of amber around his pupils. The luminous spark that makes me a little dizzy.

I shoulder my bag and drape my coat over my arm. Walk to the door on slow, reluctant feet. Drag out leaving just to have a few more minutes with him. To get another hit of his heated gaze, addictive charm, and hypnotic energy.

"I'll walk you out." He offers this every day, and not once have I declined.

"Thank you."

"T-Man," he calls across the room. "Stay here. I'll be right back."

Tucker nods then goes back to chatting with the other kids.

As Ray opens the door for me, a young woman steps back in surprise on the other side. She flashes me a welcoming smile that falters when her attention shifts to Ray. A faint blush colors her cheeks as she squirms in place.

"Hi, Chef," she says, a slight squeak in her voice.

"Hey, Cameron. The kids are still cleaning up." He jerks his head over his shoulder. "Mind giving them a hand?"

"Sh-sure." She smooths her hands over her coat in an attempt to compose herself. "I take it the pizza was a hit."

"It was. Thanks for the suggestion."

Her blush deepens.

"Cameron, this is Kaya, a… friend helping us with the classes." His pause makes my stomach flip.

"Oh." Her gaze unenthusiastically shifts to mine. She clenches then relaxes her fingers before lifting her hand. "Nice to meet you, Kaya. I work in the kitchen with Chef Calhoun."

I study her obvious beauty. Subtly scrutinize her body language and tone. Pick up on her easy attraction to Ray. Arch a brow at her territorialism—a feature Ray seems oblivious to.

I slip my hand in hers, my grip firm yet delicate, and give a slight tilt of my head as we shake. "Likewise, Cameron. Today's dish was my favorite yet." I toss out the honest compliment then release her hand. "Sorry to cut this short, but I do need to go." I avert my attention to Ray. "Ready?"

"After you." Ray gestures for me to lead the way.

We walk through the restaurant in amiable silence. Muted

music echoes around us from the kitchen where the cooks dice and chop vegetables for tonight's guests.

As we step into the sun, his knuckles graze my bicep. "Can I see you again?"

I clamp my lips between my teeth to fight a smile. "I'll be here tomorrow."

He chuckles. "You know that's not what I mean."

I shorten my stride and prolong the walk to my car. "What *do* you mean?" I ask, tone playful.

His fingers trail down my bare forearm, skim my palm, then ever so slowly lace with my fingers. My skin tingles where he's touched me; my hand in his is a live wire. Desire blooms low in my belly. A deep-rooted *need* simmers in my bones. I feel dizzy. Unsteady. Reckless. Remiss.

His thumb strokes the length of mine. "Can't stop thinking about you." He inhales a shaky breath. "Or that kiss."

Makes two of us.

"I like you, Kaya," he says without hesitation. "More than anyone in a long time." His thumb strokes mine again, softer, almost indiscernibly. "So much it scares me, but in a good way. If that makes sense."

"It does." I stop a few feet from my car and spin to face him.

"But it scares me more to not give us a shot." He widens his stance until our gazes are level. "I won't skirt around the truth." He shakes his head. "Tucker's mother did a number on me. Messed with my head for years." He tucks his chin to his chest, takes a deep breath, holds it for a beat, then meets my waiting stare on the exhale. "Lies, cheating, running off with him in the middle of the night, and…" A notable ridge forms between his brows. "I didn't come out here to dump all the heavy stuff, but it feels wrong to keep it from you."

My grip turns fierce, protective, as I step into him. "Sorry that happened to you and Tucker. Couldn't have been easy for either of you. Thank you for telling me." I caress his thumb. "If it makes you feel better, I'm scared too."

Those addictive umber irises dart between mine. "Why?"

I take hold of his other hand. "For years, I've had my life mapped out. A long list of goals to accomplish." I bite my bottom lip. "None of which include a relationship... until thirty."

"Thirty?" He visibly stiffens then relaxes. "And when will that day arrive?"

I titter. "Nice, roundabout way of asking a lady her age." I playfully roll my eyes. "Five years."

His eyes widen as he studies every line and curve of my face. As if he's seeing me for the first time.

Age hasn't come up until now. Considering Ray has a nine-year-old and soft crow's-feet when he smiles—which is often—I guess he's in his late twenties or early thirties. But maybe I'm way off.

His tongue peeks out and wets his lips. "Tell me I don't have to wait five years, Fire Eyes." The plea in his voice, the desperation in his eyes, the gravity pulling us closer tugs at something in my chest.

My heart hammers as I swallow past the building lump in my throat. He gave me one of his truths; now it's my turn to do the same. "My family has been trying to find me a husband for years."

At this, he jerks back. Red crawls up his neck and mottles his face.

I stop breathing. "What?"

His hold on me tightens then relaxes. "My parents did the same to my younger sister. The day she turned eighteen, they all but thrust her at potential suitors. Dinner parties with select Seven families. After a major clusterfuck last year, it stopped."

"How old's your sister?"

"Thirty."

Twelve years. Wow. Just... wow.

I understand and somewhat respect why my family is trying to play matchmaker. They want to be sure I land a worthy partner, someone who compliments my intelligence, ambition, and our culture.

But there is more to life than having an outwardly upstanding person at your side.

I want a true match. Someone whose personality and quirks complement mine. Whose ambitions and outlook reflect my own. Whose passion and hunger for their partner is unrivaled and not something that *builds with time.*

"Not sure how your family was with your sister, but mine has been more passive-aggressive. Hints. New dinner guests at family gatherings." I look skyward. "Next week, they want me to have dinner with a doctor in town."

"Are you?"

I inch closer to him. Step between his legs, lightly press my chest to his and subtly shake my head. "There's a conference I said yes to, but I declined dinner."

His entire body sags. "Sorry." He drops his forehead to mine, closes his eyes, and inhales a shaky breath. "This conversation went the wrong direction." He gives my hands a reassuring squeeze.

"You said younger sister," I blurt out then bite my bottom lip, my face scorching.

Why, Kaya? Why?

A smirk tugs at the corner of his mouth as he cracks an eye open. "You asking if I'm an old man, Fire Eyes?"

I squirm. "No." Those two letters hold zero conviction.

Eyes downcast, he rests a hand over his heart and mutters, "I'm sensitive about my age." For a moment, neither of us says anything. He lifts his gaze to mine, his expression deadpan as he stares. Then he laughs. Hard and loud and from somewhere deep in his belly. I want to slap him.

"Joking, Fire Eyes." He wraps my hand with his once more. "Thirty-seven next month."

Surprisingly, our age difference doesn't bother me. If anything, I find his maturity attractive. Alluring.

My thumbs caress the length of his as I drop my forehead to his chest and groan. "Gotta go." I huff, lift my head, and meet his rich browns. "See you in the morning."

He shuffles impossibly closer, his dark irises invading my vision, holding mine captive. "Say yes to another date."

The corner of my mouth twitches. "Yes."

His instantaneous smile is radiant, captivating, infectious. "Does Sunday work?"

"Sunday's perfect."

Then his lips are on mine. Soft, warm, coaxing. He licks the seam of my lips, an unspoken request for more. Tipping my head, I part my lips in silent permission and open for him. His tongue dives in and tangles with mine. He tastes sweet and savory, and like him. I groan, and he melts into the kiss.

He unfurls our hands and bands his arms around my waist. I ghost mine up his chest, around his neck, and run my fingers through his hair. The kiss lasts less than a minute but feels infinite.

"Spend the whole day with us," he says when he breaks the kiss.

Us. I love that our dates include Tucker. It's such a small gesture, but it speaks volumes. Says I'm more than someone to warm his sheets for a night or two.

"I'd like that."

His mouth drops to mine in a chaste kiss. "I should get back."

"And I'm probably late." I wince.

Totally worth it, though.

He presses his lips to mine one last time then steps back. "Go. Before I don't let you leave."

My laugh mingles with his.

"Text me later?" I unlock my car, set my bag in the back, then slip behind the wheel.

"Definitely." His grin is wide and bright as he winks. "Later, Fire Eyes."

Gooey warmth engulfs me as I take one last look at him. "Later, Chef." Then, I train my eyes forward.

I rush across town to the rec center, apologize profusely for my tardiness, cue up this afternoon's movie and pass out snacks, then settle in a chair at the back of the room. Seclude myself from the group and take what feels like my first breath since leaving Ray.

Then I do something I never would've in the past.

For the next two hours, with my phone on mute, I shamelessly watch Ray's cooking videos online. Heat licks my skin as my heart rattles in my chest. I all but drool as his fingers flick cream, chocolate, and clams in provocative ways. Practically melt in my seat as he tongues cocktail glasses and fruit slices. Start fanning myself when he plunges his fingers in citrus and papaya. Squeeze my thighs together as he spanks then strokes a large piece of red meat.

I don't dare look away. Not even when my thoughts stray to more... *delicious* places.

As for my goal of no romantic relationships... suppose that's null and void.

But if anyone's going to make me break my own rules, I'm glad it's him.

SIXTEEN

RAY

Aside from work and my videos, I don't put much effort into my physical appearance. No hair products, skincare, or modish styles. No going out of my way for the latest and greatest *whatever* trending online. No drawing extra attention to myself when I have more than plenty.

Like everyone, I have a routine—shower, brush my teeth, groom all the places, smell good, repeat. I rarely deviate from my boring schedule. And I never go out of my way to look *perfect* on a day off.

Today is the exception to the rule.

As if possessed by the spirit of vanity, I have checked my appearance no less than five times in the past few minutes. Considered changing my shirt three times. Thought of styling my hair in a way I never have twice. Sniff-checked myself more times than I care to admit.

I need a damn distraction.

Slipping on sneakers, I exit my room and poke my head through Tucker's cracked open door. He sits cross-legged on his bed with a superhero action figure in one hand and a red fire truck in the other. When he spots me, he freezes and curls his fingers to hide the fire engine in his palm.

Weird.

"Hey, bud. I'm going to do some last-minute cleaning downstairs." I glance at my watch. "We should head out soon. Come down in about fifteen minutes?"

Tucker gives me a timid smile and nods. "Okay."

Rather than ask what's on his mind and where he got the fire truck—which he had a few weeks ago, I think—I tap the doorframe twice, turn on my heel, and head for the stairs. Each step, I flit through memories of buying toys for Tucker after he moved in. I offered to buy him countless trinkets, but he wanted a fraction of them. And not a single one was a fire truck.

Maybe my parents got it for him. A gift after a tough week. The way he treasures it makes that more likely.

I switch the laundry, put the clean dishes away, and double-check I don't need anything else for dinner. As I exit the kitchen, Tucker bounds down the stairs with a toothy smile plastered on his face.

"Is it time? Is it time?" His excitement is infectious.

I ruffle his hair then smooth it out. "Yeah, bud. Let's go."

On the drive to RJ's Diner, Tucker kicks his legs and talks nonstop about putt-putt, the arcade, and how he plans to win. Meanwhile, my palms slip on the leather steering wheel as I picture my dad stepping out of the diner's kitchen to see me and Tucker with Kaya.

Seems ridiculous to be this nervous at thirty-six. But when you've had high expectations held over your head for years, it's no wonder I can't stop fidgeting.

My parents would like and approve of Kaya in a heartbeat, but a public appearance is bound to stir up questions. Ones I'm not ready to answer.

Tucker practically flies out of his seat when I park the car but waits to fling his door open. His hand in mine, he all but tugs me across the lot, talking my ear off as we head for the diner entrance. When we round the corner of the building, my steps falter.

In a cream-colored bohemian dress, Kaya is a vision. The epitome of confident and casual. Beautiful. Breathtaking.

Tucker squeezes my hand, releases it, and runs off to greet her.

Not wanting to make a fool of myself, I put one foot in front of the other and make my way to her.

Hair in soft waves down her back, she tucks a lock behind her ear as Tucker reaches her. A hint of kohl lines her eyes and makes her coppery-brown irises pop more than usual. A thin layer of gloss on her lips makes them look plumper. Mouthwatering. Luscious.

Memories of kissing her flood in, and my breath catches, my tongue heavy as I swallow against the dryness in my throat. I lick my lips, and the reminder of her taste is a new spark to the wildfire dancing over my skin, an additional whoosh, whoosh, whoosh to my pulse. But it's not until I recall her weight against me, her grip on my shirt as she pulled me closer, that a deep ache throbs in my groin.

Will the sight of her always make me react like this? Unequivocally, yes.

"*Unusakut*," she greets as I sidle up to her.

"What's that mean?" Tucker asks, his brows scrunched together.

"Tucker," I chide.

Kaya chuckles as she rests a hand on my forearm. "It's fine." Her smile steals my breath for a moment before she turns to Tucker. "I said good afternoon."

Eyes narrowed, lips puckered, Tucker nods then relaxes his pensive expression. "That's dope, Miss Kaya."

The sun glints her glossy lips, and I can't take my eyes off her mouth.

"I think so, too. Learning the language where my family comes from is fun but hard. Some words are easier than others."

Tucker's brows shoot to his hairline as his jaw drops. "Your family speaks another language?"

Kaya stands a little taller, but her expression remains soft.

"Some of us. And we only know bits and pieces. Remember the word I used for grandmother?"

Tucker fidgets in place. "Yeah."

I jog through Kaya's interactions with Tucker but don't recall hearing it. Maybe it was during cooking class or when I was out of earshot.

"It was one of the first words I learned. And because my grandmother is dear to me, it's the first I remembered."

Tucker looks up at me, an inquisitive look on his face. "Can I learn another language?"

"Sure, bud." I ruffle his hair. "Any one you want."

His whole face scrunches to the middle, an earnest air about him as he nods. Then he blinks, and every ounce of solemnity vanishes, his hazel eyes more animated. "I'm hungry."

Scratching my brow, I snicker. "Then let's go eat."

Tucker bolts into the diner and greets the hostess before Kaya or I take a step forward. He points back at us, says something, and the woman follows his outstretched arm with her gaze. I wave and she returns the gesture. Studying my face, I see the moment realization hits her. That I'm the son of the owner.

"Mr. Calhoun," she squeaks out as we enter. She nervously brushes hair out of her face and tucks it behind her ear.

I open my mouth to tell her she doesn't need to address me formally but don't get the chance.

Menus in hand, she takes off for a table. "Right this way." She seats us at a table in the back, on the side farthest from the kitchen entrance and pass-through window.

The tension in my shoulders eases a fraction. The likelihood of Dad seeing us is—

"Papa RJ," Tucker shouts as Kaya and I take our seats.

"T-Man," Dad says as Tucker rushes him. "Oof." He chuckles as his arms band around Tucker, hugging him just as fiercely. "Didn't know you were coming to see me today."

Tucker releases Dad and inches back to look up at him. "Yep." He nods enthusiastically. "We're getting lunch before putt-putt."

Sweat beads my skin as I wait for Dad to say something. To ask why we're out with Kaya. I clench my hands in my lap, then wipe my palms down my thighs.

I shouldn't be this nervous but know I'll always question if my parents think who I'm seeing is *good enough*. I shouldn't give their opinion so much weight, but a part of me will always want their approval. Seems childish, but I want my parents to be proud of my choices, whether it's work or parenting or love.

"Wish I could hang out and play putt-putt." Dad guides Tucker to his seat and takes the other empty chair. "But it's one of the busiest Sundays of the year."

Tucker leans into Dad and rests his head on his arm. "You, me, and Grandma can go a different day."

Dad wraps an arm around Tucker's shoulders. "I like the sound of that, T-Man." Dark-brown eyes identical to mine glance across the table. "Kaya, correct?"

Oh shit.

"Sorry." I wince. "Wasn't thinking." I clasp my hands under the table and squeeze until my knuckles burn. "Dad, this is Kaya Imala. She works at the school but is helping with the cooking classes this summer." Twisting in my seat, my knee grazes Kaya's thigh, and we both freeze for a breath. "Kaya"—I swallow past the desert in my mouth—"this is my father, Ray Jr."

Seems foolish to introduce them to each other. My family and the Imalas are familiar to the townsfolk. Dad undoubtedly knows Kaya's parents.

At some point, my family has fed every resident at one of our restaurants. From lattes, bagels, and breakfast sandwiches to a twist on classic diner dishes to gourmet chocolates and fine dining, the Calhoun-Kemp restaurants are a pillar in the Stone Bay community.

Aside from being a founding family, Kaya's parents are the highest-rated doctors in their field in Stone Bay. People travel here to consult with Tikaani Imala, one of the top five cardiologists in the Pacific Northwest. It's nearly impossible for residents to not know her family.

The Calhouns may not be founders, but we are synonymous with the Stone Bay upper hierarchy. A social scale my parents and grandparents care about way too much. A ladder they've been eager to climb for too many years but are now realizing they've plateaued.

Soft lines curve up at the corners of Kaya's eyes as she smiles at Dad. "Wonderful to meet you." She offers her hand. "Your homemade chili and cornbread onion rings are a secret indulgence of mine."

Dad takes her hand and gives it a gentle squeeze. "Your secret's safe with me." He winks. "Maybe one day you can teach me your family's caribou stew recipe."

What?

Here I am, shirt damp with sweat in several places, fingers drumming my thighs, heart ready to evacuate my chest... and Dad asks about a stew recipe.

What the hell is happening?

While I mentally spiral, Dad and Kaya chat as though they talk more often than we do.

The idea of coming here and bumping into Dad has had me on edge since I suggested it. I don't *need* my parents' approval for anything, but I *want* it. I figured a chance encounter at the diner would be safer than a stuffy family dinner where my parents scare Kaya off.

What I didn't picture was a smooth bump in. Seems too good to be true.

Dad unhooks his arm from Tucker's shoulders then gives the table two gentle taps. "Need to get back in the kitchen." Wood grates tile as he scoots the chair back. "Nice to officially meet you, Kaya. Hope to see you more."

Nice, Dad. Real sly.

But as he walks away from the table, a single thought rolls over and over in my head.

I hope to see more of her too.

"I am the king of putt-putt," Tucker declares as his ball sinks on the second stroke of the final hole. He throws both arms skyward and tips his head back. "Victory is mine."

Snort-laughter rips from my throat as I stare at my little man.

I don't dare stifle his ego or zeal. Don't extinguish his light by telling him to take it down a notch. If anything, I encourage this side of him. Boost it and him every opportunity I get. Add to his exuberance with a little of my own. Let him be a kid and enjoy this carefree time in his life, especially since his mother stole years of it from him.

Arms out, I bend at the hips. "I bow down to you, Almighty Putt-Putt King."

Beside me, Kaya giggles under her breath.

I playfully nudge her. "If you wish for the putt-putt gods to shower you with luck on your next game, you must bow to His Highness," I quip.

At this, she laughs harder, louder, then follows through and does a curtsy.

When we straighten to our full height, my heart melts at the cheerful smile on Tucker's face.

"Can we go to the arcade now?" And just like that, his triumph on the artificial turf is old news.

"If you're ready for me to beat your highest PAC-MAN score."

"Psh." Tucker rolls his eyes. "You'll never beat my score."

If I really wanted to win, I could do it with an arm behind my back. But I'd much rather see his smile than claim the top spot on a video game roster.

After we return our clubs at the kiosk, Tucker takes my hand and Kaya's and drags us into the arcade. The next hour and a half is a blur of bright lights, loud music, the occasional whistle of the winner's siren, and lots of victory dances.

The only thing I see with absolute clarity is her and the way she smiles at me and Tucker.

My losing streak is still firmly in place as we exit the arcade and head for our cars. As we approach her SUV, it dawns on me I didn't outright ask Kaya to have dinner with us tonight. I planned for it, bought everything we'd need, but forgot to include the idea in our conversation. I asked her to spend the day with us, and she has.

But I'm not ready for today to end. I need more time with her.

I'll always need more.

Pressing my fob, I ask Tucker to wait in the car while I talk with Kaya. Once he's out of earshot, I step into her.

"Come back to the house for dinner."

Her tongue darts out and wets her lips. Then she hums, and it goes straight to my groin.

I stiffen in my shorts, my mind on things more *delicious* than cooking dinner.

Her coppery-brown irises sparkle in the sun, rooting me in place and robbing me of rational thought.

Fuck, I want to kiss her. Take her. Claim her.

"I do like when you cook."

Yep, I'm a goner. Every inch of my body heats, my pulse deafening in my ears. "Join us." I lean in closer and caress her forearm with the back of my finger. "Please."

I've learned when it comes to Kaya, I'm not above begging. And I feel zero shame about it.

Her gaze drops to my mouth, then lowers to my throat. Up and down, again and again, her chest rises and falls faster. I swallow and those fiery irises lift and lock back onto mine.

"Please, Fire Eyes." My fingers skim the length of hers before curling and grazing her palm.

Her eyes flare as she sucks in a sharp breath and nods. "Yes."

A simple yes and I'm on the Bay Cliff Mountain peak, high on life. "Thank you." Ducking my chin, I press my lips to her forehead. "See you back at the house." Easing my hand from hers, I step back, pivot, and stroll to the car. Behind the wheel, I check the rearview mirror and my pulse soars. She's still there, befuddled, in a daze.

Same, Fire Eyes.

But my bewilderment gets a cold shower as I put the car in drive and Tucker speaks up. I should've anticipated his question but am somehow unprepared.

"Why did you kiss Miss Kaya?"

Never having been in this situation with him, I go with a generic answer. One that feels completely inadequate, but he'll understand. "When grown-ups like each other a lot, sometimes they kiss."

The real answer is a growly roar in my head.

Because she's mine.

Tucker races to his room to play more games when we get home. I offer him a spot at the counter to help cook, but he declines, still hopped up from the arcade.

As I empty my pockets and toe off my shoes, a faint knock echoes in the foyer. My answering smile is immediate as I open the door and gesture for Kaya to come in. She sets her bag down and takes off her shoes, stowing them near the door.

I linger in her orbit, a subservient moon pulled in and hooked by her gravity. Every cell in my body aches to touch her, kiss her, wrap her in my arms and memorize her soft, golden-brown skin. But I keep my hands at my sides and absorb her radiating warmth. Inhale her subtle, sweet, earthy-floral scent. Bask in the way she wakes every part of me with her proximity.

Spinning to face me, we come nose to nose. She gasps, wobbling slightly, and the buzz in my chest intensifies.

As much as I want to stay in this moment forever, I tip my head in the general direction of the kitchen. "Help me cook?" My voice a ragged blend of sandpaper and need.

She bites her bottom lip, releases it with a pop, then swallows. "Yes."

Slipping my hand around hers, I amble toward the kitchen. Lead her to the stools at the island, lift her hand to kiss her knuckles, then release her and move to the opposite side of the counter.

Fire dances over my skin as she follows my every move.

I was born to be in the kitchen, to create art with food. But her eyes on me as I cook for her... is titillating, borderline euphoric. The most delicious form of foreplay.

After a quick wash of my hands, I fetch ingredients from the fridge and pantry. Sirloin, fresh herbs, mirepoix and other root vegetables, green beans, garlic, pine nuts, red wine, and parmesan. Like second nature, I sort the ingredients in the order I'll need them. From the cabinet, I grab cutting boards, sheet pans, and pots. Knife of choice in hand, I start on the mirepoix.

"How often do you film for your followers?"

My hand pauses midchop as my gaze lifts to lock onto hers. Curiosity sparkles in those coppery-brown irises.

"Seems like you post less often than you used to."

The corner of my mouth creeps up into a wicked smirk. *Well, well, well. What do we have here?* A fresh wave of heat spreads through my veins and prickles my skin.

Doesn't shock me that the majority of Stone Bay has seen my cooking videos. I get regular commentary at work and when I frequent businesses in town. What piques my interest is when the supposedly sweet, wholesome, or proper people speak up.

The night I met Kaya, her friend made several suggestive comments that not so subtly told me she'd seen my videos. Kaya had been more reserved. Not quiet, just selective of her words.

I like that she doesn't word vomit everything on her mind.

Oddly, I can't picture her watching me in food porn mode. But damn do I love the way it makes me feel.

Eyes latched on to hers; I chop celery stalks. "Before Tucker moved back home, I posted four or five times a week. I was working at the diner with my dad and missed making gourmet dishes from culinary school." I shrug and glance down long enough to slide the carrots closer. "Dad let me experiment in the diner kitchen so long as I didn't waste food. The staff loved my creative days because they reaped the rewards."

Her long fingers trace invisible lines on the counter. "Surely no one complains when you cook for them."

There will always be someone who lives to whine and be heard. I want to tell her just how snobbish people are when they believe they've had the best of the best somewhere else. Doesn't matter what industry you work in, there will always be sour lemons in the bunch.

"Let's circle back," I say as I get to work on the onion.

"Circle back?"

"Mm-hmm." With a tilt of my head, I lick my lips. "My videos."

A luxurious shade of pink stains her cheeks.

"How do you feel about them?" At this, I drop my attention back to the cutting board. One, I need to focus on my hands while I cut the potatoes. Two, maybe it will help her open up if I don't stare. Regardless, she remains in my periphery. Always.

"Enthralled," she whispers, breathy.

With me or the food? I want to ask but keep to myself. "Enthralled is good."

When she doesn't say anything for a moment, I peek up to see her staring at my hands. I rock the knife slower on the cutting board and her brows twitch a moment before she glances up.

"What else?"

Faint lines appear between her brows as they tug together.

"What else do you feel?"

Her tongue peeks out and wets her lips before she clamps them between her teeth. The pink on her cheeks from minutes ago darkens and spreads to her neck.

My cock twitches behind my zipper.

She shifts on the stool then drops her attention back to my hands. "Fevered."

Fuck me.

"Bet there's no shortage of women at your door." Her gaze flits up. "Or men."

There is no fighting the painfully huge smile on my face. "Was... interesting when the videos first went viral. I won't lie and tell you I didn't enjoy the attention. It got me up in the morning." I shrug, not wanting to dive into those darker days when I didn't have Tucker to make me smile. "But it's all for show."

Kaya nods, her eyes still locked on my every move.

"I get to do what I love, entertain people all over, and make them fall in love with food in a new way."

Her soft chuckle filters through the air. "Oh, I'm sure they love more than your prowess and recipes."

I pause and wait until her gaze meets mine. "Not interested in what *they* love."

Her stare sears my soul a beat before she swallows. "What about me?"

Slightly confused and speechless, I tilt my head.

"Would you cook like that... for me?"

Well, damn.

At every turn, Kaya surprises me with the unexpected. She's soft but unshakable, timid yet daring, brilliant and levelheaded. One moment, she comes off as hesitant, bashful. The next, she's a fiery storm of brazen, undiluted desire.

Fuck if she doesn't make me want to dive in headfirst and drown in her.

"Definitely." With a jerk of my chin, I say, "Come here."

Her eyes dart between mine as she pushes away from the counter and eases off the stool. With slow, measured steps, she rounds the island and comes to my side.

Shuffling back, I take her hand, haul her forward until she's pressed between me and the counter, and then plant my hands on either side of her, caging her in. I lower the tip of my nose to the side of her neck, trace her soft skin, and breathe her in. She sucks in a sharp breath.

My nose trails the shell of her ear. "Pick up the knife, Fire Eyes."

She hesitates, but only for a beat. Her dainty fingers wrap around the hilt of the knife.

I shift impossibly closer. Press every inch of me to her. Mold my body to hers. Cover both her hands with mine and guide her through cutting the rest of the ingredients.

With each rock of the blade on the cutting board, her breaths come quicker, a touch louder. Shameless.

My lips hover a breath from her ear. "Tuck the tips of your fingers," I instruct, and she does. I press my lips softly to the skin beneath her ear. "Good girl."

Every nerve ending in my body is a live wire when we cut through the last piece of sirloin. Not an inch of space exists between my body and hers. My cock thick, heavy, needy as it presses her backside.

Her breasts rise and fall harsher, faster, desperate for more than just oxygen.

I set the knife aside, snake my arms around her waist, and dip my head until my lips ghost her skin. *Kiss.* "Exquisite." *Kiss.* "Divine." *Kiss.* It's on the tip of my tongue to say *mine*, but I refrain. For now. "Flawless."

Her hands on my arms loosen my hold. My pulse hammers for a different reason as she shifts in place and spins around. Before I open my mouth to apologize or ask if I did something wrong, her palms cup my cheeks as she pushes up on her toes and claims my mouth.

Ecstasy floods my bloodstream as her tongue tangles with mine. I bend slightly at the knees, engulf her in my arms, and hoist her off the floor. She tugs at the skirt of her dress a moment before her legs wrap around my waist, her arms circling my neck.

I blindly guide us to another counter and set her down. Sweep my fingers around her waist, up her sides, her neck, until they comb through her hair. An unabashed moan spills from my mouth to hers as I deepen the kiss.

Fingers fisted in the cotton of my shirt; she hauls me closer. Digs her heels into my lower back. Angles her head more as her greedy fingers dance over my chest and dip for the hemline of my shirt. Her soft, delicate fingers graze my abdomen near my waistband, and I hiss.

My cock strains my underwear, begging for relief.

Lips on her jaw, I pepper kisses to her ear, down the column of her throat. "You make me wild, Fire—"

"Dad?"

I step back immediately and help Kaya off the counter. "Yeah, bud?" We all but run back to our spots at the island.

Footsteps thump down the stairs. "What's for dessert?" Tucker rounds the corner.

Kaya bites back a smile as she tries to tame her hair.

"Berries and cream tarts. Why?"

Tucker fetches his apron from the hook and tugs it over his head. "Can I help make dessert while you cook dinner?"

"Absolutely, T-Man." I glance at Kaya and wink. "Maybe ask Kaya to cut the berries."

Crimson colors her cheeks, and I want to know what exact moment just flashed through her mind. What delicious memory set her blood on fire and stained those beautiful cheeks.

Because I sure as fuck can't get the thought of her fingers on my skin out of my head.

SEVENTEEN

KAYA

"We made the best dessert, Miss Kaya." Tucker pats his belly then sags in his chair.

This kid is too cute for words. "You get more credit than me." I load the last bite of tart onto my fork and lift it to my lips. "You did all the hard work." I pop the berries and cream in my mouth and resist the urge to moan as it hits my tongue.

I don't miss Ray's shameless staring or the fire in his eyes as the fork slides from my lips. His eyes have been on me the entire meal. Fixated on my eyes, my mouth, my throat when I swallow.

Since his *cooking lesson* earlier, a low hum has glimmered in the air between us. Subtle yet tangible. An ever-expanding bubble of anticipation. And each time I glance up to see his eyes on me, memories of him, of us, flit through my mind. The hard lines of his body pressed flush to my softer curves as he stepped into me. His breath warm on my skin, lips ghosting the sensitive flesh beneath my ear. His hands on mine, guiding me, controlling me during the *lesson*. The shiver that rolled down my spine to the tips of my limbs when he praised me with a breathy *good girl*.

"Yeah, I did," Tucker says, snapping me out of my reverie. "But you're the best helper, Miss Kaya."

I set my fork down, wipe my mouth, and smile at Tucker. "Thank you. We make a good team."

Across the table, Ray freezes.

Worry swirls in my belly as I study his blank expression. As I mentally repeat my exchange with Tucker, wondering what triggered his reaction. But I don't ruminate long.

His shoulders visibly relax as tenderness softens the corners of his eyes, his vacant expression replaced with something more affectionate. Longing. Reverence. Unrivaled tenderness. A gentle smile tugs at his lips then vanishes just as quickly.

Ray scoots his chair back and rises. "T-Man. Why don't you and Kaya go pick tonight's movie while I clear the table."

Tucker shoves his chair away from the table and fist-pumps the air. "Yes!" He scurries to my side, grabs my hand, and puts all his strength into yanking me from my seat. "Come on, Miss Kaya. Let's pick a movie."

Snickering, I move to stand. Tucker's exuberance for the simple things in life melts my heart. "Go turn the TV on," I suggest. "I'll be there in a second."

Tucker bolts for the living room.

"Let me help." I pick up my plate and glass but don't get far.

Ray rounds the table and blocks my next step, his hand cupping my elbow as he shakes his head. "I got it." He inches impossibly closer, leaning in, his breath tickling my ear.

Th-thump, th-thump, th-thump.

My heart rattles my rib cage as my lungs beg for air. Eyes rolling closed, I get lost in his proximity, the way he makes my blood sing, his sweet and spicy scent. *Him.*

Ray is the sun—radiant and warm, steady and constant, essential and boundless—and I am but a planet basking in his glow, grateful to be in his orbit, anchored by his intensity.

His fingers trail up my arm from my elbow. Unhurried. Unmistakable. A transcendental caress.

Goose bumps dance over my skin as a shiver rolls up my spine.

"Mmm," he hums near my ear. "You have no idea what that little shiver does to me, Fire Eyes."

It's on the tip of my tongue to ask, but as I inhale a shaky breath, Tucker calls me from the living room.

"Miss Kaya…" he says my name with fussy impatience. "Come on."

Ray's hand falls away as he snorts under his breath. Tipping his head toward the living room, he shuffles back and reaches for my dishes. "Go." His fingers stroke mine as he takes the plate from my hand. "Or we'll never hear the end of it."

At a loss for words, I swallow, nod, and release my grip on the plate. Blink out of my foggy state and attempt to compose myself as I spin and amble toward the living room.

Several negotiations later, Tucker and I agree on the same superhero movie. He insists we leave the lights off so it feels like we are at the movie theater. A great idea, I concur and take a seat on one end of the couch, Tucker sitting in the middle.

Salty butter wafts through the room as Ray enters with a bowl of popcorn and two glasses. He hands Tucker the bowl and insists he swaps seats with me on the couch so he's closer to the end table. Ray hands me a glass of wine, takes the now vacant seat, and presses every possible inch of himself to me. Not a breath exists between us.

The movie blurs as superheroes fly across the screen. Character conversation echoes through the speakers, but I don't catch a word of it.

In this atomic blip in time, all I can focus on is the way his body feels pressed against mine. The heat wave pulsing between us. The turbulent whir of energy beneath my skin and in my bones. The faint crackle in the air as his hand drifts closer, closer, closer. My ragged breaths mingling with his. And then his fingers weave through mine. Slowly. Impeccably. I melt into his touch, so intimate, so intense, yet nowhere near enough.

Time is measured in staggered breaths and inconsistent heartbeats. Every stroke of his thumb sparks a new fire. Every ounce of his weight has me weeping for more. The movie drags on far too long, but the entire room comes into hyperfocus when Ray shifts and leans impossibly closer, his lips at my ear.

"He's out." Inching back, his penetrating gaze pins me in place. "Sit tight while I put him in bed?"

Buzzed from his proximity, his touch, and a little from the wine, I nod.

He sets his glass on the table, pauses the movie, scoops Tucker up from the couch, and pads across the room to the stairs. When he disappears from view, my breath catches in my throat.

Since our kiss in the kitchen, every heated glance, every fevered touch, every strategically spoken word has been a match strike to the kindling that is our next step. The most tantalizing foreplay. And I'm on the literal cusp of shattering.

I want him. Need him. More than air. More than anything.

Is it too soon to take the next step? Every cell in my body screams to leap, to claim him. Unfortunately, my mind isn't fully on board.

Yes, Ray and I are the epicenter of our relationship. But it's foolish to ignore the aftershocks of each step we take. One wrong shift could set off an endless chain reaction. We may be the core, but everything we do impacts more than just us.

Before we make the first ripple, I need to know if we're both on the same wavelength. With this, we can't assume.

Light footsteps echo nearby, and I become keenly aware of Ray moving through the dimly lit room. Neither of us says a word as he resumes his spot next to me on the couch. As his leg, hip and arm wedge mine. As our heavy breaths and my thunderous heartbeat steal my hearing.

The television screen saver kicks on, darkens the room further, and I gasp. The air crackles, charges, takes on a life of its own. Perspiration licks my skin as the couch dips, and I'm hyperaware of his chest pressed to my arm. Of his calloused skin on mine as he laces our fingers.

My breaths come in short, stuttered sips as I twist to meet his gaze in the dark. And when our eyes lock, I stop breathing altogether.

Intense and palpable, his *want*, his *need*, his *ache* reflects my own.

With a single look, any concerns I had vanish.

Inch by drawn-out inch, he eviscerates the last bit of distance between us, the soft thrum of anticipation swirling in my belly. My eyes fall shut a breath before soft, warm lips sweep mine in a chaste caress. Taking a small taste. Hinting at what's to come.

Cupping my cheek, he changes the angle of the kiss, holds me steady, keeps me in his control. In a matter of heartbeats, the kiss turns unyielding, insistent. A moan rumbles his chest, his tongue darting out and trailing the seam of my lips in silent permission.

Fisting his shirt, I part my lips and let him in. Taste him for the second time tonight. Twirl my tongue with his and melt when he moans into the kiss.

Goose bumps dance over my skin as his fingers trail my jaw, my pulse point, the nape of my neck, before curling in my hair. At his mercy, he tilts my head the other way, fists my hair harder, plunges his tongue deeper. I take everything he gives me and silently beg for more.

With a yank of his shirt, I haul him closer. Moan unabashedly as his lips flutter over my jaw, the shell of my ear, the length of my throat. *He feels it, doesn't he?* My pulse throbbing under his lips. My fevered skin on his tongue. How desperate I am for air as he licks the length of my collarbone.

Head tipped back, I open my mouth to tell him I need more— of his lips, his taste, his touch—but the words die on my tongue. A shiver rolls through me as he pulls away. Confusion knits my brow as mortification eases in. I drop my chin to my chest, swallow, and keep my eyes shut.

Is he having second thoughts? Does he think this is a mistake? *God, I hope not.*

"Look at me, Fire Eyes." His voice is a seductive caress, a delicious plea.

On a shaky inhale, I ease my eyes open and meet his waiting gaze. Undiluted hunger shimmers in those dark irises. Unfiltered lust stares back, begging to be satiated. But the longer I stare, the more I realize that's not all. Past the carnality lies something... deeper. Softer. Significant. An emotion neither of us should disregard.

Apprehension.

Gaze locked with his, I lift a hand to his face. Stroke the scruff on his jaw. Caress the apple of his cheek.

His eyes roll closed as he leans into my touch. Then he twists to kiss the heart of my palm. So tender and a complete juxtaposition to the man kissing me a moment ago.

I like how romantic and kindhearted he is one moment, and libidinous and urgent the next. I like that he doesn't hide who he is from me, that he shows me sides of himself not everyone gets to see. His vulnerable side.

My thumb traces his bottom lip, my eyes following the action. "What's wrong?"

He kisses the pad of my thumb. "Need you to know I have no expectations tonight."

My gaze flits to his and holds it. "Me either."

"I dream about us, though." His hand on the nape of my neck flexes. "How good we'd be together."

Adrenaline races through my veins as an ache blooms low in my belly. Suddenly, my skin is too hot. My clothes too tight. I swallow past the pulsing swell in my throat. "Me too," I admit, voice dry, breathy.

Hunger swirls in his dark irises as they dart between mine, a litany of questions lingering in the air. But he doesn't ask a single one. Instead, he rises from the couch with my hand still in his. "Come with me?"

With a stilted nod, I tighten my hold on him and push up on unsteady legs. "Yes."

Ray guides me through the house to the stairs, our pace unhurried. One foot in front of the other, we ascend. Thrill swirls in my belly with each step. Desire pools between my thighs as we hit the landing. Hand in hand, we enter his bedroom. He closes the door behind us, the gentle snick of the latch deafening.

Golden light filters through the room and highlights a massive bed in the middle, fluffy pillows at the head, a tufted bench at the foot. An accent wall behind the headboard, as well as the wide floorboards, stained a rich brown. Cream floor-to-ceiling curtains cover the far wall and shield what I'm sure is a spectacular view of the mountains. The occasional pop from black, brass, and ivory fixtures and decor offsetting the rich, earthy tones.

As I survey the rest of the room, I feel him at my back. His heat. Every inch of his broad, muscled frame molded to the length of mine. His strong, capable hands curl around my hips. His nose dives into my hair, inhaling deeply, a faint growl vibrating his chest.

On a shudder, my eyes roll shut.

Humming, his grip on my hips softens. Inch by slow, tempting inch, his fingertips flutter up my forearms, my biceps, along my collarbones. My body quivers under his touch. Cries out for more as he sweeps my hair off my shoulders.

His breaths a warm staccato at my ear, I gasp. And for a beat, time stands still. Neither of us moves. But as quickly as it stopped, time speeds back up.

He shifts his hips and pins his impressive length firmly to my lower back. Hisses between his teeth as his hands drift down, down, down the outer swell of my breasts, the dip of my waist. When he reaches the flare of my hips, his grip turns bruising. His fingers flex and knead once, twice, and then haul me back until nothing exists but him.

Every delicious, solid inch of him pressed to me, he drops his lips to the curve of my shoulder. "I want you, Fire Eyes." He peppers kisses up the length of my neck until he reaches the sensitive spot beneath my ear. "God, I fucking *need* you."

The last of my restraint snaps.

Maybe it's the heat of him at my back, his hands in all the right places, or the sheer lust in his voice. Maybe it's all the above. Either way, it shatters my self-control.

I spin around, push up on my toes, and claim his mouth. Lick the seam of his lips and suck the bottom one with unfettered hunger. Devour his moans as he opens for me and meets me stroke for stroke. Relish in the fire that burns brighter, hotter between us as he kneads my curves and shapes my body with his in a new way.

Strong arms snake around my waist and hoist me off the floor, our kiss feral as he pads across the room. Then he lowers my legs, my feet landing on a soft rug, the edge of the bed grazing the back of my thighs. His hands coast up either side of my body, over my shoulders, along my neck to cup my jaw.

Breaking the kiss, he rests his forehead on mine, a hint of trepidation rimming his eyes. "Please tell me you want this." His gaze drops to my lips. "Tell me you don't want me to stop."

I weave my fingers through his hair. "I want this. I want *you*." I fist his thick strands and give a slight tug. "Whatever you do, don't stop."

The words are barely out of my mouth before his lips seal mine with a scorching kiss. A kiss that puts all its predecessors to shame.

Inch by mile-long inch, my hands drift down his chest to the hem of his shirt. The need to touch him, to feel him skin to skin, overrides everything. I shove his shirt up, skim my fingers over each delicious ridge and dip of his abdomen. He tears his mouth from mine long enough to tug the shirt over his head and toss it aside. Then his lips are on mine, our tongues tangling as if it's the first time. And the last.

My body sighs as he caresses the apples of my cheeks, grows hot as he trails the length of my neck, wobbles as he roams the lines of my collarbones. Delicately, precisely, his fingers slip under my dress, ease the strap off one shoulder, then the other. The cotton puddles at my feet as I tear my mouth from his, tip my head back, and gasp.

He doesn't stray from my body for a single beat. Greedy lips kiss the line of my jaw. Eager fingers caress my bare back until they reach the hooks of my bra and set them free, the lingerie joining my dress on the floor. Goose bumps freckle my skin and I shudder.

His tongue darts out and he tastes the sensitive skin beneath my ear, licks a trail of fire down the length of my neck, traces the hollow of my throat, then nips and sucks and savors the swell of my breast.

"So beautiful," he murmurs, his lips and fingers memorizing my curves. "Absolutely perfect."

A desperate ache blooms low in my belly, an insatiable hunger pooling between my thighs and dampening my panties. My nipples pinch and stiffen to hard peaks. My body vibrates, desperate for more.

Instinct takes over and I reach for his shorts, clawing at the button, greedy for more of him. Every kiss, every touch, every breath in this moment feels essential. Primal. *Feral.* It's too much and nowhere near enough.

I pop the button of his shorts and drag the zipper down the teeth. Groan when they hit the floor with a resounding *thump.* Then his mouth is back on mine, starved and wild. His hands clutch my hips, kneading, bruising. Then he eases up. Gives me more of his weight as he guides me down onto the bed.

"So soft," he whispers against my lips as his fingers caress the curve of my breast. "Delicate." His thumb circles then rolls over my nipple. He takes my mouth in another searing kiss, then nips my chin and drifts down to explore my body. I gasp as his tongue flicks and teeth graze a trail from one breast to the other.

Nip.

My fingers dive into his thick locks, my body writhing beneath his weight.

Lick.

Kneading fingers massage their way down my sides then hook in the waist of my panties.

Suck.

Frenetic energy coils around my spine, expands low in my belly, and screams for relief. With each touch, taste, hum of his approval, I crave more. Beg for more.

If I'm a dormant fire, he is the oxygen triggering my explosion.

Slowly, purposefully, he slides my panties down my hips, my thighs, then tosses them to the floor. The room goes impossibly quiet as I lie bare beneath him. Every inch of me on display, vulnerable, exposed.

Those rich, dark eyes lock with mine as he kisses his way down my body slower, with more tenderness, affection. As he worships me from my navel to the apex of my thighs. As he hooks one thigh, then the other over his shoulders.

"Dreamed of this moment," he confesses, his tongue darting out to wet his lips. "Tasting you." Fire flares in his eyes. "Fucking you with my tongue."

His admission fuels the roaring fire inside me. Makes me impatient, ravenous. More brazen than ever. "Then taste me."

His eyes flare as he clutches my thighs in a bruising grip.

Gaze anchored to his, I wet my lips and swallow. "Fuck me."

"Jesus," he mutters, giving my thighs another squeeze. Then, with his eyes still hooked to mine, he drops down and drags his tongue through my center. A feral growl vibrates against my skin as his nails bite my flesh.

My fingers dive into his hair. My back arches off the mattress. Again and again, he flicks my clit with his expert tongue. But it's not enough. I need more pressure, more of his rough stubble.

I dig my heels into his upper back. Rock my hips into him. Tug his hair.

He burrows deeper and fulfills my silent request for more. Moans his approval against my clit and devours me libidinously, without shame.

It's been too long since I've had sex. Since I've been fully immersed in the feeling of it all. Of someone else's hands and lips and tongue on my skin. Their fingers gently caressing and hungrily kneading my flesh. How different the buildup feels, especially after hours of foreplay.

I want to live in this moment forever. In my fevered skin, too tight for my body. With my lungs heaving as I pant and plead for more air. With this constant, wild hunger for more—of him, of this, of the things we have yet to explore.

His tongue teases my clit as his finger trails up and down my entrance. On the next stroke, he thrusts inside and fills me. Gasping, I bow higher off the bed. Slowly, shamelessly, he pumps in and out as he takes my clit between his lips and sucks. His eyes never leave mine as he inserts a second finger, as he curls them slightly and hits that sweet spot deep inside me.

Meeting him thrust for delicious thrust, my legs quiver and body trembles. My mind dizzies and lips tingle. Each flick of his tongue, each pump of his fingers, I climb higher and higher, my breathy whimpers the crescendo of the most luxurious anthem.

"That's it, Fire Eyes. Give me what's mine."

Tightening my grip on his hair, my knuckles burn as I dig my heels in and seek more pressure. Unabashedly, I grind against his face, his rough stubble, his formidable tongue and talented fingers. Roll my hips in time with his thrusts. Cry out as I edge closer to the precipice.

Heat ripples from the center of my chest, up my neck and blooms on my face as my orgasm swirls, expands, intensifies, takes over. "Oh, god," I mewl as the first wave hits.

He moans against my clit, his fingers unrelenting as every-thing in me tightens.

My eyes slam shut, stars dancing behind my vision as I yank his hair and clench my thighs. Tremors rack my body as I work to steady my breathing. As I slowly come down from the best orgasm of my life.

"Fucking perfect," Ray whispers as his fingers ease out and he unhooks my legs from his shoulders.

Boneless and dizzy, a lazy smile curves the corners of my

mouth. But it quickly morphs into surprise when he grips my waist and flips me onto my belly then hikes my hips up.

The *swish* of a drawer opening, followed by the crinkling of a package, floats through the room. On the next breath, I feel the thick head of his cock at my entrance. He flattens a palm on the small of my back, his hand gliding up my spine and pressing my shoulders into the mattress.

"You make me wild, Fire Eyes." His fingers thread through my hair then curl and twist. "Feral." With a swift tug, he yanks my head off the mattress. "Ravenous."

I moan and rock my hips back.

A growl vibrates the air as his other hand bruises my hip. "So eager." He licks his way up my spine, then moves to my ear. "And all fucking mine." Then he rocks his hips and fills me with his thick length.

Our fused groans ring throughout the room. I fist the bedding and revel in the feel of him, the delicious stretch between my legs, how full I am.

"God, you're tight." He eases out then rocks his hips forward again. "But damn, look how good you take all of me."

A hand in my hair and the other at my waist, he pistons his hips faster. Thrusts in and out harder. Hits that sweet spot deep inside again and again as he sets a sublime pace. Skin slapping skin bounces off the walls and mingles with our immodest moans.

He tugs my hair as his other arm bands around my waist and lifts me until I'm flush against his chest. I hook an arm back and comb my fingers through his hair. Turn into him and claim his mouth. Pin him to me as I taste and take and devour.

Deft fingers trail up my body, knead my breast, dig into my flesh, tweak my nipple.

I whimper into the kiss. Fist his hair harder. Bite his bottom lip.

"You love it like this, don't you, Fire Eyes?" He yanks my head to the side and licks the curve of my neck. "Rough." He nips my earlobe. "Filthy."

"Yes," I rasp out.

He clucks his tongue in my ear. "Such a naughty girl." He grips my chin and twists my head until his eyes lock onto mine. "*My* naughty girl."

"Yours," I moan.

He claims my mouth and rocks his hips impossibly harder, faster. Releasing my chin, his hand dips between my thighs and circles my clit. "Give it to me, Fire Eyes." He pounds my body relentlessly. "Come on my cock."

A little more pressure on my clit, and my body detonates. A relentless torrent, my orgasm pulses again and again, taking over all my senses.

"Good fucking girl," he praises, breathy, before he bruises both my hips and roars out his own release.

I drop forward on the mattress, limp and sated... and officially ruined by the man behind me.

EIGHTEEN

RAY

Disposing of the condom, I collapse on the bed beside Kaya, wrap an arm around her waist, and haul her back until our bodies are flush. The need to constantly have my hands on her, to feel her warm curves along every inch of my body, to fortify the endless hum that exists between us is heady... and terrifying.

The last time I opened myself up, put my heart on the line, let myself be thoroughly vulnerable, everything I cared about was stolen. In the middle of the night, without a sound, Brianna walked out the door with Tucker in her arms and shattered my world.

I trusted Brianna, and she used my blind faith in her as a weapon. With one simple act, she warped my perception of relationships, trust, love.

By no means is Kaya anything like Brianna. To my very core, I know this is true. But I can't help the way my head spins and heart clenches as my feelings for Kaya grow.

What I need is to snap the hell out of it. Now is *not* the time to compare the trauma of past relationships to the woman in my arms.

Closing my eyes, I burrow my nose in her hair, inhale deeply, and get lost in her scent. Memorize the softness of her skin beneath my calloused fingers. The shape of her, the way she rests her arms over mine and secures me in place.

"That was…" she whispers.

When she doesn't say more, I add, "Intense."

Her arms over mine tighten as she hums. "Intense," she repeats. "Incredible." Her hold on me loosens as she rolls over, those stunning coppery-brown eyes filling my vision. Her soft fingers delicately dancing over my jawline. "Unforgettable."

I'll never forget tonight.

And with that single thought, my apprehension from a moment ago returns with a vengeance. An invisible hand wraps itself around my unshielded heart, its poisonous, viny fingers encasing the foolish, thumping organ with ease. Clenching. Constricting. Reminding me what happened last time I let someone this close.

I dizzy from the rapid mood swing and slam my eyes shut. Like a pebble skipped across the water, a ripple of uncertainty flickers over my face.

So soft, so gentle, and perfect in every possible way, she strokes her thumb over my cheek. "What's wrong?" Trepidation coats those two words, and the grip on my heart strengthens.

No matter what I say right now, I'll come across as an asshole.

I hate it. I hate that someone no longer in my life still has a hold on me. Has the ability to affect every thought, every mood, every happy moment. To sour and darken one of the best nights of my life. More than anything, I hate that Brianna still takes up space in my head. Even if only a sliver, it remains ever-present, ready to make an appearance and steal the slightest bit of joy.

One deep breath, then another, and another. On the last exhale, I open my eyes and swallow past the boulder in my throat.

Please don't hate me for what I'm about to do. I'll hate myself enough for the both of us.

"Nothing's wrong." I brush loose strands of hair from her face and trace my knuckles along her jaw. Ignore the pang in my chest as I school my expression. "Was just thinking it's probably best you don't stay."

All the air leaves my lungs as my rib cage strangles the organs. My stomach wrings and wrenches, a dose of bile clawing its way up my throat.

The last thing I want is for Kaya to leave, for this night to end. But my fucking mind…

She jerks back in surprise, two lines forming between her brows as she studies my eyes with unparalleled intensity.

Fuck. I hate myself. Hate that I'm not strong enough to eviscerate the demons of my past. Hate that I may lose the most incredible woman to enter my life because I'm afraid of what happens next.

A frightened coward, that is what I am.

"If Tucker sees us in bed in the morning or you in the same clothes as yesterday, it'll be an endless inquisition." I clench my teeth for one, two, three erratic heartbeats. "He'll be confused, and it'll get uncomfortable."

Keep digging deeper. If I'm going to screw this up, let it be thoroughly.

Wildfire blazes in her addictive irises, but it's not a fire I'd dare step close to or try to put out. No, Kaya deserves to feel that fury-laden flame in her veins. And I deserve to be the person she burns with it.

Low, sardonic laughter floats through the room and sends a chill up my spine.

Kaya inches away, sits up, and swings her legs off the bed, giving me her back and shutting me out. Hands on either side of her, she fists the edge of the bed and shakes her head. Without a word, she stands and moves around the room, collecting her clothes and slipping them on.

I shiver—from the loss of her warmth, at the distance I feel growing between us, at the uncertainty of what happens next.

Fully dressed in seconds, she spins to face me, squares her shoulders, and lifts her chin. "You're good." She scoffs. "I'll give it to you"—her arms circle her midsection as she hugs herself with unmatched ferocity—"you had me fooled."

Fuck.

Her cool disposition snaps me out of my chaotic thoughts. I bolt up and cross the room. She shuffles back as I step within a foot of her, holding up her hand.

"No," she says, the single syllable sharp, cutting. "You don't get to make yourself feel better for throwing me out."

My hands dive into my hair as a new thread of fear seeps in and buries itself in my marrow. Full-blown panic surfaces as it dawns on me I may have destroyed my relationship with the most remarkable person to enter my life.

Aghast, I backpedal. "That came out all wrong." I close my eyes for one deep, unsatisfactory breath. Unable to filter my thoughts, I say the first thing that comes to mind. "This is so new and foreign to me."

Incredulity mars her expression. "Casual hookups?" A derisive huff falls from her lips. "I doubt that." Her arms around her middle hug impossibly tighter.

My eyes lose focus as I shake my head. An unfamiliar heaviness bears down on the center of my chest. The backs of my eyes burn as saliva pools in my mouth. "No." I bite the inside of my cheek, fighting against my next words. But they win. "Feeling so much for someone scares the shit out of me."

Kaya turns to stone, her gaze firmly locked on mine as she searches for an ounce of deception. She won't find it. Not when it comes to this.

Countless emotions dance over her expression as she absorbs my truth. "Why?"

How can the shortest question carry so much weight?

"Give me a second."

I move to the dresser, grab a pair of sweatpants, and slip them on. As I step in her direction, I mull over how much to say. Wonder how much she already knows from Tucker. Question how much more vulnerable I am willing to be with this woman.

Kaya is not Brianna, I remind myself for the umpteenth time.

"There's a reason I haven't been serious with anyone in years," I admit as I inch closer to her. God, I want to touch her. Let her know that she is the furthest thing from a casual hookup.

"Tucker?"

I tilt my head left then right. "Yes and no." As much as I want to touch her, I shove my hands in my pockets to stop myself. "I'm careful with who I introduce to him—not that there's been anyone. He's been through things no one his age should have to deal with. And I do my best to shield him from future hurt." I swallow past the thick ball of anxiety climbing up my throat. "But it's more than that."

In my periphery, she reaches out then pulls back before making contact. Her addictive gaze searches mine for words left unsaid. She shuffles closer, consumes my vision, but stays back enough we don't touch.

"I won't pressure you into telling me, but I'm here if you want to."

In no way am I deserving of this woman, her patience, her kindness, her strength. But damn, do I want her. To be deserving of her.

"Not tonight."

Her expression falls, and my frame wilts. In a blink, the softness I love about her turns defensive. "I should head home."

Before I respond, she steps back, turns on her heel, and heads for the door. As reality sinks in, Kaya exits the bedroom and slinks down the hallway to the stairs. I snap out of my muddled thoughts and bolt out the door on quiet feet, needing to reach her.

The day went from one of the best to the most cataclysmic in no time. And it's my damn fault.

I don't want her to leave, much less on a sour note. Nor do I want my insecurities to be a looming black cloud over us. "Kaya," I whisper-shout as I reach the bottom step. "Wait. Please."

Goose bumps ripple over my skin as she slips on her shoes and shoulders her bag. Head down, she doesn't meet my gaze.

Focused on her footsteps, she doesn't acknowledge my presence or plea.

Reaching for her, I cup her elbow and step into her line of sight. "Please don't leave like this."

Her fiery gaze slaps me across the face with a single look. "I didn't set this in motion." The muscles in her jaw tic as she points to her chest. "I'm allowed to feel however I want." She steps out of my touch. "Even if you don't like it."

Message received.

"Let me at least walk you out."

She doesn't deny my request. Lifting the bag higher on her shoulder, she steps around me and walks to the door, turning the handle and disappearing into the cool night air.

Barefoot and shirtless, I dash after her. Guilt floods my veins. Humiliation makes my skin itch. A thick layer of repugnance blankets my soul.

Leave it to me to fuck this up because I can't get my shit together.

Lights flash as she unlocks the car with her fob. My pulse pounds a vicious rhythm in my ears. My breaths come in clipped, unfulfilling sips.

She can't leave angry.

The thought dredges up memories of my last few months with Brianna before she stole Tucker and vanished. My hands visibly shake at my sides. I ball them into fists and shove them in my pockets.

Kaya opens the door and tosses her bag inside. Before she shuts the door, I wedge myself in the opening, duck down, and press a kiss to her cheek.

"I get why you're upset." Against every impulse, I lean back, straighten to my full height but don't retreat. "I ruined a perfect day. The best night." The last three words come out in a whisper. "But don't drive if you're angry. Pull over and clear your head." Unable to resist the need to touch her, I reach out and graze my knuckles along her arm. "Please."

Eyes forward and refusing to meet mine, her brow furrows a beat before she nods and cranks the engine.

One step back, then another, I close her car door. Gravel crunches as I fix my stare on her through the window. Headlights flash in my eyes momentarily before she puts the car in drive and slowly disappears down the unlit gravel road, headed for the highway.

When I no longer see her taillights, I fill my lungs so fully it hurts, tip my head back, take in the starry night sky, and scream, "Fuck!"

In less than a minute, it's quite possible I ruined the best thing, other than Tucker, to happen to me.

I jog back into the house, clean up the remnants of our evening in the living room, then take the stairs two at a time. Slip through my bedroom door and close it. Pick up my phone on the floor near my shorts and unlock it, tapping the message app.

My eyes lose focus as my fingers hover over the keyboard, eager to text Kaya an infinite number of apologies. I decide against it and give her the night to cool off.

I'll see her in the morning at the restaurant.

Then reality hits and reminds me there're no cooking classes this week. With Independence Day on Friday, the town is flooded with tourists. Restaurant reservations are fully booked and every server, cook, and hospitality worker in Stone Bay is working overtime.

"Dammit," I grumble as I strip back the comforter and climb into bed.

I return to my text history with Kaya and type. Before I finish the first line of my apology, my phone buzzes.

Sadly, it's not Kaya.

No, it's a message from the *last* person I want to speak with. The person I will never be rid of, no matter how hard I try. The person who sank her venomous claws so deep in my psyche she ruins every good thing in my present and future.

Somehow, I've let her have that much control over me and my heart. And I fucking hate her for it.

UNKNOWN NUMBER

hey it's Bri. can I see you and Tucker tomorrow? I need your help

And just like that, every defensive shield I own goes up and locks into place. Every ounce of distrust in my soul is seared in hellfire. Every moment I enjoyed with Kaya tonight fades away and is replaced with the haunting memories of my past.

Any peace, contentment, and affection I discovered in the past year and a half goes out the window with one text. And I ask myself if I will ever actually get a chance at true happiness.

Right now, it feels like the answer is no.

NINETEEN

KAYA

Silence is the loudest sound and says more than any string of words. When you should speak up, when you should let someone in, and all you give is silence, it is the biggest demonstration of who you are as a person.

For three and a half days, all I've gotten from Ray is silence. No texts. No calls. Nothing.

One night in his bed and *poof*, gone.

To be fair, I haven't reached out to him either. I'm also not the person who suggested I leave minutes after we had mind-warping sex for the first time. That was all him. Which is why patching up the way we left things is on his shoulders.

As a single parent who has more to worry about than himself, I understand why he asked me to leave. I never anticipated a relationship with Ray would be easy. But his delivery ripped every-thing to shreds. And his timing. The sweat barely dried on my skin before he kicked me out of his bed.

"Ugh," I huff out, shoving hanger after hanger left to right in my closet in search of something for the conference today.

Clarissa has been on the receiving end of my frustration since Monday morning. I didn't want to disrupt her vacation, but she initiated the first text, asking how cooking school was going. She followed the text with several sexually suggestive emojis and GIFs.

So, I poured my heart out. Mostly. I left out the finer details.

She offered to fly back early and beat Ray's ass with the stupid stick. I told her to stay put and do what she's always done, what I'd do for her in a heartbeat—be there for me when I need her—just from a distance.

I settle on Yale-blue slacks with a matching double-breasted blazer, a black blouse that shows a hint of cleavage, and black heels. It's rare I wear suits to work, but I enjoy the sporadic opportunity to put one on.

Slipping on the slacks and top, I cross to the bathroom and get to work on my hair. My fingers weave the long strands, braiding the length into a loose plait that rests over one side of my chest. Once secured, I dab on a light coat of makeup and lip gloss before a spritz of perfume.

Back in my room, I tie the leather cords on my quill and bead cuff bracelet, fastening it on my left wrist. Giving myself a last once-over, I slip on my heels, grab the blazer from the bed, and exit the room.

Tea-filled travel mug in hand and my bag slung over my shoulder, I walk out the front door, lock up, and slide behind the wheel of my car. Stomach in knots, the leather of the steering wheel complaining under my grip, I drive toward the Stone Bay Performing Arts Center. Ahead of schedule, I drive slower than usual. Do some breathing exercises to center myself.

Inhale... focus my energy on the seminar and how it can benefit my work. My career. My students. They are what matter. *Exhale...* eliminate every other thought and let the past go, at least for now. The past is invariant, so there is no sense in dwelling on it.

By the time I find a parking spot, a sense of calm replaces my earlier frustration. Exiting the car, I walk to the entrance and wait by the doors for my parents. In front of the three-story stone and glass building, I scan the sea of professionals crossing the lot to attend one of the largest conferences Stone Bay has held for the medical community. Unfamiliar people pass, a smile on their faces as they wave. I return the gesture and stand a little taller.

Pride washes over me as I join countless peers for a seminar some consider insignificant to my line of work. Some doctors refuse to look beyond their specific field to see all branches of medicine, including mental and behavioral health, are interconnected. The body has individual parts like a machine, but they all work in symbiosis for one purpose—to live. The sooner more medical professionals connect the dots and come to terms with how intertwined everything is within the body, the sooner we can find solutions for countless people.

Mom and Dad greet me minutes later, and we head inside to find our seats in the grand auditorium. The majority of the seats are filled, the din of buoyant chatter bouncing off the tall ceiling, mezzanine, and private booths along either wall.

We find our seats, and each pulls out our preferred method of note-taking, settling into the cushy center-stage chairs. As I scribble the title of today's seminar on a fresh piece of paper, the crowd quiets.

"Good morning," a woman greets, and I look up to see Felicity West—the current matriarch in the West family and one of the Stone Bay Seven. "I'm honored to announce our guest today, a renowned neurologist from Colorado, whose advancements in medicine are changing the way medical professionals treat their patients. His discoveries have not only saved lives but also improved them." If Felicity West could smile any brighter, we'd all pay a visit to the optometrist later. "Please help me welcome Dr. Adriel Hatathli."

The auditorium erupts into cheers as everyone rises to their feet and welcomes the guest of honor. Due to my height and that of the three men in front of me, I'm unable to see Dr. Hatathli cross the stage.

Part of me wishes I had done research before today's seminar.

An internet perusal to know the man behind the accolades. To at least know what he looks like, in case I saw him on the street.

But I've been a bit distracted.

We take our seats as the applause dies down. I set my paper and pen in my lap, poised to take notes, then glance up to see the opposite of what I expected.

Black hair slicked back and secured near the nape of his neck, a long, thin braid settles over his spine. Warm, golden-brown skin highlights his sharp jawline and soft cheekbones. Gait long and shoulders back, his presence dominates the vast stage at the head of the room.

He takes the microphone from Felicity and says something we are unable to hear. Then he turns and faces the audience, a radiant smile in place.

My stomach flips and pulse quickens.

This is bad. Very, very bad.

Not only is this man brilliant, he's beyond handsome. Which makes telling my parents I'm not interested in spending time with him that much harder.

"Good morning," he says, the baritone in his voice vibrating my bones. "I'd like to thank Dr. Sakari Imala and Dr. Tikaani Imala for inviting me to this wonderful town." He tips his head in gratitude in our direction, and we do the same. "It is my honor to share what I've learned with you all."

He shares details about himself, why he chose a career in medicine, and what he hopes everyone will take away from today's seminar. His tone is reposeful, pleasant, a timbre I could listen to for hours without tiring of it.

Everything in the room tunnels as I focus on Adriel. I mindlessly scribble notes as he lectures and goes through a slideshow. Jot down information I'd never considered with my students. More than anything, I try to focus on why I am here. But it proves challenging every now and then.

I don't miss the occasional glance in our direction when Adriel scans the crowd. The almost indiscernible tug at one corner of his lips as our eyes connect for a split second. Nor do I miss the small flip of excitement I feel with each glance.

But as fast as the exhilaration hits, it disappears. Then I am met with a heavy dose of guilt. Shame.

Since Sunday night, my relationship with Ray has been in this unbearable limbo. Regardless, the uncertainty of where we stand is a poor excuse to blatantly ogle other men. Especially a man my parents consider a suitor.

Dropping my eyes to the pad of paper on my lap, I listen and take notes. Think of ways to incorporate this new information with how I talk with my students. I keep my head down, avoid eye contact, and don't engage.

Ray and I may be in this weird place, but we're still in a relationship. Until we talk and sort our issues, everyone else is off-limits.

Of course, my parents weren't going to let me leave before introducing me to Adriel.

We shuffle forward in line, a few people in front of us, and Mom talks excitedly with Dad about integrating something with one of her patients after today's seminar. Like my parents, the conference sparked several ideas on how to approach different matters. I'm grateful my parents invited me to attend and gave me this opportunity.

But now, I'm ready to leave.

Each step in Adriel's direction spikes my nausea. Heightens my guilt. Makes me question why I didn't reach out once to Ray all week.

When it's our turn to speak with Adriel, Mom gushes over medical things outside my scope of practice. With a smile on my face, I tune out their conversation. Send a silent wish to the universe to cut their talk short.

"We'd be honored to host you for dinner this evening, Dr.

Hitathli," Mom says, and my attention snaps to her. "Please say you'll join us." With a slight twist of her posture, she angles herself toward me and Dad. "Kaya will be there, too."

His dark eyes flare for a split second, then tip up at the corners as he smiles. "How can I turn down such an invitation? The honor is mine."

A fresh wave of remorse floods my bloodstream. I step out of the line and walk up the aisle toward the auditorium doors.

I need air and a moment to think.

No doubt my parents will invite most of the family to dinner. A world-renowned doctor over for dinner is bound to excite all the healers in our family. It's an opportunity of a lifetime.

If I need to step away, there will be plenty of others to distract him.

I breathe a little easier when my parents approach, Mom practically glowing.

"Let's relax at the house before dinner." She rubs a hand between my shoulder blades. "Give us a little time to digest everything before dinner."

"Sounds great." I lean into her side and press a kiss to her temple. "Meet you there."

"It's silly to take two cars. You should ride with us, *panik*." Mom enters the living room in a sleeveless black dress with a gorgeous turquoise, white, and black pattern in a diagonal cut on the lower half.

Why did she change? Why is she so dressed up? And *why* do we need to take a car to dinner?

"Ride with you?" I ask, thoroughly confused.

She hooks beaded earrings that match her dress through her ears. "To the restaurant for dinner."

I cross the room to stand at her side. "We aren't having dinner at the house?"

A soft chuckle leaves her lips. "No, *panik*. Didn't want to over-whelm Dr. Hitathli with our wild bunch."

Something in me twists, but I shove it down. Push it away to worry over later. "Of course, we can ride together."

"Lovely." Mom glances over her shoulder. *"Aakuluk,* I don't want to be late." The term of endearment—*dear*—rolls off her tongue with love and reverence as she peers down the hallway.

Dad enters the room in all black—slacks, button-down, and suit jacket—and a bone and turquoise-beaded necklace.

A pit forms in my stomach at how formal they are dressed. "Where are we going for dinner?"

Mom ignores me as she fixes Dad's lapels. Then she loops her arm with his and leads them to the door. I follow in their wake to the car, feeling very underdressed. Dad opens the door for Mom, then for me, and dashes to his side of the car, slipping behind the wheel.

As we back out of the driveway, I try again. "Where are we having dinner?"

Mom twists in her seat and meets my gaze, a bright smile on her face. "Calhoun's Bistro. Thought it'd be a nice treat for us all."

Shit. The pit in my stomach morphs into a trench. *Please don't let him be at the restaurant tonight.*

The rest of the drive, I studiously work to calm the massive swell of anxiety beneath my diaphragm. On a deep breath, I close my eyes, count to ten, then exhale slowly and focus on the soft music playing in the car. I repeat this over and over. But regard-less of my efforts, the swirling energy doesn't settle. And when we pull into valet at the restaurant, it ratchets up tenfold.

I'm going to be sick.

Adriel meets us at the door, gestures for my parents to walk ahead of us, then rests his palm on the small of my back as we step inside.

Yep. Definitely going to throw up.

The host smiles as we approach, menus in hand as they guide us to our table.

Every step I take is calculated. My position next to Adriel concealed to purposely not draw attention to myself as we near the open kitchen. But it's pointless.

As we approach, Dad pauses and literally points the kitchen out to Adriel. And because the universe is obviously laughing at me, it's the exact moment Ray looks up and makes eye contact.

The room blurs as everything screeches to a halt. My hands shake at my sides, a chill settling in my bones. I can't breathe. Can't hear. Can't speak. But none of it matters because I witness every flash of hurt on Ray's face.

When Dad finishes his spiel and continues to follow the host, I also don't miss the tic in Ray's jaw as Adriel guides me to the table, his hand still on my back.

TWENTY

RAY

What. The. Fuck?

Four days. It's been almost four *fucking* days, and someone else already has their hands on her.

No. *Fuck no.*

My vision tunnels as she disappears from view; the little I do see is a vivid, pulsing red. Pressure builds in my chest as my nails sink into my palms. Rage I've never known radiates off me in waves.

I close my eyes, take several deep breaths, and try to find some semblance of calm while I finish my shift. But there's no relief in sight. On the fourth exhale, the image of that guy's hand on her lower back flashes in my mind's eye.

Fuck.

Unable to get ahold of myself, I walk off the line. As I pass Fin, I ask him to cover me for five minutes. I don't wait for his answer. I keep moving forward, headed for the only place I may get an ounce of respite.

Heaving the door open, I stride into the walk-in cooler, grab one of the coats off the hook, crumple it into a ball, crush it to my face, and scream. I let out every ounce of hurt from the past four days—all my own doing, of course. Let out every ounce of anger

—at myself—for ruining Sunday night, for ignoring Kaya all week. At Brianna for messaging me out of the blue and asking to see Tucker, which was a front for her actual motives. And at the man putting his hand on Kaya as though she belongs to him.

Sunday night may have ended in the worst possible way, but it doesn't change facts.

Kaya. Is. Mine.

Mine.

"Get your shit together," I chastise myself. "Rein it in, do your damn job, and deal with everything else later." Because there is not a chance in hell I am putting this off.

Hanging the coat back up, I pace the walk-in until my skin cools and teeth chatter. One final deep breath and I exit, eyes forward and attention homed in on my kitchen as it comes into view. I pat Fin on the shoulder and thank him, then resume work.

Calhoun's Bistro is busier than a typical Thursday evening. Independence Day week always brings in a crowd. Add in one of the largest medical conferences Stone Bay has seen, doctors from across the country flying in to listen to a prodigy doctor…

My hand slips and the dish I'm garnishing turns into a disaster.

"Chef Calhoun," André hollers across the kitchen. "Fix it." A muscle in his jaw tics, a rarity for him. "Now."

"Yes, Chef."

I shove my personal problems aside, focus on what matters right now, replate the dish, and garnish it without so much as a flinch. As the plate leaves the kitchen with others for the same table, a new ticket comes in. I scan the order and muster every ounce of strength I own to keep my shit together.

This is their order. I feel it in my bones. It's rare for a four-top to order only seafood entrées. What's more rare is to add the rabbit as a shared plate.

Scanning the table number on the ticket, I take a few steps out of the kitchen and peer through the dining room. I lean to the side, squint as I peek around the table blocking them from view.

My heart hammers as I take another step, the ticket crinkling in my fist.

Kaya's back is to the kitchen, but there's no mistaking it's her. Her long hair swept over her shoulder, blue jacket on the back of her chair, arms bare. To her right, with an effortless smile on his face, is the man I want to throttle. Poised in his seat, he stares at her as if she's the only person in the room.

My temper flares anew as I enter the kitchen and call out their order. Then I sidle up to Cameron, grab a frying pan from the overhead shelf, and work alongside her.

"Thank you, Chef, but I've got it," she says, a flush of pink on her cheeks.

My mouth quirks up in a half smile. "I know you do. Just need to busy my hands."

Several times, I've asked myself why I haven't found someone like Cameron. Someone who understands my way of life. Who reflects my ambitions. Who'd grasp my frustrations. Someone who'd stand effortlessly at my side. It'd be easier. So much easier.

But as I glance down at Cameron, the answer is in front of my face.

Cameron is soft, delicate, fragile—which are great qualities in a partner if that is what you want. She is a true romantic, a woman who wants to be wooed, treated with tenderness, given flowers just because—things I am not above doing.

I just don't want to do them for her. Or someone like her.

Hell, I already had that with Brianna.

I want more than beauty. I want fire. Passion. The intense weight of her gravity to pull me in over and over. To shackle me to her.

The moment I stepped up to her table, Kaya tethered my heart. I yielded to her magnetic force. Let her lure me in and hold me close. Allowed her the chance to show me what happiness looks like, what true affection feels like.

Then I fucked it all up.

And now, someone else has drifted into her orbit. Someone far more deserving of her affection.

With well-practiced breaths, I concentrate on plating and garnishing each dish. When the order is ready, I signal the server.

"Allow me to help," I offer, dismissing the other server who comes to assist.

Two lines form between her brows then smooth out as she picks up plates. "Thank you, Chef."

I take the remaining dishes and follow in her wake. As we pass tables, I smile and dip my chin at familiar faces. They return the gesture in kind. The closer we get to Kaya's table, the more I question what the hell I'm doing.

What exactly do I expect to happen as I sidle up to her table while she sits with her family?

My mind conjures every possible reason I'd have to assist a server in delivering plates to the table. Halfway through the dining room, I consider turning back and apologizing later. But I don't. I put myself in this situation, it's my mess to clean up.

Behind the server as we approach, I stay hidden from Kaya's view. But not for long. With her parents here, my appearance will spark conversation, likely about the food or restaurant.

The server sets meals in front of the appropriate person, then takes plates from me and continues.

Kaya stiffens in her seat. As if she senses me inches from her.

Yeah, Fire Eyes, I'm here.

"Chef Calhoun," Sakari Imala greets with a dazzling smile. "To what do we owe the pleasure?"

Once the plates have been placed and my hands are free, I tuck them behind my back. "Drs. Imala." I tip my head at Sakari and Tikaani, then shift my gaze. "Kaya." As vehemently against it as I am, I turn my attention to the stranger at the table, plaster on an artificial smile, and nod. My eyes return to Sakari, my gaze a touch softer. "It's a rare treat to serve our rabbit dish. I had to see who ordered one of my favorite menu items."

Lies.

"We decided to spoil our guest." Sakari gestures to the stranger, an undeniable glow about her as she gives him her full attention. "Dr. Adriel Hitathli flew in from Colorado to speak at today's seminar. A true genius in neurological medicine." Her gaze flits to Kaya for a heartbeat. "And someone I'd be honored to call family."

Every muscle in my body locks as Kaya sucks in a sharp breath. Irrational thoughts spiral as I repeat her words.

"And someone I'd be honored to call family."

Is this… a date?

Jealousy and anger flare anew. My knuckles burn as I clasp my hands tighter. A momentary wince cracks my facade as I bite the inside of my cheek. Every cell in my body screams to ask if they'd be honored to call *me* family. Instead, I swallow past the gnawing sensation in my stomach, do my damnedest to remain poised, and slip on a fake smile.

"Stone Bay is blessed to have your family, Sakari, Tikaani. Why not add a neurological genius to the bunch?" My voice is harsher than intended, but they're not the center of my wrath. I am. They just stumbled into my path of vitriol.

Needing to walk away, I take a step back. "I'll stop commandeering your time. Enjoy your meal." I bow my head. "Doctors." I glance at Kaya who hasn't moved in far too long. "Kaya."

Before any of them respond, I spin on my heel and weave through the dining room on fast feet. Rather than turn for the kitchen—where I should be—I head for the back of the restaurant, away from the noise and people. Ripping the hat from my head, I pace the back hall and drag my hands through my hair.

Undiluted bitterness and rage claw at my skin, constrict my rib cage and trample the small, maddening, thumping organ in the center of my chest. I want to scream, kick something, punch a fucking hole in the wall. And I would, were I not at work.

I fish my phone out of my pocket and open my chat history with Kaya—something I should have done days ago but didn't like a damn fool. My fingers hover over the keyboard, a million possible texts at the ready. Messages I'll likely regret later.

> Is he your date?

The moment it sends, my stomach cramps.

> I was an asshole Sunday night. And an even bigger asshole for not texting sooner. I'm so fucking sorry.

Another *whoosh* before the new message bubble fills the screen.

> I don't expect you to answer while you're at dinner with your family, but message back later. Please. There's not enough screen space for my apology.

I stare down at my phone, read the messages again and again, then berate myself for every stupid thing I've done to Kaya. I'd hate me if I were her.

> Can I see you later? Please. Just to talk.

My eyes don't leave the screen until it dims then locks. I close my eyes, count to ten and take just as many deep breaths, then open them and clear my mind.

Shoving my phone in my pocket, I slip my hat back on and head for the kitchen. André side-eyes me as I step up to my station, the muscles in his jaw tense. I bow my head, get lost in the sounds of pans clanging and food sizzling, and focus all my attention on my current priority—work.

The hours pass faster than anticipated as we serve more meals than on a typical Thursday. As the last dishes leave the kitchen, the cooks shift tasks and dive headfirst into cleaning mode. It's all hands on deck as we scrub down every surface.

Fin sidles up to me after he finishes his area, brows raised.

"You alright?" He jerks a thumb over his shoulder in the general direction of the walk-in. "Earlier…" He unbuttons his chef's coat. "Haven't seen you like that in a while."

Since the last time Brianna got under my skin, I want to say but refrain.

"Been a shitty week." I clutch the nape of my neck and squeeze the aching muscles.

He knocks my arm with his elbow. "Come out with us tonight." He gestures to a few others in the kitchen. "Have a drink. Take the edge off."

Tempting as it is, the last thing I need is to dull my senses with alcohol and make more idiotic life choices. "Pass," I say. "But thanks for the offer."

"Want to talk about it?"

I scan the remaining kitchen crew and shake my head. "Not here."

Fin drops a hand on my shoulder and squeezes. "You know where to find me if you change your mind."

"Thanks, Fin." I slap his back twice. "Now go. Have a drink for me."

As he disappears down the hall, my phone buzzes in my pocket. It could be my parents or Brianna, but I pray it's not. I unlock my phone and tap the notification, hope flaring when I see it's a text from Kaya.

So now you want to talk.

My fingers hover over the keyboard, ready to respond as another message comes through.

Now you want me. Convenient.

MY BODY VIBRATES WITH FRUSTRATION AS I STARE DOWN AT THE screen.

> I always want you, Fire Eyes.

"You have a funny way of showing it," I grumble as my fingers aggressively tap out a response.

> Could've fooled me.

> I need to see you. Tonight.

> Please

He must be joking. Four days and not a single word. Had the cooking classes been in session this week, we would've been forced to deal with what happened sooner. We may have talked like civilized people.

But it's been four days, and every minute that's ticked by has festered the wound he inflicted.

> Why?

He wants to see me, talk with me face to face, apologize in person. My nice side would give him the opportunity. But she left the building, and I refuse to make this easy for him. What he did hurt. So if he really wants me, if I am more than some conquest, he needs to prove it.

> Because apologizing in a text message is unacceptable. You deserve better.

Good start.

> At least we agree on one thing. I do deserve better.

Adriel would be an ideal match. His passion for helping people supersedes his intelligence and makes him infinitely more attractive. He's young, has a clear picture of his future—I only know this because my parents asked a barrage of personal questions at dinner—and is the most ambitious doctor I've met outside my family. I could follow my parents' insistence on a relationship with Adriel and be happy.

But in the process, I'd sacrifice other things I want in life. Like deep-rooted passion that only comes with falling in love with the person *you* choose. The fire that simmers just beneath the surface when your person is nearby. The constant need for more and feeling like you'll never get enough.

I could be happy with Adriel, but he isn't who *I* want.

If Ray craves me the way he says he does, he needs to fight— for me, for him, for us, for what we could be. His energy, his desires, need to match mine. Because I refuse to settle for less.

> Do you want him?

It's as if he hears my thoughts.

Do you really want me to answer that?

You don't

Those two words reek of arrogance. Cocky bastard.
No worries. I bite too.

Don't be so sure.

Three dots dance in a gray bubble as he types a response. Minutes pass and the screen dims. The bubble disappears and reappears again and again. By the time his message comes through, I expect a novel.

I'm sorry, Fire Eyes. Sorry I opened my stupid fucking mouth and told you to leave. Sorry I wasn't brave enough to ask you to stay. Sorry I wasn't smart enough to figure out how to explain to Tucker why you'd stayed the night. Sorry I come with baggage that seems to outweigh my rational mind. Sorry I wrecked us before we really had the chance to get started.

The backs of my eyes sting as I read the message again, as I picture him frustrated and visibly upset.

God, I want to say yes to him. Tell him he can see me tonight. Tell him to come over so we don't have to do this in inflectionless messages.

But he hurt me. And to right those wrongs, he needs to work for it. He needs to earn my time.

Tonight wasn't an "official" date, but my parents are trying to set me up with him.

As soon as the message is sent, a pang in my stomach steals my breath. Insensitive as it is to send, I won't lie to him. Tonight will not be the last time I see Adriel. Not if my parents have anything to do with it.

NO

FUCK NO

The pang is replaced with thrill as I stare at the screen. *Fight for me. If you want me, fight.*

Please, Fire Eyes. I need to see you. I don't care where, but it has to be tonight.

My thumbs hesitate as I mull over what to say. In the end, the same thought circles again and again… I want to see him. I want to do this in person. So, I cave… with stipulations.

What about Tucker?

With my parents. They'll keep him overnight.

Quickest response yet.

Fine, but I make no promises. You hurt me, and I won't forget it.

I'm not trying to be cruel, just honest. No sense in sugar-coating it.

And I'll regret hurting you every day going forward. There aren't enough apologies in existence to give you.

Before I have second thoughts, I send him my address and directions once he is on the Imala estate. He thanks me profusely and says he will see me soon.

For the next hour, I question if I made the right choice.

In a snug black T-shirt, houndstooth utility pants, and black sneakers, Ray dominates the foyer with his presence. Unlike previous times we've been in the same room together, he keeps his distance—just out of arm's reach—and looks more nervous than I feel.

"Thanks for agreeing to see me." His brow creases as he rocks back on his heels. "Can we sit?"

"Of course."

I lead us into the living room and take a seat on the couch. He sits at the opposite end with his hands in his lap. I won't admit how his distance hurts as much as his behavior the other night. But him intentionally adding distance between us is a blow to the chest.

"I panicked," he says as he runs his fingers through his hair. "I freaked out, made an irrational decision, and hurt you." Glassy brown eyes stare across the couch and pin me in place. "I will never forgive myself for what I said. For what I did. For how I hurt you. And us. The second I thought it, let alone said it, I hated myself. You have to know I regret it." He leans forward, drops his elbows to his knees, and rests his head in his hands. "If I could go back and do it differently, I would. In a heartbeat."

Frustration and devastation shape his frame as he presses the heels of his palms to his forehead.

"Then why?" The biggest question of all. If he hates what he did, if he instantly regretted it, why did he do it? Why put either of us through misery?

He turns his head to look in my direction. Dark shadows blend with sorrow and paint the skin beneath his eyes a pale purple. "Have you ever been so thoroughly destroyed by someone it warps the way you look at everyone else?"

I shake my head.

Tears rim his dark eyes a beat before he sits up and blinks them back. "I have. Not that it's an excuse for my behavior."

No, it's not. But it explains his defense mechanism. His need to throw up internal walls, mask his emotions, and keep people exactly where he wants them, in his control.

"The last time I let someone all the way in and left myself completely exposed, she kidnapped our child in the middle of the night, changed her number, and disappeared. Six years." He drops his head onto the back of the couch and sighs. "I searched for him for six years before she showed up out of the blue, signed over her parental rights, and told me she *couldn't do it anymore.*" He scoffs. "Not that she wanted to be a parent in the first place. Which is the biggest irony of all."

Closing his eyes, he pinches the bridge of his nose. "Since his return, Tucker's been in therapy. It took weeks for him to not fear me or my parents." He pauses and swallows. "We were strangers. He barely said a word the first year. Acted out daily or curled into a ball on his bed. For months, he was terrified of the dark but wouldn't let me stay in the room with him. We saw progress, but nothing monumental. The therapist said it could take several years for Tucker to recover."

He rolls his head on the cushion and meets my gaze. His dark, glassy eyes steal my breath as we simply stare at each other.

"Until you."

What?

He must see the confusion on my face.

"Tucker has opened up more in the past six months than he did the whole year prior. I attribute a few things to that." Another pause. "But since the last week of school, he's been more... of a kid. Carefree. Silly. Affectionate."

Does Ray know about my talk with Tucker? Wouldn't be bad if he did; just surprising. Most students don't relay our sessions to their parents. The only time I do is when further guidance is needed or the child is a danger to themselves or someone else.

"We haven't been seeing each other since the last week of school," I pose.

"True." A slow smile softens his expression. "But Tucker knew you by name the first day of cooking school. He hugged you. In that moment, I knew it was you. *You* brought Tucker back to life."

I'll never forget the fierceness of his hug that day, the way his face lit up.

"The only people Tucker hugs are me, my sister, and my parents. And it was months before our first."

Warmth blooms in my chest and roots itself beneath my breastbone. I love all my students, but a select few have my heart. Tucker is one of them.

"Sorry we veered off track. I just needed to put that out there. Give you some backstory."

Unable to stand the distance between us, I scoot closer to him, enough to rest my hand on his forearm. "Thank you for telling me, for trusting me with that piece of you." I stroke the lines of his tattoo with my thumb. "But it doesn't change the fact that you hurt me."

He shifts his arm and takes my hand in his, lacing our fingers. "I know. I've never hated myself as much as I did in that moment."

"I felt used." I yank my hand from his, needing zero distractions. "Like a notch on a bedpost. A convenient lay." I cross my arms over my chest and shiver. "A conquest."

He sits up straighter, turning until his knee bumps mine. "You are *none* of those things. I did not use you, and I hate that you think otherwise."

"What am I supposed to think?" I pin him with a glare. "If our roles were reversed, how would you feel?"

Silence stretches between us.

"Exactly."

He reaches for and takes my hands, his rough thumbs stroking my skin. "I learned long ago to not set expectations with other people. Hard lesson." Sadness lines his eyes as he shrugs. "But I will do whatever it takes to make this right."

"I won't make it easy." The words are out before I have a chance to filter my thoughts.

"Good. I wouldn't want you to."

A nagging voice in the back of my head says there has to be more to it. If he panicked, why would he ghost me for days? Why wait until we bump into each other to reach out?

Since he sidled up to my and Clarissa's table at the end of May, Ray has pursued me. He made his attraction to me evident. Asked for a date and wouldn't give up until I said yes. Gave me a nickname and never shied away from his feelings.

We went from all to nothing, and it doesn't line up.

"Why didn't you reach out?"

He pales and closes his eyes, inhaling a deep breath before meeting my gaze once more. "After you left Sunday, after I literally screamed at the heavens for my fuckup, I went inside, cleaned up, then considered texting to apologize."

"But you didn't."

"I didn't." He shakes his head. "Brianna messaged around that time. Said she wanted to see Tucker. That she needed my help."

My eyes widen, every protective bone in my body on high alert as I squeeze his hand. "Did she see him?"

"No." He scoffs. "She used him as an excuse, came to town, went into the diner, pestered my dad, then showed up at my work and asked for money."

An audible gasp leaves my lips. "Seriously?"

"So many times, I wish we'd never gotten involved. But then I remind myself I wouldn't have Tucker. He's the only good thing to come of her."

Couldn't agree more. "Does Tucker know she was in town?"

"No." He shakes his head. "She put him through enough hell. I won't let her do it again."

My heart hurts for an entirely different reason. I also understand why Ray didn't reach out sooner. Were I in his shoes, I wouldn't be able to think clearly either.

Hours pass in minutes as we inch closer on the couch and talk through the night. We share pieces of our past, our hearts, and what we want for our future. More than that, we open ourselves up and put our exposed hearts on the line.

As sunlight peeks through the windows, Ray promises to never hurt me again. And I believe him. He asks me for another date tomorrow—well, today—and I say yes. We agree to meet up at the festival after some sleep.

And when he wishes me sweet dreams, it feels as though things are back where they should be.

TWENTY-TWO
ERASER

Parking at the far end of town near the hardware store, I slip on a baseball cap and sunglasses and prepare to spend the day familiarizing myself with the area. Sun peeking over the mountains in the distance, I amble down the sidewalk with no specific destination in mind.

Early risers pull into the parking lot of a diner, several of the tables already full. Across the street, a line spills out the door and down the sidewalk of a coffee shop. Soft chatter mixes with the scent of bacon as I pass the open door of the diner. A hint of excitement in the air.

Before making the drive, I researched the town and some of its residents. I was promised my efforts would be fruitful. That every mile my tires ate up and dollar I spent on gas would be worth it.

By the look of things, those promises are spot on.

The farther I walk, the more this town reeks of money. I gathered as much during my online perusal but seeing it in person is quite the experience.

Quaint families decked out in pristine attire, not a single hair out of place. Not an ounce of worry on any of their faces. So innocent. So naive. So fucking stupid and careless. It will be my absolute pleasure to corrupt every one of them. All it takes is one person. An in with the most gullible of them and they fall like dominos.

I take it all in—the perfectly manicured grass, the neatly pruned plants, the colorful and welcoming storefronts, the happy-go-lucky residents. Even the town bar looks… refined, polished.

"Fucking weird," I mutter as I weave between the growing crowd.

But this is the perfect place to collect what belongs to me.

Streaks of yellow paint the powder-blue sky as I cross the street and head for the most talked about breakfast spot in town. People mosey about, smiles on their faces as they wave. Not wanting to stick out, I return the gesture. Act like every other tourist.

I round the corner and follow the street south for close to a mile. Cars line the street and spill out of the lot well before the restaurant's sign comes into view.

Good thing I have time.

The sweet scent of maple syrup mingles with the nutty aroma of coffee as I step inside, my stomach grumbling.

"Morning. Welcome to Poke the Yolk." The older woman smiles, and I return it in kind. "Just you, sweetheart?"

I remove my hat and sunglasses. "Yes, ma'am."

She waves me off. "None of that ma'am business." She surveys the dining room. "I have a seat open at the counter if that works for you."

"Sounds perfect." I glance down at her name tag. "Thank you, Trudie."

Plucking a menu from the holder at the host stand, she leads me to my seat. "You're most welcome. We should be thanking you for visiting our town."

Blending in is out of the equation. At least in places the townies frequent. Noted.

"It's a lot to take in."

Trudie smiles and rests a hand on my shoulder. "I suppose any new place can be overwhelming." Her hand falls away and she gives me the menu. "Today's special is the French toast casserole with mixed berries and cream cheese drizzle. The perfect festive treat."

With a cheek-stinging smile, I thank her, and she tells me my server will be with me momentarily.

These people are so fucking delusional. Does anyone actually believe this is reality?

Every shop in this town is independently owned and appears to be thriving. From the pictures online, all the government and community buildings are made of stone, flawlessly carved idols and monuments scattered throughout the town. The church looks like it's from the Gothic medieval era, the library not much different. The streets and sidewalks are clean enough to eat off of. And the founding families have no issue with sharing the fact they're rolling in money. Well, most of them.

Were it not for the mountain ranges, bay, and ocean surrounding Stone Bay, this place would've lost its shine long ago.

Perhaps that's why I'm here. To help it along. Nothing brings me more satisfaction than breaking people and putting them in their place.

"Good morning."

I glance up from my menu to see a pretty blonde woman across the counter, a bright smile on her face. "Good morning," I greet and glance down at her name tag. "Kirsten. What a lovely name."

The corners of her eyes twitch the slightest bit. "Thank you." Her smile shifts, still present but a touch uncomfortable. "Can I get you started with something to drink?"

"Coffee would be wonderful."

As if she's done it a million times, she turns, takes a few steps, grabs a full pot of coffee, and returns to my seat at the counter. She flips over the mug on my place setting and pours until the caffeinated brew nears the top. "Do you need more time to look at the menu?"

Saying her name made her skittish. Antsy. Aloof. She hides it well, though.

"No, I'm ready." Not wanting to draw more attention to myself, I give her my gentlest smile. "Trudie sold me on the French toast casserole." I hand her my menu.

"Good choice. Shouldn't be long."

She walks off on quick feet, stopping at a kiosk to enter my order. I study her out of the corner of my eye as I add a few packs of sugar to my coffee. A man close to her age with dark curly hair sidles up to her and says something I can't make out. A moment later, he moves down the counter alley and gives me an artificial smile as he passes.

In trying to appear friendly, I've made myself a target. But not with Trudie.

Something happened to the blonde woman. And perhaps the dark-haired man she spoke with. They watch out for each other. Protect one another.

Rather than draw more attention, I do what most people do nowadays. Get lost in one of the apps on my phone. Mindlessly scroll until a plate of food is set in front of me.

As I eat, I covertly scan what little of the restaurant I can see.

Elderly folks sip from mugs and chat with neighboring tables, uncaring how long they occupy their spot in the restaurant. Children scarf down food fast enough for a stomachache. Young adults sit in clusters with more than one carafe of coffee on their table, eyes sleepy and heads heavy.

A streak of blonde catches my eye as I swivel back toward my plate. I pause long enough to know it's my server, and she's secured in another man's arms. A black short-sleeve shirt hugs the thick muscles of his arms and chest, the word *POLICE* emblazoned on the sleeve and across his broad back.

I drop my gaze to my breakfast and eat faster than the kids nearby. Focus on clearing my plate and the reason I came to this pretentious town in the first place. To collect.

Shoveling down another bite, ready to get out of here, I make the mistake of looking for the server. When I spot her, she's still with the officer. And his studious gaze is firmly locked on me, head tilted and eyes narrowed.

Instead of waiting for the check, I grab my wallet, take out enough cash to cover my meal, and set it under the mug. Doing my best to appear unbothered, I wipe my mouth with a napkin, drop it on my empty plate, and rise from my seat. I force my shoulders to relax as I take slow, sure strides toward the door.

Trudie thanks me for stopping in as I near the door. I wave, don my hat, slip on my sunglasses, and exit the quaint restaurant without a word. I don't look over my shoulder. Don't meet the eyes I feel boring into my back.

I've already drawn too much attention. Time to accomplish what I set out to do.

The morning sun warms my skin as I trek down the road toward the park hosting the main event. I pay the attendant and enter the lavish festival. Scout the area and look for the best place to loiter while I wait for more people to arrive.

Pausing near a cluster of trees on the outskirts, I unlock my phone, go to my photos, and tap on the one with his picture. Music plays from strategically placed speakers as I study the image. Memorize it one more time.

Once I have the details of his face burned in my mind, I close the app, stow the phone in my pocket, and mosey about the event. Blend into the crowd and partake in activities. Act as though today's festivities are what brought me here and not the man I'm told will pay handsomely for someone else's mistakes.

Several songs, games, and fake conversations later, I spot him through the crowd. Genuine smile on his face, he shamelessly gawks at the woman with him, a young boy between them.

A wicked grin tugs at the corners of my mouth as I follow them with my sunglasses-covered eyes. I don't just have one meal ticket in this town. Now I have three. And the best way to get all three is the path of least resistance.

Oh, how I love learning people's weaknesses. What I love

more is the way they break as I rob them of what they hold dear, of what they love.

This man will shatter when I take what he loves. He will fold so easily. And I'll relish every moment, a pile of cash in my possession and devilish smile on my face.

TWENTY-THREE

RAY

Five hours of sleep, and I'm more awake and revitalized than usual.

Mom drops Tucker at the house a little after eleven on her way to the diner to help Dad with the influx of patron traffic. Tucker and I shower and dress in record time, fill a couple bottles with water, and make it out the door in under an hour. Before I back out of the driveway, I message Kaya.

> I know we agreed to meet at the festival but I'd like to pick you up. Is that okay?

I connect the phone to the car and shift the gear into reverse. As I exit the property, a ding echoes through the car and I tap the screen for it to read the message.

> Yes. Should be ready in ten.

With most of the residents on the opposite end of town, it isn't long before I turn onto Kaya's family's property and park in her driveway. Seeing her house in the full light of day, I enjoy the simplicity of it. Stone, wood, and stucco with several windows and tucked into the trees. Quiet, peaceful, and very much her style.

As one of the wealthiest families in Stone Bay, the Imalas live as if money isn't something to pride themselves on. As if it could vanish in an instant. Which it very well could. Nothing in life is promised, regardless of who you are.

The front door opens and Kaya steps out, the sun glinting her braided hair through the trees. In a flowy, juniper-green sundress, the skirt ending inches beneath her knees, Kaya strolls to the car with a breath-stopping smile on her face.

Damn, how I love that smile.

"Hi," she says, voice soft as she slides into the passenger seat.

"Hey." I meet her sparkly gaze and mirror her smile.

"Hi, Miss Kaya," Tucker greets with more enthusiasm than me and Kaya combined.

She peeks over her shoulder to the back seat. "Hi, Tucker. Excited for all the games and food?"

I watch Tucker in the rearview mirror. A dreamy look takes over his face a beat before his eyes widen. "I want to eat as many fried things as possible. Grandma says it'll upset my tummy, but I don't care." He shrugs as if a stomachache is no bother. "And I want to win the biggest prize at the games."

"No pressure," I mutter as I back out of her driveway and steer us off the estate.

Knowing traffic will be insane, I take the scenic route, drive farther north than the event, and loop back to the employee parking at RJ's Diner. Partial ownership perk.

A short trek down the street, we weave into the crowd within minutes. Animated chatter and delighted whoops marry with carnival game sounds and music playing through large speakers. The scents of fried foods, sweet confections, and hickory smoke float through the air.

Tucker grabs my hand and yanks me left and right to play games, pausing on occasion to eat excessive amounts of deep-fried, sugary food. Kaya and I indulge in a few, too.

Everything about today is perfect. Easygoing. Ordinary. Something I didn't know I craved until now.

At the ring toss game, I take Kaya's hand as we watch Tucker. Warm and delicate, her fingers curl around mine. An unfamiliar, desirable sense of security and peacefulness washes over me. The delicious hum I only feel with her courses through my veins. But it's when she leans into me and rests her head on my shoulder that everything clicks.

She said I'd have to work hard for her affection, for her. And I have every intention of doing so. But is it really *work* if all I want is her happiness?

The heady joy simmering in my veins, the woman at my side, my son having the time of his life... couldn't picture a better day if I tried. And I'll do whatever it takes to keep this slice of paradise.

After a few hours, the downside of my sugar high hits and my energy plummets. Not ready for the day to end, an idea sparks. The only trouble I'll have is convincing Tucker. Fingers crossed, I sway him.

"T-Man, let's get out of here before it's impossible."

"No." The whiny two-letter word sounds a mile long. "The fireworks haven't started yet."

I bend down and drop my voice. "What if I know of a better place to watch the fireworks?"

His eyes light up. "Really?"

"Yep." I nod. "And what if I told you we"—I gesture between me and him—"can also make a special dinner for the three of us? Whatever we want."

"Ooh." He rubs his hands together and bounces in place. "Anything?"

"Mm-hmm. Anything," I repeat in affirmation.

"Let's go." He grabs my hand and tugs me forward.

All I can do is laugh.

We fight the crowd—on the sidewalk and streets—for almost an hour before we reach a quieter roadway. Music filters through the car speakers as Tucker asks what he should name the massive stuffed bear he won at one of the games. He ticks off names and asks Kaya which one she thinks is the best.

By the time I turn into the vacant lot at Calhoun's Bistro, Tucker announces the winning name—Brody the Bear. Easy enough to remember.

I park in my usual spot at the back of the restaurant. Kaya side-eyes me before we exit the car and laughs.

"What?"

"Day off and you decide to come to work." She shakes her head, but the smile grazing her lips says she's anything but disappointed.

We exit the car and head for the back door, my hand going to the small of Kaya's back. Tucker stumbles a bit, Brody the Bear obstructing his view. And as we step inside, I relay why I chose the restaurant over our houses.

I put a finger up. "This kitchen is far superior to mine." I add a second finger. "The food selection is better than my pantry at the moment." Another finger goes up. "Watching me in this kitchen is a much better experience than the house." I smirk and add a fourth digit. "Easy cleanup." Final finger pops up. "And we'll have the best view of the fireworks out back past the tree line while we enjoy our picnic dinner."

I have never considered myself a romantic—not that I'm opposed to flowers, notes, and gestures; they have their place—but I've never been with someone who made me want to give or do those things. To woo them.

Until now.

Studying me from across the room, Kaya warms me in unimaginable ways. Makes me feel like the biggest tender heart. Like I'm more than eye candy online, more than my family's name, more than a single father. She stares into my soul and sees *me*. It makes me dizzy, catapults my pulse. Heats my skin. Gives me new life.

With Kaya, displaying affection through gestures comes naturally. As easy as breathing. A simple caress, her hand in mine, stolen glances, the love I pour into every dish I cook her.

As our relationship evolves, so will the ways I tell her how important she is in my life.

"A picnic during the show sounds perfect," she says, my favorite shade of pink coloring her cheeks.

I grab a chair for Kaya and have her sit where she has a full view of us. "Be right back." I wink and cross the kitchen.

Tucker's hand in mine, I guide us down the short hall toward the walk-in. A shiver ripples through him as the door closes behind us. He tugs his hand free and wraps his arms around his middle. Grabbing a coat from the hook, I help him shrug it on. I can't help but laugh when it hits the floor and drags behind him. But at least he's warm.

"Let's do something fun and easy since it's a picnic," I suggest. I ask for his ideas, and he rattles off several. We narrow it down by the ingredients we have available and get to work.

Grabbing two of the small baskets off to the side, I load up on ingredients, making sure his basket isn't too heavy. Once we have what we need, we head back to the kitchen and unload. I locate a footstool and apron for Tucker. Separate the ingredients, hand him a paring knife, and show him how to cut each item.

"Remember to tuck your fingers and take your time. Better to be slow than cut yourself."

Tucker nods. "I got this, Dad."

I kiss the top of his head, don an apron, then get to work on my own pile of ingredients. I preheat the oven and fetch a baking sheet for premade bread dough. Next, I fill a pot with water, set it on a burner, and light the element for pasta. Returning to my spot beside Tucker, I load the dough onto the pan and sprinkle herbs on top. Waiting on the oven, I chop the first of the vegetables.

And every time I peek in Kaya's direction, her eyes are on me. Captivated. Ravenous.

It scorches my skin and makes me hard.

With the dough in the oven and pasta in the boiling water, I slice and dice my remaining ingredients with swift, precise rocks of the knife. Beef filet is the only item I leave as is.

The next time I glance at Kaya, her eyes are on my hands. Curious. Spellbound. Starved. It's an instant dopamine shot to my bloodstream. An incomparable rush. Infinitely better than peer or online feedback.

Because Kaya matters. She's... *more.*

When I don't move on to the next task, her gaze lifts and locks onto mine. Lust and fire shimmer in her coppery-brown irises. A hunger that makes me want to cross the room, frame her face in my hands, and devour her.

With an arch of my brow and smirk on my lips, I wink and get back to work.

In a bowl, I whip up an oil and vinegar dressing with herbs and spices. Straining the pasta, I toss the noodles in the bowl with the dressing, coat them thoroughly, and set it aside to soak up the flavors. I add julienned carrots, diced cucumber and red onion, rough-chopped artichoke hearts and tomato, fresh mozzarella balls, and sliced olives. With several practiced flicks of my wrist, I mix the ingredients and coat everything with the dressing.

"How's it going, T-Man?" I check in with Tucker.

He sets down his knife and brushes the hair out of his face. "Almost done."

I sidle up to him and make a show of inspecting his work. "Looks perfect." I kiss the top of his head. "Good work, bud."

Once the bread is out of the oven, I heat a pan on the burner, add a large chunk of garlic and herb butter, and let it melt. Sizzling echoes through the kitchen when the filet hits the pan, my mouth watering as the umami aroma fills the air. Perfectly cooked, I transfer the filet to my cutting board to rest before slicing.

Abandoning my workstation, I kiss the top of Kaya's head as I pass her. "Grabbing some take-out boxes. Be right back."

I return with a variety of box sizes and set them out in front of me and Tucker. Pointing to each one, I tell him what we'll put in them. And it's the cutest thing to watch my little man delicately fill the boxes so his charcuterie ingredients stay neat. While he packs boxes, I slice the steak and bread.

With everything loaded in one of the walk-in baskets, I clean the kitchen in record time, grab a tablecloth, dishware and cutlery, and a bottle of sparkling water.

Ticking items off on his fingers, Tucker tells Kaya all the things he cut and that it's his best work yet.

"Can't wait to taste it all," she tells him.

The pride in his voice eases an ever-present ache in my chest, and I pause to revel in it. My vision blurs, a subtle sting behind my eyes as I listen to him excitedly share with Kaya. Tell her things he deems important or special. The entire time, she gives him her undivided attention, absorbs every word, then praises his work.

The ground quakes beneath my feet, an irrepressible tremor rattling my hands. The sting in my eyes burns hotter as saliva pools in my mouth. I swallow, blink, and inhale a few steadying breaths.

From the start, Tucker and Kaya have had this easy connection. An effortless bond. An uncomplicated relationship I never envisioned Tucker having with a woman in my life.

I want to relish it, bask in the obvious love they share, but I'm… afraid to. Scared it won't last.

Rising from her seat, Kaya returns the chair from where I got it, takes Tucker's hand in hers, and asks him what fireworks his favorites are as we head for the back door.

As we step into the fading daylight, I slip my hand into hers and close my eyes for one, two, three strides, breathing in the balmy summer air and reveling in the woman at my side. Right now, everything feels right. Perfect. Exactly as it should be. I cast my fears aside and decide to live in the moment. Capture mental snapshots of the day and store them in my memory for safekeeping. Then I send out a silent wish for many more in the future. Pray I don't forget a single minute along the way.

Winding through the trees on a foot-worn path, a table with benches comes into view, a dim light shining overhead. Waves crash against the rock face below, a hint of brine in the air as a panoramic view of the bay greets us.

When I need a mental reset during a long shift, I come out here and ignore the world for ten minutes.

"Wow," Kaya whispers, her grip on my hand tightening. "It's perfect."

My thumb strokes the length of hers, my gaze locked on her profile as the sunset dances over her skin. "Flawless." Just as I get lost in the sight of her, Tucker speaks up and snaps me out of my trance.

"Come on, Dad. Let's set everything up. I don't want to miss the fireworks."

It's on the tip of my tongue to tell him it's impossible to miss them with nothing between us and the bay. But I bite back the comment and head for the table. "Lead the way, T-Man."

Our picnic spread on the table, I fill glasses with water, hand out plates and cutlery, and take the seat next to Kaya, Tucker on the other side of her. We fill our plates with cheeses, meats, pasta salad, and bread and dine like royalty as fireworks light up the sky. Tucker oohs and awes with each explosion, saving his applause for the grand finale.

"Home for dessert?" I propose, then drop my voice as I lean closer to Kaya. "And a sleepover?"

In a heartbeat, she swivels her head and pins me with her fiery irises. Deep lines mar her brow as she silently questions my sanity, especially after her last visit. Discreetly, she tips her head toward Tucker. "You're sure it's a good idea?" A sliver of hurt edges her tone.

"Yes." I nod. "Last time, he wasn't awake for me to explain."

She swallows. "And you want to now?" Her voice softer, shaky.

Eyes locked on hers, I rest a hand on her thigh and give a reassuring squeeze. "Absolutely."

Countless emotions flit across her face as she digests this and mulls over what happens next.

A serpent coils around my heart and constricts while I wait for her next move, for her to say something. Anything. I fight the urge to beg, to insist. Saying yes is her choice, and I deserve her indecision.

She nibbles her bottom lip and inches closer. "Tucker won't freak out?"

I shrug, lean forward, and peek around Kaya. "T-Man?"

Tucker pops a grape in his mouth. "Yeah."

"Would it be weird if we had a sleepover with Kaya?"

Tucker's eyes go wide as he swallows. "For real?"

I school my expression and nod.

"That's dope." His hazel eyes shift to Kaya. "We can stay up super late and watch another movie."

Bless his enthusiasm and innocent mind. "Sounds fun. What do you think?"

Kaya purses her lips. "I think you just put me on the spot and used your son to manipulate me into saying yes."

A smirk curves my lips. She isn't wrong. "Did it work?"

She narrows her eyes. "Maybe." Her knee bumps my thigh as she twists to face me. "Do you really want me to stay over? Or is this because of a certain doctor?"

An audible growl vibrates my chest. "Yes, I want you to stay." Dropping my gaze, I take her hand and trace the lines on her soft skin. "I wanted you to stay before." My eyes sting and I swallow past the sudden emotion clogging my throat. I lift my glassy gaze to hers. "Navigating this won't be easy, but I want to try. For you. If you'll let me."

She brings a hand to my cheek, her thumb stroking my stubble. "I want to say yes."

"Then say it."

Brows pinched, she blinks a few times. "You hurt me."

Her admission stings as much as the first time.

"I understand this"—she gestures between us—"is new and

different. But if we're going to do this, I need you to promise what happened before won't happen again." She rests her forehead on mine. "You don't need to hide. Not from me. When you have doubts, talk to me. Tell me where your head is at. But please, don't run away."

My stomach flips. I suck in a sharp breath and nod woodenly. "I promise." And I mean it with every shred of my soul. "I'll probably do a shitty job, say the wrong thing, come off too harsh when I'm unsure, but I promise not to hide." I toy with the length of her hair. "Never from you. Not anymore."

A subtle smile graces her lips. "Then, yes"—she closes the distance between us and kisses me chastely—"I'll stay."

TWENTY-FOUR

KAYA

RAY HAULS ME AGAINST HIS CHEST AND HUGS THE AIR FROM MY lungs. "Thank you, Fire Eyes," he whispers in my ear. He gives a slight squeeze, loosens his hold, but he doesn't let go. Not yet.

We breathe each other in. Bask in the reality of what happens next. Give ourselves a moment to digest this step.

My pulse thrums in my ears. Rampant energy fires through every nerve ending in my body, a subtle tremble in my limbs and fingers. Effervescent thrill blooms beneath my diaphragm, a light sheen of sweat dampening my skin.

Did I really just agree to stay overnight? In his bed? With his son across the hall?

Yes, I did. And the more I think about it, the more my stomach twists in knots.

"We should get going." Ray presses a kiss to my forehead, unravels me from his hold, leans back, and shifts his attention to Tucker. "Help me clean up, T-Man."

While Ray and Tucker pack and tidy, I stare out at the bay and get lost in thought.

For years, I've held firm on my stance on romantic relation-ships. I wasn't interested. Didn't want my personal life to detract from my career. Period. I had a plan, a timeline, had constructed the path I wanted to follow. I'd never put it on paper but memorized it like the back of my hand.

And a relationship with Ray throws the plan down the garbage disposal.

But as I glance at him and Tucker picking up the remnants of our dinner and goofing off, my heart jolts to life.

The blueprint of my future can always be rewritten; I know that now. Because being with them is worth it.

Everything secured in the basket, we stroll to the car, my fingers laced with his. Ray unlocks and starts the car, hands Tucker leftovers after he situates Brody the Bear, then jogs back to the restaurant to set the basket inside.

The drive to my house is brief, quiet, and a little daunting. Ray parks in my driveway, leaves the engine running and makes no move to exit. My pulse stutters at his concession—a moment to myself. A respite I didn't know I needed, but somehow, he did.

I slip out of the car. "Won't be long."

"Take your time. I'll let Tucker entertain me with his vocal talent." I don't miss the hint of sarcasm in his voice.

The car door closes with a soft but startling *snick*. Anticipation swirls in my belly as I head for the front door. Every step forward is a heavier press on the accelerator of my pulse. As I ascend the porch steps, the fuzzy lines of reality turn crisp, clear.

Keying in the code, I unlock and open the door. Step inside and suck in a sharp breath. Close the door and sag against the wall. Exhale slowly, giving me a minute to absorb the day and consider what will change after tonight.

I agreed to spend the night at his house. To sleep in his bed. To wake up in the morning and share breakfast with him and Tucker in my pajamas.

Staying overnight is new territory. Terrain I hadn't planned on navigating for years. Yet here I am.

Hovering in the foyer, panic filters in from all sides. My stomach flips and dips, nausea clawing its way up my throat. I close my eyes, take a deep breath, and focus on something unrelated. A calming hobby or task.

Gardening.

One breath, then another, I focus on a recent memory. Let it take over and settle my nerves.

My fingers sifting through the rich earth. Glimpses of hearty vegetables in the soil, on stalks, and hanging from vines. The swell of gratitude as I fill baskets with corn, beans, sweet potatoes, and gourds. My meditative state as I prepare the land for new seedlings.

More at ease, I inhale deeply and open my eyes. Push off the wall, straighten my spine, and head for my bedroom. Flipping on the light, I shuffle to the closet for an overnight bag and sling the strap over my shoulder. I stare at my wardrobe, dazed and frozen, unsure what to pack. Apprehension trickles in as I veto one garment after another.

Do I pack normal pajamas or something more revealing?

Regular pjs. Tucker will be home.

Should I bring sexy lingerie or stick with comfy cotton?

Provocative undergarments are a guilty pleasure. Something I buy for myself and no one else. When I need a confidence boost, I slip on a lace or silk set. Let it embolden me on more difficult days.

Tonight, I may need that extra support.

I shove pajamas, lingerie, and cotton underwear into the bag. Tug a shirt from the hanger, grab shorts from the dresser, and add them to the overnighter. Head to the bathroom and load my toiletry bag. Force myself to think of anything other than the lacy panties and bra beneath tomorrow's outfit.

Jittery, I zip the bag closed, turn off the light, and walk out the door. When I step onto the porch and lock up, Ray exits the car, meets me halfway, and takes my bag to put in the trunk.

"Thank you," I say and slip into the passenger seat.

When he's back in the car, Ray takes my hand and lifts it to his lips, kissing my knuckles. "No thanks necessary."

The miles from my house to his are a blur. Tucker talks to Brody the Bear about his room and other toys. Ray caresses my hand with his thumb the entire ride. And in a matter of minutes, gravel crunches as we turn onto the driveway. Ray reaches up, presses a button near the visor, and the garage door opens.

When Ray puts the car in park, my pulse soars. *This is it.*

Perspiration licks my skin as I exit the car. My nails biting my palms as I wring my fingers at my sides. I startle when Tucker slams his door and charges inside the house. Slap a hand to my chest when Ray sidles up to me and rests a hand on my lower back.

He ducks his chin, his breath warm on my ear. "Breathe, Fire Eyes."

I nod woodenly and do as he says.

Ray shoulders my bag, kisses my temple and leads us into the house.

Tucker kicks off his second shoe as we enter and flings them toward the door in the foyer. He bounds toward the living room, flips on a light, and plops down on the couch. "I'll find a movie."

Ray and I toe off our shoes, and he straightens Tucker's next to ours. Banding an arm around my waist, he leans in and presses his lips to my forehead. "Going to put your bag in the room. Make yourself at home."

Before I say a word, he climbs the stairs and disappears, my overnight bag in his hand.

This is really happening.

I jump as intro music for the movie booms through the speakers.

Tucker dashes to my side, grabs my hand, and yanks me toward the kitchen. "We need to get movie snacks, Miss Kaya."

A task. Perfect. "What are our options?"

He opens the pantry door, drops my hand, flips on the light, and steps into the small walk-in closet–sized room. "Popcorn, licorice, different kinds of chocolate..." He pulls a bin off one of the shelves, hugs it to his chest, and moves past me to set it on the kitchen island. Package after package, Tucker dumps every possible sweet and salty movie snack on the counter. "Chips, jelly beans, gummy worms or bears, peanut butter cups."

Is the bin some magical, endless storage container for snacks?

Ray rounds the corner, his eyes wide as he witnesses the chaos of Tucker unloading all the treats. "Hey, bud. Let's pick two or three and put the rest back."

Tucker purses his lips then rolls his eyes. "Fine," he says, tone melodramatic. "Cheesy chips, gummy bears, and peanut butter cups."

"Good choices," I say, helping him put everything away.

Ray sends Tucker upstairs to change into pajamas. I take the snacks to the living room while Ray grabs drinks. Mere seconds later, Tucker flies down the stairs, beats Ray to the living room, grabs the bag of chips, and takes his spot on the couch.

Movie time is much the same—Ray and I squished together, my hand in his and our fingers laced. For an hour, I aim my attention at the screen. Do my best to focus on the show, eat a handful of gummy bears, and ignore what happens when the television shuts off.

Tucker's soft snores fill in the quieter parts of the movie a half hour before it ends. Ray kisses my temple, gives my hand a squeeze before releasing it, then carries Tucker upstairs to bed.

Unable to sit still, I take the uneaten snacks and empty glasses to the kitchen. Tidy up to distract myself.

It isn't the idea of sex that makes me fidgety. Sex with Ray is otherworldly. A literal fantasy come to life. One I want to live again and again.

What has me spinning my bracelet over and over is the emotional attachment and possible expectations that come with staying overnight. Is he ready for that? Am I?

My insides twist.

What happens when the postcoital bliss wears off? Will reality slap him once more? Will he change his mind and kick me out of his bed again?

Lost in thought, I jump and almost drop a glass in the sink when warm hands clutch my hips.

Breath tickling the curve of my neck, he mutters, "Sorry." And then his lips are on my skin. Soft. Hungry. Coaxing as they trail up, up, up the side of my neck.

I set the glass down, tip my head back, and rest it on his shoulder. Roll my eyes closed and hum as fire licks my skin, as every nerve ending sparks to life, as every worried thought vanishes.

How this man turns a string of simple kisses into torturous foreplay, I'll never know. But I ache for his touch, his lips, his bare skin on mine. The fire that exists between us.

He releases my hip, reaches forward, and cuts off the water. "Let's go to bed, Fire Eyes."

Bed.

My apprehension returns, a coiled thread twisting in my stomach. Pulsing. Shaking. Strung impossibly tight.

Speechless, I nod.

Pressing another kiss to my shoulder, he takes my hand and guides us out of the kitchen. Each step up the staircase is a jolt to the swirling anxiety in my belly. On each inhale, I remind myself this isn't new. Ray and I have been here—sex.

But this isn't like before.

Tonight, after we're boneless, breathless, and basking in our afterglow, I'll fall asleep in his arms. Buried under linens with his black amber and lavender scent infused in the cotton, we'll cross off another milestone on our relationship list.

A shiver rolls up my spine, tingles ripple down my arms, and I noticeably tremble as we reach the top landing. Ray tightens his hold on my hand, the only indication he feels the tremor.

We enter his room unhurried. The soft glow of the bedside lamp warm, inviting, familiar. Ray pauses to close the door, the soft click deafening.

My pulse soars and hands quiver.

Ray molds his front to my back, winds his arms around my

middle, and kisses my temple. "Relax, Fire Eyes," he whispers against my skin. "I've got you."

I melt into him. Let his strength and reassurance settle in my bones. Let his words quell my nerves. Closing my eyes, I take a deep breath and picture my stress withering away. On the exhale, I wrap my fingers around his forearms. Soften against every firm inch of him. Let go of my worries and give in to what I feel.

"That's my girl." He sweeps my braid aside and peppers kisses down my neck. "God, I love how soft you are." Calloused fingers dance over my shoulders in the softest caress before they wander the length of my arms.

A fiery storm simmers beneath my skin. Little sparks crackling under his touch as he traverses my body.

Ragged breath at the sensitive spot beneath my ear, his lips ghost over my rapid-beating pulse. Teasing. Taunting. A delicious form of torture a beat before his tongue darts out and tastes me.

A shiver rolls through me, goose bumps pebbling my skin, arousal pooling between my thighs.

An audible growl vibrates his chest, his hands drifting to my hips, his greedy fingers kneading, possessive. "So responsive." The tip of his nose skims the shell of my ear. "So beautiful."

Spinning in his arms, I frame his face with my hands and push up on my toes. Claim his mouth with a ravenous kiss. Show him exactly how responsive I can be.

Eager hands wander the length of my spine and curves of my ass a beat before he hoists me up. My legs circle his waist as his fingers slip under the skirt of my dress, massaging, exploring. On a groan, he breaks the kiss. "I'll never get my fill of you, Fire Eyes."

"Me either," I admit, breathy. My fingers comb through his hair, fist the thick locks, and take his mouth again.

The corded muscles of his arms flex and hug me closer as we cross the room. Pin me to his hips. Rock my core over his hard length with each stride. As he lowers me to the bed, the kiss turns frenzied. Desperate. Libidinous moans bounce off the walls as I dig my heels into his back, craving more pressure. He kisses his way up my jaw, then pushes up to hover above me, those addictive umber irises holding me captive.

An unexpected tenderness softens his expression as he cups my cheek. I don't dare ask what it means. Not now. But the flutter in my belly says I already know.

Gaze magnetized to mine, he toys with my hair and slowly drifts down the length of my braid. Tugs off the elastic band secured at the end and unravels the thick plait until he reaches my nape. Gingerly combs my locks with his fingers and hums.

On the next breath, his pupils dilate and lips part. His fingers curl into a fist at the base of my neck. And with a swift yank, my head tips back and breathing shallows as my neck is exposed.

A muffled growl floats through the room. "The ways in which I struggle..."

My brows pinch in confusion. "With what?"

He dips down and trails the tip of his nose up the column of my throat and along my jawline. "I want to be sweet with you. Tease you with the barest of touches. Watch you come undone as I move in and out of you, slowly, steadily." He grazes the angle of my jaw with his teeth. "But I also want to be rough. Knead your curves and mark your skin. Fuck you hard enough everyone in town hears you scream my name."

My breath hitches and nipples stiffen as arousal drips down my ass.

Lips pressed to the sensitive skin beneath my ear, he groans. "You like that, don't you, Fire Eyes? The idea of me claiming you." He nips my skin then drifts lower. "Marking you." His mouth opens wider, clamping down a beat before he sucks the slope of my neck for one, two, three ragged breaths. "Ruining you for anyone else." He tugs the strap of my dress off my shoulder and licks the length of my collarbone.

I tip my head to the side. "Yes," I confess, voice unrecognizable, breathy. God, I've never wanted anyone the way I want him.

He claims my mouth once more, devouring me like a starved man. Nimble fingers knead my body, massage my curves, then settle at the dip of my waist. He drives his hips once, twice, then bands an arm around my waist, pins me to his chest, and rolls us over.

Hands planted on his chest, his body at my mercy, a rush of power floods my bloodstream as I stare down at him. The shift in control is heady, potent.

Fingers trailing up my spine, he reaches the top of the zipper on my dress. Painfully slow, he drags the metal down the teeth. Parts the back of my dress and caresses my exposed skin. Rocks his hips up and grinds his erection against my center. One strap followed by the other, he peels the flowy fabric off until it pools at my waist. Snaps his fingers, releases the clasp of my bra, and tosses it aside.

Then, I'm on my back again.

He peppers kisses on the swells of my breasts, my belly, my navel as he inches down my body. Each kiss is a direct line to the ache between my thighs. A secret button press that has me weeping for more.

With a *thump*, his knees hit the floor. Hands at my waist, he drags my dress down my legs then rises to his full height. Reaches up, grabs the back collar of his shirt, and tugs it over his head. Before I can memorize the ridges of his abdomen, he unfastens his shorts and shoves them down his thighs.

My tongue peeks out and wets my lips.

The bed dips a beat before he's over me again, the heat of him pressed to every inch of my body. He kisses me once, twice, then licks and sucks and nibbles his way down my throat. Breasts in his greedy hands, he circles a nipple with his tongue then adds a little teeth. I gasp. Feel his smile a beat before he wraps his lips around the stiff peak and sucks. Hard.

I fist and tug his hair. Arch my back and thrust my breasts into his eager touch. Hiss as he gingerly bites my nipple then shifts his attention to the other.

"Mine," he growls as he releases my nipple and licks his way down to the waistband of my panties.

"Yours," I whisper then suck in a sharp breath as he grazes the skin of my lower abdomen.

Dark, hooded eyes pin me in place as he hooks a finger on either side of my panties and inches them down my legs. And then he's there, hovering above the junction of my thighs. His tongue darts out and wets his lips as he hooks my legs over his shoulders, slips his hands under my ass, and hauls me closer.

I can't take my eyes off him.

Nose pressed to my skin, he inhales a slow, measured breath. Rolls his eyes closed and hums. "Divine." My body vibrates as he drags his tongue up my center, his fingers bruising the insides of my thighs. "The only taste I want on my tongue."

I lose all sense of reality as he flicks and sucks my clit, then dips lower and spears me with his skillful tongue. Eats me savagely. Each shameless slurp and lap of his tongue edges me closer but is nowhere near enough.

I need more.

Cupping my breasts, I roll my nipples between my fingers. Give them a slight tug. Gasp as I relish the bite of pain.

He groans against my pussy, the vibration better than any toy in my arsenal. Rooting his fingers in my flesh, he devours me, his smoldering gaze locked on my breasts.

Focused on his fiery stare and the throbbing ache between my thighs, I miss the shift of his arm. As I rock dangerously close to the edge of my orgasm, he slips a finger into my pussy. Followed by a second, and I whimper.

"Give me what's mine."

He pumps his fingers, again and again, his mouth relentless on my clit.

I detonate. Fist his hair and the bedding. Cry out, then cover my mouth.

But he doesn't let up. Resolute and insatiable, he sucks my clit harder. Pistons his hand faster until I reach the other side of my orgasm. "Stunning," he mumbles against my skin.

My eyes fall shut, my arms collapsing at my sides as I attempt to catch my breath. Goose bumps dance over my skin as his hold on me loosens and the heat of him vanishes. My pulse soars at the sudden chill, a wave of panic blanketing me as my eyes fly open.

What I'm met with vanquishes every ounce of dread.

Thick and pulsing, his cock juts out, a bead of precum glistening the tip. A soft *swish* followed by the crinkling of foil hits my ears.

I push up on my elbows. "Wait."

Fingers paused on the wrapper, his eyes dart to mine with silent concern.

Sitting taller, I reach for and take the condom. Swallow past the sudden lump in my throat as I lock onto his intoxicating umber eyes. "I'm on birth control."

A flurry of emotions flickers across his face. Lust. Yearning. Thrill. Fear. It's the last one that gives me pause.

"Hey." I drop the condom on the bed, scoot closer to him, and take his hand. "Just wanted you to know." Bringing his hand to my lips, I kiss each of his fingertips. "But if you feel better using a condom, I am on your side."

Deep lines form between his brows then smooth out. "It's just that…"

Not using a condom is probably how Tucker came to be, and he doesn't want to risk it. He put his trust in someone else's hands, and it flipped his world upside down.

"I know." Eyes on his, I pluck the condom from the bed, tear it open, toss the wrapper, and lift the latex to his weeping cock. "May I?"

His dick twitches inches from my face as his lips part. Desire replaces the fear in his eyes. Cupping my jaw, he presses the pad of his thumb to my bottom lip, adds a little pressure, and sweeps across it. "Never have to ask, Fire Eyes."

Leaning forward, gaze firmly locked on his, I stick out my

tongue and slowly lick the head of his cock. Moan as the salty precum dances over my taste buds. Bask in the way his eyes roll back and hips rock forward.

Inching back, I pinch the end of the condom and roll it down his length. Cup his balls and roll them in my palm once, twice, then stroke his length root to tip.

"Mine." The single syllable a bold declaration.

Soft grip on the underside of my jaw, he tips my head back and bends at the hips until his breath paints my lips. "Yours," he growls. Then he claims my mouth.

We're a frenzy of urgent touches, fevered skin, and hungry mouths. Easing onto the bed, he leans back against the headboard and holds out his hands. I crawl closer, take his hands, and straddle his thighs.

Hands on my hips, he bruises my flesh. "Ride me, Fire Eyes." He palms my ass and hauls me forward until I hit the base of his cock. "I want to watch you take me. Need to see that fire burn in those gorgeous eyes."

Gripping his shoulders, I lift and inch forward. Press my mouth to his in a searing kiss as I ease down and his tip nudges my entrance. Thread my fingers through his hair and deepen the kiss a breath before I sink and take his entire length at once.

We gasp in unison, breaking the kiss. My eyes roll back as I revel in how full I feel in this position. Yet it's still not enough.

More. I always need more of him.

Dropping my forehead to rest on his, I rock my hips back, then glide forward until I can't take him any deeper. He shudders beneath me and fists my hips. I repeat the move again and again, each stroke faster than the previous. Sweat pebbles our skin. Our moans blend with the slap, slap, slap of our bodies.

His grip on my hips turns ruthless as he guides our thrusts. Drives them harder, faster. A loud *thwack* echoes through the room, my ass cheek hot and tingling.

I lean back and drop a hand on the bed. Grab his arm with my other hand. Ride him like a rodeo champion. Cry out when his lips wrap around my nipple and suck. Moan unabashedly when he adds teeth. Miss the feel of his mouth when he releases the tight bud with a *pop*.

"Look at you," he croons, pistoning my hips faster up and down his length. "Taking my cock like a good fucking girl."

He licks from my cleavage to my chin, slides his hands up my sides, and brings me closer to him. An arm bands around my lower back as the other hand snakes up my spine and pauses at the nape of my neck. He nips my bottom lip then kisses it. "You're close."

Clinging to him, I tip my head back, close my eyes, and roll my hips. "So close."

His hand on my lower back shifts, his finger slinking between my ass cheeks, lower and lower. He slicks the digit with my arousal then shifts back. "I want you dripping down my cock," he purrs. "My balls." His finger grazes the hole between my cheeks. "Come for me, Fire Eyes." His finger slips inside a place no one else has been, and it's like a match to a fuse. "*Mine*."

Stars dance across my vision as I gasp. Wave after perpetual wave, the orgasm rolls through me with the promise to never stop.

One, two, three more quick thrusts, Ray shatters beneath me, his fingers bruising my ass as my name spills from his lips. Body shuddering, he wraps me in his arms and secures me to his chest until our breathing levels out.

Silence echoes around us, but it's comfortable. Perfect in the moment.

He eases me off his lap, goes to the bathroom to dispose of the condom, and returns with a warm washcloth. Every touch is gentle, unhurried. Pressing a kiss to my forehead, he takes the cloth to the bathroom, goes to the dresser, and comes back with pajamas for us both.

Everything about tonight feels natural. Routine. Sublime.

We slip under the covers, Ray turns off the light, and we adjust to the new sleeping arrangement. His front to my back, an arm around my waist and his lips pressed to my hair, he takes a deep breath and sighs. Content. Happy.

Eyes heavy, body sated, the weight of sleep lulls me under. Just before it does, he whispers into the dark.

"Never met anyone like you." He kisses my hair with reverence. "Won't lose you." He hugs me closer, tighter. "You're mine, Fire Eyes." A hum vibrates between us. "And I'm yours."

Lazy smile on my face, I drift off to sleep.

TWENTY-FIVE

RAY

"Great job, everyone." My cheeks sting as I scan the room and meet each of the students' eyes. "You've made me proud this week."

Like any school or class, the work gets more challenging with each step forward. This class is no exception. But these kids blew me away with their skills this week. The recipes we selected for the program range in difficulty—none of them too hard—but many are tedious and take patience. I imagined the kids huffing or groaning at the process. They proved me wrong.

I gesture to the platters along the front counter. "These are extraordinary. Be proud of yourselves." I clap, André and Fin joining my applause before everyone else. "Now, come up here and fill your plates."

For the last day of lunch and appetizers, each group was given a different recipe. André, Fin, and I also had our own order to fulfill. The result is five different slider-size sandwiches and an appetizer for everyone to enjoy. From mini burgers to barbecue pulled chicken to smoked trout, we made picture-worthy, mouth-watering meals.

The kids form a line and shuffle along the counter, adding one of each to their plates. Kaya pulls up the rear, a radiant smile on her face as she meets my waiting gaze.

Since meeting Kaya, I've seen so many of her smiles. But the one she wears now is my favorite. She's worn it every day since waking up in my bed Saturday morning. And like a lovesick idiot, I return it with equal fervor. It's impossible not to.

Once everyone has gotten their share, I fill a plate and join Tucker and Kaya to eat.

"How is everything, bud?"

Tucker swallows his bite and washes it down with water. "So good." His jaw slackens as he makes this drool-worthy expression. "This one's my favorite so far."

Shocked by his choice, I do my best to school my features. Whenever I introduce new foods to Tucker, I remind him the flavor may not be something he's used to, so he may not like it… at first. But I ask him to be open to trying it again, made a different way.

Tucker isn't big on fish, but I've discovered new ways to make it and him enjoy it. The banh mi–style smoked trout sandwich was not something I expected him to put on his plate, but I'm glad he did.

I taste the fish sandwich for the first time and moan. "You've got good taste buds, T-Man." The smokiness of the fish, the sweet and pungent flavors of the pickled vegetables, and the hint of heat from the peppers make for a killer combination.

Smile on his face, Tucker leans closer to Kaya and talks about the sandwich they made today—the ultimate veggie. With animated gestures, he demonstrates the different cuts he made for the vegetables. His bright eyes and rushed words are the absolute highlight of hosting this class.

No one indicated they ate plant-based, but I wanted to show them how flavorful and delicious vegetables can be. When most kids picture a vegetable on their plate, it's bland, overcooked, and by itself. A lot of kids only know of a handful of vegetables—corn, peas, green beans, carrots, potatoes—and cringe at the sight of them.

I want them to love food, whether it's plant or animal, fresh or fried. If they know new ways to eat it, the possibilities are endless.

My eyes lose focus as Tucker carries on with Kaya. His comfort with her... makes my heart warm and melty.

When I got him back, Tucker was angry and scared. All the time. It broke my damn heart. But he had a reason to be furious, to be frightful. Brianna treated him worse than trash. She used him. Left him on his own for days with no promise of returning. Convinced him I didn't want or love him. Brianna perpetuated the lie enough that Tucker believed her. It took months of therapy and me constantly proving I would be there to disprove her lies.

After the damage she caused, I worried Tucker would have trust issues. Being with Mom often helped, Abigail too. Having loving feminine figures in his life has been the biggest saving grace. Adding Kaya into the fold has been life changing.

Tucker smiles, laughs, and comes alive more since Kaya entered the picture. As do I.

Her leg nudges mine beneath the table. "You're staring," she whispers then chuckles. Her cheeks flush as she clamps her lips between her teeth, fighting a smile.

I lean in and lower my voice. "You're mine to stare at, Fire Eyes."

With a roll of her eyes, she shakes her head. "At least *try* to be inconspicuous."

Wiping my hands and mouth with a napkin, I pinch her chin between my fingers, turn her until we're nose to nose, close the distance between us, and chastely kiss her. Beside us, Tucker makes kissy sounds. "Not a chance." I kiss the tip of her nose. "You're also mine to kiss. Best everyone knows that."

Her blush darkens to a beautiful shade of red as she lifts a hand to her lips. "Yeah, I suppose so." This time, she doesn't fight her smile.

With full bellies, the kids fill take-out boxes and clean up the room.

Kaya removes her chef's coat and stows it in her bag before shouldering it. "I should get going. Finger-painting day at the rec center." She winces. "Thank goodness it's water-based, or I'd never get it out of my clothes."

"I'll walk you out." I glance over my shoulder and mouth to Fin I'll be back. As I open the door, Cameron is on the other side, hand reaching for the handle. A sense of déjà vu hits, and I mentally stumble back.

"Chef," she croaks, her admiration coloring her pale skin. "Glad I caught you."

I rub my jaw. "Can it wait a minute?"

She holds up an envelope. "Just came to bring you this. It was taped to the door."

Every muscle in my body stiffens as I reach for the envelope. My name on the face in a handwriting I'll never forget. "Thanks, Cameron."

Passing her, I study the envelope as we move through the dining room, a chill rolling down my spine. "Fuck," I mutter.

Kaya hooks her arm through mine and guides us to the front door. "What is it?"

I inhale a jittery breath. Clench my jaw until my molars throb. Swallow past my fear and let rage take its place. "Brianna," I snarl. "I've ignored her since the surprise visit." I wave the envelope in front of us as we step outside. "Highly doubt this is her asking about Tucker." Irritation forms like a cancer in my gut.

Why won't she leave us the hell alone?

Brianna detested motherhood, despised being *chained down*. Yet here she is again, back for more.

Just crawl into a hole and let us move on.

I owe Brianna nothing. Not visitation. Nor a conversation. And certainly not money.

"Are you going to open it?" A beep sounds as we approach

Kaya's car. She tosses her bag in the back but makes no move to get in.

"Whether I want to or not, I have to." I pinch the bridge of my nose. "She doesn't care about Tucker and will use him every chance she gets. Do whatever it takes to get what she wants."

"Money," Kaya mutters.

I tip my face skyward, blink a few times, then level my expression. "And she has no remorse manipulating or exploiting Tucker to get it." My stomach cramps at the idea of Brianna committing heinous acts.

"What can I do?"

A simple question, yet it eases some of the agony.

Lifting a hand to her cheek, I step into Kaya and press a soft kiss to her lips. "Don't let me lose myself." I swallow. "No matter what happens, don't let me become someone I'm not because of her."

Kaya frames my face, her soft thumbs stroking my cheeks as she stares into my soul. "I've got you." Her shimmery gaze holds mine. So steady. So consolatory. "Lean on me. Share the burden." She pushes up on her toes and presses a soft kiss to my lips. "Let me help you carry it."

I drop my forehead to hers. "Don't want her to ruin this. Us."

"Not going to happen." Confidence laces her words.

And damn, do I want to share her optimism. To believe everything will be okay. Unfortunately, I've glimpsed Brianna's dark side. Seen how low she'll go to get what she wants. And it terrifies the shit out of me.

"Want to open it before I go?"

I should let Kaya leave for the rec center. Let her play with finger-painting kids and not wreck the rest of her day. But selfish me wants her here, at my side. She asked me to lean on her, and I should. If I want this to work, I need to share the stress and hurt I've carried for so long on my own. Let her be part of my support system.

"Yeah." I nod and ease out of her hold. "Sure."

On a sharp inhale, I slip a finger under the envelope flap. On the exhale, I tear it open. A dingy, crumpled piece of paper stares back at me, tormenting. Nausea roils in my belly as I slide it out and unfold it.

Need that money.

Three words. One demand. A lifetime of her always lurking in the shadows for more.

Bile burns the back of my throat. Dropping my hands to my knees, I inhale for a count of five, hold it for three, then exhale for five. My rib cage strangles my lungs, suffocating, unrelenting. The thunderous *whoosh, whoosh, whoosh* of my pulse clogs my ears. The ground wobbles and spins beneath my feet, and I close my eyes to steady myself.

And then Kaya is there. Her gentle hands on my face, grounding me. Her warm voice in my ear, snuffing out my panic as she coaches me to breathe.

"Give me some of that hurt." She presses a kiss to my forehead. "Give me some of that fear."

The backs of my eyes burn as I lift my gaze to hers. Pain explodes in my knees as I drop to the ground and fall back on my haunches. Tremors shake every muscle in my body as I stare into her eyes and relinquish a fraction of the heartache I've shouldered for far too long.

One fallen tear is all it takes for the floodgates to open. And for the first time in years, I rip open my chest and expose my heart fully. I put my vulnerability on the line and pray Kaya keeps it safe.

Crawling onto my lap, she wraps her arms and legs around me in the middle of the parking lot. Hugs me so fiercely it hurts. But I want nothing less.

I squeeze her to my chest and cry into the crook of her neck.

Spill my anguish in a rivulet of tears onto her skin. Release an ounce of my dread as I fist her top and keep her close. Minutes tick by, but she doesn't let go. Doesn't complain. Doesn't shove me away. If anything, she strengthens her hold. Runs her fingers through my hair. Rocks us gently. Hums softly in my ear.

When the tears run dry, I loosen my hold of her and lean back. Sniffle and wipe my nose on the sleeve of my coat. "Thanks, Fire Eyes."

Her fingers trace my hairline, then comb through the thick strands. "Any time."

I love how she means it.

"You should get going." I stand us up and smooth out her hair.

"I'll stay longer if you need me to."

My fingers toy with the end of her braid. "I'm good now." A sad smile tugs at my lips. "Need to see if my parents or Abi can watch Tucker for a bit." I wave the note between us. "Barron Law handled Bri's parental rights surrender paperwork. Maybe they can help with this."

"Hope so." Kaya lays her hands on my chest over my heart. "Might be good to talk with the police or Tymber Woulf Security, too." Lines mar her forehead. "If you're worried about Tucker's or your safety."

I hate that it's something I need to think about, let alone worry over. But Kaya's right. Better to err on the side of caution.

"Thanks for the suggestion, Fire Eyes. I'll go there afterward."

"Hurts to leave you like this," she admits, a breath above a whisper.

Eyes on hers, I press a chaste kiss to her lips. "If it makes you feel better, I don't want you to go. But I know you need to." I take a step back, toy with her braid then release it. "Come over after the rec center."

She nods. "Nowhere else I'd rather be."

I inhale a shaky breath. "Thanks for catching me, Fire Eyes."

Tears rim her glittery eyes. "Always, Chef." She slips into the driver's seat. "See you soon."

I lift a hand and wave. "Soon," I repeat.

And until her car disappears from view, I remain rooted in place, my fear from minutes ago trickling back in.

Scarlett Barron assures me Brianna cannot touch Tucker—legally.

"Your paperwork is ironclad. If she so much as talks to Tucker without your permission, you have the right to seek legal counsel and protection." She skims the note one last time then returns it. "As for this, I'd talk with Chief Emerson. From our previous conversations, we both know Brianna is unstable. Someone who'd go to extremes. And that's dangerous." With a dip of her head, she gestures to the note. "The money she demanded... she's in deep. You don't want that trouble knocking on your door." She hesitates for a breath. "Or disrupting Tucker's life. Not any more than it already has."

Elbow on the conference room table, I drop my head in my hand and mutter a curse. Squeezing my temples until pain shoots across my forehead, I drop my hand and sit up.

"I wish I had a more positive solution for you." A sympathetic smile curves her lips. "Go see Emerson and get everything on paper. If she continues to harass you, the documentation helps build your case."

Fuck.

"Police station was next on my list." I shove the note in the envelope. "Have you worked with the new security firm? Was thinking they could investigate Brianna more. Maybe give me an idea of what I'm up against."

"Tymber and Levi are an asset in the community. Worth every cent." Scarlett's praise of the small security and investigation company eases some of my stress.

"Appreciate your candor." Wheels whisper over wood as I

push away from the table, rise from my seat, and offer my hand. "I'll let you know if anything else comes up."

Scarlett takes my hand and braces it with her other in a show of support. "We're always here for you. If I'm unavailable, don't hesitate to ask for Emery." Pride shines in her eyes at the mention of her daughter. "She will go to battle and come out the victor." Scarlett gestures to the door. "I'll introduce you on the way out."

My conversation with Emery Barron is brief but enough to let me know who she is as a person. Determined, bold, kindhearted. Having either Scarlett or Emery—or both—in my corner is an honor and privilege and assuages my anxiety more. With them, I feel like I have a fighting chance.

At the police department, I'm directed to the other Emerson—Travis, the chief's son. Over an hour passes as I recount my history with Brianna and her recent reappearance. Travis types furiously on his computer, documenting every word. When I finish and inhale my first full breath since walking through the door, he gives me a well-practiced smile.

"Your call, but a restraining order should be put in place." Travis leans back in his chair, his fingers tapping the arms. "It's another layer of protection for you and Tucker."

"Really think we need it?" Would a restraining order do anything? It's a piece of paper, not a steel wall.

Travis rests his forearms on the desk and leans forward. "Will it keep her away?" Pursing his lips, he shakes his head. "No. What it will do is tell a judge you are concerned for Tucker's well-being and your own." A look of understanding crosses his features. "For your son's sake, I hope it's unnecessary. But if something does happen, that piece of paper works in your favor. It's ammunition to put her behind bars."

Never imagined myself in this position—filing a restraining order against someone from my past. An online stalker? Sure. I've seen followers turn obsessive, possessive. But someone I once cared for? Never. And the reality of it makes my stomach churn.

"Fine," I acquiesce. "Do it." While Travis fills out paperwork, I ask him about the security and investigation firm. If he's worked with them and his opinion. "Wanted to see if they'll dig into Brianna's past. Maybe find something I can leverage. Possibly what her life was like when she had Tucker."

"We worked with them on recent cases. Top-notch. Thorough." His fingers pause over the keyboard. "Levi's a buddy and genius-level smart, but don't take offense if he doesn't work your case. He's been through some stuff."

I may not know the case details, but I do know Levi was part of a major investigation last year that turned his life upside down. And the only reason I know that much is because my parents spoke with the West family often, on an endless mission to join my sister and Levi in holy matrimony. It was doomed from the start but got infinitely worse when Abigail took it too far. Since then, interactions with the West family have been... strained.

When Tucker ran up to Levi's boyfriend, Oliver, at the Memorial Day Festival a couple months ago, I wanted to apologize to Levi—for what happened to him, for the way my family and his treated him, for every absurd dinner he was forced to attend at my parents' house or his. No one deserves what he went through. I'm in awe of his strength and perseverance.

I acknowledge with a nod. "I have no expectations. Only hope."

By early evening, I wrap up with Travis and drive around the block to Tymber Woulf Security and Investigative Services. Tymber walks me into his office, closes the door, and asks me to share my story.

I leave nothing out.

Tymber says he'll run lead on my case. That Levi, with his extensive research skills, will likely join later. "If there's a trail, we'll find it. You have my word." Tymber walks me to my car. "We're damn good at what we do."

Relief washes over me as I unlock the car. "Thanks, man. Your help is priceless. Pass my appreciation on to Levi."

"Will do." He pats my shoulder. "I'll be in touch. Reach out with any updates, no matter the hour."

Twilight indigo paints the sky as I exit the parking lot. For the first time in years, confidence and optimism outweigh fear and hurt, and I breathe easier.

The road forward may be bumpy, but at least we will reach the other side unscathed.

TWENTY-SIX

KAYA

Tucker, Erin—the other student at our table—and I add the finishing touches to our s'mores camping cake. As I arrange rock-shaped chocolate candies and mini pretzel sticks for the campfire, I peek over at Ray as he travels the room and praises the kids. His smile is endearing, kind, but doesn't reach his eyes.

Since Brianna's note, the light has dimmed in Ray's eyes. In less than two weeks, I've watched him go from confident and exuberant to leery and downcast—though he puts on a good front —and it breaks my heart. No one should have to live like this—in fear or constantly looking over their shoulder.

Brianna weaseled her way into town and demanded an obscene amount of money from Ray. The attorney, police, and security firm all say not to respond to the letter. That Brianna likely dug herself deep and is pressuring everyone for help. Replying will only lead to more problems.

God, I want them to be right. I want to have faith in Stone Bay law enforcement and Ray's legal team. But I also can't ignore the twinge in my side. The constant pinch telling me to be cautious, alert, vigilant. Because we already know how calculating and heartless Brianna can be.

Ray steps behind Tucker and rests his hands on Tucker's

shoulders. "Looks incredible, T-Man. You, Erin, and Kaya did a great job."

Tucker sits taller and Erin blushes, both gleaming under his approval. Erin puts the last of the rock candies on the outer edge of the cake while Tucker skewers mini marshmallows on toothpicks and sets them on the mini peanut butter cups.

For a heartbeat, Ray glances my way, and the wariness fades. For a fraction of time, I see a hint of fire in his gaze. But as quickly as it appears, the glint vanishes.

Ray heads for the front of the room and assumes his position behind the counter, facing the group. "Maybe you all should teach the next class," he teases, and everyone laughs. "Seriously. Your work has been inspiring. Be proud. Brag about your accomplishments."

He claps and everyone joins in, a few rowdy cheers from the preteens.

"Add your final touches then bring the cake to the front for everyone to see. Then we'll eat."

We were all given the same ingredients, but each cake looks different. I love how creativity works that way.

Cakes finished, the kids fawn over them, complimenting each other. As they get sliced, Fin enters the room with a loaded cart. At the end of last week, the kids were given a lunch survey for this week. Fun as it would be to eat only cake for lunch, sending the kids home buzzed on sugar was not the best idea.

Fin delivers sandwiches on crusty bread to everyone while Ray slices cakes.

When he's done, Ray joins us with his own lunch, sitting between me and Tucker. His hand on my thigh, he listens to the conversation between Tucker and Erin but doesn't engage. Any time someone glances his way or tries to spark a conversation, Ray gives an artificial smile then stuffs his mouth.

Seeing him like this—despondent and so unlike the man I met —lights a fire in my veins. A furious, brutal flame I want to launch at the person responsible. Brianna has stolen so much from Ray, yet she feels entitled to take more. As it stands, Ray rarely leaves the house. Work and absolute necessities are all he's willing to go for.

I loathe her for how vulnerable and insecure she makes him feel. How, with one move, she cuts open every wound she inflicted on him—that hadn't quite healed—and disregards the painful aftermath.

For the past twelve days, I've bottled my feelings. Kept my tone calm and light. Resisted giving my opinion unnecessarily. Because Ray needs support, not bitterness.

But damn, do I want to scream my irritation to the heavens. Uncover Brianna Werner's whereabouts and have law enforcement slap cuffs on her wrists. Gift Ray and Tucker the peace they deserve.

I've never experienced anger like this. But I've also never cared so deeply for someone—in this case, two people. And I'll do just about anything to keep them—happy, healthy, safe, and *mine*.

Ray's grip on my thigh tightens a beat before he leans into my side. "Coming over after the rec center?"

With Ray on self-imposed lockdown, I've spent my free time at his place. Our weekday evenings have been low-key, and Tucker seems oblivious to Ray's protector mode. Somehow, we've kept Tucker entertained. He asked once last weekend why we weren't going anywhere, and Ray played it off as a long, tiresome week.

I rest my hand over his, slowly stroking his knuckles with my thumb. "Yes, if that's okay with you." With all the chaos, I leave all decisions up to Ray. If he wants a father-son night with Tucker, I don't want to intrude.

He loosens his hold, flips his hand over, and laces our fingers. "Always, Fire Eyes." He presses a kiss to my temple. "Always," he whispers softly.

Strengthening my hold, I rest my chin on his shoulder and give him my weight. "I'll be there."

When lunch wraps up, Ray asks Fin to keep an eye on Tucker while he walks me to my car. Although I've assured him I can handle myself—I never go anywhere without pepper spray or an eleven-inch pocketknife—he insists on escorting me to my car.

Secretly, I love his overprotective nature. The discreet way he says he cares.

"Text me when you get to the rec center." He steps into me, frames my face, and kisses me as if he'll never have the chance again.

Cuffing his wrists with my hands, I promise to message him. "See you soon." I push up on my toes, kiss him chastely before releasing him, and slip into the driver's seat.

I watch him in the rearview mirror as I exit the lot, his arms crossed over his chest and eyes on my car. With every cell in my body, I wish for a way to assure him I am safe. But you can't ease someone's anxiety with a finger snap or well-intentioned daydream.

An upbeat song plays in the background as my tires eat up the miles between Calhoun's Bistro and Stone Bay Recreation Center. Sunlight beams through the windshield, a handful of clouds off in the distance. Pine and salt dance in the air as the breeze filters through my partially rolled-down windows. Business parking lots are jam-packed, smiling children yanking adults' hands as they head toward their next adventure in town.

Everywhere, I see happiness. People enjoying the summer sun on their skin. Others hand in hand as they stroll down the sidewalk. Children laughing as they play chase in the shaded, fenced yard of the rec center.

I want this for Ray and Tucker. For them to move about in the world without worrying what happens next.

Reversing into a space at the back of the rec center lot, a pang forms beneath my diaphragm. I put the car in park and scan the surrounding cars. Press the lock button on the door and peer through untinted windows. Take a deep breath, then another, and another.

Not a soul lingers in the parking lot, but I *feel* someone watching.

Cutting the engine, I unbuckle my seat belt, shoulder my bag, take out my pepper spray, and exit the car. With confident, quick strides, I cross the lot on constant alert.

When I make it to the front door, I exhale the breath I'd been holding, stow the pepper spray, and step inside.

But the twinge in my gut lingers.

I turn around and study the parking lot through the tinted doors. Survey the vehicles from a different vantage point. Look for anything out of place.

Nothing… yet the cramp remains.

Pulling out my phone, I send a quick message to Ray.

> At the rec center. See you in time for dinner.

As I hit send, something moves in my periphery. By the time I look up, it's gone.

During my entire shift, I fight the urge to be sick.

TWENTY-SEVEN

RAY

Elbow on the table and cheek in his hand, Tucker pokes the barely eaten cannoli cream-stuffed French toast on his plate. Either he isn't feeling well, or he's bored out of his mind. My guess is the latter.

For the third weekend in a row, we haven't left the house. Tucker has no idea why, but he's miserable over my decision. But I'd rather him be frustrated and safe than scared and hurt.

"Not hungry, bud?" I point at his plate with my fork. "Best stuffed French toast I've made."

Lips pursed, Tucker gives a half-hearted shrug. "It's fine." His tone says otherwise.

I hate that I have to fake enthusiasm to keep Tucker sheltered from all the bullshit in my life, but the chaos that is his mother is not his burden to bear.

Leaning toward him, I nudge his arm. "It's fine," I mock then chuckle.

Tucker doesn't react. He just keeps swirling the fork tines through the filling.

"Talk to me, bud."

On a dramatic huff, he drops his fork, shoves back from the

table, crosses his arms over his chest, and stares at me as if I'm dense. Several minutes pass in silence, each more strained and awkward than the previous.

Heartache blooms beneath my sternum as I hold his narrowed hazel eyes. In keeping Tucker out of the line of fire, by keeping him in the dark and sheltering our lives to stay safe, I've undone all the good in his life in the past year and a half. One day, one note, one demand is all it took to destabilize my life and, consequently, his.

I've never detested someone the way I do Brianna Werner.

Fuck her.

Tucker's gaze flits to Kaya, his body softening for a brief second. When his eyes meet mine again, I see every ounce of anger, frustration, and hurt. "Did I do something wrong?" The tinge of sadness in his voice breaks every barrier I have up.

Reaching across the table, I lay my hand near his plate. "No, Tucker." I shake my head for emphasis. "You've done nothing wrong."

"Then why am I being punished?" His fists tighten beneath his elbows.

Wood scrapes tile as I shove away from the table and inch closer to him. I reach for him again, but he pulls back. The single move is a knife to the chest, but one I deserve.

I want to tell him why I've kept us home for weeks. Why my mood has been trash. Why I have trouble sleeping at night. But the thought of him stressed over something completely out of his control makes me sick.

It's reasonable to want my son to have a carefree childhood. To live with joy, laughter, and peace in his heart. No child should have to worry over the bad decisions adults make. They deserve to not suffer because of others' poor choices.

All my protection of him has done is cut a fresh wound. Because I didn't explain *why* our lives suddenly went from fun and wonderful to dull and dreadful, I've brought his own insecurities and painful memories to the surface.

"Sorry if I've made you feel that way, bud." I take a deep breath, hold it for three heartbeats, then exhale. "I've been under a lot of stress and not handling it well. I promise you've done nothing wrong."

In my periphery, Kaya drops her gaze to her lap. I don't know if it's because of my answer or lack thereof.

Tucker's arms remain rigid against his chest as his eyes narrow to slits. His silence in response is a well-deserved slap to the face.

How do I make this better? I want—*need*—to make it better.

"Maybe we can go to the pool with Grandma today," I suggest.

This softens his frame a bit. "I miss Jordan and my other friends at the skate park."

A shiver rolls up my spine, but I do my best to ignore it. My decision to not leave the house comes from a good place, but I'd be a fool to not see the negative impact it has made on him.

"Let's plan the skate park for another weekend."

Disappointment blankets his expression.

"That way you can make sure Jordan will be there," I add.

"Okay," he says, understanding but disheartened. "Can we do *something* today? Please."

I bite my cheek to hide my wince as I mull over a solution.

"May I offer a suggestion?" Kaya speaks up for the first time since we sat down to eat.

Please don't be something outlandish or risky. Swallowing past the expanding ball of nervous energy in my throat, I nod.

The apple of her cheeks plump as a soft smile curves her lips. Her coppery-brown irises sparkle as they shift from me to Tucker. "How about we start with lunch at RJ's? If your dad feels better and is up to it when lunch ends, we'll do something fun."

Tucker's hands drop to his lap as his face lights up. "Like what?"

I'd like to know as well.

"After breakfast"—Kaya aims a pointed look at Tucker's plate —"your dad and I will talk about it. Not eating this delicious French toast is a deal breaker."

Damn, she makes following the rules sexy.

Tucker cuts into his French toast, stabs the piece, and shovels it into his mouth. One bite after another, he clears his plate. The entire time, I stare at Kaya, utterly astonished.

I'm still not keen on leaving the house, not until Travis Emerson or Tymber Woulf give me good news. But if we go anywhere, a familiar place, one I know inside out, is the best option.

Tucker bolts up the stairs to shower and dress for the day. Kaya helps me clear the table and clean up in the kitchen. A few minutes after the shower turns on, Kaya sidles up to me at the kitchen sink.

"Things have been up in the air, especially since you haven't heard from her again, but you need this. Both of you."

I hand her a rinsed plate for the dishwasher. "I know." Rinsing the next dish, I take a deep breath. "I've never been big on gut feelings, but something still doesn't sit right."

She loads the next dish I hand her. "We'll be right there with him. At all times."

"Not sure I can handle anywhere besides the diner," I admit.

"And that's okay." She presses a kiss to the top of my arm. "But in case you're up for more, where should we go?"

I mull over the possibilities, and anxiety creeps in as I picture the crowds. "Not sure. I'll think on it."

Kaya wipes her hands dry then passes me the towel. "Come on, Chef. We need to get cleaned up and ready."

Tossing the towel on the counter, I wrap my arms around her waist and hoist her off the floor. Laughter fills the air and is a balm to my soul.

"Only if I get you dirty first," I mumble against the sensitive skin beneath her ear.

"Yes, please."

I climb the stairs two at a time with Kaya in my arms and deliver on my promise.

It's been far too long since life felt this normal.

Tucker tells a corny joke, and my full belly laugh draws the attention of nearby patrons. I don't care, though. It feels great to laugh, to experience this light, whimsical sensation in my chest. In this moment, life is good, carefree, perfect.

And I owe it all to Kaya.

I may have been hesitant to leave the house, but I'm grateful we did. Kaya is right. Tucker and I need to get out and live. Existing in the constant state of *what-if* only ends in regret and missed opportunity. I don't want that for me or Tucker.

Dad stops by the table and chats with us for a few minutes. He tells Tucker about the new bikes he and Mom bought. "We need to test them out, make sure they're good. Want to go biking after cooking class tomorrow?"

Tucker's gaze shoots to mine, a hopeful look in his eyes. "Can I go?"

"Of course, bud." I trust Tucker will be safe with my parents.

Dad ruffles Tucker's hair. "I'll let Grandma know."

"Yes!" Tucker pumps his fist in the air.

"What else are you up to today?" Dad aims the question in my direction.

"Not sure," I answer honestly.

The lightness in my veins has me eager to do something. To go out, have fun, and see Tucker smile and laugh more. He is my sunshine, my brilliant ray of hope, my light in the dark. He deserves the world, and I want to give it to him.

And it's in this moment I decide I am done letting Brianna control my emotions, my fears, my life. It's time to be brave, put my foot down, and say no to her. No more living in a constant state of panic. No more giving up my happiness for an insignificant person. No more letting her dictate my future.

Tucker is mine. My life is mine. And I'm taking both back.

"We haven't gone bowling in forever." Tucker exaggerates the last word.

Kaya, Dad, and I laugh at his dramatics. But damn, I wouldn't want my little man any other way.

"True." I plant my forearms on the table and lean in Tucker's direction. "Can I use the bumpers?"

Tucker rolls his eyes. "No. They're only for kids."

"What if I'm a kid at heart?"

He sips his root beer float. "It doesn't count."

"Fine," I huff out. "No bumpers."

He pushes his drink away. "So we can go?" The hope in his eyes is all I need to see to answer him.

"Yeah, bud, we can go bowling."

Tucker wiggles in his seat. "Woo-hoo!"

That right there is all I need—my happy little man.

"It's a miracle," Kaya declares, hands on either side of her head.

"What?" I sit next to her as we watch Tucker approach the foul line.

"I found something you're not perfect at."

Glancing at her, I arch a brow. "It's been a while. I'm still warming up."

She tucks her lips between her teeth and fights a smile. "Hmm. Okay."

Tucker hollers, "Yes!" Then, he's in front of us doing a celebratory dance. Eight frames in, he's gotten two strikes and two spares. And he's winning.

I hold up my hand for a high five. "Great job, T-Man. Showing everyone who's boss."

He slaps my hand, then Kaya's, plops down in his seat, and guzzles his drink, an endless smile on his face.

We bowl the ninth frame—Kaya knocks down nine pins, I hit seven, and Tucker gets another spare. The energy is high, and

Tucker is antsy to claim his winner's trophy for game one—he picks dessert tonight.

"I need to go to the bathroom," Tucker says as he rises from his seat.

"Come on, bud. I'll take you." I press a kiss to Kaya's crown. "Be right back."

We reach the bathroom and I follow Tucker inside. He spins around and raises his brows.

"I can pee by myself, Dad."

A hearty laugh spills from my mouth. "I'm aware."

"Go." He waves me away. "I'll be back in a minute."

Every instinct in my body screams to ignore him and stay put. But I don't want to ruin today. Shoving down the niggling fear in the back of my mind, I nod. "Come straight back to the lane. No stops."

"I will."

The first step is the hardest I've taken in a long time. My feet fight it, but I force myself out the door. For a moment, I loiter outside the bathroom and wait. No one comes out or goes in. I glance around to see everyone talking, taunting, cheering, and having a good time.

He's safe. No one here wants to hurt him. I repeat it until my anxiety wanes a little. And then I amble four lanes down to where Kaya waits.

She sits up straight, her eyes darting around. "Where's Tucker?"

I spin around and face the bathroom, my eyes glued to the door. "In the bathroom."

"Alone?"

Curling my fingers into fists, I nod. "I didn't want him to think I was hovering."

Kaya sidles up to me and rests a hand on my arm. "He'll be okay."

The voice in my head gets louder, expressing its disagreement. "I know." I say the words but don't believe them. Not fully.

The booming sound of balls knocking over pins clashes over and over. As each minute passes with no sign of Tucker, my anxiety blooms anew. *He's fine.* But after five minutes, I can't stand here and not know if he actually is okay.

"Be back in a sec."

Before Kaya responds, I bolt for the bathroom. Cross the carpeted space in seconds. Push through the bathroom door, only to be greeted by an empty room. No one at the urinals. No one in the stalls. And no one at the sinks. Empty.

Where is he?

"Tucker," I call out.

No response.

"Fuck!" I storm out of the bathroom and scan every face in the building. Nothing.

Kaya runs up to me, her eyes wide and skin pale. "He's not in there?"

I grind my molars and glare at her. "No," I bark out, then rush past her.

She quickly catches up and keeps pace a step behind me.

Passing a large group, I breathe a sigh of relief when I spot the back of Tucker's shirt. "There you are," I say as I reach him. "You had me—"

It's not Tucker. A young boy so similar in height, hair color, and overall appearance... but it's not Tucker.

The backs of my eyes sting as the boy stares at me, frightened. "Sorry," I say. "Thought you were someone else."

Freaked out, the boy runs off.

My limbs shake as my stomach bottoms out. "Where are you, Tucker?" The question is barely a whisper as I search the sea of faces.

"What can I do?" Kaya asks.

I spin on her, my worst nightmare resurrected. "Anything!" I shout. "This is your fault." Deep down, I know Tucker missing is not on Kaya. But if we would've stayed home like I wanted to,

Tucker would be safe. "This was a bad idea. We shouldn't have come here."

Tears spilling down her cheeks, she opens her mouth to say something. Before a single word gets said, I bolt for the front desk and alert the attendant. Then I pull out my phone and make the worst call of my life. Again.

Please let him be okay. I can't lose him. Not like this. Not again.

TWENTY-EIGHT

KAYA

The tears won't stop. Neither will the throbbing ache in the center of my chest. But I deserve to feel every second of it.

I did this.

Ray wanted to stay home, and I encouraged him to leave. Said going out would lift both his and Tucker's spirits. And it did. For a few hours, they were the happiest I'd seen them in weeks.

Then Tucker vanished, and the world went dark.

Panic I've never known shadows every line, muscle, and angle of Ray's face as he paces the sidewalk near the bowling alley entrance. A sense of dread only a parent feels when something traumatic or devastating happens to their child.

Of course, I'm unsteady. Dizzy and bewildered. Hysterical and apprehensive. But what I feel is inconsequential. Utterly insignificant compared to what Ray is going through. So I slip on my mask. Shove my emotions into the recesses of my mind and promise to keep them there until I'm alone.

Roger Emerson—the Stone Bay police chief—and Travis Emerson—Roger's son and the officer Ray spoke with a couple weeks ago—ask Ray a barrage of questions.

"Do you have a recent photo of Tucker?"

"Can you give us a detailed description of Tucker—hair color and style, eye color, height, weight, definable marks?"

"What was Tucker wearing today?"

That question brings on a new wave of tears.

After Ray called 911, he took off his bowling shoes, slipped on his one the attendant didn't keep, and went to the front desk to return them for his other shoe. When they set his other shoe on the counter, he froze. Gaze fixed on the sneaker, his hands shook at his sides, not in anger but bone-deep terror. Beside Ray, I held Tucker's lone black skateboard-style sneaker.

The moment Ray stormed off for the door, I begged the attendant for Tucker's other shoe, no matter the cost. Several cubby searches later, I walked out the door with the shoes tucked in the crook of my arm. As soon as Ray spotted them, his lip curled. In three long strides, he ripped them away from me and hugged them to his chest.

Since then, I haven't moved from my spot on the bench. And Ray refuses to acknowledge my existence.

Can't say I blame him.

Ray Jr., Angel, and Abigail rush toward the entrance from the parking lot, panic-stricken expressions on their faces. Angel hugs her son with unparalleled ferocity while he fists her shirt and cries into the curve of her neck. Ray Jr. barks orders at Chief Emerson, demanding the police do something other than stand here with their thumbs up their asses. Abigail lingers nearby, uncertain who to console or how to help.

Right there with you, girl.

Chief Emerson's jaw muscles tic as Ray Jr. steps into his personal space. He clutches the radio attached to his uniform at his shoulder and presses the call button.

"Attention all units, code 10-65. Male. Caucasian. Nine years old. Four feet tall. Dark, curly hair. Hazel eyes. Last seen at Strikers Bowling Alley at 15:47 in a blue shirt, denim shorts, and bowling shoes. Name: Tucker Dean Calhoun. Possible suspect: Brianna Werner. Thirty years old. Caucasian. Female. Thin build.

Approximately five foot five. Possibly armed, proceed with caution."

Bile claws its way up my throat as officers acknowledge the call. Ray collapses on the ground, his sobs deafening and heartbreaking. Every cell in my body screams to go to him, to hold him, shush his cries, and whisper in his ear that I'm here, that we will find Tucker.

But my comfort is the last thing Ray wants. Although it hurts to envisage, I wouldn't fault Ray if he never wants to see me again.

I may have put us in this precarious position, but I want Tucker returned safely too. If he is hurt—or worse—I will never forgive myself.

Ray bolts up from the ground and shoves a hand in his hair. "I can't just fucking sit here," he barks as he paces the walkway. "Being here accomplishes nothing. I should be on the road, searching the sidewalks and scanning cars." His hands fall to his sides and curl into tight fists. "Something!"

Travis steps in front of Ray and braces his shoulders. "You're in no state to drive."

Ray twists out of his hold and waves a hand toward his family. "Then one of them can drive. I don't give a fuck, Emerson."

"I'll drive you," Abigail offers.

Momentary relief washes over Ray's face. "Thank you."

"We'll stay here in case he shows up or someone has more information," Angel states.

It's her words that stir life into my body. I rise from the bench and cross to where they're grouped together. Ray sneers at me and it twists my insides.

He'll never forgive me, but at least I can do this one thing.

"No, Angel." I shake my head. "You and RJ should be out there looking, too. I'll stay here. If I see or hear anything, I'll call immediately."

"Yeah, you should be the one to stay," Ray snarls. "Your damn fault we left the house in the first place."

I take every verbal lashing without protest. He's hurt, angry, terrified, and I am the person who nudged him to let down his guard. Today's outing is one hundred percent on my shoulders. I accept it.

"I know, and I'm so very sorry."

Angel shakes her head. "No one here is at fault." She faces her son. "You have a right to live a worry-free life. So does Tucker." She shifts her attention to me, a sympathetic smile on her face. "And you are not to blame for someone else's heinous behavior." Leaning closer to me, she lowers her voice and repeats, "It's not your fault."

Her words hold a modicum of truth, but I don't dare voice it. Now is not the time or place. And saying as much won't lessen my guilt. Nothing will except Tucker's safe return and Ray's forgiveness.

"Let's go!" Ray shouts as he sprints for his car.

When he is out of earshot, Angel asks, "Do you have my number?"

I shake my head.

She takes out her phone and asks for my number. I rattle it off and she sends me a quick text. "I'll keep you updated, and you do the same."

The backs of my eyes burn, an emotional lump thick in my throat as I slowly nod. "Promise I will."

Reaching for my hand, she takes it and gives a gentle squeeze. "Once Tucker's back and safe, he'll cool off." Her eyes dart between mine, a softness in her gaze. "Just give him time."

Before I'm able to contradict her, she turns and walks off. After a quick exchange with the officers, Angel and Ray Jr. head for their car and drive away.

All but one officer leaves, her sunglasses-covered eyes scanning every inch of the parking lot and person that passes.

I dig through my bag for my phone, unlock it, and add Angel to my contacts. Then I open the group chat with my parents and siblings and type out a brief recap of what's happened. Considering my family has no idea Ray and I have been dating, I'm about to open the door to Pandora's Box.

> Was out with Ray Calhoun and his son, Tucker. If you haven't heard yet, Tucker is missing. Please keep an eye out and spread the word. Please don't ask questions about me and Ray. Not now. I'll tell you everything soon. Let me know of any updates. I love you.

Unease swirls in my belly as I stare at the sent message. Mentally, I prepare for an onslaught of questions but know my parents will hold off.

The screen dims then brightens as a breath-stealing alarm blares from my phone. My stomach pitches then plummets as I read the notification.

AMBER Alert
Stone Bay, WA AMBER Alert: Child Abduction Emergency White male, 9 years old, Tucker Dean Calhoun, possibly in the company of a 30-year-old woman, Brianna Werner and other unknown subject(s). Last seen at Stone Bay Strikers Bowling Alley at 3:47p.m. PST. Dark hair, hazel eyes, approximately 4'0" in height, blue shirt, denim shorts, bowling shoes. No identifiable vehicle.
Do not take action. Call local law enforcement or 911 immediately.

When I tap the notification, a recent image of Tucker fills the screen. My vision blurs as tears stain my cheeks. I bring a hand to my mouth as a sob rips from my chest.

My fault.

Beneath Tucker's photo is another. A woman with curly dark-brown hair and identical eyes to Tucker. *Brianna.* Ray has talked about her, but I've never seen *her*. As healthy and vibrant as she appears in this photo, it's outdated. An image of a woman before she lost her way.

Seeing her makes this more real. It also alleviates some of my guilt.

Leaving the house may have been my idea, but I am not to blame for Tucker's disappearance. That onus falls on Brianna.

This nightmare... her fault. Tucker's mental and emotional hardships... a result of her long list of poor life choices. As are Ray's inherent trust issues and deepest afflictions.

She is the reason Tucker is missing.

Brianna. All of this is *her* fault.

Not mine.

And I won't rest until Tucker is home and safe. Until she is in cuffs and prosecuted for what she has done.

Whatever it takes.

TWENTY-NINE

TUCKER

MY TUMMY HURTS LIKE IT DID THE TIME I ATE TOO MUCH ICE CREAM and threw up on myself.

I tuck my legs to my tummy and hug them. Lay my head on my knees and squeeze my eyes shut.

"There's my boy." Her voice is scratchy but one I've heard before. "Mommy's so happy to see you."

Lifting my head a little, I peek between the front seats of the big van. The sunlight hides her face some, but I think the lady is my mom. But she looks… different. Skinnier. Scarier.

"Mom?" I barely hear my voice.

Her cracked lips form a smile. It makes my tummy ache more.

"Yeah, Tuck. It's Mommy."

I haven't called her Mommy in a long time. Not since her second boyfriend after Dad. He was a bad man that made fun of me for calling her Mommy.

"Where am I?" My body shakes as I look around the inside of the van. Food wrappers, empty bottles, and dirty clothes cover the floor. And it smells really bad. "I'm scared."

"I just wanted to see you. I've missed you, Tuck."

When Mom left me with my dad, she told him I was always in her way. A pest. That she should've abandoned me when she did him. She must not remember saying that. Or she thinks I didn't hear her.

I shiver when I look at the man driving. He's big. Really big. He makes me want to throw up more. "Wh-who is he?"

Mom turns to look at the man and smiles. "This is Mommy's friend."

I don't know who he is, but I don't like him. The ring on his finger is the same one I saw before the bathroom went dark.

He's not a good man. Not at all.

Mom faces forward in her seat and talks quietly with the man. I can't tell what they are saying.

I hug my legs tighter and stare out the front window. Tall trees and a cloudy blue sky. It looks happy outside.

I want my dad.

Does he know where I am? Is he scared too?

Laying my cheek on my knees, I close my eyes and make a wish. I wish for Dad to rescue me from my mom and the bad man. I pretend like I'm at home with Dad and Miss Kaya, eating snacks and watching a movie. I pretend like I'm not scared.

The van wobbles and makes my tummy hurt worse.

"Ready for vacation, Tuck?"

I don't want a vacation. I want my dad.

"Mommy and her friend found this supercool cabin to stay at until it's time to see your dad again."

My eyes hurt like they do just before I start to cry. I want my dad now.

The van stops. Mom and the man get out. A door on the side opens and Mom waves at me to come out.

"This place is nice, Tuck. Come see."

I don't like this van, but I don't want to see the cabin either.

Mom leans into the van, grabs my arm, and tugs. "I said come on, Tucker."

I stumble out of the van and trip over a rock as she leads me to the cabin.

When we get inside, she lets go of my arm and huffs. "Always difficult," she mumbles then points to a chair. "Go sit down."

The cabin is one big room with a bed, kitchen, bathroom, table, chairs, and a fireplace. It's nice, but I still don't want to be here. Not with her or him.

"This is how we get the money," Mom says, her dirty finger pointed at me. "We don't hurt him." She shakes her head. "You make the call, and his family will pay."

I don't understand what is happening.

Who is he going to call? What are they paying for?

The man gives Mom a mean look then grabs her throat.

I taste throw up in my mouth.

"Better be right, Cook. Or this is where it ends for you."

Mom smiles at him. "I am right. They'll do anything for Tuck. Make the call."

The man lets her go and she falls on the floor. He taps on his phone then holds it to his ear. "Is this Ray Calhoun?" He doesn't say anything for a moment. "I got your boy. If you want him back, you'll have to pay."

THIRTY

RAY

My phone rings in my pocket and I dig it out, my heart pounding in my chest. *Unknown Number* flashes on the screen and my stomach drops. I accept the call and bring the phone to my ear.

"Hello?"

"Is this Ray Calhoun?"

"Yes, this is him." *Please let Tucker be okay. Please, please, please.*

"I got your boy. If you want him back, you'll have to pay."

"Whatever you want. Just please don't hurt him."

"Glad we're on the same page. Hundred thousand."

"Ask for more," a familiar female voice says in the background. *Brianna.* "They have it."

My vision tunnels at the request. Fire roars in my veins at hearing her tell him to ask for more. The world tilts beneath my feet as the truth sinks impossibly deeper.

Brianna has absolutely no love for Tucker. Not a single ounce. To her, he is a tool to feed her addiction or fix her problems.

I will fucking kill her.

"No tricks. No cops. Or he dies." He says it with such ease. As if life means nothing. As if Tucker isn't the first kid he has abducted and held for ransom. "I'll be in touch with more details soon."

The call disconnects.

"Who was it?" Abigail glances my way from the driver's seat.

"Pull over," I mutter.

"Was it Brianna?"

Bile inches up my throat. "Pull the fuck over!"

Tapping the brakes, she jerks the wheel right and steers us onto the shoulder. When the car slows enough, I unbuckle my seat belt, fling the door open, and vomit. My body doesn't stop retching after I empty my stomach. Minutes pass in painful dry heaves.

When the convulsions stop, I slowly sit up and close the door. Grab a napkin from the glove compartment and wipe my mouth. Swallow past the sour taste in my mouth and focus on what matters.

"Head for the police department."

Abigail glances over her shoulder, checks the road for traffic, then makes a U-turn. The engine revs then shifts gears as Abigail floors it. Buildings and pedestrians pass in a blur as we drive well over the speed limit through town.

Unlocking my phone, I scroll through my contacts and tap Mom's name. She answers on the first ring.

"Did you find him?"

I wish that was the reason for my call. *Soon.* "No, but I did get a call. Abi and I are headed to the police station."

"We'll meet you there."

I hang up before Mom says something hopeful. Moving down the list, I tap *Call* on Tymber Woulf Security and Investigative Services.

When the call connects, Tymber skips the pleasantries. "Update?"

"Got a call a few minutes ago. Man asking for ransom." I pause and inhale deeply. "Brianna was with him. Told him to ask for more."

I have never hated someone with every fiber in my body the way I do Brianna Werner. She is human trash.

"How much?"

"Hundred thousand."

"How long was the call?"

"Not long. A minute, maybe."

"I'll have Levi pull up your call history. We won't get an exact location, but we'll know which of the towers bordering town the call connected to. It'll narrow our search."

"Thanks, Tymber. We'll be at the police station in a few."

"I'll head over with news once I have it."

The call disconnects.

On instinct, I open my chat history with Kaya and stare down at the screen. My fingers hover over the keyboard, eager to type a message and tell her about the call. But I don't. I close the app, lock my phone, and drop it in my lap.

I *know* this isn't her fault, but I'm still too fired up. I don't trust myself to be kind right now. Not while Brianna is using our son— *my* son—as a bargaining chip.

What sort of person does that? Who kidnaps their child, the one they openly admitted to never wanting, and offers to return them for an obscene amount of money? What kind of person thinks death threats toward their child are acceptable?

The worst kind.

Abigail turns into the police station lot and parks near the entrance. As I step onto the sidewalk leading to the door, my parents park next to my car. They jog to catch up as Abigail opens the door and holds it for us.

A blast of cool air hits me as I step inside. The scent of stale coffee and day-old donuts filters through the room as I cross to the reception desk. A man with dark hair lifts his gaze from the computer screen, a smile on his face that falls when our eyes meet.

"Mr. Calhoun." He sits taller. "I'm sorry, but we don't have any updates."

I glance down long enough to read the badge on his chest. "Well, I do, Officer Fritz. I need to speak with Emerson."

His brows twitch then smooth out. "Which one?"

Irritation roars in my chest. "Does it matter? Pick one. I don't care which." I roll my eyes. "For fuck's sake."

"Sweetheart," Mom mutters, her tone half-sincere, half reprimanding.

"Don't," I growl. "You can scold me later when Tucker's home."

Thankfully, she backs off.

Chief Emerson strolls through the bullpen, opens the door separating the lobby from the officers, and gestures for us to come in. Before I step through, I tell Officer Fritz Tymber should be here soon. Fritz agrees to send Tymber back when he arrives.

Emerson walks us into a small conference room and shuts the door. "Talk to me."

"Got a ransom call about ten minutes ago."

He pinches the bridge of his nose, closes his eyes, takes a deep breath, then meets my gaze. "How much?"

"Hundred thousand." My insides wring as I tell him what some sick fuck thinks my son's life is worth.

His hands curl into fists at his sides as his jaw works back and forth. "They say anything else?"

Bile sinks its claws in my throat once more. I cover my mouth with a loose fist and inhale a slow breath. "He threatened Tucker's life."

Mom gasps. "Oh god."

Dad wraps an arm around her shoulder and tugs her into his side. But that's the end of his consolation. He doesn't offer uplifting words or vacant promises. Not when things are so up in the air.

"Talked to Tymber on the way here. He's got Levi on my call history to see which tower their phone pinged. Should be here soon."

Emerson rests his hands on his duty belt, one on the butt of his sidearm and the other over a collapsed baton. "You try calling the number back?"

Why the hell didn't I think of that?

"No." I unlock my phone, go to the call history, tap on the unknown call, and put it on speaker.

"The number you have dialed is no longer accepting calls."

Dammit.

"Was worth a shot, but I assumed it wouldn't go through," Emerson states.

A knock echoes through the room and startles everyone. Emerson opens the door and Tymber rushes inside. Out of breath, Tymber slaps a piece of paper on the table and points.

"Call pinged the north tower."

An ounce of relief trickles in and gives me premature hope. "Where exactly is the north tower?"

"Not far from the Freeman Estate," Emerson states.

"So he's still in Stone Bay?" There's no way to mask my optimism.

Tymber shakes his head. "Possibly, but not guaranteed. The tower has a fifteen-mile radius." He leans over the table and draws a circle on the paper with his finger. "The call came from somewhere in this range."

I wince at the size of the circle.

"It's something to work with," Emerson says. "And it's more than we had before you walked in the door."

"What now?" I ask, desperate to move, to do something, anything, that will bring Tucker home.

Emerson glances around the room. "I update my officers, then we divide and conquer." He points toward the printed map on the table. "We pair off and search every inch of this fifte-mile radius." Emerson levels me with his gaze. "Did the caller say when they'd reach out again?"

I shake my head. "No, just that he'd be in touch."

Tymber growls. "Piece of shit."

My thought exactly.

"Until the next call, we search as if Tucker's life depends on us," Emerson states with too much ease. "We stay in constant communication. No matter how insignificant you think something is, share the details of anything you find." He holds my gaze. "It'd be best if you rode with an officer or Tymber."

I nod and look to Tymber. "Mind if I join you?"

"Not at all." Tymber dips his chin in my direction.

Everyone starts for the door, but Emerson steps in front of it and holds up a hand. "Do *not* engage if you find them."

Muttered agreements echo through the room.

"I mean it. We don't know who this person is or what they're willing to do. Tucker's life is at risk. We can't make impulsive, reckless decisions. As far as we're concerned, this man is dangerous."

We exit the conference room, weave through the bullpen to the lobby, and walk out the front door.

Before I follow Tymber around the block to TWSIS, Abigail hands me my keys and says she will ride with our parents. Dad tells me where he plans to start, and Tymber shares which area we will scout. We promise to check in via call or text every thirty minutes or sooner if we find something.

Mom steps up to me, frames my face, and holds my stare. "We will find him." She nods. "He'll be home and safe soon."

Her words repeat in my head until her proclamation settles in my bones.

We will get him back safely, swiftly.

THIRTY-ONE

KAYA

Goose bumps dance over my skin as a bone-deep chill settles in. An inescapable bitterness that grows colder with each passing hour.

I wake my phone for the millionth time and swipe the screen to see if I missed a notification. Nothing. Like every previous time. No missed calls. No voice mails. No text messages.

The officer stationed at the bowling alley hasn't left her post. Several times, I've heard the crackle of her radio but couldn't make out what was said. Her expression, however, has me on edge.

People come and go from the bowling alley with smiles on their faces. I hate how completely oblivious or indifferent they are to the horror existing in town. It only adds to my frustration, my anger, my hurt.

Mom offered to come keep me company. I declined. Dad said he'd speak with the Seven and help in whatever way possible. That eased some of my nausea.

The higher the crescent moon rises in the sky, the longer I sit on this bench and wait for an update, the more my insides grow hollow.

Deep in my soul, I am convinced Tucker's disappearance isn't my fault. I mentally repeat as much a dozen times a minute. But my heart isn't fully on board. Guilt continues to gnaw at the beating organ. And that remorse has my mind in a perpetual Ping-Pong match of culpable and innocent.

I'm tired of sitting on this damn bench. I need to leave. To scour the town for Tucker. To do *something*.

What I need is a car. And someone to spill my frustrations to.

Unlocking my phone, I scroll through my contacts and tap *call* on the one person who'd run through fire to rescue me. The call connects after the second ring.

"Saw the AMBER alert a little bit ago. What's going on?" I've never heard Clarissa so serious or distressed. "Talk to me." I love how she skips the pleasantries. How she gets right to the point.

The backs of my eyes sting as I open my mouth to tell her everything. But the words catch in my throat.

"Kaya?" My name comes out edgy yet affectionate.

An ounce of concern is all it takes for me to fall apart. The sting behind my eyes strengthens a beat before the first tear spills down my cheek. I cover my mouth with a hand as a whimper slips between my lips. "Will you come sit with me?" I ask, voice borderline unintelligible.

"On my way." Muffled sounds echo through the phone line. "Are you home?"

I swipe my cheek. "No, the bowling alley."

The line goes quiet a moment.

Please don't ask. Not now.

"Have you eaten?"

My stomach grumbles in response, but the last thing I want is food. "No. Maybe later."

"You sure?"

I sniffle. "Yes."

"Kay. Be there in ten."

"Thanks, Rissa."

Clarissa obviously defies all traffic laws because she pulls into the parking lot seven minutes later. As she rushes across the lot, warmth expands in the center of my chest. Worry mars her expression, but she also looks ready to take down anyone in her path.

"I'm here." Her purse falls to the ground in front of the bench as she sits and wraps me in the fiercest hug. "I've got you."

I ignore the world around us and fall into her. Go boneless and let her hold me steady. Cry until my eyes puff up and my throat turns hoarse. Tremble in her arms until her warmth seeps into my bones and stamps out some of the cold.

Over and over, she rubs between my shoulder blades. Strokes the length of my hair and tucks the occasional wayward strand behind my ear. Hugs me harder to her chest and gently rocks us. She doesn't push me to talk. Once this emotional release ends, she knows I'll spill everything. Well, as much as I'm willing to share on a public bench.

When it feels as though I can't cry another tear, I ease out of her hold. She reaches for her purse, fishes out a travel pack of tissues and hands me one.

"Thanks." I sniffle and blot around my eyes.

She plucks a few more tissues from the pack and sets them on my lap. "Always." And I know she means more than always having tissues. The single word means she will always be there for me, no matter the hour or day or circumstances.

So I dive in headfirst and tell her everything. I start at the beginning and don't leave a single detail out. Some of it, she already knows, but it bears repeating.

I tell her about the dinner dates with Ray and Tucker. The cooking lessons that were infinitely better than any of Ray's online videos. Spending more time with Ray and Tucker—at the restaurant during cooking school, but more often outside of that time. Dinner with Adriel and my parents, and how jealous and angry Ray was at seeing us.

And the sex… I all but melt as I tell her Ray has ruined me for other men.

Then I change topics, my expression and mood more solemn. I

tell her about the past couple of weeks and the panic Tucker's mother provoked. A visit and the note that tilted Ray and Tucker's world sideways.

All I wanted was to level it out a little. Give them a touch of levity. Let them ignore their troubles for a few hours.

My eyes sting again as I say leaving the house today was my idea. My nose burns when I tell Clarissa how perfect our lunch date was at the diner. How Ray's dad came to the table and talked with us. How *normal* it felt to be with Ray and Tucker, out in the open. When I share Tucker's excitement over beating his dad at bowling, my throat starts to close.

I admit how my heart plummeted when we couldn't find Tucker. How my insides shriveled when Ray yelled and spit the blame in my face. How my chest hollowed when Ray gave me his back, so angry and terrified. And how empty I've felt since Ray got in his car with his sister and drove away.

Painful as it is, I will find a way to accept his never wanting to see me again after this. If it's what he truly wants, I will let him go. Even if my heart disagrees, refuses.

A throbbing ache settles in my chest, and I press the heel of my palm to my breastbone. The thought of never seeing Ray or Tucker again…

One dreadful pang, one hollow notion, is all it takes for the subconscious truth to surface.

I love Ray and Tucker.

I am *in love* with Ray.

"What do I do?" I cover my face with my hands. "I messed up."

"No, Kaya."

My hands fall to my lap as I twist to look at her. My brows pinch together. "What?"

"I said no."

I open my mouth to ask what she means, but she holds up a hand and cuts me off.

"You will *not* shoulder the blame." She vehemently shakes her head. "You will *not* take responsibility for some asshole's actions." She crosses her arms over her chest. "No, Kaya. Hell no."

"But—"

"No," she says louder then softens her expression. "You're allowed to live, Kaya. Ray and Tucker, too." She takes my hands in hers and gives them a gentle squeeze. "Our time on this messed-up planet isn't long. We can't predict what will happen today, tomorrow, or next week. All we can do is live in the present. Enjoy life. Go out in the world and be happy. If we crawled in our caves every time something bad happened, we'd never come out."

Clarissa's right. Pausing life because someone else *might* do something isn't living; it's existing in a constant state of fear.

I'd rather live a short life and die happy than live a long life and be miserable.

But how do I get Ray to see that perspective?

"You're ri—"

My phone rings in my lap, Ray's name on the screen. I fumble to pick it up, and with a shaky hand, I answer.

"Ray?"

"Hey, Fire Eyes."

God, he sounds exhausted. Wait. He called me Fire Eyes. Does this mean he's no longer mad at me?

"Sorry I was an asshole earlier. I didn't mean what I said."

The backs of my eyes sting for the umpteenth time today. "Thank you."

He has no idea how much I needed to hear his apology. And once everything is back to normal, I intend to make him grovel. A lot.

"Did you find Tucker? Is he okay?"

He sighs, and his agony bleeds through the phone and settles in the center of my chest. "Not yet, but we have a lead. Will…" He pauses, and I picture him with his eyes closed as he composes himself. "Will you come to me and help us?"

I glance around the parking lot, then at the officer stationed just out of earshot. "What about the bowling alley?"

"The cop will stay, but Emerson and Tymber don't think they'll return there with Tucker."

They?

I'll ask later. "Where are you?"

"Tymber Woulf Security. We're regrouping while we wait for another call." He groans. "Shit. You don't have your car. *Fuck.*"

"Don't worry about it. Clarissa's here. She'll give me a ride."

Clarissa nods as she rises from the bench and digs out her fob.

"Fuck, I'm sorry. So damn sorry."

"Later," I say, not wanting the focus to shift from what matters right now—finding Tucker. "I'll be there soon."

"I..." Ray starts, then stops. "Drive safe, Fire Eyes."

A little more of the chill vanishes from my bones. "Promise," I whisper.

THIRTY-TWO

ERASER

Heat licks my lips as I light a cigarette and inhale deeply. Rich earth and the addictive sting of menthol burn my lungs. It does little to curb my irritation, but not much has since this bitch entered my life.

Once this is done, once I have my money, she's gone. I don't need or want her fucking bullshit. Bitch has been more of a headache than anything else.

Rocks and pine needles crunch beneath my boots as I pace the length of the cabin. The only light for miles glows through the curtain-covered window, another reminder of why I am done with this cunt.

Nothing like an addict roping her kid in to pay her debt. Fucking soulless trash human. I have nothing against kids. They just aren't something I want in my life. I double wrap my dick for more than one reason, but knocking a bitch up is the first.

My parents weren't bad people. I had everything I needed as a child—food, shelter, clothes, affection. But that is *all* I had, and by the time I realized more existed, I owned several bully-inflicted mental scars.

The first opportunity I had to earn money, I took it. Sold anything and everything to make a buck. Skunk, ice, downers, uppers, televisions, laptops... the list goes on. Once I was more *established*, I upped my game. Pharm parties and making my own product.

Stacks of cash crowd my safe; I have everything I've ever wanted. And I love my fucking life.

This bitch, though... I will slit her fucking throat if she robs me of it.

I storm toward the cabin, climb the steps, and dig out the slip of paper in my pocket. Pushing through the door, I swipe another burner phone from the table, dial the number written on the paper, and bring it to my ear.

The desperate idiot on the other end answers on the first ring. "Hello?"

Eyes averted from the bitch that got me in this mess, I pace the cabin. "You got my money?"

Shuffling sounds in the background on his end. "Most of it. Can't exactly go to the bank on a Sunday night."

"I don't give a fuck what day or time it is. You want to see your kid again, get the fucking cash."

"Let me see he's okay. Send a picture." His breath grates the phone mic. "Please."

I scoff. "Did I give the impression I play by anyone's rules other than my own?"

"One picture and I'll get your money."

"Train yard in one hour. Come alone. If you don't, the kid dies." I drop the call.

The current bane of my existence crosses the cabin and blocks my path. "What did he ask for?" She tries to put her hands on me, but I step back out of her reach.

"Does it fucking matter?"

"Maybe." She shrugs. "I know him. All he wants is Tuck."

I eye the kid curled in on himself on the bed. If I had feelings, he'd have my sympathy. No doubt this bitch has scarred him for life. She's probably screwed over everyone who's met her.

Gripping her jaw, I lean in and drop my voice. "Don't care

what *he* wants, Cook. Right now, all that matters is what *I* want." Lifeless eyes stare back at me as I tighten my grip on her face.

"I know." Her eyes dart to the boy, then meet my gaze. "All I'm saying is if he asked about Tuck, he'll get the money faster if you give him whatever it is."

Shoving her away, she falls to the floor. I curl my lip at her, hold up a hand, and pinch my thumb and forefinger close together. "I'm this fucking close to paying off your debt with my blade. Don't push it."

I've considered dropping her off in the middle of nowhere once I have my money. But she will just make someone else's life hell. No one needs her brand of insanity.

So once this is over, I'll take the scenic route home. Find a dark, desolate stretch of land and pull over. Then, I'll erase her from the world.

Moving toward the bed, I tap the camera icon, lift the phone, and snap a picture of the kid. Opening a new text, I type in the man's number, add the photo, and hit send. Then, I drop the phone and smash it with my boot.

THIRTY-THREE

RAY

Headlights flash through the windows at Tymber Woulf Security and everyone inside turns to see who pulled in. I don't know the car, but familiarity hits when the passenger exits the vehicle.

I bolt from the conference room for the front door. It swings open as I round the corner, Kaya coming into view. For the first time in several hours, I breathe a little deeper. When I have Tucker back in my arms, I'll breathe fully.

Puffy, red-rimmed eyes greet me, and the sight breaks my heart for a different reason.

I was such an asshole earlier. Yes, I was in full-on panic mode. But it's a poor excuse for my behavior. Tucker's abduction is not Kaya's fault, nor mine. Letting her carry an ounce of guilt for what happened was a dick move on my part, and I'll do whatever necessary to make it up to her.

Swathing Kaya in my arms, I hug the air from her lungs and breathe in her comforting, earthy rose scent. "So, so sorry, Fire Eyes. I wasn't thinking."

If I have to, I will apologize every hour of every day until Kaya tells me to stop. Inching back, I cup her cheeks and bend at the knees so we're eye level.

"Please tell me you believe I didn't mean it." Thumbs stroking her cheeks, I drop my forehead to hers.

"I believe you."

My shoulders cave forward.

"But I won't let you forget."

The corner of my mouth twitches. "Better not."

"Tré," Tymber calls from the conference room. "Phone."

"Shit." I take Kaya's hand, spin around, and jog across the office. "Come on." We enter the room, and all eyes are on my phone on the table.

Tymber glances up, his expression unreadable. "Think it's a text with an image."

I swipe my phone from the table and tap on the notification. A second later, a low-resolution image of Tucker appears on the screen, and I enlarge it. Curled in on himself, he looks so damn scared. I soak in the sight of him and let the fact he is alive soothe an inkling of my panic. Then I shift my attention to the space around him—the bed, the edge of the lampshade, the picture on the wall behind him.

None of it looks familiar.

Where are you?

Setting my phone on the table, I keep my eyes on the screen. "It's him. He's okay." I point to the image. "Wish I knew where this is."

Everyone leans closer and squints at the picture. Time stretches out as they stare and pick apart the background. The solemn look on their faces as they stand back up is all the answer I need.

They don't know the place either.

"Can I?" Kaya points at the phone. When no one responds, she picks it up and narrows her eyes as she brings the phone closer. Her brows pinch as she tilts her head. A beat later, her eyes widen.

I crowd her. "Do you know this place, Fire Eyes?"

Slowly, she shifts her attention to me and nods. "Think so."

Relief slams into my chest. "Where is it?"

"Several years ago, I went hiking with my family just north of the Stone Bay border. We happened upon this old cabin in the woods. Looked like no one had lived there in a while." She stares back down at the image. "We hiked the same area a few months later and someone was cleaning up the place. We stopped and spoke with them. They showed us the inside and said they planned to rent it to tourists." She points at the painting on the wall in the picture. "This floral painting... I asked about it." She meets my gaze. "It's the only reason I remember this place."

Clasping her arms, I bite the inside of my cheek to resist sounding impatient. "Where is it?" I ask again.

"A couple miles outside of town, there's a dirt road"—she closes her eyes and pinches them tightly—"I can't remember the name."

"It's okay," I assure her as hope trickles into my bloodstream. "What else?"

"There's maybe a mile between the highway and the cabin. The train tracks are another half mile or so east of it." Kaya winces. "Rough guess."

I drop my mouth to hers in a chaste kiss. "It's more than any of us had. Thank you."

Papers shuffle on the table. I turn to see Travis spreading out a map. Everyone leans in as he points at an area.

"From her description, I estimate the cabin is here." Travis draws a circle on the map with his finger. "Train yard is here. We have"—he checks his watch—"forty-eight minutes until the meetup. Tré?"

I meet his gaze across the table.

"Go to the train yard. Take your family or anyone Tucker is comfortable around. If they make the exchange, we need someone he feels safe with to protect him."

It's on the tip of my tongue to argue. Knowing Brianna, she will hide Tucker at the cabin with the intent of using him again in the future. But I don't get a word out.

"I'll go to the train yard," Kaya offers. "Tucker feels safe with me."

Her bravery makes my pulse soar. Just another reason to... care deeply for her.

"We'll be there, too," Dad states as he hugs Mom to his side.

"Perfect. Officers will be split between the cabin and train yard. Tré's the only one visible for the exchange. Everyone else hides in the tree line or shadow of the buildings. You'll have a duffel filled with bundled paper that looks like cash." Travis levels his gaze with mine and holds it. "You do *not* hand over the bag until Tucker is released. Once they know there's no money, shit will go sideways. Tucker needs to be out of the way first."

"Got it," I say.

"Once Tucker is safe, officers will make their presence known. I suggest you get as far away from Brianna and the man as possible. We want to apprehend them but will take them down if necessary."

Sweat dampens my skin as my stomach cramps. All I can do is nod.

"Let's head out," Travis orders. "Best if we get there early and hide any signs of other people." Travis turns to Tymber. "You good going to the cabin with my group?"

"Absolutely." Tymber pulls out his phone. "Let me update Levi and hit the head before we go."

"Meet you outside in five," Travis says then exits the conference room.

I turn to Kaya. "Sure you're okay with this?"

Her brows knit together, her coppery-brown eyes locked on mine. "I need to be there. And he's going to need all of us."

Taking her hand, I lace our fingers. "As long as you're sure."

We leave the conference room and head for the front door, Mom and Dad behind us. Outside, we cram into my parents' SUV to lessen the number of vehicles to hide.

The drive to the train yard is quiet. Every possible scenario plays in my head as the miles disappear. As we approach the building, an officer flags us to stop and directs us where to park. One visible vehicle is expected. The cops contacted the yard's manager and were able to access a building to park two cars in.

Kaya and my parents duck just inside the closest building.

I stand out in the open on an empty patch of dirt between the building and the tracks, a black duffel in my hand. Sweat soaks my shirt as my heart pounds viciously in my chest. My gaze roams the trees, the tracks, the sides of the buildings, the street that ends at the station.

I tighten my hold on the bag. Take a deep breath, then another. Count to ten in an effort to settle my nerves, to calm the nausea clawing its way up my throat.

Light bounces off one of the buildings as the sound of gravel crunching hits my ears. A commercial van rolls closer, and I swallow past the fear-shaped lump in my throat.

Get Tucker to safety. That's the only thing that matters.

THIRTY-FOUR

RAY

The van comes to a stop at the end of the drive. Bright beams light up the tracks and faintly touch the tree line.

Feet rooted to the earth, I grip the duffel straps tighter and never take my eyes off the van. The passenger door opens, my breath catches in my throat as I wait to see who steps forward.

Please be Tucker. Please, please, please.

As the person clears the door, my heart sinks. It isn't Tucker. This person is too tall, too scrawny. *Brianna.*

She steps in front of the van, blocks one of the headlights, and maintains considerable distance. "You have the money?"

Have the drugs completely rotted her brain?

What kind of person does this to their own child? Who holds their son for ransom, inflicts enough trauma for a lifetime, suggests asking for more money, and doesn't give a single fuck how it will impact their future?

It's beyond me how I felt any positive or loving emotions for Brianna Werner.

When I was oblivious to her escapades, I often pictured a future with her. A beautiful house with a huge backyard, another child or two, smiles and laughter, both of us happy in our careers, growing old and gray. Watching our babies have children of their own.

For more than a year, I relished those fantasies. To me, they were real, tangible, perfect. Unfortunately, I had been a fool. An ignorant man too lost in daydreams to see reality as it unfolded.

The saddest part is I'd do it all again just to have Tucker.

I lift my arm and shake the bag. "Of course I do. Where's Tucker?"

She takes a step closer and holds out her hand. "Give me the money."

With a shake of my head, I snort. "You're fucking joking, right?" I swing the duffel behind me and clutch it with both hands. "You don't get shit until I have Tucker."

"I don't trust you to give me the money if I hand him over." Her hands tremble at her sides, presumably from lack of a fix and not nerves.

"Does it look like I give a damn if you trust me?" I swing the duffel around, hold it up, and dangle it between us. "The only way you get this bag is if I have Tucker in my arms. Period."

A curse leaves her lips as the driver's door opens.

I squint to make out the person but see nothing with the headlights aimed my way.

They walk around the back of the van. The screech of metal scraping echoes through the balmy night air and bounces off the trees. Gravel crunches as the other person mutters something unintelligible. A beat passes before two figures come into view, and I know with absolute certainty one of them is Tucker.

Thank goodness.

But as quickly as relief floods my veins, it vanishes.

I get a better look at the man and Tucker as they sidle up to Brianna. With broad shoulders, thick muscles, and pure malice etched into his features, the man's presence screams *don't fuck with me or I'll kill you.* He holds Tucker by the back of his shirt. In his other hand, lazily at his side, is a hunting knife.

"Here he is," the man shouts as he thrusts Tucker forward, but not letting him go.

Tucker whimpers, and the sound shreds a piece of my soul.

"Now give me the fucking money, or I'll take matters into my own hands." He lifts the hand holding the knife and waves it.

My heart plummets as I look from Tucker to the man. "Don't hurt him." The backs of my eyes sting as my throat closes. "I'll toss the bag if you release him." I lift a hand in surrender. "No games, I swear." I extend my arm and hold out the bag. "Just, please, don't hurt him."

Brianna nudges the man and says something I can't hear. The man's jaw flexes a beat before he says something back to her.

"On three, you toss the bag and I'll let him go," the man states.

"On three," I repeat.

He starts counting, the moment he reaches three, I swing my arm back then forward and let the bag fly.

Tucker runs my way, slams into me, and wraps his arms around my waist. I hug him harder than any other time, bend at the waist, and whisper in his ear so only he hears.

"I love you so much, bud." I stroke his hair. "But I need you to run for the building."

He startles in my arms.

"Kaya, Grandma, and Papa RJ are in there. I need you to go until this is over." I kiss his hair. "Now, bud. Please."

As I straighten my spine, I relax my hold on Tucker. Tears spilling down his cheeks and chin wobbling, he looks up at me and nods. And then he bolts for the building.

In my periphery, the man lunges forward with the knife. Time stutters to a stop as he dives toward Tucker.

In a microsecond, I die a thousand deaths while being hit with the sudden urge to take a life.

Time speeds back up as he misses Tucker and falls to the ground. Knuckles burning, I rush forward with the intent to beat this man until he no longer breathes. But I never land a punch.

Out of nowhere, Brianna collides with him. The man tries to

shove her off, but she locks her legs around his waist. They tumble in the dirt, two different metals glinting in the headlights as they roll and punch and fight for dominance.

Stepping back, I glance toward Tucker, who has paused at the top of the stairs on the platform. I jog over to him and wrap him in my arms again. Kiss his hair. "Don't watch, bud." I give him one last squeeze and point to where I know my family waits. "Go find Kaya, Grandma, and Papa RJ."

"I'm scared."

I frame his small face with my hands. "Me too, bud. It'll be over soon. Go."

Grunts and wails bounce off the building as I turn back and slowly make my way back down. Fists clenched at my sides, I keep my distance. The tussle between Brianna and the man slows until it stops altogether. The first sign of blood stains Brianna's shirt and the ground.

I approach on slow feet, my eyes darting from him to her while also searching for the knife.

Who is bleeding?

Are they dead?

Will someone lunge if I get close enough?

Brianna is dead weight as she lies on top of him.

I take another step and she stirs, a gurgled groan breaking the silence. I freeze, then step back.

Brianna rolls off the man and falls to the ground beside him, the butt of his knife protruding from her stomach. My gaze darts to him and narrows as I scan his paralyzed expression.

Boots thunder over foliage, earth, and gravel as I step closer. Shouts and clicks echo through the trees as my gaze shifts to the man's neck, where a dull piece of metal sticks out. Goose bumps erupt on my skin as a chill coils around my spine when I glimpse the man's lifeless eyes staring skyward. With a fork jabbed into the side of his neck, a dark-red puddle encircles him on the ground. He doesn't blink. Doesn't move.

Is he... dead?

I am not the type to wish death upon anyone, but I will make an exception for him.

Pain shoots down my shins as my knees crack the hard earth, but I ignore the throb.

Tucker is safe.

This man will never hurt him again.

And neither will Brianna.

THIRTY-FIVE

KAYA

Red and blue lights strobe off the trees, the buildings, and every surface between. Frigidity sweeps through the air that has nothing to do with the gentle breeze coming off the bay. Muttered conversations blend with the quiet whimpers coming from the woman on the ground with a knife in her belly. Cameras flash as photos are taken of the scene, small numbered tent cards in various places on the ground.

Arms banded around my neck and legs wrapped around my waist; Tucker trembles against my chest. Since leaping into my arms, he hasn't stopped shaking. Our cheeks pressed together, I strengthen my hold on him and slowly sway. Ray's parents stand inches from us, Angel stroking Tucker's hair and Ray Jr. whispering how much they love him.

When the police rushed through the trees and took control of the situation moments ago, we stepped out of the shadows and onto the platform. The worry on Angel's face told me I wasn't alone in needing a clear view of Ray to see he was unharmed. The second I knew both my guys were safe, I took my first real breath in hours.

While we console Tucker, Ray speaks with the police.

"Is my mom okay?" Tucker tries to turn in my arms and look

for his mother.

More lights bounce off the trees. Doors slam then gravel crunches. EMTs come into view with two stretchers. They pause in front of Ray and the officers. Ray points toward us and says something we can't hear.

"I don't know," I tell Tucker. I want to ask him how not knowing makes him feel, but I refrain. It's not the time.

Small pack slung over their shoulder, an EMT jogs up the steps, gives us a sympathetic smile, and points to Tucker in my arms. "Is this Tucker?"

Tucker glances over his shoulder at the medical technician then turns away and ducks his head.

"If you don't mind, I'd like to ask a few questions and check you for injuries. Is that okay, Tucker?"

Tucker gives an infinitesimal shake of his head.

I rub a hand over his back. "How about this, Tucker?"

He peeks up at me.

"What if they ask and you whisper the answer to me, Grandma, or Papa RJ? Can we do it that way?"

Tucker strengthens his hold on me and nods.

The EMT asks one question after another, and we relay answers. Except for being terrified and traumatized, Tucker is otherwise okay. No scrapes, cuts, bruises, or physical injury.

Although this day will live with and haunt him for years, I breathe a sigh of relief he won't have physical scars.

Handcuffs on her wrists and latched to the stretcher, Brianna is wheeled off to an ambulance. The remaining EMTs load the man into a black body bag, zip it closed, and hoist him onto the other stretcher. As they wheel him away, I keep Tucker's gaze averted.

Ray strides across the dirt and up the steps, sidling up to us. He presses a kiss to Tucker's hair. On the next breath, Tucker loosens his hold on me and reaches for Ray. The world stills and quiets as the two embrace each other in the fiercest hug.

The backs of my eyes sting a beat before tears stain my cheeks. Ray's parents and I crowd him and Tucker, wrapping them in our arms. A tremble ripples from one set of arms to the next as we weep happy tears.

We may have a lot of stress and hurt to work through in the coming months, but at least we have each other to lean on. So long as we stick together, everything else will work out.

Ray presses a kiss to Tucker's temple, then turns and kisses my cheek. "Let's go home."

Except for taking a quick shower and changing his clothes, Tucker hasn't left Ray's arms. He asked Ray to stay in the room as he did both. Can't say I blame him.

Well past Tucker's bedtime, we sit on the couch with the television on, the volume almost inaudible. On Ray's lap, Tucker rests his head on his dad's shoulder. Ray offered to make something to eat when we walked in. But none of us has an appetite.

"Is my mom okay?" Tucker asks for the second time.

Ray takes a deep breath and shifts Tucker so he can look him in the eye. "I'm not sure, bud. She was really hurt when the ambulance took her to the hospital."

A deep groove forms between Tucker's brows. "Is she in trouble?"

With a nod, Ray answers truthfully, "Yeah, bud. Your mom did some bad things." What he doesn't say is if she lives to see tomorrow, Brianna will spend a long time behind bars. "Do you want to talk about what happened?"

Tucker ducks his chin and shrugs.

I lay a hand on his pajama-covered shin. "It's okay if you don't want to talk about it, Tucker. What happened was scary for all of us." I gently stroke the side of his leg with my thumb. "Sometimes it helps to tell someone what you remember and how it made you feel. Sharing doesn't make it go away." I bring my hand to his hair and run my fingers through the soft curls. "But each time we talk about it, it hurts a little less."

Tucker's lips twist as he mulls over my words. "Can I tell my fire truck?"

In my periphery, confusion lines Ray's forehead.

"Of course," I assure him. "You can tell your fire truck whatever you want. Always."

Tucker's shoulders relax a little.

"But you need to talk with your dad, and maybe other grown-ups, about what happened today."

Tucker stiffens, and Ray hugs him closer.

"He's been through enough today," Ray says, voice low and edgy. "Don't pressure him."

Releasing Tucker's curls, I ease back and add a little space between me and Ray. He means well. Deep down, I know he does, but encouraging Tucker to suppress how today made him feel will blow up in his face later. Like his former experiences with his mother, what happened today will stay with him a long time. Better to let some of it out now than have him screaming in the middle of the night.

And didn't he just ask Tucker if he wanted to talk about it? Not that I'll point it out. Now isn't the time to highlight his hypocritical behavior.

Maybe I should go home. Give them time alone together. But as the thought crosses my mind, I can't find the strength to get off the couch, grab my shoes, and call someone for a ride. So, I move farther down the couch. Back off and put some distance between me and them.

"Don't leave, Miss Kaya." The shaky plea in Tucker's voice tugs at my heartstrings.

A half-hearted smile curves my lips as I give an imperceptible shake of my head. "I won't leave if that's what you want."

"I want you to stay." Tucker rests his head back on Ray's shoulder and stares across the room. "Mom was acting weird."

Ray freezes for three heartbeats, then takes a slow, deep breath. His mouth opens then closes a few times before he rolls his lips between his teeth. When he opens his mouth again, he doesn't get the chance to speak.

Tucker elaborates on how Brianna was behaving as he stares at Ray's shirt. He talks about the man and how he was in a bathroom stall at the bowling alley. How the man said he knew Tucker because he was friends with his mom. That his mom and dad were outside talking, and he was supposed to bring Tucker to them. Tucker says he wasn't scared until he didn't see Ray with Brianna and she made him get in the van.

Until he reaches the end of his side of the story, Tucker spills his heart. As each truth comes out, Ray hugs him closer to his chest. The more they embrace, the more I feel like an interloper.

Turning my head off to the side, I look anywhere but at them.

I should leave.

When Tucker finishes talking, I scoot to the edge of the couch, fist the cushion for a breath, then rise from my seat. I keep my eyes ahead and move around the couch. My stomach twists more with each step, but I continue forward.

"Where are you going?"

Pausing, I close my eyes. Tucker is not going to let me leave. Regardless of how much I feel like an outsider right now, he will find a way to keep me here.

Sweet, sensitive soul that he is, Tucker has tethered my heart without effort. I love him for that.

"It's been a long day," I say. Opening my eyes, I meet his anxious gaze. "I'm tired."

"Can I sleep with you tonight?" Anticipation glitters in his eyes as they dart between me and Ray.

"I don't—"

"Of course, bud," Ray cuts me off as he rises with Tucker in his arms. He rounds the other end of the couch and blocks my path. "Kaya and I need your snuggles, too." He sets Tucker on his feet. "Go brush your teeth. We'll be up in a minute."

Tucker wraps his arms around my waist and squeezes with all

his might. Then, just as quickly, he releases me and heads for the stairs. "Don't take long."

"We won't, bud."

"'Kay."

The moment Tucker is out of earshot, Ray invades my space and hauls me to his chest. "Sorry. I didn't mean to snap at you." He tucks his face in the crook of my neck and inhales deeply. "I reacted without thinking." On the exhale, he leans back and cups my cheeks. "All I want is to protect him. Please tell me you understand."

I rest my hands over his and meet his veiny, tired eyes. "I do." Twisting, I kiss his palm. "But protecting him isn't always shoving the bad stuff in a box and burying it." Meeting those wary brown eyes once more, I lean into his touch. "You asked him if he wanted to talk about it. When I nudged, you punished me." I drop my chin to my chest, count to five, then continue. "Although it's hard, talking about it safeguards his mind and liberates him from guilt or shame. It gives him the chance to let go of the pain." Reaching up, I take his face in my hands. "Yes, he needs to feel physically safe. But he also needs validation. He needs to know any time he has a nightmare or flashback, it's okay to talk about it without feeling like an imposition."

"I would never make him feel like a burden," Ray says, defensive.

"Not intentionally." I shake my head. "But if you tell him he doesn't have to talk about the hard stuff every time it comes up, you're inadvertently saying to keep those things to himself."

His brows pinch together as he mulls over my words.

"You love Tucker more than anything. I know this. But loving someone also means letting them share their pain." A corner of my mouth curves up in a sad smile. "It's how we heal and move forward."

Ray leans in, runs the tip of his nose along the length of mine, then claims my mouth with his. The kiss is slow, deep, a brand on my soul. And all too soon, he breaks the kiss to rest his forehead on mine. "You have no idea how much I need you."

My breath catches in my throat as my pulse soars. "I need you, too. Both of you."

His calloused thumbs caress my cheeks. "Love you, Fire Eyes."

I gasp as my heart stutters. My vision tunneling as I wobble in place.

He loves me?

I try to wrap my head around his confession. Question if it's real or a proclamation fueled by fear.

"If you're not ready, you don't have to say it," he says after a moment. "But after today, after all I've been through, what we've endured, I need to say it." He drops a chaste kiss to my lips. "I love you, Kaya. More than I've loved anyone." He pulls back then kisses my forehead. "It scares me to death, but that's how I know it's real." His hands on my cheeks tremble. "Let's try to get some sleep. Tomorrow will be another long day."

Slipping my hand into his, he guides me up the stairs and to the bedroom. We take turns changing in the bathroom, then crawl into the bed with Tucker between us.

And until I drift off to sleep hours later, his confession replays in my head.

"I love you, Kaya. More than I've loved anyone."

THIRTY-SIX

RAY

I spear the last piece of fruit on my plate and force myself to eat it.

The last time my appetite was this absent was the first time Brianna ran off with Tucker. I ate maybe once every few days and only because someone insisted. Mom would shove a piece of peanut butter toast in front of me and say, *"How will you find Tucker if you keel over?"*

Tucker sitting within arm's reach is the only reason I can stomach food this morning. Seeing him in the flesh, hearing his sweet voice, hugging him to my chest and breathing in his outdoorsy smell, knowing he is home and safe… soothes my soul in a way nothing else does.

Yesterday shook us all to the core.

For hours, I lost my shit. I went off on Kaya, screamed at people I love, and felt compelled to knock out a few who seemed to dally. Horrors filtered through my mind as I sent infinite pleas to the universe—*don't let them hurt Tucker*. Nausea simmered in my belly the entire time Tucker was gone.

For the second time, my worst fear pointed its proverbial finger at me and laughed in my face.

I am a bad father.

Panic ensued the day Brianna told me she was pregnant. Neither of us knew a thing about being a parent. We were still in the *fun* phase of our relationship—the wild, uninhibited, let's-have-sex-ten-times-a-day period. We were monogamous but not serious. I had my place and she had hers. Both of us were focused on our culinary careers. Marriage, children, and settling down were nowhere near our radar.

Two positive pregnancy tests changed Brianna and me forever. While I went from panicked to queasy to optimistic to elated, Brianna went the opposite direction.

From the beginning, she voiced her disdain. Was adamant in her stance on motherhood—quiet and uneasy at first, beyond deafening and adamant during our last fight—she did not want to be a parent. I tried to do the right thing. Suggested we live together and work opposite shifts so our lives and careers didn't take as heavy a hit.

Brianna slapped me with her scorn often, and I took every hit without complaint. At the time, I felt I deserved it.

While I sought ways to improve our relationship, Brianna searched for a way out. While I busted my ass to be the best father possible, Brianna plotted ways to use Tucker to her advantage. Who wouldn't help a homeless single mother with a toddler and no money?

I'll give it to her; Brianna knows how to play everyone for personal gain. But it ends now.

"You don't have to go," I say to Kaya. Last night, we talked about going to the hospital to speak with Brianna. Kaya hadn't given me a clear answer on whether she'd go with us. "If you need to be at the rec center—"

"No," she cuts me off. "I want to go." Her expression softens. "You and Tucker need me there." She reaches across the table and takes my hand. "*I* need to be there." Those last words come out almost inaudible.

Like it or not, Brianna hurt Kaya. By coming after and hurting the people she cares about, Brianna left Kaya with a fresh wound.

Over time, the scar it leaves behind will smooth out and be less noticeable, but it will always exist.

The first step to heal invisible wounds… closure.

Kaya needs to see Brianna, maybe speak with her to move forward. Tucker and I need this visit, too. It may not be the last time we see her, but knowing Brianna's no longer a threat is the major suture in a lifelong wound.

Turning my palm up, I cradle her hand in mine and mirror her gentle strength. "Then we all go." I shift my attention to Tucker and inhale a shaky breath. "If it upsets you, bud, you don't have to go. Grandma and Papa RJ said you can hang out with them."

Still in this edgy cloud of apprehension, Tucker pokes at his scrambled eggs with his fork. After a fitful night of sleep, I didn't expect him to eat much today. He's eaten half of what I put on his plate. I'll call it a win.

The silence is broken when the clang of Tucker's fork hitting the plate bounces off the walls. A huff spills from his lips as he slouches in his seat and drops his hands in his lap. His dark brows scrunch together as he stares at his plate.

I mentally prepare for a hundred different scenarios, but mainly for him to go off. I've seen and experienced every emotion except true anger from him regarding his mother. All the unnecessary chaos Brianna thrust into his life, he should be angry—at her for putting him in those situations and not caring how it made him feel, at me for not doing more to find and rescue him the first time.

Do I want my little man upset or angry? Never. The idea makes me sick.

But he must harbor *something* for all the heartache he's been through. It's normal. Human. Whether it's with me, Kaya, or a therapist, Tucker needs to get it out.

"I need to go, too," he finally says. "I want to say goodbye to Mom."

No child should have to be so brave. Not this early in life. Not with someone who should love them unconditionally.

"Okay, bud." I swallow, school my features, and exude strength I don't feel. "Let's clean up and get ready."

Antiseptic stings my nose as a blast of cold air dries my eyes. Hushed conversations drift through the waiting area. The weight of a hundred stares bores into the back of my head, but I keep my eyes forward. Tighten my hold on Tucker and Kaya and picture invisible armor around us as we step farther into the hospital.

Can't say I blame the townies and gossipmongers for being curious. Just let us get through today. Let us catch our breath. There will be plenty of time to plaster our names in the town paper later.

I steer us toward the front desk and don an artificial smile.

The receptionist glances up from their computer. "May I help you?"

"Brianna Werner's room number, please."

They study me with scrutinous eyes. "Are you family?"

My gut twists. "Yes. This is her son, and I'm his father."

Several clicks on the keyboard, an identification check, and phone call to Brianna's floor later, we are given the room number and directed to the correct elevator. Solemn smile on their face, the receptionist says we will have to be cleared by officers before entering the room.

Each elevator ding on the ride up spikes my blood pressure. I clench then relax my fingers. Wipe my palms on my thighs. Swallow past the nauseating cramp in my stomach. Every cell in my body screams to pick Tucker up and hug him to my chest, but I don't want to scare or worry him.

Sensing my discomfort, Kaya takes my hand with a reassuring squeeze and gives me some of her weight.

Damn, I fucking love her.

On a louder ding, the doors whoosh open. Feet rooted to the linoleum, my gaze darts from one person to another. Machines beep in the distance. Bleach lingers in the air. The corridor bright white from the overhead LED lights. People pass in different-colored scrubs—blue, green, gray, pink, various patterns.

My breakfast threatens to make a comeback, so I close my eyes and take a deep breath. Focus on my contact with Kaya, then Tucker as he slips his hand into mine.

Five breaths pass and the bulk of my unease settles. I press my lips to Kaya's crown. "Thank you," I murmur.

She tightens her hold on my hand. "Always." A press of the button for the floor and the door opens again.

We head down the hall and go through all the checks with the police guarding Brianna's door. Once we're cleared, an officer tells us we only get ten minutes. It's on the tip of my tongue to tell him I only need five, but with Brianna, who knows what bullshit she'll pull.

Stepping into the room, I note a third officer guarding from the inside. The boulder in my stomach shrinks to a manageable rock.

I owe Travis and Roger Emerson and Tymber Woulf a lifetime of gratitude—for how quickly they acted, for putting up with my outrageous behavior, for wanting to bring Tucker home as much as I did.

"Are you happy?"

My attention snaps to the woman cuffed to the bed. Cheeks hollow, nostrils flared, lips cracked, her face is covered in red marks. Pupils blown wide, her lifeless gaze rakes over me as if *I* am the problem.

I refuse to let her spin this whole scenario. She will *not* gaslight Tucker or me into believing her habits and life choices are our fault.

"For the first time in years, yes"—I steel my spine—"I am happy. You'll finally be held accountable for what you've done."

Brianna scoffs. "What *I've* done?" She grinds her teeth. "My life was perfect until *you* came along."

I do my damnedest to stay calm and keep a level head. "No, Brianna, it wasn't."

She opens her mouth to interject, but I keep talking.

"No one's life is perfect. We all have our own stuff to deal with. If we'd never met, it'd be someone else who *ruined* your life."

"Didn't get pregnant on my own." She rolls her eyes. "You pricked the condom, didn't you? Wanted to keep me imprisoned, so you poked a hole in it and forced your kid on me."

Anger boils under my skin. I open my mouth to tell her to go to hell, but the words never surface. Tucker beats me to it.

"I hate you!" Tucker yanks his hand out of mine and stomps closer to the bed. Small fists at his side, his face turns red and blotchy. "If you never wanted me, why did you steal me from my dad?"

Brianna's cracked lips curve up in the most repulsive smile. "Your *dad* stole my dreams, so I robbed him of his. Plus, the only way anyone would give me a place to stay or food was if I gave them a sad story." She lifts her hands from the mattress and shrugs.

In a blink, Tucker is inches from the bedside. He grabs the extra pillow propped against the frame, lifts it over his head, then brings it down with a *whack*. He gets in two solid hits before I swoop in and pull him away.

Hugging him to my chest, I drop my mouth to his ear. "I know you're angry, bud." I close my eyes and pour every ounce of love I have for Tucker into my embrace. "But don't let her take away your happiness. Don't let her fill you up with all the ugly."

Opening my eyes, I set him on his feet, take the pillow, and kiss his hair. I squat down, spin him so we're eye to eye, and rest my hands on his shoulders.

"You're my favorite person, T-Man." I nod for emphasis. "I will never love anyone as much as I do you." Lifting a hand, I comb my fingers through his hair. "You are so brave and strong. Even when you shouldn't have to be." The backs of my eyes sting as I hold his gaze. "I'm proud to be your dad and promise to love you enough for two parents."

Tears rim Tucker's eyes, the first one spilling down his cheek a breath before he wraps me in a fierce hug. "I love you," he whispers, his voice cracking.

"Well, isn't that fucking adorable," Brianna says, sarcasm thick.

I rise to my full height and turn toward Kaya. "Take Tucker into the hall? I need a minute alone with her."

Compassion softens Kaya's expression as she nods. She offers her hand to Tucker. "Let's go see what kind of candy they have in the vending machine."

Tucker takes Kaya's hand, and they exit the room.

When the door clicks shut, I count to ten in my head to make sure Tucker is out of earshot. The second I hit ten, I pivot and step up to the foot of the bed.

"Blame me all you want for your shitty life decisions, Bri"—I point toward the door—"but don't you fucking dare blame him. Ever." My molars ache as I clench my jaw. "We all make choices, and you made yours. Deal with the consequences like a big girl."

I grip the footrail until my knuckles burn. "I thank whatever cosmic force brought Tucker into my life. If you were a decent human being, you'd see beyond yourself and how incredible he is." Releasing the rail, I take a step back. "Your loss."

She opens her mouth to feed me some line of bullshit, but I cut her off.

"No, Bri," I bellow, holding my hand up. "You've done more than enough damage." I point to the ground. "From this day forward, you keep Tucker's name out of your mouth. Hell, don't even think it. You never wanted a kid?" I clap my hands in front of my face then spread them out. "*Poof.* You don't have one." Narrowing my eyes, I tilt my head. "In case you need a reminder, you have no parental rights. *He is mine.*"

Needing distance, I take a step toward the door. Then another. An arm's length from the door, I peer over my shoulder. "If you so much as look at Tucker again, it'll be the last thing you see."

"Did you just threaten me in front of a pig?"

I glance at the cop. "Did I just threaten her?"

He tips his head from side to side. "Technically, no."

Gripping the door handle, I take one last look at Brianna. "Have the life you deserve." Then I fling the door open and walk away.

Unfortunately, I will see her again… when her case goes to trial. But hearing her sentence and knowing she won't be anywhere near Tucker for many years to come is the final piece of closure I need.

Headed back the way we came, I find Tucker and Kaya at the vending machines. Tucker has a can of soda, two different types of chips, and a few sugary snacks. Kaya has two drinks—one she hands to me—and a bag of pretzels.

"Thanks." I tip my head toward the elevator. "Let's get out of here."

The trip back to the car goes much quicker. As if the universe says *you've been through enough, let me make the rest easier.*

In the car, we buckle up, but I don't start it. Before we leave the lot, I want everything out. All the anger, frustration, and hurt, it all needs to be out in the open so we can move forward.

"It might be hard to talk about, but I need to know how you feel, Tucker," I say. "What happened will stick with us for a while, but we shouldn't keep it to ourselves."

He's quiet, thoughtful for a moment. "Will I ever see my mom again?"

I twist in my seat to look at him. "Probably not, bud. She's done a lot of bad stuff and has to take responsibility for it." I contemplate leaving it at that but decide it's best he's aware of the other reason he won't see Brianna again. "And when she brought you here last year, she signed a special paper that says she doesn't want to be your mom anymore."

Insufferable heartbreak contorts his sweet face. "Why would she do that?"

The part of me that never wants Tucker to be in pain, whether physical, mental, or emotional, wants to sugarcoat the truth to soften the blow. But not ten minutes ago, Brianna spewed bitter, cruel words with Tucker mere feet from her bed.

Brutal honesty hurts, but it's better to experience the momentary stab now than be left in the dark for a long time and be irreparably devastated years later.

"Brianna didn't want to be a mom, and that's not your fault. Never was, never will be." I spin the soda can in the cup holder. "We cared about each other and were happy. That's how you came into our lives." I reach between the front seats and rest a hand on Tucker's knee. "I've loved you since the moment I knew you existed. Brianna struggled with being a parent."

I make a point to call Brianna by her name rather than Mom. She signed away her right to the title, not that she ever deserved it. In my eyes, she lost the moniker eight years ago, maybe before that. But Tucker has only ever known her as Mom. So perhaps, if I say her name enough times instead of Mom, it will shift his mindset and help him move forward.

"I've always wanted the best for you, bud. And that will never change. But I wish I would've known sooner that both parents being together doesn't always equal a happy life."

Tucker drops his gaze to his lap and wrings his fingers. "Is she going to jail?"

I want to say yes and mean it, but ultimately, the decision is out of my hands. After all she has done, it'd be a shock if she didn't go to prison.

"Probably, bud. How does that make you feel?"

He relaxes his hands then lifts his chin. Tears glaze his hazel eyes. "Glad." He blinks and sits a little straighter. "I hate her."

His reaction and response are a knife to the chest, but I'd never rob him of his feelings. Brianna treated him poorly from the start and didn't care how it would impact his life. She deserves his wrath, but I'll find a way for him to channel it without hurting anyone else.

"My brave guy." I run my fingers through the curls near his temple. "I'm sorry you had to go through this." Peeking at Kaya from the corner of my eye, I take her hand. "I'll always be here for you. If you need to yell, cry or hit something, you come to me and let it all out. And if you don't want to do those things with me"—I squeeze Kaya's hand—"you can sit down and talk with Kaya."

Her grip on my hand is severe as she nods. "It would be an honor."

A smile lights up Tucker's face and it's as if the sun came out for the first time in years. Who knew such a simple action could conquer the dark?

Tucker leans forward and lays his hand over our joined ones. "You're the best, Miss Kaya. I love you."

And now, Kaya Imala has the love of two Calhoun men.

THIRTY-SEVEN

KAYA

The past few days have been a whirlwind. Full of ups and downs. Joy and chaos. A strange blend of predestination and uncertainty, thrill and horror. Each moment made me breathless. Some had me fearful. Others made my pulse throb in my ears.

But they all served as a reminder of how fortunate I am.

I still get to wake up next to a man I care for deeply. Still get to see Tucker's smile, hear his laughter—although both are rare since the incident with Brianna. Still get to make memories with two people I never expected to enter my life, but I am glad they did.

Since the showdown at the train yard, Ray, Tucker, and I haven't spent a moment apart.

Although it pained him, Ray asked for the week off during the final days of cooking classes. André didn't blink at the request and told Ray to come back when he was ready.

I reached out to the rec center, gave them an abbreviated version of what happened, and requested a week off. Since summer camp is almost over, they told me to focus on myself, Ray and Tucker and preparing for the new school year.

Again, beyond fortunate.

In the days since the incident, we've had time to talk—with each other and a therapist. Spilled our hurt and exposed our wounds. Allowed ourselves to be vulnerable in an unprecedented way. In doing so, we've also strengthened our bond and made each other a safe space.

"Spatula." Ray tugs open a drawer then closes it just as quickly. "Where do you keep your spatula, Fire Eyes?"

When I mentioned needing to come home for clothes yesterday, Ray made the outlandish suggestion we stay at my place for the night. From our first date, all at-home events were at Ray's place. I've never been opposed to time at my house, I just wanted Tucker comfortable, and that meant him being surrounded by familiarity.

I opened my mouth to tell Ray my house was crampy and not as entertaining or enjoyable as his home. But I was cut off by an enthusiastic Tucker who thought a sleepover at my house would be fun. Couch forts and junk food. Board games and a little playful rivalry.

I didn't have it in my heart to open my mouth and question Tucker's zeal. The last thing I wanted was to stifle an ounce of his happiness.

Months from his tenth birthday, Tucker's already endured more than most two or three times his age. I can't help but wonder if his superficial gaiety is a defense mechanism.

Unless Tucker gives me reason to worry, I shut off my psychologist brain and let him express himself however he chooses.

"Erm…" Gaze on the fruit I'm cutting, I wince.

In two swift strides, Ray crowds me at the counter. Inches impossibly close. Dips his chin and trails the tip of his nose along my jawline, the heat of his breath like velvet on my skin.

I suck in a shaky breath.

A harsh *clang* echoes through the room as the knife falls from my hand to the cutting board. Sparks dance under my skin as his fingertips graze my bare arm, my collarbone, the hollow of my throat. Eyes rolling back, I melt into his touch. He nips then kisses the angle of my jaw, and it's an instant jolt to my heart. Ache blooms low in my belly a beat before arousal pools between my thighs. His talented fingers thread through my hair at the nape of my neck, curl into a loose fist, and tug.

Breath hot on my lips, erection thick and hard against my hip, his fiery gaze brands my soul. Lost in his riveting umber eyes, the world disappears.

He is all I see, all I feel, all I want.

Nose to nose, gazes locked, his lips ghost mine. "Tell me you have a spatula, Fire Eyes."

What?

I blink several times, confused. "Huh?"

"Cooking implement used to scoop and flip food," he says, tone teasing as his brows lift. "Flipper. Turner. Inverter." The corners of his mouth twitch as he fights a smile. "Often used for pancakes, burgers, fish, omelets." Humor dances in his eyes as he bites his bottom lip.

The urge to laugh bubbles to the surface, but I resist long enough to tease him in return.

Brows scrunched, I purse my lips and stare at him with mock confusion. "Inverter?" I look up and to the left, pretending to think. "Like the box for my solar panels?"

His head jerks back as lines mar his forehead. "Uh, no." He pinches my side and I squeal. "You know exactly what I'm talking about, Fire Eyes."

I playfully roll my eyes. "Sorry." Lifting a hand, I wiggle my fingers next to my head. "All the kissing and stroking and teasing jumbled things up." I bat my lashes. "The spatula is in that drawer." Pointing across the kitchen, I add, "I think. Don't cook much for myself."

Ray drops a chaste kiss on my lips, pushes off the counter, and walks backward until he reaches the drawer. He opens it, looks down, then smiles as he digs out the barely used spatula. Pointing it at me, he says, "So what I'm hearing is you need more cooking... lessons."

Heat hits my cheeks and I duck my chin. "Suppose I do." I pick up the knife and get back to work on the fruit.

As Ray pours the last batch of pancakes into the pan, Tucker shuffles into the kitchen, rubbing his eyes. He mutters, "Good morning," then sidles up to Ray at the stove.

Tucker woke up twice in the night. The first time, in a cold sweat as he gasped to catch his breath. The second time, Ray had to wake him. Tucker twisted in the sheets and kept muttering that he wanted to go home. When Ray finally woke him, he was disoriented and asked what happened. More than an hour of snuggles and countless whispered assurances, Ray lulled him back to sleep.

Either Tucker doesn't remember, or he forces himself to forget.

Ray asks me to get drinks while he assembles his famous pancake charcuterie board loaded with fruit, bacon, and a few other things he found in my cabinets. When he sets it in the middle of my small dining table, I gape at how he made something so simple look extravagant—especially with my limited kitchen supplies and ingredients. Thank goodness he brought a handful of things from his place.

"What would you like to do today?" Ray asks then shoves a loaded fork in his mouth.

Tucker says he wants to hang out with his friend from the skate park.

Ray's lips flatten into a grimace for a split second and I'm glad Tucker's too busy trying to spear a blueberry to notice. After a deep breath, Ray nods. "Sure, bud."

He won't admit it, but Ray will have Tucker in his sight the entire time. A habit for the foreseeable future. When school starts in a month, Ray will struggle. Tucker will, too, just not in the same way. But thankfully, I'll be able to check in with Tucker's teacher often and relay updates.

"Yes!" Tucker does a fist pump. "I miss Jordan."

Ray ruffles Tucker's hair. "I bet they miss you, too."

A buzz interrupts us, and I glance toward the living room to see a new notification on my phone. Deciding whoever it is can wait, I load my fork with another bite and listen to Tucker's skateboarding stories. He's in the middle of telling me about the time he scraped the underside of his chin when my phone buzzes again.

"Sorry." I wince, wipe my hands and mouth with a napkin, and retrieve my phone.

ANAANA

Checking in. How are you? How are Tucker
and Ray?

Bring them by for dinner on Sunday. I'd like to
formally meet them.

It's been days since I messaged my family and said I was out with Ray and Tucker. Respectful of my wishes, they didn't pry. Help was offered without questions or opinions.

But now the dust has somewhat settled. And my family meeting Ray and Tucker is imminent.

"Everything okay?"

I glance up from my phone and am met with Ray's curious, concerned gaze. I nod. "My mom's checking in. Asked how we're doing."

Ray tilts his head and studies the lines of my face with more interest.

I nibble my bottom lip. "And she suggested I bring you to dinner on Sunday."

Ray's eyes flare, the corners of his mouth tugging up the slightest bit. "Tucker and I would love to join your family for dinner, wouldn't we, bud?"

"Mm-hmm," he mumbles around the food in his mouth, his head bobbing.

My stomach flips and churns. "Great," I say with zero enthusiasm.

Thunderous laughter fills the room as Ray shakes his head. "What's the matter, Fire Eyes? You look a little pale."

My lips flatten into a straight line. "Shush, you." I turn my attention back to my phone and type.

> We're good. Taking it one day at a time. We'll see everyone on Sunday.

I stare at the *delivered* status below my message for far too long. By the time I look up, Tucker is no longer at the table, his plate taken to the sink. Ray studies every inch of my face while he masks his own emotions.

"Why are you worried?" he finally asks.

Setting my phone down, I reach for his hand and take it when he meets me halfway. I let the rough yet gentle brush of his calloused fingers on my skin soothe me as I fumble over my thoughts.

"I'm not worried."

His brows shoot up, his eyes wide. A silent *"Really?"* heavy in the air between us.

I close my eyes, take a deep breath, then meet his apprehensive gaze on the exhale. Strengthening my grip on him, I lean across the table, duck my head, and kiss the back of his hand. "Promise." I kiss his knuckles. "I'm not worried."

The wood legs of his chair protest as he scoots closer. "Then what is it?" His knee bumps mine under the table. A second later, his other hand is on my thigh.

The answer repeats in my head and sounds childish. But my heart knows Ray will empathize. After all, his family spent more than a decade playing matchmaker for his sister with one of the Seven.

"I've never introduced anyone to my family," I confess in a rush. "Let alone two people."

The corners of his eyes soften as his mouth curves into a compassionate smile. "Me either. Well, except for you. But that wasn't planned."

My eyes widen in shock as I lower my voice. "Your parents didn't meet Brianna?"

He shakes his head. "We started dating shortly before I graduated culinary school—if you call getting drunk and hanging out often dating." He winces. "Things weren't serious until she was pregnant. Even then, it was touch and go."

"They never met after Tucker was born?"

Lips pursed, he shakes his head again. "When they visited, Brianna made excuses to leave. It was… uncomfortable."

Wow.

"Makes me a little less queasy about bringing you to Sunday dinner," I say and laugh without humor.

"If it makes you uneasy, we don't have to go."

I'd be a fool to miss the disappointment in his voice. "No." I squeeze his hand. "I *want* you to meet them. It's just…"

When I don't continue, Ray cups my cheek. "Just what, Fire Eyes?"

I wince. "My family is much larger than yours. And they'll probably ask… embarrassing questions."

Ray lifts his other hand to frame my face, his thumbs slowly caressing the apples of my cheeks. "I can't wait to answer every single one of them."

"You're sure?"

He closes the distance between us and presses his lips to mine. "Only if you promise you're still mine afterward."

The backs of my eyes sting as emotion pools in my mouth. "I promise."

THIRTY-EIGHT

RAY

Tucker hasn't left my side in a week.

I love how much closer we've gotten, how he opens up without hesitation, how he wants to spend all his time with his dad. What worries me is how skittish he is around other people now.

We met up with Jordan at the skate park yesterday. Tucker had been so excited to see them. The entire drive there, he spoke animatedly about all the things he wanted to try on his skateboard. But when it came time to hang out with Jordan, Tucker's hands started to shake. His smile was all wrong.

I told him we didn't have to stay. We would come back another day.

But Tucker wasn't having it. He vehemently shook his head. *"No. I have to do this."* His voice had been so stern, determined.

I didn't have it in me to insist otherwise.

The entire hour, he was glued to Jordan's side. They talked, skated, and sat on a bench for a bit.

It warms my heart to know Tucker feels safe with Jordan. That he has someone other than family, Kaya, and a therapist to speak with about what worries him. He is braver than I ever was at his age.

"Do I have to wear this shirt?" Sour expression on full display, Tucker tugs at the stiff, snugger-than-he's-used-to-wearing sleeves of his button-down. "It's so itchy"—he scratches the nape of his neck—"and tight," he whines.

"You don't *have* to wear it," I say, and he sags in relief. "But I'd like you to." I fasten the last button on my own shirt and sit on the edge of the bed. "Come here. Let's see if I can help."

He shuffles forward with a hint of hope in his eyes.

"Hold out your arm, bud."

He does as I ask, and I unbutton the cuff. One flip after another, I roll up his sleeves until they are just beneath his elbows. Then I reach up and pop the top two buttons at the collar and relax the cotton away from his neck. With two simple adjustments, his entire frame loosens.

"Every once in a while, we have to put on a dress shirt and look extra nice." I smooth my hands over his shoulders. "Especially when we want to impress people."

His brows drop down and scrunch together. "What does impress mean?"

I run my fingers through his curls, fix a few wayward locks, and make a mental note to get it trimmed soon. "Impressing someone means you put in extra effort to look nice or do something special for them. You want them to remember how handsome or thoughtful or wonderful you are after spending time together." I study his quizzical expression. "Does that make sense?"

Eyes narrowed and lips puckered, he slowly nods. "I think so." Softening his features, he adds, "You want Miss Kaya's family to like us."

"Yes, bud." I roll up my sleeves to match his. "I want them to like us." *More than anything.*

Since the start of my culinary career, my primary objective has been to deliver the best dish possible and make a lasting impression on the recipient. Others' approval has been a top priority more years than not. The pressure to be perfect is nothing new.

But I've never had to impress others—definitely not a girl-friend's family—with *only* my personality.

When Kaya said her family wanted Tucker and me to join them for dinner, an unexpected surge of adrenaline flooded my bloodstream. Meeting the parents is a big step in any relationship. Granted, because our families are prominent figures in Stone Bay, the Imalas and Calhouns are somewhat acquainted… in a generic, impersonal way.

Tonight's dinner will shift the dynamic, hopefully for the better. Regardless, I want Kaya's family to like us, accept us, and know we're worthy of her affection.

I asked if I should make something for dinner, and Kaya said her family had the meal covered. My skin crawled at the idea of walking into her family's home without an offering. Food is my default but not an option.

So when Kaya left for her place after lunch, Tucker and I dashed to the florist and created the perfect thank you arrangement. Vibrant peach and yellow roses, bold orange ranunculus, dark-pink camellias, blossoming succulents, sprigs of lavender, and a soft bed of moss in a rustic wooden box. Beautiful and breathtaking yet unique and modest.

"You ready to go?" I pocket my wallet, phone, and keys.

Tucker rushes out of my room and across the hall. "Just a minute."

As I reach the stairs, he sidles up to me, a toy fire truck in his hand.

"Where'd that come from, bud?" I've seen the fire truck a few times but have yet to ask where he got it.

He hugs it to his chest as we descend. "Miss Kaya gave it to me at school."

I stay quiet until we reach the bottom of the stairs. "That was nice of her. It's a cool fire truck."

With a little bounce in his step, he walks ahead of me for the door leading to the garage. "It's special," he says, his voice full of wonder. "When I have a bad day, I share my secrets with it." His lips twist. "But sometimes, I just take it with me. Like a friend."

Speechless, I mentally fumble over what to say. I don't want to make him uncomfortable by not responding. But I also don't want to say the wrong thing.

"Well, I'm glad you have it." I unlock the car and open the door for him, feeling like I should say more but have no idea what. So, I stay quiet.

Tucker bops his head to a few songs on the way to Kaya's house. As I park in her driveway, she steps onto the porch and locks the front door. Tucker flies out of the car while I take my time grabbing the floral arrangement.

A low groan rattles my chest, my dick straining against the zipper as I swallow at the sight of her. Hair down and in loose waves, it cascades over her breasts and a very revealing, formfitting sleeveless black top, the point of the *V* at the base of her cleavage. High-waisted khaki pants hug her middle and flare wide on her mile-long legs, sweeping the ground. A large turquoise pendant rests beneath the hollow of her throat, her bead and bone cuff bracelet secured on her wrist.

Without effort, Kaya robs the air from my lungs and ruins me for any other woman. How I went half a lifetime without her, I'll never know. But damn, am I grateful and honored to have her now.

Slipping my arm around her waist, I lean in and whisper in her ear. "You look incredible."

She clutches the side of my pant leg. "Thank you." Inching back, her fiery irises peek up and lock onto my gaze. "If it's okay, I thought we'd walk to the main house."

Tucker takes her hand. "Lead the way, Miss Kaya."

Weaving through the trees, Kaya guides us along a foot-worn path. Our fingers laced, I take it all in.

Crisp pine mingles with the salty breeze from the bay. Birds chirp in the distance while chipmunks forage on the forest floor.

Sunlight filters through the tree canopy, a soft glow on our skin and surrounding woodlands.

I love how the Imala family has gone out of their way to preserve as much of the land as possible. With one large home in the center of the property and several smaller homes scattered throughout, they've kept most of the estate as it once was—trees and earth. In a world full of concrete jungles and noise, it's lovely to see places such as this still exist. It's peaceful, energizing, a way to reconnect with nature and reset.

The trees thin and open to a two-story home constructed of wood and stone. Large windows frame much of the south wall— an open deck on the second floor and covered patio beneath, spanning the entire side. Roughly twenty feet of cut grass surrounds the house, but the remaining exposed land is beautified with ponds, a grand firepit, and lush gardens.

My heart is in my throat as we walk between two large vegetable garden beds and I glance toward the house, an older man sitting in a chair on the patio. From here, it's difficult to read his body language or expression. For all I know, the man could have a smile on his face. Either way, it wouldn't ease my nerves.

I strengthen my hold on Kaya, and she gives me a gentle squeeze in return.

"There she is." The man rises from his seat as we approach, a warm smile wrinkling the corners of his eyes. "My favorite *irngutaq*."

"Grandchild," Kaya translates a beat before she steps into his open arms. It's easy to see his embrace is soft, loving, everlasting. The kind you want more of. When they break apart, Kaya introduces us. "Ray, Tucker, this is my *ataatasiaq*, grandfather, Nanook Imala. Nan for short. *Ataatasiaq*, this is Ray and his son, Tucker."

I shift the arrangement and offer my hand. "Wonderful to meet you, Nan."

His weathered, calloused hand is warm, his grip firm yet full of tenderness. "Nice to see my Kaya with a caring man." The affectionate comment catches me off guard, but before I can ask how he knows what type of man I am, he pulls Tucker into a hug. "And what an honor it is to meet you, young Tucker." The soft lines by his eyes deepen as a fond smile brightens his expression.

The way he speaks to and of us, it's as though we've been a part of his life for years. It assuages my unease, makes me feel more welcome than I anticipated.

Nan releases Tucker and meets Kaya's gaze. "Everyone's inside and eager to meet these two."

Kaya inhales deeply and nods. "Let's not keep them waiting."

I love that she is as nervous as I am. It says she cares about us and how her family will receive me and Tucker.

We follow Nanook inside and I am struck speechless at how open and alive the home feels. Wood and stone repeat throughout the interior, pops of color on the walls from simple yet powerful pieces of art. Pleasant neutrals and earth tones given more life from the natural light streaming through the windows.

"This place is dope," Tucker whispers.

Kaya and I chuckle.

"Yeah, bud, it is."

When we reach the dining area, I stop breathing. In the heart of the room—and the house—is a lengthy, live edge table with several chairs tucked underneath. It'd be a tight fit but could easily seat more than a dozen people. Most would look at it and complain about how such a large table shrinks the room. To me, it's a warm, inviting space that keeps everyone connected.

Food is my passion, but having an appealing, welcoming place to share it is equally important.

Lost in thought, I fail to notice the turn we take toward the kitchen, blindly following Kaya's lead. When my attention snaps and focuses, I momentarily stumble, lost for words once more.

Mesmerized, I scan every inch of the kitchen. No shiny top-of-the-line appliances that look unused. No pristine countertops covered with perfectly placed pictures, books, or gadgets. And no aesthetically pleasing, pointless trinkets.

A dusting of flour, sporadic baskets, and heaps of vegetables take up much of the counter surface. Mouthwatering herbs and spices float through the air. The distinct sound of a knife rocking against a cutting board hits my ears. Generosity, mirth and deep affection radiate from the walls.

With only what it needs and nothing more, the kitchen is the core of this house. Pure love. The place where Kaya's family shares a piece of their heritage and soul.

I never want to leave this kitchen.

"*Panik,*" Sakari Imala says as she rounds the long island.

"Daughter," Kaya translates. "Hi, Mom." Their embrace is as warm as the one Kaya shared with her grandfather. "You remember Ray Calhoun."

"Of course." Sakari turns toward me and gives an unexpected hug around the arrangement. Inching back, her attention shifts to the other side of Kaya. "And you must be Tucker." Bending at the knees, she makes it so they're eye level. "I've heard many wonderful things about you. Nice to put a face to the name."

My ribs constrict and steal the air from my lungs. An unfamiliar reverence blooms beneath my sternum, the *whoosh, whoosh, whoosh* of my heart pounding in my ears.

Kaya talks with her family about Tucker.

Damn, do I love this woman.

Sakari introduces Ahnah and Liuna, Kaya's grandmother and great-grandmother. I present them with the arrangement then offer to help in the kitchen. When they wave me off, I ask if they mind me watching them cook.

Kaya leans in and rests a hand on my shoulder. "Will you be okay if I show Tucker around?"

I lay my hand over hers and twist to meet her shimmering gaze. "Absolutely. You have no idea how much I love to sit and learn."

With a squeeze of my shoulder, she releases me and chuckles. "I'm sure I can guess."

The moment Kaya is out of earshot, the three women begin

their interrogation. I expected nothing less. Just wondered who'd ask all the questions. Turns out, they share the duty.

"How long have you been a chef?" Ahnah asks as she forms dough into small cakes.

"I got my culinary degree ten years ago but have loved being in the kitchen since I was a kid."

Ahnah smiles, then sets some of the cakes in a large skillet over a low flame.

"How have you managed working such strenuous hours with a young child?" Sakari adds minced garlic and ginger to a meat mixture and folds it in.

"Tucker was with his mother for several years. When he came to live with me, it was an adjustment, but my family and I made it work. And since the summer cooking school was a success, Chef Beaulieu announced I'll be head of year-round cooking classes. The change will give me more time with Tucker."

"What are your intentions with our Kaya?" Liuna lifts the lid on a large pot, stirs the contents, tastes the broth, then adds a pinch of salt.

"I am very much in love with her."

All three women stop what they are doing and turn to look at me, a mix of joy and surprise on their faces.

"Have you told her this?" Ahnah flips over the cakes in the pan.

"I have, yes."

Ahnah's brows lift as her eyes widen. "And... what did she say?"

Kaya's grandmother has the type of energy that makes me want to smile all the time. "She hasn't said it back, which is okay. When she's ready, she'll tell me." I press a hand to my chest. "But I know how she feels."

"Kaya is very passionate and headstrong. As stubborn and unmoving as a mountain"—Sakari leans in and talks softer—"which is what her name means." Sakari fills wonton wrappers with the meat mixture, spoons on a small amount of fish roe, pinches them into pouches, and puts them in bamboo steamer basket trays. "Until you and Tucker came along, all she cared about was work."

"When you love what you do, it's hard not to put all of your energy into it," I answer.

Until a few months ago, I didn't want to change my ways either. I love being in the kitchen. I love taking simple ingredients and making a masterpiece. But most of all, I love hearing and seeing people's reactions to my dishes. Their praise and admiration fuel my soul.

But I'm excited for the next leg of my journey. Thrilled to discover a new love for food by teaching others.

"True," Sakari says as she stacks the trays over a pot of boiling water. "But I'm happy she's on a more balanced path now. You've given her that, and I thank you."

Once again, I'm struck speechless. Thankfully, the awkward silence doesn't last long.

Kaya and Tucker return and the conversation shifts. She sidles up to me and wraps her arms around my waist from behind. "Did they ask all the invasive questions?"

I rest an arm over hers and chuckle as Tucker plops down on the seat to my left. "Not all of them, but plenty."

"Sorry," she whispers.

"Don't be." I caress her skin with my thumb. "I expected it."

Kaya releases me and joins the three women on the other side of the counter. She plucks a handful of berries from a bowl, picks up an ulu, and slices the fruit. She works with the crescent-shaped knife as if she has done it thousands of times. Once all the berries are sliced, she adds them to a casserole dish, squeezes fresh lemon juice on top, and sprinkles them with a heavy amount of sugar— no measuring.

Watching her is enthralling. How she moves with such ease. How she makes baking look sexy as fuck.

Is it like this for her with our roles reversed? Because I definitely want to watch her in the kitchen a hell of a lot more.

She takes some of the remaining dough her grandmother used for the cakes and adds it to the top of the fruit. As she wipes her hands on a towel, she peeks up at me from beneath her lashes. "Quit staring," she mutters, the corners of her lips twitching up.

"Not a chance, Fire Eyes," I say nowhere near as quietly.

She rolls her eyes then steps away with the casserole dish, puts it in the oven, and removes a sheet pan with huge dill-coated salmon filets on cedarwood.

My mouth waters.

Everything other than the large pot's contents is added to serving platters. Kaya goes to the fridge and pulls out a salad that must've been made before we arrived. Dishes get carried to the table and set in the middle, and I take one without asking, wanting to help.

Other family members appear out of nowhere. Hugs and greetings get exchanged, then we all take a seat. Tucker keeps to himself unless someone speaks directly to him. But he doesn't appear overstimulated or panicky.

Plates and bowls are filled and Kaya relays to me and Tucker what's on tonight's menu. Bannock—a bread that can be eaten with savory or sweet dishes or on its own. Ground fish, shrimp, and goose wontons. Bison stew with root vegetables. Slow-roasted cedar plank salmon.

Tucker picks at his food until he decides he likes all of it. I love his adventurous spirit.

Conversation erupts around the table, everyone sharing details of their lives since their last gathering. I anticipate more questions, maybe from Kaya's father or brother, perhaps an uncle, but am asked none.

When the oven timer goes off, Kaya excuses herself. As she enters the kitchen, her mom meets my gaze from the other end of the table and raises her glass.

"Thank you for joining us, Ray and Tucker. We all see how much light you've brought into Kaya's life. It overjoys us to see her so happy."

Kaya takes her seat next to me and mutters, "Mom."

Sakari carries on. "We'd love to see you both more often. During family dinners or nights when our schedules align."

My heart rattles my rib cage as emotion clogs my throat. "Tucker and I would love that very much. Thank you." The underlying anxiety I had about Kaya's family accepting us fades more and more with each kind sentiment.

"But we'd like you to take it slow," Sakari adds. "Get to know each other better."

I wring my napkin in my lap as my unease slips back in.

Kaya sucks in a sharp breath and gingerly sets her fork down. "We've spent the last two months getting to know each other. We have taken it slow."

I mentally tip my head side to side. *Kind of slow.*

"For someone who was adamant about not being in a relationship, your sudden shift on the subject is interesting." Sakari takes a sip of her drink. "I just want you to be careful, *panik.*"

Kaya's shoulders relax as her expression softens. "When have you ever known me to be anything other than cautious?"

Tikaani takes Sakari's hand and gives it a gentle squeeze. "She's right, my sweet. We must trust her instincts and let her walk her own path."

Sakari purses her lips then sighs. "Yes, I suppose we should, *aakuluk.*" She lifts her glass once more, this time higher and toward the center of the table. "*Inuuhiqatsiaq*! Cheers and to good health!"

A mixture of *inuuhiqatsiaq* and cheers erupt around the table before we all take a drink. Dessert is brought to the table and devoured faster than the main meal.

The second the cobbler hits my tongue, I tell Kaya she is in charge of dessert going forward. She simply laughs.

After a long line of warm embraces, we wish everyone a good night and take the path back to Kaya's house, the fading sunlight illuminating the trail.

"That went better than expected," she says as her house comes into view.

"I like your family. It's good of them to ask or say all the hard things. Means they love you." I trail my fingers down her arm and lace them with hers when I reach her hand. "What'd you think, T-Man?"

"Your family is lit, Miss Kaya."

"From dope to lit. Oh, how we evolve," I say on a laugh.

Kaya leads us to her front door and unlocks it. "Be right back. Need to grab my bag."

As Tucker opens the car's back door, Kaya steps out with a stuffed tote. I stow it in the back seat next to Tucker then slip into the driver's seat.

The miles fly by as we head to my house. But before I turn off Fossil Mountain Highway, Kaya takes my hand and twists in her seat to face me.

"You know we can go at whatever pace *we* want, right?"

I flip the blinker on, ease off the accelerator, and press the brake. "Of course, Fire Eyes." I turn onto the road for the Calhoun estate and keep my speed slow. "It's not something we've talked about, but I'm open to it."

She stares out the windshield, contemplative a moment. "Yes, we still have a lot to learn about each other. But the same can be said for people who've been together years." Her eyes are back on my profile. "I just don't want someone to mold our relationship according to their ideals. Does that make sense?"

I bring her hand to my lips and kiss her knuckles. "Makes perfect sense."

Pressing the button for the garage door, I steer the car inside and put it in park. Tucker bolts from the back seat and runs inside the house. He'll probably have a movie queued up and a handful of snacks ready by the time we walk through the door.

"I feel like we've gone slow enough," Kaya whispers into the dark. "I'm ready to go a little faster."

My pulse thrums in my ears. "You'll have to guide me, Fire

Eyes." I lean over the center console and kiss her. "My version of fast probably looks different than yours."

Cupping my cheek, she softly strokes my scruff with her thumb. "I love you, Ray." She presses a chaste kiss to my lips. "You and Tucker. Don't know who I'd be without either of you."

Dopamine hits my bloodstream in a rush. I frame her face with my hands and take her mouth in a fevered kiss. "I love you, too." I drop my forehead to hers and bask in the swirl of energy between us.

A thunderous boom from inside the house garners my attention. Probably an action movie playing through the speakers, but you never know.

"We should get inside before he eats his weight in sugar."

Kaya chuckles and reaches for her bag in the back. "Yeah, we should."

At a leisurely pace, we enter the house and go about our nightly routine. After a quick change of clothes, we're on the couch, movie ready, and in one big snuggle with Kaya at the heart.

Life may not be perfect, but this is as close as it gets. All I need is right here. So long as I have Tucker and Kaya, I have everything.

EPILOGUE

KAYA

PEACE COMES IN MANY DIFFERENT FORMS. KIND GESTURES OR SOFTLY spoken words. Simple touches or warm embraces. Solitude in your favorite place. Getting an answer you've waited a long time to hear. Spending time with someone you care about. Accomplishing something you've worked hard on.

People and places can gift peace. But when something significant happens, respite only comes from one source.

Last week, after years of heartache, frustration, anger, and torment, after weeks of wondering how this chapter would end, Ray and Tucker were able to breathe easier.

A few rows back in the courtroom gallery, Ray, Tucker, and I sat in silence, our hands clasped and hearts pounding. Beaufort Langston sat behind the bench in the judge's chair, his enigmatic expression giving nothing away as his eyes scanned the paper in his hand.

Then he read the verdict. "Guilty on all counts."

My eyes stung as I turned to look at my guys. Tucker had his arms around Ray, his face buried in his father's chest. Sweet relief spilled down Ray's cheeks as he hugged Tucker and held my gaze.

Guilty.

Judge Langston slapped the highest sentence on each count, and the list was far from short.

While Brianna awaited trial, Ray helped build a case against her. And Brianna made it too easy. By the time her court date arrived, she had zero chance of freedom. My stomach twisted tighter as each charge had been read. Kidnapping, child endangerment without intent of harm, child endangerment with intent to harm, child neglect, aiding and abetting, violation of a restraining order, second-degree manslaughter, extortion, possession of a controlled substance, possession of drug paraphernalia, and drug manufacturing.

As it stands, Brianna will be in jail the rest of her natural life. The only person upset with the sentence is her.

A little more than a month has passed since Brianna brutally scarred our lives. Yes, it will take years for us to recover fully, but I love the small strides we make each day. When our smiles and laughter come a little easier. The days Ray looks over his shoulder less often. Or when Tucker acts more like the boisterous boy I met a few months ago.

I hug each of those moments to my chest and cherish them. Those are the memories I choose to keep close.

"Is Papa RJ working?" Tucker asks as Ray parks at the diner.

"All day." Ray puts the car in park.

"Yes!" Tucker unbuckles his seat belt and whips the car door open. "He makes the best milkshakes."

"Hey—"

Tucker shuts the door then stands on the other side of Ray's, tapping on the window. "Hurry up, Dad."

"I make better milkshakes," Ray mutters as he opens his door.

I laugh under my breath as I exit the car. When I reach him and Tucker, I loop my arm with his. "Everything you make is better."

He turns and kisses my temple. "Nothing but truth comes out of those gorgeous lips, Fire Eyes. Another reason why I love you."

The diner is slammed with residents enjoying the last week of break before school resumes. Teens huddle at tables and laugh over who knows what, their joviality infectious. Younger kids enjoy burgers, finger foods, and milkshakes with family as they ask for one more back-to-school outfit.

I breathe it all in and mentally prepare myself for another great year of doing what I love.

We're seated within minutes and told the specials. Tucker bounces in his seat and begs Ray to let him have the special milk shake—Cookie Monster extreme—and not a *boring* one. Ray agrees, but only if Tucker eats his lunch and drinks it slowly. We place our order and Sandi, the server, says it shouldn't be long. Then she scurries off to another table.

"You ready for fifth grade, *kuluk*?" The term of endearment— dear one—rolls off my tongue as if I've said it all of Tucker's life and not a handful of times.

A few days after Ray and Tucker's first gathering with my family, Mom and I chatted over the phone. She told me how cute and dear Tucker is and it stuck. Later that night, when Ray, Tucker, and I ate dinner, I called him *kuluk*. He asked what it meant. When I told him, the biggest smile plumped his cheeks.

Tucker sits taller in his seat and puffs out his chest. "I'm the big kid on campus now."

"Yeah, you are." Ray pats Tucker's shoulder. "Just remember to be nice to the little kids."

He draws an X over his heart. "Promise."

"That's my T-Man."

Tucker ducks his chin a little. "But I'm also scared."

Ray pulls him in for a side hug. "Want to tell us why?"

His lips twist then relax. "What if people make fun of me again?" Lines form between his brows as he lifts his chin. "What if they're mean to me because of Mo"—his eyes water—"Brianna?"

Ray runs his fingers through Tucker's shorter curls. "If they treat you with disrespect, they're not your friends. Which is their loss." Ray kisses the top of Tucker's head. "But then you let your teacher or Kaya know how they're acting. Bullies aren't allowed at school." Ray presses his nose to Tucker's hair, breathes him in, then straightens in his seat. "Whatever you do, don't lose your cool. Don't let them turn you into someone you're not."

Tucker nods. "'Kay."

A few smaller tables next to us clear out and are pushed together. I mentally cross my fingers a large group of rowdy teens aren't taking the spot. Before I can scope out our table neighbors at the door, RJ sidles up to our table with a sugar-laden monstrosity in his hand.

"I hear my grandson ordered the Cookie Monster extreme." RJ sets down the fluorescent-blue milkshake rimmed with chocolate and topped with whipped cream, chocolate chip cookies, and blue drizzle. "Hope you're ready for the aftereffects." He looks pointedly at me and Ray.

"Will he need his stomach pumped later?" Ray asks, tone teasing.

"Only if he chugs it on an empty stomach," RJ jokes back, laughing. "I need to get back to the kitchen but wanted to pop out and say hi." RJ kisses Tucker's head. "Let's do something fun on Friday, little man. Just you, me, and Grandma."

Tucker plucks a cookie from the whipped cream. "Mm-kay." He nods and shoves the cookie in his mouth.

"Love you." RJ gives him another kiss. "Easy on the shake."

"Love you, Papa," Tucker mumbles.

RJ disappears back into the kitchen, and we get a full view of the group next to us. Some familiar faces—Travis Emerson, Phoebe Graves, Delilah Fox, Levi West, and Oliver Moss, the drummer for Stone Bay's local rock band, Hailey's Fire—but a few I don't recognize.

"Whoa," Tucker whispers as he elbows Ray. "That's Mr. Ollie!" Tucker glances back to the group then goes wide-eyed when Oliver meets his gaze.

Oliver whispers something to Levi, gets up from his chair, then moves to a seat closer to us. "Hey, Tucker. What the heck is that" —he points to the milkshake—"and how do I get one?"

Tucker appears starstruck and it's the cutest thing ever. He fumbles over his words but manages to tell Oliver what he's drinking.

Oliver glances over his shoulder and says, "Moje srce." Levi meets his gaze. "Order me this Cookie Monster milkshake." He points to the shake. "Just the buzz I need before tonight's show."

Levi winces, nods, then shakes his head.

"You have a show tonight, Mr. Ollie?"

Oliver gives Tucker his full attention. "Yep. At the park by the post office. Let me know if you'll be there. I'll get you a backstage pass."

Tucker twists in his seat and peers up at Ray, so much anticipation in his eyes. "Please, Dad. Can we go?" He clasps his hands together. "Please, please, please."

Ray appears casual as ever. "Only if your stomach's not upset from this shake."

Tucker shakes his head. "It won't be." He says it with absolute certainty.

The woman across from Oliver taps his arm and says, "The cookout."

A bright smile stretches Oliver's face as he looks at me then Ray. "We're starting a new tradition this year. End of summer cookout." Oliver jerks a thumb over his shoulder. "If it's too weird because of the history with Levi and your sister, I get it. But if you don't have plans on Sunday, you're welcome to join us."

As one of the Seven, I'm in the loop of what happens with the other founding families. Unless it impacts me, my family, or people I love, I usually steer away from town politics, drama, and the Seven in general.

But in the past two years, a lot has come to light. Many in my generation of the Seven want change. And they're slowly unveiling the town's secrets. Bringing unsavory facts to the surface. Recent corruption and financial scandals. Buried truths since the "founders" names were penned on paper. Truths that involve the other half of my family—the Stonewater tribe this town is named after.

As each skeleton surfaces, I speculate whether the scandals will be buried in a deeper grave or examined with a fine-tooth comb and addressed impartially.

Only time will tell.

Since I've managed to avoid town squabbles and theatrics to focus on work, my circle of friends is small. But I'd love that to change. It'd be nice to form more friendships. To have more people to lean on. To chat with like minds and build lasting relationships.

I glance across the table at Ray. "A cookout sounds fun, but only if you're comfortable."

Ray nods then shifts back to Oliver. "I'll give you my number. Text me the details and let us know what to bring."

Oliver hands Ray his phone to exchange numbers. "Only decision we've made is Travis is hosting." Oliver winks at Tucker. "So bring your swimming trunks."

Ray hands back Oliver's phone. "Lounging by the pool is the perfect way to end summer. Thanks for the invite, man."

Sandi sidles up to the table and sets down our lunch.

"Won't bother you anymore. We'll chat later." Oliver taps the table then gets up and moves back to the seat next to Levi.

"That was really nice of him," I say as I cut my smoked salmon burger in half.

"My dad is friends with a rock star," Tucker says with so much pride.

Ray leans into Tucker and lowers his mouth to Tucker's ear. "So are you, bud."

Tucker's eyes widen as realization sets in. "Dope AF."

"Nope." Ray shakes his head. "No AF. Just because you don't say the actual curse word doesn't mean you're allowed to abbreviate it. Not yet, bud."

"Fine." Tucker rolls his eyes. "I guess it's just dope."

I can't help but laugh at his lack of enthusiasm.

Our table quiets as we dig into our lunch. Halfway through, Ray suggests we go see the new superhero movie at the theater. Tucker fist-pumps the air then wiggles in his seat. When our bellies are full, Ray asks for a to-go cup for Tucker's shake and the bill.

RJ comes out to say goodbye before we leave. As Tucker jumps up and wraps his arms around his grandpa, Ray's head jerks to the front door.

I peek over my shoulder to see who caught his attention. "Who is that?" I whisper, my gaze darting between Ray and his father.

"Not sure," Ray says.

RJ releases Tucker and huddles in closer. "Guess Old Man Freeman had some secrets he took to the grave." He tips his head toward the man now at the take-out counter. "That would be Maddox Freeman. Stone Bay's newest resident."

Another town secret exposed. How much longer until all the skeletons are set free?

Almost Four Months Later

"Why did I agree to this?"

I snake my arms around Kaya's waist, drop my nose to the crook of her neck, and lift her off the ground. "Because you love me."

"Hmm. Maybe not as much as I used to."

Snow flurries around us as I set her back on her feet. "Nah. You love me more."

Kaya spins around, rests her palms on my chest, and narrows her eyes. "Moving while it's snowing does not make me love you more." Her lips curve into a wicked smile. "Guess you'll have to make it up to me later. Several times."

In two weeks, Kaya and I will celebrate seven months together. And yes, I am the corny one in the relationship that makes a big deal out of each milestone. Flowers, gifts, cooking *lessons*, decadent dinners, orgasms… I shower my woman with it all. And she loves every second.

Heat licks my veins as I frame her face and erase every inch of space between us. "How about we start now?"

A blush hits her cheeks as she swallows. "Maybe in the shower once we unpack."

Groaning, I duck my chin until my lips ghost hers. "Wet and naked and ready…" I close my eyes and will my dick to go down. "How am I supposed to load boxes with that image in my head?"

She sucks my bottom lip, takes it between her teeth, then releases it. "Consider it motivation." With a slap of my ass, she steps back, turns toward her old house, and calls over her shoulder. "Let's not make our friends do all the work."

I stare at the sway of her hips and groan loud enough for her to hear.

She laughs in response then disappears inside the house.

Tipping my head back, I let the flurries land on my face and cool my overheated skin. Count to ten and think of anything other than Kaya's naked body in our shower.

"Everything alright?"

I level my head and turn toward Travis. "Should be asking you that."

Stone Bay has been complete chaos the past couple of months, but I hope it settles down soon. A lot has changed in such a short period, but it's all for the better. Kaya's family seems to think the worst of it is over, but I won't hold my breath.

Travis sets a box in the bed of his truck then leans against the open tailgate. "I'm good. Adjusting to the new norm." He scoffs. "So much is different, but a lot remains the same. If that makes any sense."

Kaya kept me in the loop of all the news. Since the changes impact what Stone Bay has considered as the founding families for generations, most of the details have been kept under wraps. But I wouldn't put it past Phoebe to publish a special edition in the Stone Bay Gazette once the dust settles. Her recent stories have certainly ruffled a lot of feathers.

"It does. If you need a night out to blow off steam or vent, you know where to find me." I slap and squeeze his shoulder, then tip my head toward the house. "Should probably go help before Kaya gets upset and changes her mind about moving in."

It will never happen. Kaya has slept in my bed all but a few nights since the beginning of August. I'd have to do something monumentally stupid to fuck that up.

Travis laughs. "Let's get the last of her things and get you two home before the snow gets worse."

We finish loading up our vehicles, leaving the large furniture items in the house for the next Imala or Stonewater family member. In a four-vehicle convoy, we drive the last of Kaya's things to *our* house.

A light dusting of snow blankets the town with a promise of heavier snowfall later tonight. Winter events carry on, but many of the residents have steered clear this season. With all the recent disorder, can't say I blame them. Most of the townsfolk are at the grocery store, clearing the shelves, saying this will be the biggest storm Stone Bay's seen in years.

If only snowstorms and heatwaves were all this town needed to worry about.

Flipping on the blinker, I turn off the highway and onto the personal road for the Calhoun estate. I lift my and Kaya's joined hands to my lips and kiss her knuckles. "Sure you're up for everyone staying for dinner?"

"Absolutely. If they won't let us pay them for their help, we'll feed them instead."

"Love you, Fire Eyes."

"Love you too, Chef."

The garage comes into view, and I press the button to open it. We take turns backing into the driveway and then get to work unloading everything into the garage. Boxes stacked and out of the way, I close the garage door and we all head into the house.

While everyone relaxes with a drink, I get to work on burgers, grilled fish, vegetable kabobs, potato wedges, and a massive salad. Knowing we'd be worn out from hauling boxes, I did most of the prep work this morning. And before anyone finishes their first drink, I load up platters and carry them to the dining room.

"Where's Tucker?" Oliver mumbles around his burger.

"Parents took him for the weekend so we could move and unpack without worrying about him." I dunk a potato wedge in garlic-curry aioli. "Mom said they're making homemade chocolates and candies. She'll send dozens home with him."

"Ooh," Kirsten, Travis's girlfriend, and Skylar, one of her best friends, say in unison then laugh.

"Promise I'll sneak some for you," Kaya tells them.

Light conversation about the holidays floats through the room as we finish dinner. Everyone offers to help clean up, but Kaya and I turn them down.

"Should probably go before the snow gets worse," Travis says.

"As much as I love you all, I don't have the energy for a sleepover," I tease, and everyone laughs.

Hugs are exchanged and we tell everyone to drive safe. When the last set of taillights disappears from view, Kaya and I head back inside and clean up. With the table cleared and dishes in the dishwasher, I take Kaya's hand and lead her out of the kitchen, turning off the light.

We ascend the stairs in comfortable silence, amble into the bedroom, and turn for the bathroom. Cranking the shower, I take my time peeling off her layers. She strips me with equal care, her fingers tracing my tattoos.

I guide us into the shower and shut the door. Wash her hair and massage her scalp. Caress every single curve and inch of her addictive body as I wash her head to toe. After she returns the favor, spending more time soaping and stroking my cock, I rinse off with my lips pressed to hers.

I lick and suck, bite and claim. Then I spin her around, hike up her leg and plant her foot on the bench. Snake an arm around her waist and dip my fingers between her thighs. Circle her clit then slip my fingers inside her hot, sweet pussy.

"You make me wild, Fire Eyes." I rub the length of my cock along her ass. "In the best fucking ways."

Her whimpers bounce off the shower walls.

"Need you to come for me." I flick her clit then sink my fingers into her pussy again. "Give me one before I fuck you with my cock."

Kaya groans and rocks her hips, fucking my fingers. She loves when I talk dirty. When I demand her orgasm. And I love when she gets like this. Greedy. Desperate. Insatiable. We may be exhausted from the day, but she'll come at least three times before we collapse and pass out.

She reaches back and fists my hair. Drops her head on my shoulder and mewls, her brown nipples stiff and thrust up.

I pump my fingers faster. Stroke her clit with more urgency and pressure. Knead her breast with my other hand. Clamp down on the curve of her shoulder with my mouth and suck hard.

Her cries grow louder, faster, needier. And then her pussy strangles my fingers. She fists my hair and whimpers as she rides out her orgasm.

"Such a good fucking girl, Fire Eyes." I bring my fingers to my mouth and suck the taste of her off them.

Once she catches her breath, I cut off the shower, towel dry her hair and skin, then carry her to the bed. The mood is playful at first. Smiles, laughter, tickling. But as I hover over her and toy with the damp strands of her hair, the air crackles between us.

I claim her mouth. Kiss her slowly, passionately. Stroke her tongue with mine. Taste her as I wrap her in my arms. Hum a beat before I break this kiss and rest my forehead on hers. "Love you, Fire Eyes. So fucking much."

Her delicate fingers trail my jawline as her coppery-brown irises stare into my soul. "Love you too, Chef." She presses her lips to mine in a chaste kiss. "As nice as this moment is"—she bites her bottom lip—"I need you to fuck me."

A growl rumbles in my chest. "I love when you demand sex."

She reaches between us and strokes my cock. "I know."

Then she flips me over, lifts up off my waist, grabs my cock, and lowers herself onto it. We sigh in unison as she sinks down and takes me to the hilt.

I fist her hips and set the pace. Drag her up and down the length of my cock. Get lost in the sight of her, the feel of her pussy choking my dick, the sound of skin slapping skin and our libidinous moans. The smell of her arousal in the air.

Full tits pushed up and bouncing, hands planted on my chest and nails in my pecs, she rides me hard. And then the pitch of her moans shifts, gets higher, more irregular.

Bruising her hips with my grip, I lift and slam her on my cock. Meet her thrust for wild thrust until her limbs shake and orgasm drenches my balls.

Exhausted and breathless, I flip her onto her back and slow the pace. Sit back on my haunches and lift her legs over my shoulders. My eyes dart between hers and where my cock slides in and out of her pussy. The sight is erotic, addictive, and absolute perfection.

Thumb on her clit, I draw slow circles and add just enough pressure. "I'll never get my fill of you, Fire Eyes." I rock my hips forward and moan as I disappear inside her. "Not fucking possible."

She cups her breasts and gently pinches her nipples. "Never," she whispers on a moan.

And when I come, it's with her name on my tongue.

IMALA
family tree

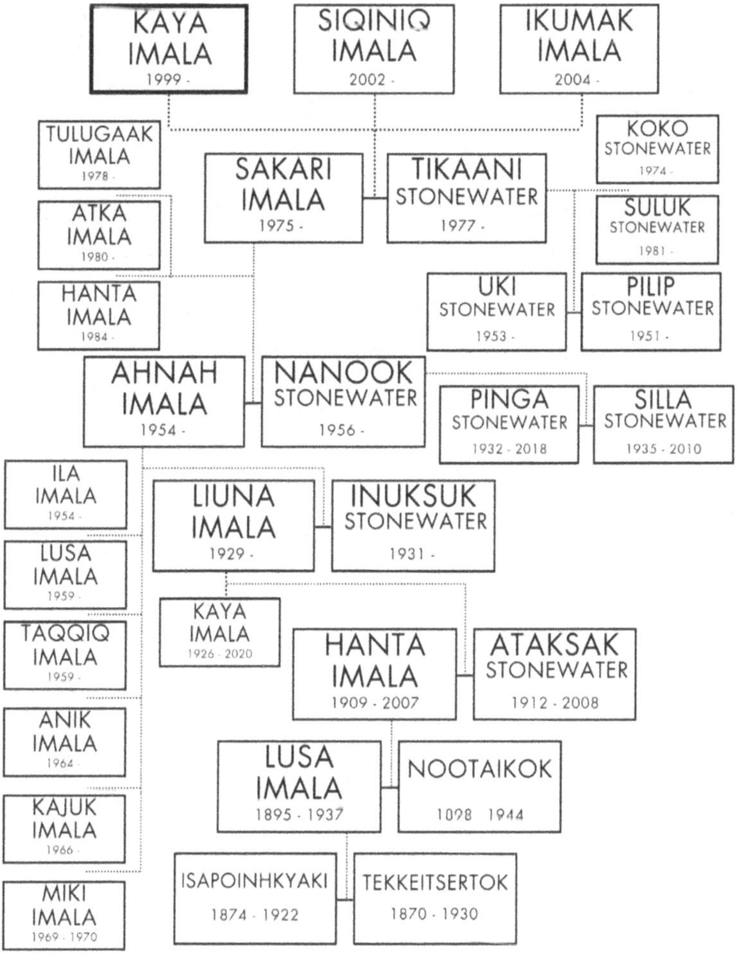

KAYA IMALA
1999 -

SIQINIQ IMALA
2002 -

IKUMAK IMALA
2004 -

TULUGAAK IMALA
1978 -

SAKARI IMALA
1975 -

TIKAANI STONEWATER
1977 -

KOKO STONEWATER
1974 -

ATKA IMALA
1980 -

SULUK STONEWATER
1981 -

HANTA IMALA
1984 -

UKI STONEWATER
1953 -

PILIP STONEWATER
1951 -

AHNAH IMALA
1954 -

NANOOK STONEWATER
1956 -

PINGA STONEWATER
1932 - 2018

SILLA STONEWATER
1935 - 2010

ILA IMALA
1954 -

LIUNA IMALA
1929 -

INUKSUK STONEWATER
1931 -

LUSA IMALA
1959 -

TAQQIQ IMALA
1959 -

KAYA IMALA
1926 - 2020

HANTA IMALA
1909 - 2007

ATAKSAK STONEWATER
1912 - 2008

ANIK IMALA
1964 -

LUSA IMALA
1895 - 1937

NOOTAIKOK
1098 - 1944

KAJUK IMALA
1966 -

ISAPOINHKYAKI
1874 - 1922

TEKKEITSERTOK
1870 - 1930

MIKI IMALA
1969 - 1970

Every Thought Taken

As young children, an unshakable friendship brought them together. As teens, they discovered an undeniable love. Then life pulled them in different directions–into darkness and light–and slowly ripped them apart. Years later, he returns home in the hopes of a second chance with his first love and to conquer the demons of his past.

Distorted Devotion

Free-spirited Sarah lives life to the fullest. When a new love interest enters her life, she starts receiving strange gifts and letters. She doesn't want to relinquish her freedom or new love, but fears the consequences.

Transcendental

A musician in search of his muse and a woman grieving the loss of her husband. Two weeks at an exclusive retreat and their connection rivals all others. Until she leaves early without notice. But he refuses to give up until he finds her again.

The Click Duet

High school sweethearts torn apart. When fate gives them a second chance, one doesn't trust they won't be hurt again. Through the Lens (Click Duet #1) and Time Exposure (Click Duet #2) is an angsty, second chance, friends to lovers romance with all the feels.

Broken Sky

Their eyes meet across the bar, but she looks away first. Does her best to give him zero attention. But when he crowds her on the dancefloor, she can't deny the instant chemistry. After one night together, he marks her as his. Unfortunately, another woman thinks he belongs to her.

Shattered Sun

When your heart is split in two, how do choose who to love more? While Ben—her childhood best friend—and Travis—the hottest cop in Stone Bay—fight for Kirsten's affection, someone else has their eye on her. When she questions everyone and everything, Ben and Travis vow to protect her. In the process, she falls for both men. Before it's too late, she needs to decide which man she loves more.

Fractured Night

Shallow. Heartless. Egocentric. The top three words people use to describe Phoebe Graves. Somehow, I've always seen past her icy facade. Seen beyond her callous exterior. And those minor glimpses… they make me want her more. The moment my fantasies start becoming reality, I question how long it'll last before Phoebe abandons me for something bigger.

Fallen Stars

An underlying current has always existed between us. An undeniable bond that keeps me tethered to my best friend. My person. The man I have loved in secret for years. I've wanted to tell him how I feel. Countless times, I've considered crossing the line but have resisted. I'd rather love him in secret than lose him forever. As our love story begins, one test after another is thrown at us. As we fall deeper in love, our world becomes a living, breathing nightmare.

STOLEN DREAMS PLAYLIST

Here are some of the songs from the **Stolen Dreams** playlist. You can find and listen to the entire playlist on Spotify!

Between the Wars | Allman Brown
Rescue My Heart | Liz Longley
Don't Let Me Go | RAIGN
Lost It All | Jill Andrews
Wide Eyed | Billy Lockett

CONNECT WITH PERSEPHONE

<u>Connect with Persephone</u>
www.persephoneautumn.com

<u>Subscribe to Persephone's newsletter</u>
www.persephoneautumn.com/newsletter

<u>Join Persephone's reader's group</u>
Persephone's Playground

<u>Follow Persephone online</u>

instagram.com/persephoneautumn
facebook.com/persephoneautumnwrites
tiktok.com/@persephoneautumn
bookbub.com/authors/persephone-autumn
goodreads.com/persephoneautumn
amazon.com/author/persephoneautumn
pinterest.com/persephoneautumn
threads.net/@persephoneautumn

ACKNOWLEDGMENTS

To my family… I love you so much! Your infinite support of my writing and publishing journey makes my heart so full. I wouldn't be who I am without you and wouldn't continue this author dream without your encouragement and love.

Rose at Fairy Proofmother Proofreading! Thank you for always making my stories sparkle and shine. You wave that magic wand and put all the commas in the right place. I am forever grateful for you! Love you!!

Abi of Pink Elephant Designs! Your artistry knows no bounds. I love that every time I get a cover from you, it takes my breath away. Thank you for being so incredible. I'm sending you all the hugs!

A huge thanks to Lindee Robinson for the stunning model photography for Stolen Dreams. The moment I saw Angel, I wanted her for my cover. And Brian, he is absolutely perfect next to her.

To all the bloggers and ARC readers that continuously promote my stories, get excited about books I'm terrified of putting out in the world, or read and love my words. I love you all so much!! Your support means more than you know. I love seeing your posts and joy about my books, and am forever humbled.

To every person that picks up one of my books, I love you! Whether Stolen Dreams is your first Persephone Autumn book or your 30+ book, I never take a single one of you for granted. All the fucking hugs!!!!

ABOUT THE AUTHOR

USA Today Bestselling Author Persephone Autumn resides in Washington state. A proud mom with a cuckoo grandpup. An ethnic food enthusiast who has fun discovering ways to vegan-ize her favorite nonvegan foods. Most days, you'll find her with a tea latte or fruity concoction in her hand. If given the opportunity, she would intentionally get lost in nature.

For years, Persephone did some form of writing; mostly journaling or poetry. After pairing her poetry with images and posting them online, she began the journey of writing her first novel.

She mainly writes romance and poetry, but on occasion dips her toes in other works. Look for her nonromance novel publications under P. Autumn.